# THE DIVINITY BUREAU

Tessa Clare

Asset Creative House

PORTLAND, OREGON

**Asset Creative House**
**PO Box 6841**
**Portland, OR 97228**
**www.assetcreativehouse.com**

Publisher's Note: This is a work of fiction. Names, characters, places, and incidents are a product of the author's imagination. Locales and public names are sometimes used for atmospheric purposes. Any resemblance to actual people, living or dead, or to businesses, companies, events, institutions, or locales is completely coincidental.

Book Layout © 2017 BookDesignTemplates.com

**The Divinity Bureau/ Tessa Clare**. – 2nd ed.
ISBN 978-1-947015-00-5

# CONTENTS

## CHAPTER ONE

# ROMAN

'*L*eave it to Finn to waste taxpayer money on an asinine piece of crap,*' I grumble to myself when my Mobiroid goes off. It's not the best time for me to be taking phone calls, not while my hand is inside a million sterling machine.

"Withered piece of..." I begin, but I stop myself when I realize that I've caught the attention of a chairman for District 202. He's passing me by with a cup of joe in hand, so I use my free hand to give him an awkward wave. Hopefully, it doesn't kill me.

Most days, I'm glued to the translucent device, literally. I wear it on my wrist, but a wireless earpiece is connected to it so that I can make calls, listen to shows, and make commands. Maybe that's why I forgot to take it off before I started my work on the control panel.

The good news is that it didn't touch any of the wires, so I didn't electrocute myself to death. The bad news is that I lost grip on the wire on my hand, so all my hard-earned progress from the last two hours has been lost.

The automatic door is in its sixth straight month of giving me hell. I'm one breakdown away from tearing it down and replacing it with a fucking curtain. Per my boss, Finn Hannigan, it's supposed to be better for the sake of security and convenience. We work for the Divinity Bureau, and it's necessary to have state of the art protection.

Behind that intimidating metal door is the headquarters for The Divinity Bureau's Midwest state. This office houses all the bureau's Chairmen who have districts within our state, 140 districts out of the 560 interspersed throughout the Confederal Districts. It's also the central office for our Regional Chairman, Gideon Hearthstrom. Life and death decisions are made behind these doors, and Finn thinks that it's necessary that the people making those decisions are well-protected. I can't say I disagree.

The problem is that it never works. When we first got the machine, I had to upload the facial images of every single employee that work for the Bureau, which was about twenty-five hours of repetitive grunt work. After that, the sensor broke – twice. Then the deadbolt broke, and we had twelve full hours of virtually no security. Today, the final straw came when I found out that the camera's screen broke. In this day and age, that shouldn't even be possible.

I clench my jaw. The vibrating on my Mobiroid is still going. I'm not in the mood to talk to anyone, especially now that I know that my plans to leave at five o'clock have been tossed out the window. Still, I probably should see who it is. I give my wrist a glance. Immediately, I'm startled out of my bad mood.

*Gideon Hearthstrom.*

Seeing that name on my wrist is like seeing a ghost. There must be a huge mistake. For one, I don't know how he has my number. Two, as our Regional Chairman, I'd think that he wouldn't have time to be dealing with someone as low on the totem pole as me. He's supposed to be busy with appeals, meetings, and making sure that our state doesn't overpopulate.

I briefly entertain the thought of letting it go to voicemail, but it takes half a second to realize my career might be resting on this one phone call. I clear my throat, press the "Accept" button that's flashing on my wrist, and the call forwards to my earpiece.

"IT, this is Roman."

There's a long pause on the other end.

"I thought you were the office assistant," comes a deep, gruff voice on the other end.

I glance at the caller ID again. Maybe I *am* being prank-called.

I'm slow and deliberate in my words. "I'm.... I'm an IT Technician."

I might as well be an office assistant, considering I make twelve sterling an hour. In this economy, that's barely enough to pay my rent.

"Oh," Gideon says. "Finn says that you're an office assistant."

I smack my head against my hand. It nearly knocks out my earpiece.

"I don't know why," I say, all but seething. I clear my throat. "Is there anything I can help you with?"

"Yeah, can you tell me where I can find Finn?"

I wonder if I'd feel better if I threw my earpiece off. It's the size of a coin so it may not make an enormous impact. "He's gone for the day."

"Does he not work on Wednesday's?"

"He's usually gone by four."

"Why doesn't anyone seem to work past four these days?"

"*I'm* working," I point out, a bit self-serving. I hear a huff on the other end. In my earpiece, it sounds like he's breathing in my ear. I shake off a shudder.

"Well, the chairman for the two hundred and twentieth district thought that it would be a fantastic idea to pay the West state a visit during election time," Gideon says begrudgingly. "I was under the impression that I could run the election report – and yet, apparently, I don't have permission! I'm the Regional Chairman!"

I shift my feet. Technically, Gideon isn't supposed to have permission. Running the election report for individual districts is a job for the district chairmen, but technically, Gideon is over them. Does that mean I should grant him access?

"Do you need me to fix it?"

There's a pause. As soon as the words come out of my mouth, it hits me that I shouldn't have mentioned that. My resume indicates that I have a Master's degree in Information Technology, so it's obvious that I know how to bypass security. I also have Finn's log-on information. Neither seems like things that I should have in a government agency.

"Get a hold of Finn," Gideon says after a moment of silence. "He should have access. If not, I guess Hemmingsworth's constituents will deal with long lines and traffic for the next three months!"

There's a click on the other end, followed by silence. I let out a breath that I didn't realize I was holding.

∎∎∎∎∎∎∎∎∎∎∎∎∎∎∎∎∎∎∎∎∎∎∎∎∎∎∎∎∎∎∎∎∎∎∎∎∎∎∎∎∎∎∎∎∎∎∎∎∎∎∎∎

Two hundred years ago, there was a place called North Amerigo (or was it North America? I can never remember the name). Once, it was the home of the greatest scientific discoveries, from space travel to quantum physics to genetics. The most significant development of them all was the discovery of BIONs, which allowed for human immortality. For the first time, people were healthy, young, and immortal – but this development came at a cost.

Soon, the population exploded into levels that were hardly sustainable. The overpopulation problem in North Amerigo was only fueled by global warming, which caused rising sea levels and a dramatic loss of land. A war ensued between the upper-class citizens – who were immortal and had obtained much of the remaining resources to sell for profit – and the lower-class citizens – who were poor, unable to afford these resources, and usually unable to afford immortality. From the chaos, a country called the Confederal Districts emerged.

The Confederal Districts did two things: they divided the region into five hundred and sixty districts, which split into four states. They also lowered the cost of immortality to make it accessible, while establishing the Divinity Bureau to control overpopulation.

The Divinity Bureau holds an election every quarter. Every quarter, by random selection, a certain number of names are picked (there used to be a lottery ball machine, but then the district chairmen grew tired of selecting thousands of names and paper became a scarce resource; so, they use a computer now). That number is determined by factors such as the birth rate, population growth, and so on – all determined by the district's chairmen.

If you can afford immortality and you choose to opt into it, it comes at a cost: you will be put on this list. And if your name is selected, you will die by lethal injection. Fortunately, with millions of people on the list, your odds of being selected are low – at least, until fate catches up with you.

If you haven't opted into immortality, you will be placed on the list as soon as you turn one hundred – and the only ones that don't opt into immortality are the ones that can't afford it.

Fortunately – or unfortunately, depending on the time of year – I'm one of those people.

■■■■■■■■■■■■■■■■■■■■■■■■■■■■■■■■■■■■■■■■■■■■■■■■■■■■■■■■■

I spend all of forty minutes trying to figure out why Gideon's not able to run the report. I'm locked out of the permissions system, and by the time I'll be able to figure out how to bypass security, it'll be too late to call Gideon back and let him know that he can run the report. Instead, I use Finn's log-on information (which he sent me in an email about six months ago, after he couldn't figure out why an advertisement to "Meet Real District 520 Women" kept popping up – in my mind, I could see my Network Security professor shaking his head).

The report isn't complicated. It uses a query to select a list of people randomly. The people are sorted by last name, first name, and birth date. The people on the list are known as "elects," and they have thirty days to report to the closest regional headquarters – from the Western state in District 530, the Eastern state in District 1, the

Southern state in District 333, and, finally, the Midwest. We're in the windy, smoky District 200.

I'm trying not to think about the fact that thousands of lives are in my hands. It's a necessary evil. The world is overpopulated, and there's no way around it. I breathe polluted air, live in a crippled economy (I have a Master's degree, and I still only make twelve sterling an hour), and spend an hour in traffic just to drive five miles. The worst part is that every time I step over a sleeping homeless person outside my apartment building (which happens at least once a week), I'm forced to think about how lucky I am to have a two-hundred-square-foot apartment in a building with hallways that smell of smoke and urine. It could always be worse.

With that in mind, a sheet of data appears in front of me. 10,421 names on the list. *Easy.* I can't believe that chairmen and chairwomen spend their careers stressing over this every quarter.

I'm in the process of drafting an email to Gideon to let him know that I finished the report (though I conveniently leave out the part about how I did so), yet before I can hit the "send" button, curiosity gets the best of me. Who is on the list?

I do a search on my name. Irvine is a distinguishable last name, and the only people with it is my family in District 402. It's silly, as I know that it's not possible for me to be elected; but I want to see it with my own eyes.

I do see one familiar name: Neal O'Donnell. He's an actor for a thriller movie series known as the Insomnia series. What a shame, as I was looking forward to the next installment.

Still – there isn't anyone that I know or recognize, which isn't a huge surprise. The only people I know in the Midwest is my ex-girlfriend and her three friends, and I'm not on good enough terms with either of them to be horribly sad if I see them.

I'm ready to log out for the day when I see a name: April McIntyre. I casually glance at her birth date and stop, certain that my eyes are deceiving me. In a list of ten thousand names, the girl I'm looking at is nineteen years old.

That can't be right. Doctors won't inject BIONs in anyone under the age of twenty-five, as her brain hasn't finished developing. Maybe a filter is broken. As an IT Technician, isn't it my job to fix it?

*No,* a voice in the back of my head tells me. *The Divinity Bureau is a government system that's been running for as long as I could remember.* It can't be an accident.

She's meant to be on the list.

She's expected to die.

I try to shake the gnawing feeling inside of me. Computers have glitches all the time. If they didn't, I wouldn't have needed to go to school for it for seven years. My specialty, Network Security, is solely dedicated to exploiting those glitches. And yet, I can't find anyone else on the list that stands out the way she does. Most of the people on the list are over one hundred years old.

On impulse, I copy her name from the list and into a search engine. A second later, the profile of a girl with dark brown hair and a smile appears on my screen.

*April McIntyre*

*Birthday: April 30th*

*Parents: Henrik McIntyre and Macy McIntyre*

Henrik McIntyre. I know that name. He's a famed politician in the Republic party. Outside of District 200, he – and other Members of the Republic Party – aren't very popular, primarily because they still use the old methods of individual reasoning to make decisions. Other parties defer to more advanced forms of decision making, ranging from AI to computer polling systems.

The last time I saw him in the news was a year ago when he was elected – and not in the way that Henrik was likely accustomed to every eight years. He was the youngest person in nearly a century to be chosen by the Divinity Bureau. Reportedly, it was because of his position on the Committee for Population Regulation. It explained so little – and so much.

I bring my attention back to April. She's a freshman at the Midwest University, located in District 201. She works part-time at a coffee shop near her campus, though I'm having trouble figuring out why the daughter of a wealthy politician would need to work for minimum wage. Her social media platforms contain few posts but plenty of pictures of herself – ranging from selfies in her car to photos with friends (though her activity seems to have dwindled in the last year). There's a lot of selfies. A lot. The conclusion that I've come to is that she's a typical nineteen-year-old girl – which is why it doesn't make sense that she's on the list.

But I can find out why. I have a degree in Network Security. I've spent years studying this. Breaking into systems that I'm not supposed to see is my specialty – and kind of a hobby if I'm entirely honest with myself. The downside is that I'd need to find the glitch. Once I unlocked the encryption, I'd need to scroll through layers upon layers of code to figure out where the injection happened – something that I don't have time to do. Deleting her name, on the other hand, would only take minutes. The problem is that I'm not sure if I should.

I'm stuck. The last thing I want to do is anger Gideon, but I can't let an innocent girl die on my watch. The only options I have is leaving it alone – or fixing it and hoping for the best. But without knowing who April McIntyre is, I can't make that decision.

And yet I have access to her social media platforms, I realize.

An idea hits me. It's the worst idea I've ever had, and I may get arrested for it. My hope is that karma is in my favor.

■■■■■■■■■■■■■■■■■■■■■■■■■■■■■■■■■■■■■■■■■■■■■■■■■■■■■■

I leave the office quickly, like a criminal trying to sneak away from the scene before I get caught - so quick, that I forget to put on my face mask. But the smell of smog and dust is a reminder; I pull my plastic cover out of my jacket.

"Watch where you're going, you BION bot!"

I look at my feet and notice a sleeping bag under my feet. Curled up inside the sleeping bag is an old man – wrinkled, gray-haired, and wearing a flimsy paper mask. He's obviously not immortal, and he thinks he's insulting me by calling me the common term the have-not's call the immortal (the idea was to infer that they weren't fully human because a good portion of their body consisted of nanobots). My ex-girlfriend, Jenneka, used to respond by calling them "weathered wastes." But I'm not immortal, so I'm not willing to sink that low.

"Sorry," I mutter, then walk away as quickly as I can.

I have a plan in place to meet the girl. The way I'm going to do that is by visiting her workplace, which she has clearly listed on all her social media platforms. Twenty minutes ago, it sounded way less creepy in my head; but now that I'm walking out of the building and into the parking lot, I'm sure I'm making a huge mistake.

All I need is sixty seconds with the girl. With those sixty seconds, I should have an impression of whether I should delete her name from the list. From there, I can either return to the office or go home. Either way, I should be able to rest easy tonight.

I take an elevator to the top floor of the parking garage. My car is a parked on the roof, where I hope every day that there's enough sunlight to charge my car. My vehicle resembles a pod. It only fits two people, and the reflective glass doubles as a solar panel to power the vehicle. The problem is that I had gotten into a car accident six months ago. There's a dent on the right side of the car, which makes it almost impossible for it to charge from that side. Thus, I have to keep it on the roof and hope that there's enough sunlight to power it throughout the day. I also must hope that it doesn't die in the middle of traffic.

April works at an old-school coffee house called Dang Coffee, located near Midwest University in District 201. It's ten miles away – a short stretch where I used to live, but one that takes nearly an hour in the daily traffic of the Greater District 200 Area. It's been close to a decade since I've been to an old-school coffee house. My hometown in District 402 had one that had survived the Confederal War, but it was primarily a tourist stop. Most coffee shops these days have been dominated by automation. You punch in an order, any customizations, and a machine makes it for you. It's faster, easier, and cheaper than waiting for some kid to make it.

My best guess is that April is a maintenance technician, though April doesn't seem too tech-savvy. Still, first impressions can always be wrong.

As it turns out, my first impression is wrong.

After battling a self-driving luxury Benz for a parking spot, I walk into a coffee shop. The aroma of freshly brewed coffee infiltrates my nose. I look for a machine and a head of brown hair, but instead, I see a counter, a blonde-haired boy – and a strung-out line.

I shuffle my feet awkwardly. I step on my toes to see if the girl is hovering behind the counter, but I don't see anyone but the blonde boy. I recognize him from a few of April McIntyre's photos. He has curly blonde hair and bright blue eyes, which makes him impossible to miss. Still, no sign of the girl.

Well, shoot. This trip was obviously a terrible idea. I suppose the best thing I should do is what I should have done all along: leave it alone. It's not my battle to fight.

I fall in line to grab a cup of coffee before I head home. I'm standing behind a group of college students, and the line is moving at a sluggish pace – far slower than if a computer had run the store. I also can't help but notice how expensive the drinks are. Five sterling for a cup of joe?

"How do we order?" I ask a boy standing in front of me.

The boy glances at his friends then back at me. A bemused grin crosses his face. "You tell the cashier, naturally."

"Wouldn't it be easier if we could just punch it into the kiosk? Why is he punching it in for us?"

A friend of the boy in front of me snickers. "You see, Quinn? *This* is why our society has so many problems! People don't know how to talk to each other!"

"Yeah," the boy chimes. "Back in the day, they didn't have coffee kiosks."

I stare at the boy blankly. Of course, I know that coffee kiosks are an invention of the last century; but I also know that people used to create paintings on caves. It doesn't mean that those traditions need to continue, particularly since other mediums in both forms developed. Still, it explains why the coffee shop is still in business. Located near a university, it clearly caters to that demographic.

When it's my turn to order, I ask the blonde-haired boy for a hot caramel macchiato. The cashier marks the cup and sets it in a line that's practically overflowing off the counter. I glance at the row of irate customers. If I'd gone to a regular coffee shop, I'd already be on my way home.

Knowing that I'm going to be waiting for a long while, I turn my wrist to check my text messages while I wait for my order. I don't have enough friends in the Midwest state to warrant many messages, but my mom does text me on a weekly basis. This time, it's because my student loan payment is due.

The thought makes a pit form in my stomach. Would I ever catch a break? Once, I had hoped that a Master's degree would guarantee me a chance at making it in this poor economy; but at times, I think it made it worse. Sure, I have a job. I have a roof over my head, yet all my money goes towards food and bills. I may be able to make a living, but I would hardly call it making a life for myself.

I'm in the middle of replying to my mother's text message when the back door flew open.

"Where the hell have you been?" the cashier barks, loud enough that my head shoots up in the air.

"Shut up, Tate. I'm here."

As soon as I see her, all thoughts of replying to my mother's text message are lost. Her pictures have not done her justice. The first thing I notice is her eyes: steel-gray and a bit too large for her face. Her hair is pulled into a loose braid, a few strands flying free as she races towards the espresso machine. She picks up my empty caramel macchiato cup, and I get a glimpse of her up close. She's not wearing any makeup; or, if she is, it's subtle. She meets my gaze as she tops my drink off with a sprinkle of caramel sauce. She smiles – a subtle upwards turn of her lips that may not be directed at me, but I don't care. As soon as I see it, my stomach churns.

I need to say something. Anything. I can talk about the weather, but that's cliché. I try to think about what interests I had seen on the girl's social media.

The realization hits me like a punch in the stomach, knocking the air out of my lungs.

Oh God, I've seen her social media profile.

*I followed her to work.*

I am the worst human being on the planet. Can I redeem myself after this? The only conversation topic that comes to mind is about coffee.

"Can you make that decaf?" I blurt out, not thinking about the implications.

The girl glances at me and back at the near-completed drink in her hand. Her brows furrow in annoyance. "Excuse me?"

Her grey eyes meet mine. My heart is thumping in my chest, reverberating in my ear. I don't know how to talk to attractive women – especially one that looks as infuriated as she does at that moment.

"Well, I – uh – I just realized that it's past seven o'clock," I say, word vomiting the first thing that comes to mind. "I can't fall asleep when I drink caffeine. Not that I mind staying up late. I just need to work early in the morning." Pause. "Sorry, I'm used to going to real coffee shops..."

If I wasn't already nailing the coffin, then I'm sure my last comment would put me six feet under. April is glaring at me as she pours my drink down the drain.

"I'm sorry," I say meekly. "That – that came out wrong."

"It's fine," April responds, though her tone says that it's anything but. Maybe the boy in line was right about people not being able to talk to each other. If that's the case, then I can blame society for my lack of ability to talk to beautiful women.

I'm ready to run out of the coffee shop and back into my work-sleep-pay-bills routine. But then I remember why I'm there. The girl that's glaring at me right now has no clue that I can save her life. That thought makes me feel like I have a lot more power – something that I've lacked for my twenty-five years of existence.

I glance back at her, right as she's pouring steamed milk into my cup. I swallow a lump in my throat and try again. "So – uh – do you go to school around here?"

I know the answer already, but it's an easy topic of conversation.

April shrugs. "Sort of. Why?"

Her answer is confusing. Didn't I just read that she was a freshman at Midwest University? "Sort of? What does that mean?"

"It means that I haven't fully committed to it."

She's being vague, dodging questions in the way a girl that's grown up in the limelight would. I can also tell that she doesn't fully trust me. That's understandable. She did just meet me, and I haven't given her any reason to trust me. I decide to try another angle.

"That's smart. College is expensive. I mean – not undergraduate school, if you go to a public university..." More words are coming out, faster than I can think. "Which I didn't, because I'm a dumbass. I was hoping that if I studied computers for six years, I'd be able to find a good job, which is like finding bigfoot in this economy. My mom thinks that I just signed up for graduate school to procrastinate on the entering the real world. I don't belive she's wrong. I just think –"

I stop when I realize that April had stopped making my drink. Instead, she's staring at me – holding a hand up to her mouth and attempting to stifle a giggle.

"Are you laughing at me?" I ask, my face heating.

The words make her laugh come out in full force. I don't know what I did – or if I should do it again.

"Sorry," April apologizes. Her cheeks are pink from laughter. "It's just, well, your face is pretty red right now."

Maybe I shouldn't say anything more. Maybe I should just crawl into a hole.

"Sorry," I say, unsure if that's the right thing to say. She did just apologize to me. "I didn't mean to…" I trail off. The ideal situation in my head is to say that I didn't mean to make myself sound like an idiot in front of a gorgeous woman, but that would be cheesy.

April shakes her head. "You don't have to apologize. Haven't you ever heard the ancient phrase, 'the customer is always right?'"

"No, but I've heard different variations. The one I hear most frequently is that the customer is an idiot."

April giggles. She turns her attention back to my drink, but I want to keep her talking.

"What's your name?" I ask, even though I already know it.

"April," she replies. "Yours?"

She pauses, glancing at the drink in her hand.

"Oh wait. Does it relate to an ancient empire of some sorts?"

"It's Roman. I'd be impressed, but I can see it clearly written on the cup."

April puts her hands up in the air in mock surrender. "You caught me, Roman." She turns her attention back to the drink, and the annoyance appears to have diminished. "I still haven't figured out what I want to do with the rest of my life. My…" She glances at me, no doubt internally debating on how much information to give me.

"My mom wants me to follow in my dad's footsteps. You see, he passed away last year, and his career was..." She pauses, eying me. I don't divulge that I know that her dad is Henrik McIntyre. "Well, I guess you can say it was a family legacy. I'm not sure if it's for me; so, I'm just taking two classes and working here. It's not a bad way to pass the time."

If I had any doubts about April's mortality, they're diminished with her words. Even if she had found a doctor to render her immortal – and I'm certain she could, given her family's connections – she doesn't even know what she wants to do with her life. Immortality is out of the question.

The thought crosses my mind of how fortunate she is that she can decide whenever she wants to be immortal. She can pick an age and stick to it. From what I knew about Henrik, he continued his aging to appeal to the voters that wanted someone that looked older. For most, the choice isn't given to them.

"You still have plenty of time," I say. I expected the tone to come out more bitterly, but it doesn't. "I didn't declare my major until my junior year. Both of my parents are potato farmers in District 402. I decided early on that it wasn't the life for me, but I didn't know what I wanted to do."

I leave out the part about moving halfway across the country to be closer to my then-girlfriend, Jenneka. We split up six months ago, so it's hardly relevant.

April laughs. "Potato farmers?"

"Yeah. I'll never eat another potato again." I still associate my childhood with agrichemicals and greenhouse skyscrapers.

She hands me a cup of a steaming hot caramel macchiato. In the look she gives me, I understand why people pay extra to come to an old-fashioned coffee shop. The human touch – and the subsequent human connection at that moment – can never be replicated in a machine. I can see myself coming back.

April glances at the line of cups behind her. "I suppose I should get back to work. I guess I'll see you around?"

I take a sip of the drink and give her a nod. Perfection. I'm *definitely* coming back. "Yeah. You'll definitely be seeing me."

She has no idea how true those words are, nor does she know how I'm about to make sure that it happens. But first, I need to make a returning trip to the office.

## CHAPTER TWO

# APRIL

"What do you think?" I ask, holding a poster board in front of me for Tate to inspect.

I'm not artist – primarily because paper is difficult to come by these days. I only lucked out because I found a cardboard box in the dumpster near my work and a handful of permanent markers near the coffee shop's cash register. Still, I managed to get by. I drew a black hourglass. On the bottom, surrounded by grains of sand (colored with a red permanent marker), were the words "No Justice in the Divinity Bureau." The idea is to symbolize time running out, much like the way I feel life slip through my fingers. Unfortunately, Tate doesn't seem to be getting the message.

"No Justin?" he asks skeptically. "Is he one of your failed one night stands?"

I slap him across the shoulder. "Can you not read?"

It's the Divinity Bureau's Election Day. Throughout my life, there were two kinds of elections. There were the "good" elections: the kind that would determine whether my father would have an office for the next eight years. My mother had insisted that those elections were essential to our wellbeing. Then there were the "bad" elections: the kind that determined whether you'd live to see another quarter.

Neither Tate nor I have anything to worry about. Neither of us is immortal, nor are we close to the age of one-hundred. But we know people that are.

This quarter, the elected that comes to mind is Neal O'Donnell. I don't know him, nor have I seen any of his movies (which is probably a good thing, as the last one ended on a cliffhanger and the world would likely never see its ending); but plenty of people do. A protest is being held today in front of the Divinity Bureau's Midwest Headquarters.

"It's a terrible idea," Tate says bluntly, crossing his arms to affirm his point.

"I asked for your opinion on the sign – not on my life decisions."

"It looks awful! You really should invest in an art class. But while we're on the topic of your life decisions…"

I set the sign down and attempt to brush past him. I hope that it's the only clue he needs that I'm not in the mood to listen to one of his lectures, but he follows me anyways.

"What?" he calls out, following me into the stockroom. "You don't want to relive getting arrested and biting the police officer that tried to take you away?"

"Shut up."

The last protest I had attended was when my father, Henrik McIntyre, was elected. Last year, he got stuck with one of the "bad" elections. It was a shock to us all, so I did the one thing that I hoped would give me some control of the situation and make him proud: I raised hell. I was never politically active, despite early exposure to the inner-workings of political life; but my dad's connections to the political world resulted in demonstrations behind held across the Midwest state.

"There's going to be a line of cops keeping you from getting close to the building!" Tate reminds me, despite my attempts to ignore him. "You got lucky last time; but this time? Do you want to risk jail time?"

"I'll a hire a lawyer," I say stubbornly. I should probably say that my mother will; but given the last year, she may also let me rot in a jail cell.

"And risk your pretty head sitting in a jail cell? Last time, you complained that their toilet sprays didn't work."

Tate knows me too well. We've known each other since we were freshmen in high school, and our friendship only strengthened when most of our mutual friends left the Midwest. I don't want to argue with him. I don't want to dwell on the fact that today is the one-year anniversary since my father's election, nor do I want to think about the fact that my last attempt to make my dad proud had ended with my arrest. All I know is that it's something that I need to do.

Fortunately, the shop's automatic doors come to life. We have a customer. Tate and I exchange a look to debate on who would be taking care of it – something we frequently do whenever neither of us feels like working – but I catch a glimpse of curly dark hair. I recognize it from the day before.

"I'll take care of it," I say, too eagerly to not be noticed by Tate. He watches me skip to the front counter like an animated character – all smiles and blushes. All that's missing is a whistle to a happy tune.

"Hey Robert," I say, my heart skipping a beat.

The boy's face immediately contours to confusion. "Robert?"

Whoops. I've never been good with names. It just wouldn't be my nature to have nailed it the first time around. "I totally screwed that up, didn't I?"

"Just a little."

"Let me think," I say, searching my memory. I know I learned it yesterday, but my mind is a myriad of faces and tedious tasks. "You were named after an ancient empire."

A memory comes to mind. *"It's Roman. I'd be impressed, but I can it clearly written on the cup."*

I grin at the memory. "Roman."

"That's the one."

"Roman," I repeat, to solidify it into my memory. The last thing I want is to embarrass myself again. "A hot caramel macchiato. Decaf."

"That's right," Roman says, a hint of redness spreading across his cheeks. Is he blushing?

"Same thing?" I ask. I briefly make eye-contact with Tate, who's watching the scene unfold from the backroom. He's watching like he's engrossed in one of his soap operas.

"No, thanks," Roman says, oblivious to the silence exchange between Tate and me. "I'll take a vanilla latte. Make that a medium."

I turn my attention back towards Roman and try to pretend that Tate isn't there. "Decaf?"

Roman laughs. "Yes, please."

I ring him up. While Roman is fumbling to get the machine to register his thumbprint, I catch Tate eying me with a coy grin. Even though we disagree on some things, I can always count on Tate to appreciate my taste in men. Luckily for me, he has a boyfriend.

As subtly as I can muster, I mouth, 'He's cute.'

Tate laughs. 'Get his number,' he mouths back.

I bury my face in my sleeve to stifle a giggle. Roman clears his throat, interrupting our silent exchange. "So, April..."

I turn my attention back to him, shaking the thoughts out of my head. "Yeah?"

He looks like he wants to say something; but instead, he watches me for a long moment. I wasn't kidding when I told Tate that he was good-looking. Sure, he's a bit awkward, but he has a handsome face and an aura of sincerity. I wait for him to say something, but I don't think I can look away if I tried.

Roman can, however. He's the first one to break the silence. "Sorry. I – uh – I forgot what I was going to say."

I realize at that moment that I haven't begun making his drink. I queue two shots of espresso and start steaming a cup of milk. I try to lighten the conversation by saying, "Were you about to compliment my fantastic drink making abilities?"

"Yes!" Roman exclaims, a bit too quickly. A blush forms when he realizes what just happened. "I mean, no – that wasn't it. But that is true."

"I'm glad you think so," I say, a bit proud. It may be a minimum wage job, but it still feels good to be complimented on it. The drink is almost done, but I wanted to hold onto it for a bit longer so that we can keep talking. "Where do you work, Roman?"

At those words, Roman immediately tenses. He looks away. "Err – around…"

His sudden shift in mood is alarming. "Are you always this vague?"

"No," says Roman, shifting his feet. When I don't say anything further, he elaborates, "I work in IT."

"A computer science guy!" I exclaim. It's not a unique profession (in my College 101 class, it's one of the most common majors), but I've spent my entire life around politicians and businesspeople. The steamed milk is done, so I pour it into an empty cup. Casually, I ask, "Do you like it?"

Roman shrugs. "Sometimes."

"Again, with the vague answers," I observe. The drink is finished, so I hand it to Roman. Maybe he doesn't want to talk to me as much as I initially thought he did.

"Sorry," Roman apologizes. He eyes the drink, but he doesn't take it. "I'm not trying to be vague. It's just…" He pauses, then he runs a hand through his hair. "I'm not used to talking to gorgeous girls. It's a little nerve-wracking."

I nearly drop the drink. *Sweet Hades.* That hair is going to be the death of me.

"Did that come out weird?" Roman asks, his face turning pink. His face turns to horror. "That definitely sounded creepy! I'm sorry. I swear, I'll leave you alone if you want me to…"

I shake my head. "No, that's not it at all." I glance at the cup in my hand. Tate told me to get his number, but I feel like being a little more creative. "I need a minute."

I quickly move to the back office – brushing past Tate, who is watching the scene unfold before him with keen interest. It reminds me of a picture I saw in a museum: a man sitting on the edge of his seat with a bowl of something called Pop Corn. Tate eyes the drink in my hand.

"What are you doing?" he asks.

I search the desk for a black marker. "Following your advice."

I scribble on the cup: 'Life is short. Don't waste a single moment.' Underneath it, I scribble my Mobiroid number. I think I'm done, but then I see Tate standing in the corner. I think of when he made fun of my hourglass drawing; and, to prove a point to him (and myself), I draw a miniature hourglass on the side of the cup.

"Nice," Tate nods in agreement. He chooses not to comment on my added touch.

I practically race to the front of the shop with the cup in hand. By then, I'm certain that the drink is cold. I'm keeping my fingers crossed that Roman is too awestruck to notice.

I hand Roman the cup. He takes it, though he looks confused by the happy expression on my face.

"Don't forget to keep the cup," I say with a wink, before seeing him off.

■ ■ ■ ■ ■ ■ ■ ■ ■ ■ ■ ■ ■ ■ ■ ■ ■ ■ ■ ■ ■ ■ ■ ■ ■ ■ ■ ■ ■ ■ ■ ■ ■ ■ ■ ■ ■ ■ ■ ■ ■ ■ ■ ■ ■ ■ ■ ■ ■ ■

I can't say that the rest of the day was eventful. We had a mid-afternoon rush; and by the time it was over, I had forgotten all about Tate and his idiotic lectures about my life decisions. I'm no longer irritated with him by the time I'm ready to go home. We re-bonded over an afternoon session of experimenting with different coffee concoctions (the most notable being a peppermint and passion fruit combination that I'll probably never recover from). When it's time for me to leave, he corners me in the backroom office.

"You know you're my only friend out here, right?" Tate says. His face is pensive, but his blue eyes are wide and inquisitive. He's looking for validation like he always does. I can never tell if it's because he needs it or wants it.

I want to remind him that he's my only friend as well, but my pride won't allow it. I swallow. "I know."

Tate crosses his arms. "That means I'm going to be pretty pissed off if I have to bail you out."

I roll my eyes. Whatever validation Tate was hoping to get from me has officially gone out the window. "You know that I'm the daughter of Henrik McIntyre, right? Bail money would hardly make a dent in my massive trust fund."

It's a shame my parents had grounded me and blocked me from accessing it.

The thought of my late father only reinforces why I want to do what I'm about to do. My dad was only fifty years old when he was elected. He lived a good life, but fifty years is still young. There were rumors that he hadn't even opted into immortality (of course, I knew that was a lie). He wasn't known to be a pleasant person, but a demonstration in front of the bureau's Midwest headquarters still erupted. I suspect that the general public's outrage has less to do with his life and more to do with the fear that it can be any of us.

I put on my facial mask; then I check the weather report on my Mobiroid before I head out the door. Clear skies, 70 degrees, and – most importantly – an Air Quality Index of 150. Not bad.

My car is parked in a public parking garage that's located three blocks away. I use a remote to queue one of the doors to open for me, before stepping into the interior of a vehicle that smells of peppermint. The thought brings me back to the passion fruit and peppermint concoction that I had just a few hours previously. I try not to vomit.

A robotic voice purrs: "Hello, Miss McIntyre. Please enter your destination."

I enter the Divinity Bureau's headquarters into the screen next to my seat.

My car drives and parks itself, as it's illegal for people to be driving manually on public roads. Typically, I use this time to watch TV and surf the net; but today, I'm staring out the window and contemplating about what I'm about to do. It should be easy. Hold a sign, show my support, and try not to get arrested. It's been a year since I've been on television, so I'm hoping that no one recognizes me.

My mind wanders to the last protest I had attended: the one after my father was elected. At the time, I had been proud of what I was doing. I was standing up for what I believed in, which is something that my father had dedicated his entire life to do. But when my dad bailed me out, he cursed me out for spending his final weeks embarrassing him ("Biting a fucking police officer?" he had said in astonishment. "I passed laws that would make that a federal offense!"). He cut me off from my trust fund until I learned to "take responsibility" for my actions. I spent the remainder of his life resenting the fact that I had been grounded, forced to attend weekly therapy sessions, and obliged to get a minimum wage job that hardly allowed me to live the extravagant lifestyle that I once had.

A glass building comes into view – one that I remember quite clearly from my nightmares. The Divinity Bureau's Midwest Headquarters is a twenty-story skyscraper shaped like an isosceles triangle. The building appears to be made of glass, but I heard rumors that the glass is bulletproof. The roof was shaped to look as though it pointed towards the heavens, which is said to symbolize the bureau as a stairway to heaven. I can't help but be amused by the irony.

Parking is never easy in District 200, not even with a car that parks itself. In the end, I find a pay-per-hour garage several blocks away.

From a distance, I can hear the chants of protesters and the drumming of a snare drum.

"Hey, ho! The Divinity Bureau has got to go!" a voice enhanced by a microphone calls out.

The crowd quickly repeats the speaker's words: "Hey, ho! The Divinity Bureau has got to go!"

*What?*

I glance down at my sign, suddenly unsure of myself. I grew up in a world where changes – from policy making to parenting decisions – occurred behind closed doors. Standing in front of the bureau with nothing more than a crudely-drawn sign, I feel overexposed.

To be honest, I'm not even sure if I want the Divinity Bureau to go. Logically, I know that there is something wrong with the idea of a government agency deciding who lives and who dies; but what else needs to happen? Billions of people live in this world, and hardly anyone is leaving it.

I take another look at my sign. If I hadn't spent two hours drawing the hourglass design and more time sitting in traffic for this protest, I would have turned around in a heartbeat. But I did.

A realization hits me: I'm getting ahead of myself. I'm not a policymaker. I'm not even a politician. Solutions for things like overpopulation are for people like my father. All I need to do is make an appearance, show my support, and, when it was over, cross one item off my bucket list. What do I have to lose?

With newfound determination, I follow the chants. I contemplate standing in the back, but police officers surround the area. Instead, I find myself standing in the middle of the crowd.

An array of senses overtakes me. I can smell tobacco smoke and sweat, even through the supposed protection of my face mask. The sound of drums is pounding in my ears. And the sights! Everywhere I look, there's something new to look at – the pointed building, the brick courtyard, and the protesters. I can tell that most of the protesters aren't immortal. Most have gray hair and wrinkles. One man is holding a sign from his wheelchair. And the unfortunate reality is that many haven't opted out of immortality by choice.

Police officers surrounded every corner. The sight nearly sends me running back to my car. Am I supposed to be there? Would I get arrested?

But once my mind adjusts to the activity around me, I take a closer look. The police officers – covered from head to toe in black metal gear that makes it look like they're more prepared for war than a protest – aren't arresting anyone. Some are even joking and laughing amongst themselves.

I'm not doing anything wrong. I have every right to let my voice be heard. Even if I'm intimidated by the protesters that surround me, the protest itself is peaceful. They – like me – have been impacted by the Divinity Bureau, and we all deserve to be here.

Despite my mixed feelings, I find myself chanting along: "Hey, ho! The Divinity Bureau has got to go!"

Halfway through the protest, I notice the air quality clearing up – or maybe I've just grown accustomed to it. Still, it's not often that I can breathe in fresh air, so I pry the plastic mask off my face. I'm not ashamed of what I'm doing. I can't be – not if I want my voice to be heard. That means that I shouldn't need to hide my identity.

I'm watching a woman dance in the middle of a drumming circle when I hear a familiar voice call out: "Excuse me! Excuse – oh! I'm so sorry! Excuse me, sorry again!"

Geez, I don't think I've ever heard anyone apologize so much in such a short period. No one, except...

*Oh.*

In the corner of my eye, I see a head of dark curly hair attempt to push his way through the crowd. When I glance in his direction, I rub my eyes to make sure my eyes aren't deceiving me.

It's him: Roman. I hardly recognize his face through the face mask, but there's no mistaking his voice and head of dark hair. He has a black laptop bag swung over his shoulder, while his other hand is holding a badge. I think about calling out to him; but by the time it crosses my mind, he's already at the front of the crowd.

*Please don't tell me he works for the Bureau.*

You'd have to be heartless to make a living killing hundreds of thousands of people every quarter. I gave him my number because I thought he was sweet, sincere, and even a little sensitive…

But when he makes his way to the front door, and a police officer lets him inside without a second thought, there's no mistaking it.

Roman works for the Divinity Bureau.

## CHAPTER THREE

# ROMAN

The Divinity Bureau's Election Day is a federal holiday. Banks and federal offices – including the bureau's headquarters – are closed for the day. I have the day off, so I used it as an opportunity to visit my new favorite coffee shop. The banter alone had been worth an hour of traffic, but when she handed me a cup with her phone number, I thought that I'd hit the jackpot.

I was standing outside my car, in the process of inputting her phone number, when I felt a vibration on my wrist. A text came through: "I can't get my computer's projector to work. Is that something you can fix?"

It was my neighbor, Marla. She lives in the apartment below me. I've hardly ever interacted with her – occasionally, we've made light conversation in the elevator – but I guess that she had gotten my number from someone else in the complex.

It's not a secret that I'll barter my skills in computer engineering for food and money. It's more exciting than my day job, and there's no way that I can survive on twelve sterling an hour without a little extra side cash coming in. The message came at the right time, as I was starting to run low on cat food.

It took another thirty minutes of sitting in traffic, but I made my way home to pick up the computer. I knocked on Marla's door, and she invited me to her apartment to look at the computer.

The computer itself was only a keyboard and a wireless mouse, but there was a button above the keyboard that would project a computer screen wherever she wanted. Unfortunately, according to Marla, whenever she pressed the button, nothing would happen. Immediately, I know that it's a hardware issue. One of the connectors looks like it's fried. I'd need to fix it at the bureau, as I didn't have the appropriate equipment at home.

I cringed at the idea of sitting in more traffic.

"I don't need it for another few days," Marla offered when she saw the look of dread on my face. "Maybe you can fix it while you're at work tomorrow?"

"I can't," I say through gritted teeth. "My work has a non-compete clause. I can't do any computer work for anyone while I'm still working there."

It's complete bullshit. I can hardly make a living from my government paycheck. Still, that doesn't mean that I'm not going to do it anyways.

The best time to do my work is today, Election Day. The building will certainly be empty. Even if it isn't, the protestors will draw most the attention. Another hour of traffic, but maybe I'll be able to splurge on real meat instead of the lab-grown crap that I feed myself with every day.

That brings me to now: pushing myself through a crowd of protestors while I fumble to find my badge. In an area surrounded by police, the last thing I want is to be mistaken for a protestor. I finally make it onto the front steps of the bureau when a familiar face in the corner of my eye catches my attention.

April.

For a second, I think that I've gone crazy. April McIntyre is standing less than twenty feet away from me. She's not wearing a face mask, which is a horrible decision. The place reeks, and the pollution level is still at haphazard levels. She almost blends in with the crowd – almost.

"April!" I call out, my heart thumping in my chest.

She gives me a side eye, but she doesn't respond. Maybe she doesn't recognize me in my face mask.

"April!" I call out again. I make my way towards the crowd to reach her.

Once I'm close enough to see her, a smile crosses my face. She can't see it, thank heavens, because I'm sure I look like an idiot.

"Hey," I say, a little out of breath. "So, I meet you at your work, and now you're following me to mine? Is that what's happening here?"

I assume she knows that I'm joking, but she huffs and crosses her arms.

"Sorry," I say, raising my hands up defensively. "I didn't mean to offend you. I just…" I trail off when I see the sign that she's holding.

It's dangling sideways from one of her clenched fists. I need to tilt my head slightly to read it. When I do, its meaning is loud and clear: No Justice in the Divinity Bureau.

She's protesting the Divinity Bureau. More accurately, she's protesting the organization where I spend forty hours of my life, and that pays my bills. That's a huge problem.

"April?" I ask, realizing that she hasn't said anything to me.

Maybe I'm better off letting this one go. There are billions of people in this world, and I'm bound to meet the right girl eventually. But I *like* this one. Is chemistry enough to see past what is possibly a glaring red flag?

"I can't believe you work for them," April spits out, immediately dashing my hopes.

"I don't know what you're talking about," I say, hoping denial might help my case.

April's eyes narrow. "You know *precisely* what I'm talking about! You work for a bureau of murderers!"

"I…"

"God," she groans, tugging her hair. "I'm such an idiot. I can't believe I gave you my number!"

I stare at her, unable to understand why she's upset. She has no idea how close she had come to sharing her father's fate. She would have if it weren't for me. I saved her life, and it's not fair to group me in the same category as a "Bureau of murderers."

"That's rich," I say dryly, unable to stop the words from coming out of my mouth. "Coming from the daughter of Henrik McIntyre!"

April's mouth falls open, and it hits me that she hasn't told me about her father. I know that my biting words are going to come back to haunt me.

She storms off before I can say another word, and I'm left to stand there dumbfounded.

The chants of the protesters surround me: "Hey, ho! The Divinity Bureau has got to go!"

■■■■■■■■■■■■■■■■■■■■■■■■■■■■■■■■■■■■■■■■■■■■■■■■■■■■■■

I regret my words as soon as I see her walk away. Shortly after I see her, I text her: "Hey. I just wanted to let you know that I'm sorry about what I said. I want to make it up to you and explain the situation."

With those words, April has my number if she changes her mind. I don't know what I'd tell her, but I feel like I deserve a chance – even if she doesn't know the reasons why.

Still, the weekend comes and goes. Before I know it, ten days have passed.

I've spent the first half of that time trying to tell myself that I've done the right thing. It shouldn't matter if I jeopardized my job for a girl that, now, isn't even acknowledging my existence. I've saved a life, and karma is going to reward me for it.

The second half is spent pacing my apartment and berating myself for being that stupid. I have rent to pay, a mountain of student debt, and I'm sure that I can go to jail for obstruction.

By day ten, I've realized that I'm going to need to tell someone about what I've done. Anyone with a background in Computer Science is going to be able to figure it out, and it's better for me in the long run if I come clean. I wake up early that morning with my mind made up. I'm prepared to face the wrath of my bosses.

"Okay, listen, Finn and Gideon," I begin, a layer of sweat starting to form on my scrunched face. "I did something stupid, and I know you aren't going to like it. I know you guys trusted me to run the election report, which probably wasn't the best move – not that I'm blaming you guys," I add hastily. "It's all total my fault. Anyways, it might be a little too late for this, but you might need to add someone. You see, I took a girl out. Also, I might have followed her to work, and she might have given me her number. That's okay, though, because she's not answering my text, and it's been over a week. Talk about mixed signals." I attempt to laugh at the joke, even though it's too depressing. "Anyways, please don't arrest me or fire me, because I have student loans to pay and a family to feed. Yes, a cat totally counts as the family..."

My cat, an orange tabby that I named Neville, meows in response.

At the moment, my cat is the only member of my audience. I only have a few minutes before I need to leave for work, and I'm still struggling to find the right words to say. I try to envision myself standing in Gideon's high-rise office, but when I open my eyes, I'm standing in a cluttered two-hundred-foot studio apartment. It's not exactly the most motivating scenery.

I lean down to rub my hand through Neville's fur. "I might have to bring you to a shelter."

Neville purrs, stretching his back against the linoleum floor.

I rub his furry stomach. "Sorry, boy, but I won't be able to afford to feed you if I go on unemployment."

I shudder at the thought. Unemployment isn't guaranteed; and even if I do qualify, it only gives me forty percent of my income for six months. I can hardly support myself on one hundred percent; and given this economy, I'm not sure if I can find a job in six months.

Neville rolls over and rubs his head against my hand, resulting in a resigned sigh from me. "Okay. Maybe I'll starve for you," I say, rubbing the cat's head before preparing to start the day. "You're lucky you're cute. Wish me luck."

The cat tries to follow me out the door, but I give him a gentle nudge back into the apartment. I lock the door behind me and prepare myself for a long day.

I live on the twentieth floor of a Chinatown building that's designed only to have ten. The building used to be a motel; but when the real estate crisis came into effect, the owner decided to renovate the building and add several floors to accommodate more housing. Occasionally, I see people sleeping in the hallways. The front door isn't quite secure; as a result, the occasional homeless person will trickle in. Coming from a farming city, this used to terrify me. Nowadays, I brush it off as a regular occurrence.

As I make my way to work, I allow myself to think that losing this job might be a blessing in disguise. I have a Master's degree from West State University and two years of working at the Divinity Bureau under my belt. I might be able to get a job that will pay me more money. Maybe I'll even get health insurance!

My optimism is crushed by driving through downtown, where reality hits me in the face. On every street corner, I can see people living in tents and panhandling for spare sterling. One man on the side of a freeway is holding up a sign that says: 'Former Investment Banker Looking for Work.' It's true that there's a chance I might be able to get a better job if I lose the one that I'm at, but there's an even greater chance that I'll end up on the streets. Am I ready to take those chances?

I park my car in the headquarters' parking garage – on the top floor, as usual. I wait for someone to notice that something is wrong. The guilt on my face is stunningly clear to me, and I expect someone to pick up on it. Still, the parking attendant lets me through the gates. I'm greeted by a security guard as I make my way into the building. The facial recognition software still allows me into the office (though, if I'm completely honest with myself, I don't think the facial recognition software will ever lock me out – not when I'm the one that programmed it in the first place).

I set my computer up at my workstation, determined to clock in as many hours as possible before facing the fire. I start the day off by checking my emails. Three tickets to work on, and a handful of emails. It's enough to keep me occupied.

As the day progresses, the anticipation is overwhelming. I find myself walking into several conversations, wondering if any of my colleagues had caught onto what I had done. Are any of them gossiping about me? Maybe I'm paranoid, as many of them don't know the first thing about databases. But what if someone does? By lunchtime, I can't focus on my work. After staring at the same email for a half hour, I've finally decided to close my computer and get it over with sooner rather than later.

Gideon's office is on the top floor of the tower. The building is shaped like an isosceles triangle, and the narrow point is his floor. I step into the elevator. When the elevator door closes, the last thing I see is bland gray walls and call center agents dressed too fancily for their line of work. When they re-open, eighteen stories later, I'm staring at a panoramic view of the city. The sight temporarily distracts me from what I need to do – until I catch sight of Gideon as he's walking out of his office.

Gideon is a pepper-haired man of about one hundred and fifty years old. Every time I see him, he's wearing a blue suit jacket and a black shirt; but he varies up his tie selection. Today, he's wearing a green tie that reminds me of illness, probably the sickness that I'm feeling in my stomach.

He's a member of the Gerontocracy Party, which holds onto the notion that elders should hold onto power. Because of this, he's been in office for over fifty years. He also didn't opt into immortality until he was much older – approximately seventy-five. His brown eyes make him look much older.

"I need to talk to you," I say as soon as I catch up with him.

"It's about time!" Gideon snaps. He isn't slowing his pace, and I'm struggling to keep up with his long strides. "I can't do my job with this damn virus on my computer!"

I stare at him. "A virus?"

"Didn't you get the email?"

"What email?"

"The one I sent Finn three weeks ago!"

"Did you make a ticket?" I ask, mostly out of habit. I'm technically supposed to use the ticketing system to prioritize tasks.

Gideon stops to stare at me as though I had just asked him if the sky rains marshmallows. "Of course, not! God, I hate that ticket system. It's such a hassle to navigate – plus why do I need to put my IP Address on the ticket? Isn't it your job as an office assistant to figure that stuff out?"

"I'm not –" I begin to correct him, but then I decide that it isn't worth it.

"Have it ready in two hours," Gideon calls out as he resumes his pace, ignoring me completely. "I expect it to be usable in time for my meeting at two o'clock."

I stare at Gideon's back, dumbfounded and at a loss on my next course of action. I don't want to spend two hours fixing Gideon's computer if he's just going to fire me right after. At the same time, maybe getting rid of the virus will be enough to make Gideon happy enough not to fire me once the truth comes out. I turn my heel and head towards Gideon's office.

Almost everything about Gideon's office looks sleek – from the view of the city to the black and white artwork on his walls. The only thing that doesn't look well-kept is Gideon's desk, which looks as though a tornado had hit it. Papers are scattered everywhere. I don't even think that I can see the plastic surface of his desk.

*Wait, paper?*

Paper is a rare commodity; and far too expensive to be worth the investment. Gideon has piles of them like they're going out of fashion. One stack is enough to pay for a year's worth of my salary. I could get a raise, but Gideon prefers to busy himself with a useless commodity.

The worst part is that I can't even find his laptop underneath the rubble. I shift a few papers to see if it's buried anywhere, careful to make sure I put everything back into its cluttered spot. When I don't see it on his desk, I open a few drawers. I think it might be there, but it's not. I walk around the room to see if it's not a shelf. Nowhere.

Without any luck, I'm ready to give up on the search altogether – until I see a white hard drive sitting on his desk, blending in with the pile of papers. A button is on top. Curious, I approach the device and give the button a light tap. A computer desktop projects in front of me, one that takes up the entire room. I take a step back, unable to believe my eyes.

Gideon's work computer is a Universe TX3000 – a top of the line computer whose manufacturer boasts a combination of portability and power. It utilizes a top-of-the-line high-definition projection system that's completely touchscreen-based – thus making the computer as portable as a wallet. Its processing speed is nearly ten times faster than the bulky computer that I keep at home – and despite its small size, it has access to a cloud-based storage system that gives Gideon virtually unlimited storage space. I never believed in love at first sight until this moment.

I turn off the screen and bring the computer downstairs into my cubicle. I adjust the resolution settings so that the projector would fit into my workstation. Before I can get started, I receive an instant message from Finn: "Hey, do you have a minute to talk?"

I feel my face heat.

It wouldn't be hard for Finn to realize what I've done, as I ran the report under his account. Still, I was hoping that I'd have the chance to come clean and explain the situation in my words before anyone found out.

Begrudgingly, I reply: "Be right there."

I'm rehearsing my speech as I walk down the hallway and into Finn's office. "I have student loans and a cat to feed..."

I knock on his door quietly, to which Finn responds by telling me to come in.

Finn Hannigan's official title is 'Director of Operations.' He reports directly to Gideon, and I report directly to Finn. While every district chairperson has an assistant or two to help manage the workload, Gideon has Finn Hannigan. Finn, in turn, helps make sure that the Midwest region is running smoothly – especially the headquarters' operations. Other than the fact that Finn is responsible for evaluating my job performance, this is as far as I know about the nature of his work.

Finn tells me to take a seat, and I willingly oblige. I feel as though I might have a heart attack.

"So," Finn begins, letting his folded arms sit on his desk. "I heard from security that you've been coming in after hours."

"I can explain!" I blurt out, though this is before I realize what Finn said. "Wait, what?"

"We've got a record of you on camera," Finn explains. "According to security, you told them that you were fixing the internet. I'm just confused on why you'd need to repair the internet no one is in the office, to begin with!"

I blink, unable to believe that this is happening.

"I had a ticket," I say lamely, even though we both know that that's not the case.

Finn turns his head and gives me the side eye. "Is there something you need to tell me?"

It's my opportunity to come clean about everything that's happened with April – except I'm distracted by the fact that Finn is confronting me about my non-compete clause. I've been coming into the office after hours for two years, and I'm only being confronted about it now?

"No," I say flatly.

"You're on camera."

"I don't know what the big deal is."

I can't believe I've spent all day being afraid of this man. He's a guy that forgets deadlines, pesters me for help on the simplest of computer tasks, and he even needs me to remember his password for him!

Finn sighs. "Listen, Roman. I don't know how to break this to you, but security thinks you're using the bureau's facilities for outside business."

"Outside business?"

"Making money on the side," Finn clarifies. "That's a violation of your employment contract with the Divinity Bureau."

"Doing what?" I fume, even though it's not far from the truth. It's a rule, but it's an unfair rule! "Who can afford a computer repair technician these days?"

The fact that Finn, of all people, is accusing me of violating my employment contract makes me seethe. I wouldn't need to do extra work if they paid me more than twelve sterling an hour!

"Listen, Roman," Finn says slowly. "I don't care what you do in our free time, but now that I know about it, I have to address it. I'll let you off with a warning; but don't let it happen again. You might want to tell your business to go elsewhere."

With those words, I'm trapped. I can't survive on my meager paycheck from the Divinity Bureau. I can nod my head and agree with the hope that I'd be able to continue my business without getting caught – especially since Marla's computer is still in the passenger seat of my car – but if I did, they'll surely fire me.

The thought was enough to make me seethe. How can the Bureau refuse to pay me more money so that I can survive, but fire me for trying to supplement that income? I spend eight hours a day ensuring that the bureau's technical systems stay running. Sometimes, I even take calls on my days off. I can fix technical issues before the Bureau's IT department looks at their ticket queue. I even ran the election report! I didn't need to, and yet...

A thought occurs to me. One look at Finn's face, which is still waiting for a response, confirms what I'm about to do. "So, listen. I might have done something."

Finn raises an eyebrow in astonishment. "What's that?"

"Well..." I begin, thinking back to the phone call with Gideon. "Gideon called me a couple of weeks ago. He needed someone to run the election report, so I might have done it."

Finn pales. It takes several moments before he finds his voice. He grits out, "That's fine," though his tone indicates that it's anything but.

"I used your log-on," I say slowly.

Finn jumps out of his seat. "Are you kidding me?"

Something's not right about Finn's reaction. I've had his log-on information for six months. We've never had issues.

I should stop talking, but I've been preparing myself for this moment for the last week. I continue, "I also took a name out. Her name is April McIntyre. I'm not sure if you know her, but she's about five feet tall. Age nineteen. Brown hair –"

Finn goes from white to red. "Roman, you better be fucking with me!"

Now I know that something's not right. "Do you know her?"

I wait for Finn to say something. Anything. He's supposed to deny knowing the girl. She's nineteen years old, for heaven's sake! But I'm met with suspicious silence. Something is wrong.

"Finn?"

"That system is hard-coded," Finn murmurs. "You shouldn't have been able to do that."

I'm astounded by his answer. "I have a Master's degree in Network Security." I pause, letting the last few minutes' sink in. "Do you know her?"

"You shouldn't have done that," Finn says, his tone cold and evading my question. "Obstruction with the election report is a federal offense that can land you in prison."

"She's a nineteen-year-old girl!" I say defensively. "I thought it was a glitch!"

Finn remains silent. I'm positive that I'm about to be fired in the next few minutes if I don't break the tension quickly.

"Is it alright if we just keep it between the two of us?" I squeak. I hoped that I'd sound more convincing, but I'm too nervous to think. "I know I can get fired, but I have student loans to pay and a family to feed." Pause. "And yes, a cat totally counts as family."

Finn looks as though he wants to say few words, many of which begin with the letter 'F.' He finally grumbles out, "Fine."

I feel as though a weight is lifted from my shoulders. I make a hasty exit out of Finn's office, happy that I'm not going on unemployment anytime soon. Still, questions swirl in my mind.

Who is April McIntyre?

What does the Divinity Bureau want with her?

I'm in the process of taking deep breaths of relief when I feel a vibration on my wrist. Confused on who would be calling me during my work hours, I glance at my wrist and notice the caller identification.

*April McIntyre.*

This day just keeps on getting better.

CHAPTER FOUR

# APRIL

*Earlier that day...*

I'm sitting in the therapist's office, and my stomach is in knots. I was fifteen minutes late to my appointment – which Dr. Darcy Gray brazenly reminded me.

"I was stuck in traffic!" I say defensively.

Dr. Gray, a brunette woman who typically reeks of cigarette smoke, raises a perfectly groomed eyebrow. "Are you positive about that?"

Of course, I'm positive about that! Practically everywhere we go is surrounded by traffic!

But of course, I know that that's not the full truth. I'm late because I don't want to be here. The only reason why I'm sitting in this office is that the district judicial court – and, of course, my mother – will hear all about it if I don't show up.

My weekly sessions with Dr. Gray began a year ago. Shortly after my arrest at the protest for my father's election, the judge forced me to choose between three months in jail or a year of probation. I, of course, took probation without a second thought. Part of my probationary terms was that I was required to undergo a year of therapy. Seeing Dr. Gray – and her condescending, know-it-all attitude – makes me wish I chose jail time instead.

"Of course," I affirm. "It's not like I didn't just spend the last hour sitting in it."

I catch a glimpse of a red light blinking in the corner of my vision, and it takes every ounce of willpower not to break the plastic device that's sitting on Dr. Gray's end table.

The device is the primary reason why I hate my sessions with Dr. Gray. Sure, she's blunt and pompous; but to be honest, I am as well. It's not even the fact that she's my mother's best friend, even though that detail can get annoying at times. No, the reason why I dread every single Monday morning is the plastic device that Dr. Gray keeps a few feet away from me. It uses motion sensors to blink a red light whenever it detects a lie-indicating micro-expression. I can't get away with anything, no matter what I do.

Still, Dr. Gray chooses not to comment on my fib – which is probably smart on her part, because I'd raise hell if she did. She unlocks her tablet and meets my gaze. "So, tell me – how are things going for you?"

"Still working at the coffee shop."

Dr. Gray nods. "How's that working out for you?"

This is what she does: she asks the same questions every single week in hopes that the answers will be different. They're usually not.

"Well, my mother hasn't granted me access to my trust fund. I'm assuming I'm doing something wrong."

"What do you feel your mother wants you to do?"

I don't know, lady. You're the one who grabs drinks with her every Friday.

"Work hard," I seethe through gritted teeth.

The blinking light goes off. Dr. Gray's maroon-colored lips tilt upwards as she gives me a knowing look.

"Okay," I say, trying again. "My mother is trying to teach me a lesson." The blinking light goes off again, distracting me from my train of thought. "You've got to be kidding me."

"Let's try something else," Dr. Gray offers. "Do you feel that you've learned the value of hard work?"

"Yeah, most definitely!" I say immediately. It sounds like I'm saying it with sarcasm, but I'm as genuine as I can be. I've learned the value of hard fucking work. I've got the coffee stains and broken nails to prove it.

The blinking light goes off again.

"I'm done," I groan, standing up and moving towards the door. "I think that plastic thing is broken."

Dr. Gray shakes her head. "It's not broken. The device is programmed to catch all forms of lies – even the ones that we tell ourselves."

"I'm not telling myself anything!"

Other than how much these sessions fucking suck.

"Please take a seat, April."

Under Dr. Gray's firm gaze, I don't have a choice other than to resume my place on her coach. I eye the plastic device conspicuously, still not too certain that it isn't broken.

Dr. Gray's voice softens. "Have you taken your medicine?"

I shoot a glare in the doctor's direction. I can't answer because the device will give me away – and the thing I hate more than anything in the world is being accused of being a liar. As the daughter of an infamous politician, I've got enough of that in my blood. Still, my silence is all Dr. Gray needs.

"April, we've gone over this several times."

I let out a laugh, but it sounds hollow in my ears. I've given Dr. Gray the same explanation, time and time again, and she still refuses to listen to me. "Listen, doc – let's get one thing straight: I'm not crazy." I shoot a glance at the plastic device. It's not blinking. Good.

"See, even your toy agrees with me. You can ask my friends. You can ask my sister. Ask anyone except for my mother!"

No, my mom is the one that held me back one year in elementary school because I wasn't as physically developed as the rest of the students in my grade. Rather than being the smallest, I was the tallest – and the oldest. She's the first person to look for a quick fix at any sign of trouble.

"April, please calm down," Dr. Gray says, even though I think it's bullshit.

"I'm totally calm!" I insist, causing another red light to go off. That's it. I walk over to the shelf and take the device into my hand. I should throw it out the window. No, I should throw it on the floor and crush it underneath the heels of my black leather boots! Or maybe –

My thoughts are interrupted by the sight of Dr. Gray in my peripheral vision. She's the one that taught me to take deep breaths whenever I'm upset, which is something I need to do right now. Breathe in, breathe out. I glance at Dr. Gray and set the device back down on the shelf. This time, it's facing away from me so that its sensors can't detect my micro-expressions. I fold my arms in front of my chest, still standing in front of the shelf. I'm not willing to sit down any longer.

Dr. Gray presses her lips together before she turns her attention back to her tablet. I can't see the screen, but the way the doctor's eyebrows scrunched together indicates that the notes about me aren't favorable.

"What are you writing about me?" I ask.

Dr. Gray peeks at me through black-rimmed glasses that I'm sure are fake. "Denial is merely a symptom of delusional disorder – as is paranoia."

"Denial? Hang on…"

"When you opt into immortality," Dr. Gray interjects, ignoring my protests. "The final dose of BIONs, where are designed to trigger neurogenesis, should be enough to cure any chemical imbalances in your brain. Until then…"

"I don't have any chemical imbalances!"

Dr. Gray shakes her head. "I understand that it is normal not to think that anything is wrong with them, but no one is perfect. Sometimes, we all just need a little bit of help."

I stare at her, utterly dumbfounded. I'm a perfectly functional young adult! I have good grades in school and a part-time job that I perform relatively well at! I don't need any more help than the average person.

Dr. Gray hits a button before turning her attention back to me. "I'm sending a record of your prescription to the pharmacy in District 220." A smile – so subtle that I barely even notice that it's there – crosses her face. "Try to use it this time."

Once the prescription is sent off, Dr. Gray escorts me out the door.

I put on my face mask and storm to my vehicle. Several passersby give me side glances as they watch me march to the parking garage with clenched fists, but I'm too irritated to care. When I finally unlock the car and climb inside, I slam the button to turn it on.

"Hello, Miss McIntyre. Please enter your destination."

I move my finger to the computer screen on my dashboard; but then I realize that I don't know where I want to go. The logical answer would be to my house in District 220, but I don't feel like dealing with my mom and Autumn just yet. I'm still salty that my mom's been forcing me to go through these weekly therapy sessions that don't seem to have an end in sight. I can also head to school, as I have a biology class later this afternoon; or I can make a stop at the coffee shop.

And yet, I don't have any place I want to be other than in the depths of my thoughts. I don't get enough opportunities to feel sorry for myself. Sometimes, I wish I had more time to think about how much it sucks to be the daughter of Henrik McIntyre, how I wish I wasn't an idiot that got arrested last year, and how I want both Dr.

Gray and my mother would stop trying to change me. I decide to sit in the parking garage with nothing more than my thoughts.

Maybe Dr. Gray is right. Maybe I am delusional. But does it make a difference if I am? My thoughts create my reality, and it doesn't give me the closure that I've been seeking. The only thing I can do is speculate and let my imagination run its course. There's only one cure, and that's answers – reliable ones, not the half-ass excuses that my mother's been giving me for the last year. Unfortunately, everything at the Divinity Bureau is top secret. The only way anyone would be able to give me answers is if they had access, and that would take –

Wait.

A realization hits me. Images of curly black hair and a coffee shop float through my mind. Hadn't the boy mentioned that he worked in IT? If anyone can give me solid answers, it's him.

That is if he'll talk to me again.

I won't blame him if he doesn't. I did burn that bridge pretty quickly. Hell, I burnt that bridge before it was built. I hadn't even given him a chance to explain himself. The job market is tight in our current economy. I'm fortunate to grow up in a well-to-do family, so it hardly affects me, but the world is difficult for most people out there. And I can't even picture him to be the cold-hearted killer that I had implied him to be in front of the Divinity Bureau. To be honest, I only said that because I was angry and felt like I had been betrayed.

Not that he owes me an explanation in the first place.

*God, I'm an idiot!*

After the way I had treated him, I won't be surprised if he never wants to speak to me again. As good looking as he is, it won't be a surprise if he's already dating someone else and has forgotten all about me. But I don't see any harm in trying. I move my wrist in front of me and sift through the prompts to find the text message that he had sent me last week: "Hey. Just wanted to let you know that I'm sorry about the other day. I want to make it up to you and explain the situation. Please, can we talk about it?"

I'm an idiot. I want to tell him that I'm sorry. I had jumped to conclusions, and that's my fault. But everything I say over text sounds ridiculous. 'Hey, sorry that I was a bitch to you – can you use your Divinity Bureau connections to dig up information about my old man?' That's not going to cut it.

Without a second thought, I sift through more prompts on my wrist and hit the "call" button. The call is transferred to my earpiece. Five rings in, and I start to hope that it goes to voicemail. I don't know what I'd say to him; yet on the seventh ring, I realize that I'm never lucky enough to get what I want.

"Hello?"

I inhale a sharp breath. "Hi, is this Roman?"

"Yes, it is."

"Hey, Roman," I say, feeling a bit silly. "It's April. I'm, uh, the girl from the coffee shop."

Roman's voice suddenly gets squeaky high. "April! Hi! How are you doing?"

I can sense the nervousness in his voice, which makes me giggle. "Not bad. I'm…" I glance around the empty parking garage, unable to ignore Dr. Gray's office building looming around the corner. "Just waiting to start class. How about you?"

"Nothing much! Just trying to write an IRL command that's compatible with the TX3000 operating system so that I can execute it and run some diagnostics and pull the browser's history from the system's database before my boss's boss gets out of his meeting."

I stopped listening halfway through all of that. "That's…. interesting."

Roman lets out a nervous laugh. "Long story short: I'm trying to find a virus. Not that you can actually 'find' a virus; but I guess…" He pauses. "Never mind. Yes, I'm trying to find a virus."

"Oh, that's cool!" I say, realization dawning on me. "An actual computer virus?"

"Yeah," says Roman. "Gideon said he needed help. I'm not sure if you know who he is. He's the Regional Chairman of the –"

"I know who Gideon is," I reply, sharper than I had intended. When my father had won an appeal through the district chair, he was required to go through the regional chairman to ensure immunity. Gideon had outright rejected his request and sentenced him to die. I shake the memory away and clear my throat. "Is that who has the computer virus?"

"Yeah. For some reason, Gideon keeps getting hit with advertisements for BION treatment of erectile dysfunction."

I giggle. Despite the disturbing mental image and my adversity to the Regional Chairman, I can't help but laugh.

"It sounds like you're busy," I finally determine. "I can call you back later."

"No, it's okay!" Roman insists. "I…" There's a pause. "Okay, I can talk for three more minutes. It's great to hear from you, though. I thought for sure that I had struck out."

I shuffle my feet. "Yeah – look, I just really wanted to apologize. What I said to you was uncalled for."

There's a long pause, which makes my heart rate pick up.

"I have my issues, which might be a huge turn-off," I ramble on, determined to fill the silence. "But I swear that I'm working on them. I…" I stop as I peer over the parking garage ledge to watch Dr. Gray walk out of her office, unaware that I'm still there.

The doctor's words come back to haunt me. *I understand that it is normal not to think that anything is wrong with them, but no one is perfect. Sometimes, we all just need a little bit of help.*

I sigh. "I want to make it up to you, though. Let me take you out for dinner – on me. We can go somewhere really awesome, and we can talk more about –"

I hear a gasp on the other end.

"April, I'm sorry. But I have to go."

I take a deep breath as the sting of rejection washes over me. "Okay, I understand." I close my eyes. "I totally understand. I really..."

"No, it's not that," Roman interjects quickly. "I just found something on Gideon's computer that I need to investigate."

I'm not sure how to react. "Oh."

Roman laughs at my dumbfounded tone of voice. "Dinner sounds nice, though. Are you busy on Thursday night?"

I can't help the broad smile that's beginning to grow on my face. I look like a blushing schoolgirl. "I suppose I am now."

"Cool," Roman says breathlessly. I can picture the grin spreading across his face. "I'll see you on Thursday at seven. How about if you message me your address, and I'll pick you up?"

"That sounds good," I agree. "I'll see you then. I, uh..." I pause, unsure if my next words even make sense. "Good luck on your virus hunting."

Roman laughs. "Thanks."

CHAPTER FIVE

# ROMAN

A s soon as I got off the Mobiroid with April, I dove straight back into work. My assumptions are correct. Gideon's virus stemmed from downloading something that he shouldn't have. But I was completely wrong about the content that the download contained. I prepared for a few videos that may not be safe for work, and I had my speakers muted in anticipation. Instead, I found a batched hack job on a personal computer.

I don't have a name on the would-be victim. All I can see is an IP Address. Still, it's obvious that Gideon didn't know what he was do-ing. I have years of specialized training, and it'd take me weeks to do what Gideon had attempted to do. Based on the timestamps on his computer's log history, he tried to do it in a few hours. I assume his knowledge of network security came from the internet.

The biggest giveaway is that Gideon used a program that's incom-patible with his computer – not a huge surprise since his computer uses a highly-specialized operating system. All programs need to be specially coded for it to work. Another giveaway is that he attempted to bypass the security on a computer that had yet to be compromised. He must have sent a link or document to a person's email, and the per-son had yet to open it. When Gideon attempted to hack into the unknown person's computer, the link or document went to Gideon's computer – thus, compromising *his* security.

It won't be hard to reverse. All I need to do is uninstall any programs that appear to be suspicious, including the software Gideon was using. I'll also need to do a scan on his computer to look for anything with an odd extension. The process should take less than an hour.

But I can't ignore my newly sparked curiosity. Who can be important enough that Gideon would risk compromising his own security?

With no one around, I open Gideon's email processor and do a quick scan. Most of Gideon's emails are to high-ranking government officials and the chairmen within the Midwest state. I notice several emails to Nolan Fitz, the Minister of Population Regulation. I resist the urge to nose around. At last, I come across an email that contains a link to compromise the owner's security.

*Henrik McIntyre.*

Why am I not surprised?

I'm starting to question whether April's name showing up on the election report was an accident. Finn's reaction to hearing her name earlier comes to mind. Coupled with Gideon's apparent interest in her late father, April's near-election can't be a coincidence. But I don't understand why the Bureau would be interested in killing off a nineteen-year-old girl. It doesn't make any sense. Even if it's still confusing to me, my instincts tell me that April's name – and possibly her mother and sister – are going to show up again. It's only a matter of time.

I glance at the time. My two hours are nearly over, and Gideon is going to need his computer back soon. Panic swells in my chest. I'm so close to having answers, and they're about to be ripped away from me. I need to do something – fast.

Without a second thought, I find a hard drive and begin the process of backing up everything that I can: documents, emails, and bookmarks. I'm in the course of downloading the cookies on Gideon's browser when a voice comes from behind me.

"Hey, Gideon says that he's looking for you."

I nearly jump from my seat. Finn is shifting his feet, avoiding eye-contact and undoubtedly still reeling from our earlier conversation. I feel guilty. It's not in my nature to blackmail people. But it's also not in my nature to let innocent people die under my watch.

"Tell him that I'll be there. I just need a second," I say. There's nothing else that I can say, and I hope that Finn will forgive me in time.

Despite the risk, there are skeletons that I need to uncover. The question is whether those skeletons exist in the closet of the Divinity Bureau – or April McIntyre.

■■■■■■■■■■■■■■■■■■■■■■■■■■■■■■■■■■■■■■■■■■■■■■■■■■

By five o'clock on Thursday evening, I am more than ready. I clock out and make my way into the parking lot before the security guard can finish saying, "Have a good afternoon."

After a quick shower and a shave, I stand in front of the mirror as I button up a dark long-sleeved shirt. I tousle my hair with gel. It's curly, and it's a beast to maintain. I wish I had chopped it off before tonight, but it's too late for that now. I attempt to give it some form, but it doesn't make any difference. It ends up looking like it usually does: like I just rolled out of bed. If anything, the gel just makes it a little shinier.

April lives in District 220, which is approximately thirty miles north of where I live. I leave early in anticipation of the usual heavy traffic; but once I'm fifteen miles out of District 200, the drive is smooth sailing. Once I turn onto her street, I'm shocked by the sights in front of me: yards and sprawling mansions overlooking the late. I haven't seen green lawns since I left District 402.

Black gates greet me when I pull in front of April's house. While the large lawn overtakes most of the property, her house is hard to miss. The white mansion – which, from afar, looks more like a dome – can easily take up a block in the city.

My vehicle sits stiffly in the driveway. I'm positive that I have the wrong address. I've always known that Henrik McIntyre was wealthy, but I didn't realize that the government representatives made enough money to afford a mansion. I, too, am a government worker; and my meager paycheck couldn't pay for one bar of these fancy gates.

After spending several minutes gawking, I send April a text message: "Hey. I'm in the driveway." I pause, glancing up. "At least, I think it's your driveway. It looks to more like a parking lot."

I've just finished hitting the "send" button when a loud honk startles me. I look up to see a shiny yellow car waiting to get into the driveway. Black tinted windows cover the car, except for one that's hanging open. A dark-haired woman is hanging her head out through the open window with a cigarette between her teeth.

"Are you lost?" she asks.

I glance between the foreboding gates and the woman. "I… uh… I'm trying to find the McIntyre residence."

The woman crosses her arms. "Oh yeah? May I ask why?"

Through the open window, I get a glimpse of the interior of her car: tan leather, windows, and even a television. There's no steering wheel. Instead, the driving is done through a series of commands and prompts on the television screen. It looks more like a living room than the interior of a vehicle.

Despite the cozy inside, the exterior is intimidating. The steel bumpers can quickly squash my frayed vehicle, and one look at the woman makes me think that she wouldn't think twice about it. I look away. "I'm supposed to be picking up April McIntyre. She and I are… well, I guess you can say that we're friends…"

The woman's eyes immediately go wide. "Oh! You're here for April! Let me give her a call." She presses a few buttons on her car's dashboard before her car pulls to the side of the road. A moment later,

I can see her dialing a command on her Mobiroid. "I'm Macy, by the way – April's mother."

The information takes a moment to register; but once I take notice of the pointed chin and steel eyes, it makes sense. I wonder why she isn't wearing a face mask until I look at the greenery that surrounds me.

"I'm Roman," I respond as Macy sifts through her contacts. "You don't have to do that. I've already sent her a message."

I'm too late. Before I can get another word out, I can hear the phone dialing through the speakers of Macy's car.

*Ring.*

Macy turns her attention back to me. "How do you know April?"

*Ring.*

"We met at her work."

*Ring.*

"Oh, that's nice! April didn't tell me that she met someone."

*Ring.*

"Well, it's a funny –"

"Hello?" a voice interjects, blaring loudly through Macy's speaker system. It echoes and screeches, forcing me to cover my eyes. I can hear a groan from the other end of the speakers. "Mom, would it kill you to turn your speakers down? I can hear it all the way from inside the house!"

Macy turns a knob. "Well, how do I –"

The screeching only increases. I squirm in pain.

"Well, anyways!" Macy hollers, once the noise stops. "Why didn't you tell me that you had company coming over?" Macy's voice is nearly as loud as the speakers. "I nearly had a heart attack when I saw his beater pod in front of our house! I thought someone was coming to rob us!"

I glance down at my car, slightly offended. Sure, there's still that dent on the right side; but I don't think my two-seater has enough luggage space to rob anyone!

"Did you tell him about your curfew?" Macy goes on. "Also, he better not go into your father's study! He should understand that –"

"Roman," April's voice blares through the speaker, cutting her mother off. "I'll be down in just a second."

She hangs up without another word, leaving Macy and me to eye each other for a few moments of uncomfortable silence. Not wanting to take part in awkward small talk any longer, I turn the key in my ignition. "Let me get out of your way."

Macy nods her head, before pressing a button on her dashboard. I can hear a computer say, "Please enter your destination," which Macy overrides.

The gates open just in time for me to get a glimpse of April. She's walking across the front lawn. The first thing I notice is her merlot-colored dress, tight around her chest and loose around her knees. Her brown hair is in a loose bun. She's wearing crimson lipstick that's a mere few shades off from her dress. As she comes closer into view, I notice her eyes: dark eyeshadow covers them, bringing out their steel color.

I don't think I'll be able to recover from the flurry of butterflies that are in my stomach. I stare in awe, barely noticing when April attempts to open the door to the passenger side. She gives me an awkward wave, and I realize that the passenger door is still locked. Hastily, I unlock the door for her.

"Sorry for the mess," I immediately say. It just doesn't seem right for a girl like her to be sitting in my cramped and dirty car.

April laughs as she scoots into the front seat. "It's alright. I should be apologizing to you for having to put up with my mother."

"She's nice," I say. While she intimidates the hell out of me, I don't see any reason to dislike her. I put my hand on the transmission. "So, where are we going?"

April's eyes dart around the dashboard. "Where's your GPS?"

"Don't have one."

April looks as though I had just told her that the earth doesn't revolve around the sun. "What do you mean, you don't have a GPS? How do you get around?"

I point to the transmission stick. "By driving."

The ability to drive is a rare skill nowadays, as self-driving cars have taken over. But April doesn't look impressed. "That's illegal."

That is also true. A two-ton machine is, per the Department of Motor Vehicles, too dangerous to be left susceptible to human error, so cars are required to be in a self-driving mode in public spaces. But the self-driving motor had broken on my car five years ago, and I don't have the money to fix it. I've also managed to survive the last seven years without an accident.

"I know," I say with a grin. "Hang on. It's probably going to be a bumpy ride."

"Maybe we should take my car," April begins, but she's cut off by the sound of my engine roaring as we speed down the street. Normally, I'm a lot more cautious; but it's been years since I've driven down a road that wasn't polluted by traffic. District 220 doesn't seem to have a lot of it, so I take advantage of the free space.

I know that she's nervous, especially when I speed past a yellow light that's on the verge of turning red. But by the time we make it onto the freeway, she's laughing through the bumps as I swerve between cars and bypassing the self-driving cars that are cruising at the speed limit.

Whenever I can, I sneak a few glances at her. Her laugh is contagious. Every time she giggles, it makes a warm feeling erupt through my chest; and we find ourselves laughing for no reason at all. Even the sight of her smile is addicting. I want to continue putting that smile on her face throughout the night; and maybe even longer, if she'll let me.

When traffic starts to slow, I find myself reaching for her hand. She shoots a curious glance in my direction as I grasp her fingers between mine. My heart is thudding in my chest – so loud, that I can feel it reverberating in my head. I'm tempted to brush it off as an accident; and I nearly do, until her fingers wrap themselves around mine.

*I'm definitely in trouble.*

April chose an upscale steakhouse called Promenade. As it turns out, we're forty-five minutes late to our reservation, still holding hands as we walk into the establishment. April spends several minutes arguing with the hostess that had given away our table, but we manage to secure a seat at a table situated next to a window. I don't let go of her hand until I'm pulling out a fabric covered chair for her.

The waiter sits a menu in front of us, which I take eagerly. My enthusiasm falters when I see the prices. I'm sure that the cost of one steak can feed me for an entire week. But April doesn't seem to be taken aback, and she had insisted on paying for dinner. Still, the idea makes me feel inadequate.

"So, Roman," April begins, pulling me out of my dark thoughts. She bursts into giggles before she can get another word out.

"What's so funny?" I ask, suddenly self-conscious. Was this all a joke?

April brings her hand to her mouth to cover her giggles. "It's nothing. I just..." She sighs. "Well, you see, I have this friend of mine that made me memorize this long list of questions that I'm supposed to ask on a first date. I totally thought that I'd be asking all of them like it's some job interview. Though now that I think about it, the idea is ridiculous."

I cock an eyebrow. "What kind of questions?"

"It's nothing."

"You just said that you have them memorized."

"Yeah, but we can talk about something else."

"What if I don't want to talk about anything else?"

April turns pink. "You're not going to let this go, are you?"

I grin. "Absolutely not."

April glances around the room, looking for a way out of her dilemma. I don't know what the big deal is, though. I don't have anything to hide.

April nods. "Okay, first question: what is currently in your refrigerator?"

Never mind, these questions are ridiculous.

I answer by telling her the truth: my fridge contains a six pack of beer, a bottle of hot sauce, and a can of condensed milk (which I think is expired – but April doesn't need to know that). I also tell her about the last book I read (a book on coding), my favorite childhood memory (when I won a brand-new VR system in fourth grade), and whether I'd prefer to fight a horse-sized duck or one hundred duck-sized horses (a horse-sized duck, of course).

"Why a horse-sized duck?" April asks in between bites of steak. "All that thing would need to do is sit on you!"

I shrug. "I'd much rather fight one animal than having to keep track of a hundred."

"You could just step on a duck-sized horse."

"Yeah, but then their duck-sized guts will get all over the place!" I exclaim, even though it's probably not the best thing to point out while she has steak in her mouth. I shudder at the thought. "I'd rather not clean up that mess. I spend enough time as it is by cleaning up people's computer messes for work."

Like Finn's.

I expect April to laugh as she had done all night, but she immediately falls silent. She turns her gaze away from me. I get it. The nature of my work is a sore subject, but I can't sweep it under the rug. No matter how well tonight goes, it's a conversation that we'll need to have at some point.

I take her hand and turn my head so that she's looking at me. "April, I know you think I work for a bureau of murderers. I don't deny that death happens within the Bureau because I know it does." I sigh. "But it's a job. It pays the bills. It's nothing more, I swear. Without it, I'd be stuck living as a potato farmer in District 402."

It hits me that she doesn't know how awful it is to live as a farmer in District 402. The textbooks that I picked up in college portray farming as happening in open fields and underneath blue skies, but that's far from the case. Farming occurs in skyscrapers made of greenhouse glass, standing as tall as the bureau's headquarters. Falling is a common occurrence, but the most dangerous hazard is the agrichemicals. For those that can afford BION treatment, it's not a big deal – but most people, like my family, can't. Most people don't live older than the age of fifty. Going to college was my only opportunity to escape that life.

April gazes at our conjoined hands. "I'm sorry. I still feel horrible for yelling at you."

I laugh, attempting to diffuse the tension in the air. "If it makes you feel any better, I've heard a lot worse."

But the tension isn't relieved. April looks away.

"My dad was elected a year ago," she admits. "He made the news for being the youngest person elected in the last century."

The findings on Gideon's computer come to mind.

"There are a few different stories on why it happened," April continues. "The official explanation is that they occasionally pull from the younger pool when there aren't enough candidates for election. But I think he was targeted."

I lightly rub her knuckles. "I'm sorry."

"I'm not supposed to talk about it," April confesses. "My family thinks I'm crazy." She glances back at him, her eyes full of anxiety. "Which is why I'm hoping that you might be able to help me get answers."

I watch her warily. Everything is clicking into place: her apology, the lavish dinner, and her interest in me after ten days of ignoring me. I thought she had a change of heart, but reality is slapping me in the face.

I pull my hands away from her. "Is that what all of this is about?"

She only wants something from me.

April stares at me, confused. "What do you mean?"

I'm not willing to play that game. No. I'm an adult with responsibilities, and I don't have time for mind games. "God, I'm such an idiot. Here I thought that we had something – but the reality is that you just wanted me to be your little spy for the Divinity Bureau!"

April turns white. "That's not it at all!"

"Then what is it?" I exclaim, throwing my hands up in the air. "It doesn't take a Master's degree to figure what's going on here." When she doesn't say anything, I pull out my wallet and pull out a handful of sterling. "So, I'm going to cover this meal..." I cringe at the thought. My bank account is going to punish me for this later. "And we'll call it even."

"Roman –"

"I hope that you get the answers that you're looking for," I interject as sincerely as I can muster. "But I can't be the one to give it to you. I can't. I have bills to pay, a cat to feed, and responsibilities to take care of." I stand up from my seat. "We need to go."

April eyes me incredulously. "We?"

"I'm taking you home," I say slowly. As upset as I am about the night's turn of events, I'm not enough of a jackass to leave her to find her way home.

April looks like she wants to protest. I'm sure my resolve would have wavered if she did. But without another word, she reaches for her purse and stands up from her seat. This time, I don't reach for her hand. There aren't any laughs or smiles as I drive back to her house – not even an utter of "good night" as she opens my car door and slams it closed. Once she's inside the comfort of her home, I punch the dashboard as hard as I can.

For the first time since I had begun working for the Divinity Bureau, I hate my job.

CHAPTER SIX

# APRIL

I wake up to a person in my bed. My Mobiroid's alarm had gone off at eight in the morning, vibrating and ringing on my wrist. I try to press the snooze button, but the touchscreen doesn't recognize my sloppy movements. Irritated, I push the wrist against a pillow to mute the sound, but the pillow appears to be occupied.

"Ow!"

I freeze. I've snuck plenty of guys into my bedroom during my high school years. So far, my record of getting caught has been clean, and I prefer to keep it that way. Except I haven't gone out as often since I was cut off from my trust fund, and it's been months since I've brought a guy home. The last guy I had gone out with was Roman; and considering the disaster of our date, I don't think I can expect to be seeing him in my bed anytime soon – or ever. I have only one other possibility.

I pull the duvet off the bed. A figure wearing a pink nightgown is underneath it. Like me, the figure has brown hair and gray eyes – but that's where the similarities end.

"Autumn, how many times do I need to tell you that you can't sleep in my bed?"

The little girl yawns, stretching her limbs in the process. "Bad dreams. Couldn't sleep."

I'm skeptical of my sister's excuse. "Didn't you just turn thirteen? How many teenagers still need to sleep with their older sisters at night?"

"I'm eleven," Autumn mumbles.

I open my mouth to retort, but my sister's snores resume before any words can come out. I give Autumn a light nudge, but I give up when she doesn't bulge. I roll to my side and attempt to fall asleep, but my sister's snoring is distracting. That's why I don't let her sleep in my bed! Letting out a disgruntled sigh, I sit up and clutch my legs to my chest. I can feel a headache coming on.

It's been four days since I last saw Roman. He hasn't texted or called, and I haven't either. I'm still aghast that he thought that I was using him. Who does he think I am? I thought that I hated being accused of lying more than anything in the world, but that night with Roman made me realize that that's not the case. What I hate is being accused of manipulating. Both of those traits are prevalent in the McIntyre bloodline, and I don't want any part of it.

I sit up from my bed and make my way towards the kitchen. I take the elevator, as it's too early in the morning to shuffle down three flights of stairs. I'm prepared to say good morning to the maid, but I'm greeted by a slab of polished metal instead.

"What do you think?" my mother asks as she comes around the kitchen corner.

I stare at her. "What is it?"

"It's CLEO," my mother replies, a proud grin on her face. "Our new housekeeping system."

I circle the slab of metal. I'm not sure how the block is supposed to keep our three story mansion clean. "Where's Charlotte?"

"Well, we had to make some arrangements," my mother says nonchalantly, as though it's not a big deal that we let our maid go into a world of high living costs and low employment. "Charlotte is just one person, and she gets tired fairly quickly. This machine does all the same work that Charlotte did, but it can run 24/7. All we need to do is charge it once a week."

My mouth drops in horror. "Hang on! You replaced our maid with this piece of crap?"

"It's not a piece of crap! See…"

She moves in front of me to press a blue button on the side of the slab. Instantaneously, coiled arms and a cone-shaped head pop out, causing me to jump back. My mother looks straight into the machine and instructs, "Make me scrambled eggs with bacon."

"Certainly, Miss McIntyre," a deadpan robotic voice answers. It wheels over to the refrigerator, where it uses clawed hands to pry the fridge open.

My mother gleams with excitement. "You see? It's nice, isn't it?"

"Would you like real bacon or synthetic bacon?" the robotic asks in monotone.

"Real bacon," my mother clarifies, causing me to wrinkle my nose. The idea of eating animals seems when synthetic bacon tastes almost the same seems barbaric to me.

I watch as the machine pulls out the ingredients to fulfill my mother's request. I cross my arms in a huff. "I can't believe you fired Charlotte."

My mother waves a hand dismissively. "She'll be okay. I'm sure she'll be able to find work."

"In this economy?"

My mother looks up to contemplate this. "She'll just have to find new skills. Housekeeping is practically a dead profession. She's lucky to have been with us for as long as she did."

"You act like the job market isn't as tight as it is," I say pointedly. "Roman has a Master's degree, and he's still stuck working as an entry-level technician at twelve sterling an hour."

As soon as my mother's eyes go wide, I regret the mention of my failed date.

My mom had been married to my father for twenty years, up until his passing. Their relationship was tumultuous, at best. My dad lived in District 1 for nine months out of the year, and my mother had no desire to move our lives out east. Vows to visit every weekend turned into promises to visit once a month. Even those promises were often broken. Over the years, I've grown skeptical on love. I know my mother deeply regrets this. The hope in her eyes is all too apparent.

"No," I say as soon as my mother's mouth opens. "Don't even start."

"Come on!" she urges. "He's cute!"

"He's also ridiculously insecure."

"Would you rather go for someone that's ridiculously arrogant?"

My eyes narrow. "Says the person that married a politician!"

My father is still a sore subject. On the one hand, my mother did grieve for him once he passed; but it didn't change the nature of their relationship. When silence fills the air, I know that the conversation is over.

"Your scrambled eggs are ready, Miss McIntyre," CLEO interjects, setting a plate of eggs on the counter. The aroma hits my nose, and I'm tempted to ask the robot for the same thing, but I'm still upset that it cost our former maid her job.

"I'll just pick something up on my way to work," I say as I make my way towards the elevator.

■■■■■■■■■■■■■■■■■■■■■■■■■■■■■■■■■■■■■■■■■■■■■■■■■■■■

Tate is in the middle of a morning rush when I waltz through the door. He's in the process of adding whipped cream to a latte when I step behind the counter, ready to help with his line of orders. He glances at his Mobiroid and back at me. "You're early."

"Don't look so surprised."

"Your shift doesn't start for another hour."

I eye the line of empty cups behind the counter and queue a shot in the espresso maker. "You're welcome."

He doesn't say anything more.

After twenty minutes of struggling to control the line of orders that are quickly accumulating, we begin to bicker after we both make the same drink for the same customer ("I started working on it first!" Tate insisted, even though I handed the man his iced mocha before Tate could finish measuring how much milk should go into it). After a heated debate that nearly cost us a few customers, I send Tate to work on the opposite side of the bar. These are the times when I wish my mother would grant me access back into my trust fund.

It takes two hours before the rush finally dies. When it does, I queue myself a double espresso. I shoot it down my throat before my mind can register the bitter taste; though when it does, it hits me full force. I cough in my sleeve, my throat burning. Tate walks into the bar as soon as my eyes begin to water.

He rushes behind me to give me a pat on the back. "Are you okay?"

I'm still coughing, but I nod as I pour myself a cup of water. Tate gives me a few pays on the back as I chug the water down as though it's a lifeline.

"It's just not your week, is it?" Tate asks.

I wipe the tears in my eyes and shoot him an incredulous look. "What do you mean?"

"Well, for one, you're not wearing any makeup."

My jaw drops. "I was in a rush! And I don't need makeup."

"You always wear makeup," Tate points out dryly. "Something about boosting your self-esteem, which I don't think you need. Your ego is high enough as it is." I roll my eyes. Tate continues, "And you can't have been in a rush, since you were over an hour early."

Tate crosses his arms, the biggest giveaway that he's about to approach a subject that he knows I'm not going to want to talk about. I try to busy myself by wiping down the espresso machine.

"Did my questions work?" Tate inquires. "You never did say how your big date went. Did he say that he would fight a horse-sized duck? That's a dead giveaway if he's the wrong guy for you."

"I don't want to talk about it."

"That's another sign that something is wrong," Tate points out. "You always want to talk about it – at least, to me. Last time a date went sour, you burst through the door and said that his junk smelled like urine – quite loudly, I might add." He wrinkles his nose at the memory. "Don't tell me that you caught feelings on the first date."

I turn red. "No! I…"

"You totally did!" Tate gasps. "I knew that there was a hopeless romantic in you somewhere."

"I did not!" I contended, turning my back to him as I wipe the espresso machine down. "Besides, even if I did, I don't think that he'll be calling me back anytime soon."

Tate lets out a sigh that's almost as bad as Roman's rejection. "What'd you do?"

"I didn't do anything," I say in annoyance. "He's just insecure."

"So, reassure him about whatever he's insecure about," Tate says blatantly, as though it were elementary school math. "It's easier to spend a few extra minutes telling a person that you like them instead of spending a lifetime in regret."

"He thought that I was using him," I admit, biting my lip. I keep my eyes glued to the espresso machine, unwilling to look at Tate. "I think I was, even if I didn't want to admit it to myself."

Tate's expression softens. He puts a hand on my shoulder. "If you were just using him, then why is it still bothering you?"

I open my mouth to answer, but I don't get the opportunity. A woman with three children walks through the door, forcing me to put on my best smile. Soon, I have a substantial order of blended mochas to keep my mind occupied.

I spend the rest of the day attempting to distract myself. Once I finish the order of drinks, I take the espresso machine apart and clean its coffee-grind infused inside. Tate leaves two hours before my shift ends. When the last fifteen minutes of my shift comes around and I don't have any projects that I can finish in that span of time, I'm forced to acknowledge the fact that Tate is probably right.

I close my eyes as I think about the way Roman's hand felt on mine. There was something different about it, but I can't explain what it is. He has the same number of fingers as anyone else. He had grasped my hand the same way that anyone else would. And yet, no one had caused the same amount of tingling that he did. No one had made me laugh the way he did. No one made me feel comfortable with myself as quickly as he had. For the first time in my life, I didn't have the McIntyre name to live up to. It takes a few minutes before I decide what I want to do; but once my mind is made up, there's no turning back.

I queue three decaf shots of espresso before grabbing an empty cup. I make a decaf caramel macchiato that I finish just in time for my relief (a middle-aged woman that I hardly ever speak to) to take over for me. Soon, I'm putting on my face mask and making my way towards the car with the decaf creation in my hand. When the robotic voice asks for my destination, I enter the Divinity Bureau headquarters.

It's 4 o'clock on a Tuesday afternoon, which puts me right in the middle of rush-hour traffic. I hope that I can catch Roman before he leaves for the day. But the never-ending line of cars stretches ahead, and time ticks ahead. Before I know it, the drink is cold, and it's five o'clock. I'm sure that Roman is just about to leave the office.

"Sweet Hades," I curse. By the time I reach the exit, it's already 5:30 PM. Roman is certainly gone by now. My best bet is to turn the car around and let my heartfelt declaration wait until tomorrow.

"Now exiting the I-205 freeway," the car's robotic voice says as it makes a right turn.

I need to change the vehicle's destination, but the map of the road is populating the screen. I attempt to press the back button, but my fingers slip. I press the wrong button.

"Now transitioning into manual drive mode."

I freeze. "No, no, no!"

I have no idea how to drive. Not only is it illegal, but I don't have a reason to. By the time my car finishes transitioning into manual mode, I'm in the middle of city streets and ahead of three impatient drivers. My eyes search the vehicle for what looks like a steering wheel, and I press the closest pedal that I can find – the gas pedal. I jolt forward as the car speeds down the street, causing a shriek to erupt from my throat. I am certainly going to die.

Buildings are passing me by faster than I can acknowledge that they're there. I swerve past a line of cars by driving on the sidewalk. I come across a traffic light, but I can't stop quickly enough to avoid passing through the intersection. When I'm finally in the clear, and there aren't any cars behind me, I slam my feet on the brakes. My head collides with the steering wheel.

It takes a few minutes to calm my racing heart. Am I alive? The pounding in my head answers that question. *Yes, I'm still alive.* When I'm finally at ease, I press a button on the dashboard to revert to auto-drive mode. Still saved as the last destination that I had entered, the robotic voice says, "Auto-drive mode reinstated. The destination is the Divinity Bureau."

I take a deep breath. I would need to input my home address, but my mind is still racing.

"You have arrived at your destination."

My eyes fly open. I turn my head to study my surroundings; and sure enough, the pointed tower of the Divinity Bureau's headquarters is in front of me. I can't believe my luck.

I glance at the coffee cup. I'm not going to drink it, and it'd likely go to waste. Maybe I should just see if Roman is working. I'm already here; and if he isn't, then there isn't any harm or foul. I think about how crazy it is that I'm following him to where he works. He'd never follow me to mine!

Without any protests happening in front of the bureau, there aren't any police to block the entrance. I make my way through the revolving doors with ease.

Security is another issue. A conveyor belt sits in the middle of the lobby, along with a giant machine that I'd need to stand in to make sure that I don't have any weapons on me. All of this is guarded by a man in a white button up shirt. He's wearing a badge and gun like a medal of honor – and he's eying me suspiciously, keeping a hand on his gun.

"You need to remove your mask," the guard says.

"What?" I ask, confused. Then it hits me that I'm still wearing the facial mask that I wear to protect my face from smog. "Oh, this? Sorry…" I pull it off quickly and clumsily.

"Do you have a badge?" the guard asks.

I clench the drink tightly. "No, I, uh…"

"Well, for one, drinks aren't allowed in the building."

"I was bringing it for a friend that works here," I explain. "I'm not sure if he's here. His name is Roman, and he works in IT…" I drift off, certain that my visit was a terrible idea.

"Did your friend not tell you that drinks aren't allowed in here?"

I shake my head. "No, he doesn't know that I'm here." That's the wrong answer, and I realize it when I see the look on the guard's face. "It's nothing like that, I swear. We went out on a date a few nights ago, and he got mad at me. I wanted to bring this to make it up to him." The guard presses his lips together. "I'm not a crazy stalker, even though it probably sounds like I am." The guard tightens his grip on his gun. "You know what? I think I should probably go…"

A voice stops me from going anywhere. "April?"

Both the guard and I turn our heads towards the source of the voice, where Roman is standing on the other side of the machinery. He has a messenger bag swung over his shoulder, and his feet are angled towards the exit. The guard looks as shocked to see Roman as Roman is to see me. At the same time, the guard and Roman ask, "What are you doing here?"

I answer first. "Well, I was in the neighborhood. Thought I'd stop by to bring you coffee and possibly see if I can convince you not to hate me just yet." I hold the cup of coffee up. "I brought you a caramel macchiato. Decaf."

Roman takes a step towards me. "I don't hate you. I just…"

"Roman," the guard interjects. "Loitering in the building is against bureau policy. Why are you still here?"

Roman glances at me before averting his gaze to the guard. "An operations coordinator got terminated yesterday. I needed to see what was on his computer to make sure that he didn't have any sensitive data that could be exposed to the public."

If I wasn't so mentally exhausted, I would have picked up on the fact that Roman is *definitely* hiding something. He has a cover story, but he's staring straight into the guard's eyes as though he doesn't want it to be obvious that that's what it is: a cover story.

"It couldn't wait until tomorrow morning?" the guard asks.

"It seemed like it could be urgent," Roman says. He turns his attention back to me. "April, can we go outside?"

I nod, eager to get away from the guard. The man is shooting glares into the back of our heads as we pull on our masks and walk through the revolving door. As soon as we're outside, I let out a breath of relief; but the relief disintegrates as soon as Roman turns to face me.

I open my mouth to speak. "Look, I…"

"I'm sorry," Roman says immediately. "I shouldn't have gone off on you like that."

My mouth nearly drops in shock. I had spent two hours in traffic to apologize, and Roman was offering the apology on a silver platter. I hold the cup out to him. "I brought you coffee. I put it in an insulted cup, but it might still be cold by now."

He laughs, taking the cup from my hand. "Thanks. I needed the caffeine. It's been an exhausting day."

I bite my lip, unsure if I want to break the news to him. "It's decaf."

Roman's eyes widen, though the appalled expression on his face quickly turns to amusement. "I see."

"Well, I thought you didn't drink caffeine in the afternoon!" I say, a bit too defensively. "So, I made it decaf."

"Of course it is," Roman says, his cheeks red. A chuckle erupts from him. Soon, that giggle turns to a loud laugh that leaves him bending over. "Go figure!"

I'm standing over him, confused. "I don't understand what's so funny."

"Well," Roman admits, wiping the tears of laughter from his eyes. "The thing is, I have an iron caffeine tolerance. Sometimes, I'll chug an energy drink at two o'clock in the morning while I'm in the middle of a major battle – a video game battle, by the way, not a real one – and I can still fall asleep a half hour later. I honestly just had you remake it so that I could spend a little extra time talking to you."

My jaw drops. "Are you kidding me?"

"I know," Roman says sheepishly. "I feel like we've spent a lot of time apologizing to each other."

"So, don't," I say breathlessly. "This is who you are, and this is who I am. And I still want to be here."

Roman shakes his head. "Being an ass isn't in my nature. I want to make this one up to you."

I smile. I want to protest, but I can't say no to that. "What do you have in mind?"

"Are you doing anything this weekend?"

"No," I say breathlessly, even though I'm positive that I'm scheduled to work. "What do you have in mind?"

That's one lie that I can be okay with – and I'm positive that I can convince Tate to take my shift.

Roman grins. "You'll see. I'll pick you up this Saturday at noon?"

I nod. "That works for me." I turn my heel, prepared to head back into my car. Then a thought hits me. "Roman?"

"Yeah?"

I attempt to sound serious, but a smile still makes its way to my face. "This makeup date better be epic."

CHAPTER SEVEN

# ROMAN

It's three minutes past noon when I find myself parked outside the gates to the McIntyre estate. A vehicle – though it looks more like a spaceship, it's cylinder shape covered in reflective glass and tinted windows – is parked on the side of the road. As soon as I pull up, one of the doors slowly lifts open, revealing April. She's wearing a sundress, sitting cross-legged inside the vehicle. Tan leather and computer screens take up most of the backseat of the car.

"Is it okay if I drive this time?" she asks.

I agree, but I want to tell her that typing an address into a computer isn't driving. But I step into the vehicle anyways, happy to trade my stick shift and roaring engine for a half hour of relaxation.

It's been a long week.

It's been three weeks since the bureau's election report was released – almost a month – which means that those who are on the list are rapidly approaching their thirty-day deadline. The district chairmen and women have been running around wildly in an attempt to get through all their hearings; which, in turn, leads to their staff running around wildly as well. I glance at April, who is nonchalantly flipping through channels on the television in search for the weather report. Had I not noticed her name on the election list, she would probably be scrambling as well.

I push the thought aside. While it makes me feel better to know that I saved her life, it doesn't entitle me to anything. And that's why I still haven't told her.

When I'm not working on the latest broken system, I'm analyzing the data from Gideon's computer. So far, I have yet to find anything of interest. I managed to skim through every single picture on Gideon's computer, most of which are pictures of him at conferences and events. The most notable photo is one of Gideon and Macy McIntyre, which made me shudder. I spent hours researching any possible connections that the two might have had. I learned that the picture was taken at a fundraiser for Henrik McIntyre's campaign. At best, it was a publicity stunt. At worse, it was another dead end. Maybe I'm better off giving up. It's fruitless, and I doubt April will appreciate me nosing into her family history.

My mind is brought back to the present when I recognize the cross streets of our destination.

"We're here," I say.

"You have arrived at your destination," a too-loud robotic voice purrs.

I jump, still not used to the luxuries of a self-driving car. My worries worsen when the car attempts to parallel park. I grip the steering wheel, but it's locked in place. I glance over at April, who's checking something on her Mobiroid, barely even noticing the car moving. She doesn't even look up when it stops suddenly (at least, it feels sudden to me). I glance behind me to make sure we haven't hit another car. We haven't, but we're still too close for comfort. I can't believe April lets this thing drive her around every day.

Our destination is a hovering skyscraper that is rumored to have the best observation deck in the country. I've never been to the top. Jenneka was afraid of heights, and I never had the guts to go on my own. But I've always wanted to go, and after living in the Midwest region for two years, I'm figuring that it's time I cross that item off my bucket list.

Once I'm certain that the car will stop moving, I glance in April's direction. "Are you ready?"

She closes the app on her Mobiroid and starts digging through her purse. "Just give me a second to find my mask."

I already have mine pulled out of my pocket, and I put it on while April's digging for hers. It takes her a few minutes, and I soak in the view of her unmasked face. She's so beautiful. I chose the location because I heard the observation deck is indoors, which means that she won't need a mask. We can take in the view, and maybe I can know what it's like to kiss those full lips…

I shove the thought aside as she pulls out her mask and puts it on. She nods in my direction, and we step out of the car.

The observation deck is a historic landmark. A century and a half ago, it was the tallest building in the world. Though that was before carbon nanotubes, 3D printing, and robot swarm construction, so that title has long passed elsewhere. One also used to be able to see for miles, even all the way to the 70th district, but the atmospheric changes have reduced the view to mostly the 200th district. Still, I figured it'd be interesting to watch how people used to work back in the 21st century. And even with the smog, I still expected the view to be magical.

Unfortunately, when I glance in April's direction, I can see that she isn't sharing my enthusiasm.

My face falls. "What's wrong?"

April holds her hand out to point at the crowd standing in front of us. People are lining up around the corner, heading towards the building's entrance. Her voice is muffled through her mask, but I can still hear the dejected tone. "We're never going to get in."

"Yes, we will," I say optimistically. I don't care if I need to wait in line. "We just need to wait a little bit."

April raises a perfectly groomed eyebrow, skeptical on my interpretation of 'a little bit.'

"Maybe we should grab lunch and come back?"

"We'll get lunch after this. I promise."

April lets out a groan, a loud indication that she doesn't want to wait that long. But I'm optimistic that we can get in and out fairly quickly. While there's a hoard of people entering the building, there are sure to be just as many people leaving it. Once we're inside, all we'd need to do is take an elevator to the top, take a few pictures, and (hopefully) share a romantic moment.

Unfortunately, the look on April's face is anything but romantic.

I find the last person in line and fall behind them. April begrudgingly trails behind me, adjusting the strap on her face mask. To distract her, I unlock my Mobiroid and start to pull up the guidebook I'd downloaded. "Did you know the windows are made of glass and rubber?"

She raises an eyebrow.

I keep going. "They redid it during the Great Rebellion of District 500. Apparently, the windows took some damage, so they redesigned them to be bulletproof."

April raises an eyebrow. "You didn't know that? I had to learn about the tower's windows to pass the third grade."

"*What?* How? At that age, I was learning about the history of genetically modified potatoes!"

April looks at me as though a lightbulb had just turned on in her mind. "You know, that makes sense."

"What makes sense?"

She points to the guidebook that is now occupying the screen on my Mobiroid. "Only tourists download these. I had to listen to the guided tour for my elementary school field trips – twice."

"There's a guided tour?" I ask, suddenly excited. "How much is it?"

April shakes her head. "It's not worth the money." She pauses, still skeptically eying the line in front of us. "Where are you from again?"

"The 402nd District."

"Where is that?"

"West State," I answer. "Near the Rocky Mountains. I went to college in District 530, though I couldn't get a job out there. I ended up moving here for an old girlfriend."

"Interesting," April says flatly, though her tone indicates that she doesn't want to talk about my ex-girlfriends. She goes on, "Two of my grandparents were chairmen for the Divinity Bureau district in the surrounding districts near 530."

"I know," I say instinctively, resulting in a tilted head from April. I learned that detail from Gideon's computer, but I'm not ready to delve into that yet. "Err – I read it somewhere."

April nods, appearing to accept my answer. This brings me to my next question.

"You've asked me all these questions," I point out. "But I still don't know a thing about you." Other than bits and pieces on Gideon's computer.

April shrugs. "There's not really a lot to know. I come from a long line of politicians. My family is wealthy. All you have to do is think of your stereotypical rich girl, and you've probably figured out a majority of who I am."

"My stereotype of a rich girl doesn't involve a minimum wage job at a coffee shop."

April laughs, a hint of pink staining her cheeks. "I got cut off from my trust fund." I raise an eyebrow, waiting for her to continue. "What do you want to know?"

*Everything.*

"What's your favorite color?" I ask.

April bursts out laughing. "Really? Is that all you want to know?"

"Oh, there's more," I warn with a grin. "I'm just asking the first thing that came to mind."

"Red," April replies.

I think about it for a moment. "That makes sense. The lettering on your protest sign was red. I thought you were trying to make it look like blood."

"Do you have any idea how hard it is to find things to write with?"

"Not at all, actually," I answer. "I don't know why we'd need to. We have computers and telecommunication devices." I flash the wrist that has my Mobiroid attached to it. "There's no point in wasting your time and money."

"True. Next question."

The next question comes easily. "Would you rather fight a horse-sized duck or one hundred duck-sized horses?"

April throws her head back laughing. "A horse-sized duck. Your mention of duck-sized guts really turned me off. Next!"

"What did you want to be when you were a kid?"

"A politician."

I'm taken aback. I thought that being the daughter of Henrik McIntyre would turn her off from a political career. "Are you serious?"

April thinks about it. "Well, actually – I wanted to be the Queen of the Confederal Districts. Unfortunately, that job doesn't exist."

"Is politics still something that you want to do?"

"I don't know," April admits. "You should have seen my dad. He was always so... secretive. And the way he talked was like..." She looks away, lost in the memory. "Well, he had a really monotone voice. He always chose his words carefully. I think most of his success was because he could bore you to death. I don't think I'd be good at that." She pauses. "My feet hurt. Let's sit."

I don't have the chance to utter another word before April plops herself onto the concrete ground. She immediately pulls her heels off her feet as soon as she's comfortable. I feel awkward hovering over her, so I find a spot next to her and plop onto the ground.

"You know," I say, circling back to our conversation. "From what I know about you, I think you're a badass. And I think you can be good at anything that you want to be good at."

April turns to look at me, a wide smile on her face that's making my stomach churn. "Do you really think that?"

I wrap an arm around her tiny frame and pull her closer to me.

"I really do," I answer softly, and I mean that.

She lets out a breath as she leans her head against my shoulder.

"Cool," she says, her voice light. "I think that I want to be good at cutting lines to tourist attractions."

It takes an extra second to comprehend what April is saying; but when I do, I burst out laughing. "That'll just make you an expert at being an asshole."

"I can live with that," she says with a grin. Despite her claims, though, she doesn't appear to have any desire to move from her spot — and neither do I.

The moment of calm is shortly interrupted by a stomach growl. I'm not sure if it came from me or April, but April is the first to voice my thoughts. "I could really use some food."

I agree, but I'm worried about losing our place in line. The crowd behind us is only getting bigger, and I don't want to wait any longer than I need to.

April sits up first. "How about if we just hit up a café and come back? By then, the line should have died down a little..."

I stand up behind her, though I tug on her arm to keep her from leaving the line. "No, no, no. We're already moving..." April gives me a skeptical look that I purposefully ignore. "I have an idea. How about you save our spot in line, and I'll run across the street and grab us some food? We can eat while we wait."

April hesitates. I'm guessing that she'd rather enjoy her meal inside a warm café instead of the smoggy streets of District 200. But she eyes the ever-growing line behind her and concedes. "Alright, fine."

I grin. "Anything in particular that you're in the mood for?"

April shrugs. "Surprise me. I'm not picky – just as long as it doesn't have marinara sauce, pickles, or anything spicy." She pauses. "Also, extra bonus if it has pesto."

"Okay," I agree. "I'll be back in ten minutes – twenty minutes, tops. Don't go anywhere without me."

I give her a kiss on the cheek, causing her eyes to widen. I make my way across the street. When I turn to glance at April, she has a hand on the cheek where I had kissed her.

I order a grilled chicken panini for April, requesting for extra pesto to be added to her sandwich. I got a ham and cheese panini for myself.

When I make my way across the street ten minutes later, I notice that April isn't where I left her. I scan the line before finding that she had moved several feet forward, much to my delight. Unfortunately, April doesn't share my enthusiasm.

"The line attendant came by," she says, taking the sandwich from my hand. "She said that it'd be a three-hour wait."

My eyes widen. "A three-hour wait? That's absurd!"

"I guess we shouldn't be surprised," April says lamely. "It is the weekend." She takes another look at the line in front of us and sighs. "Listen, Roman. Do you want to just take a raincheck on the observation deck? Maybe we can go to the park or the pier…"

I shake my head. "No, no. It can't be three hours. We've already been waiting for an hour, so it must be three hours for the people behind us. Besides, I'm sure it'll clear out. The line will probably empty out when people get tired of waiting."

April takes another look at the line, not seeing any signs of it clearing out anytime soon. "Roman…"

"Come on," I plead because I'm excited about this and I have no problems with waiting – just as long as I get to wait with her. "It won't be too bad. Besides, it'll give us time to hang out."

I'm positive that she's going to say no, and I won't blame her if she does. There's plenty of things to do in District 200, and I'd be happy to take her anywhere that she wants to go. But to my surprise, she agrees.

"Alright fine," she says, unwrapping the sandwich in her hand. "I'm hungry, though."

She takes a seat on the sidewalk, and I sit next to her. She takes off her face mask, giving me an unobstructed view of her. We eat in silence, devouring our food. Technically, we're not supposed to eat outside (something about the smog making its way into our food). But I know she's hungry, and I am, too. Every once in a while, we need to scoot a few inches forward to keep the line moving, but I don't think that a few inches will matter. I'm halfway through my panini when April crinkles the wrap that her sandwich had come in.

"This was good," she says heartily. "Thank you."

I turn to glance at her, noticing a streak of green on her chin. "You have pesto on your chin."

She wipes her chin with a handkerchief, but she had only succeeded in spreading the green.

I laugh, bemused by the confused expression on her face. "Here, let me help you with that."

I take the handkerchief from her hand and press it against her chin. She turns her head so that she's facing me. As I wipe all traces of green from her face, I can't help but notice how close her face is to mine – and how her steel eyes keep darting towards my lips. I can hardly breathe. All it would take is a few inches to close the distance between the two of us, but I don't want our first kiss to be in line while April has basil on her chin. But I'm having a hard time pulling away.

April is the first to break the moment.

"How old are you?" she asks suddenly.

The question makes me burst into a coughing fit, and I'm not sure if it's because of the smog. I start digging through my pocket for the face mask.

"Does it…" I start to ask, not wanting her to think I'm avoiding the question, but I'm interrupted by another coughing fit. "Does it matter?"

At 25, I'm not abhorrently old, but at nineteen, she might disagree. It's not uncommon for couples to have several decades between them; but it's still relatively taboo.

"It does to me," April replies, looking away. "Look, I'm only nineteen. If you're old enough to be my dad, that's going to be weird to me."

I shake my head. "I'm not old enough to be your dad."

"Then you should have no problem answering the question."

"Twenty-five," I say. "I turn twenty-six in November. I haven't even stopped my aging."

April laughs, but she appears more relieved than amused. "You might want to do it soon. My mom says that it's all downhill once you reach the age of thirty."

I look away. The primary reason why I haven't stopped my aging is that I can't afford it. Immortality is a luxury that my wages from the Divinity Bureau are, ironically, not enough to cover. I also don't want to end up on the Divinity Bureau's Election List. But it goes deeper than that. I want children; and in a world where overpopulation is an issue, I feel selfish for it. But even if I had the option, I don't think that I can bring myself to do it.

"I'm not there yet," I reply hesitantly. "I'm not sure if I want to be twenty-five for the rest of my life." I pause. "Maybe if twenty-six ends up being a good year, I'll do it."

April shrugs. "It's up to you. Though as a cautionary tale, my mother was forty when she decided to stop her aging. She vomited up everything she ate, lost a lot of weight, and fainted a few times. She had to be hospitalized for a week."

My stomach suddenly feels queasy. "Thanks. I'll keep that in mind."

I'm not sure if I'll be able to finish my panini, but the idea of wasting food makes me cringe – and there's no way that I'll be able to bring it into the tower. Once I feel recovered from my coughing fit, I pull off my mask and stuff it down; then I take the garbage from April's hand. I ask her to save my spot while I search for a trash bin, which I oblige. When I come back, I find that she has moved a few feet forward.

"It looks like we're finally moving," I note.

April shakes her head. "I think our wait just got a little bit longer."

She points to the entrance door, where a small group has formed a second – and smaller – line. The group consists of a group of men wearing tuxedos and women in ball gowns. The smaller line gets into the building without a second thought.

"Is it a private event?" I ask.

"Looks like it," April says dryly. "We're never going to get in."

"Yes, we will," I say, brow furrowed in determination. "We've already waited for over an hour. If we leave now, it'll all have been for nothing."

"Roman, I…"

I cut her off, knowing that she's going to want to leave. "I have an idea. How about if we play a game?"

"I can't. My Mobiroid will die if I spend three hours playing –"

"Not those kinds of games," I interject, even though a part of me wishes that I had thought of that earlier. "Have you heard of Two Truths and a Lie?"

April shakes her head. "No. What is it?"

"Okay," I say, as I attempt to gather my thoughts. "I'm going to tell you three statements. Two of them are going to be truths, and one of them is going to be a lie. You need to guess which one is the lie. Are you ready?"

"Yeah, I guess so," says April, but her face indicates that she isn't. I'm sure she'll catch on.

"So, the first statement is that I have a cat named Neville – who, by the way, is the greatest cat in the world."

"That's a lie," April blurts out quickly.

"You might want to wait until I give you all three statements to make your guess," I tell her, though her determination is endearing. April's cheeks redden. I continue, "The second statement is that I have a Bachelor's degree in History. The third statement is that I used to be a blonde."

April takes a moment to contemplate her answer. "The second statement is a lie. You have a degree in computer science – or something technical."

I shake my head. "Actually, that's a truth. I initially went to school for History, but it ended up being a terrible major. I couldn't get a job that I could use it in, so I went back to school and got a Master's degree in Information Technology with a specialty in Network Security." I smile, unable to resist throwing a moment to brag. "I went to school at Western University and got admitted into a specialized program for Network Security. I spent a year learning how to hack any computer on the planet, then another year learning how to safeguard against those hackers. I graduated at the top of my class." I pause. "I was never a blonde, though."

"Why would you major in History?" April asks skeptically. "Especially in this economy?"

"That's a question for another time," I say, unwilling to admit that it was because I was an eighteen-year-old idiot that just wanted to escape the life as a farm boy. "You're up, Miss McIntyre."

April glances around, as though she's hoping that her surroundings would give her a clue on what information she should share. She begins slowly and hesitantly, "Okay. The first statement is that I've had dinner with the Prime Minister." My jaw nearly drops in disbelief, though April continued, "The second thing is that I was a cheerleader in high school. And last, I have six trophies from playing the piano."

As it turns out, April was never a cheerleader.

She did, however, meet the Prime Minister; and when I stare at her in disbelief, she reminds me that she's from a family of politicians.

The story was that she was twelve when her father had been invited to a fundraising event for one of the Prime Minister's backers. In an attempt to sway her into following in his footsteps, he had brought her along. Instead, his plan had backfired. Rather than persuading her into a career of power and money, April had thrown a tantrum, and the two of them were forced to leave early ("That's when I realized that I shouldn't be a politician when I grew up," April admitted sheepishly). She joked that her father had never forgiven her for embarrassing him in front of the leader of the free world, but a part of me wonders if it still bothers her.

"What made you start working at the coffee shop?" I ask. I'm curious why a girl from a wealthy family would spend twenty hours a week serving coffee for minimum wage. Even if she had been cut off from her trust fund, she still had to be living comfortably.

April looks away. "It's a long story."

"Well, we've got nothing but time."

April shakes her head. "Actually..."

In the time that we've been talking, we've been pushed from the outside corner of the building to the interior. I can see the ticket booth in front of us, and we're close to hitting our destination.

"What time is it?" April asks.

I glance at my Mobiroid. I can't believe how much time has passed. "Half-past four."

April's eyes widen. "I thought they said that the wait was only going to be three hours?"

I haven't minded the wait. It's been a great excuse to spend more time with April and get to know her better. She's beautiful, fascinating, and our conversations have been intriguing. With newfound bravery, I find myself grasping her hand. "Didn't even notice."

We're still holding hands when we finally make it to the ticket counter. I buy two tickets, but April has to coax me out of spending the rest of the money I made in overtime on a guided tour.

"Alright, time to see what this observation deck is all about," I say as we present our tickets to the ticket checker. I turn my attention to the checker. "Is the view worth the three and a half hour wait?"

The checker shakes his head. "You won't be going to the top of the building yet. There's a presentation about the history of the observation deck, which has a line. Also, there's a line to get into the elevator."

"You've got to be kidding me!" April exclaims. "We waited in line for three and half hours, just to pay to wait in more lines? What do I need to do to get to the observation deck?"

I pull her forward before the man has a chance to answer.

"It won't be for much longer," I promise. "We already made it this far."

She groans when she sees the line for the presentation, but the trivia on the wall soon captures her attention. We take turns taking silly pictures in front of a cut-out of the world's tallest man before a passerby sees us and offers to take a picture of us together. We're in the middle of posing for a photo when we're ushered into a dark theater.

The presentation is a movie projected on a screen that details a history of the building. A monotone narrator explains that the building was designed to house a major corporation and accommodate its rapid growth. We take turns attempting to mimic the narrator's voice – deep, to the point that it sounds cartoonish – bursting into laughter until we're nearly kicked out by a security guard.

The narrator finishes the presentation by explaining that the building's rich history is what brings us there, and how he's so happy to have everyone there (though he sounds anything but enthused). When the movie ends, the staff ushers us into another line to the elevator.

"This is it," April says with a grin. "After an entire afternoon of waiting."

"Yeah, no kidding. We've been here for five hours now."

When it's our turn, we're crammed into an elevator with a group of tourists. The elevator has two hundred stories to reach, and I prepare myself for the change in elevation. It takes another twenty minutes for the elevator to make it to the top, and we stand in silence while we try to avoid getting trampled in the crowd. April and I exchange glances as we wait to reach our destination.

When we get to the top, specks of orange, purple, blue, and pink give us a magnificent greeting. We've arrived just in time to see the sunset, as it sets under the horizon and illuminates the city in an array of colors. The buildings – many made of glass – reflect these colors back, painting District 200 and brightening it like a paintbrush on a blank canvas.

"Wow," I breathe.

April nods. "Yeah."

I grab her hand and take her near a window. The city buzzes to life underneath us as we watch in complete awe. From above, we can see the millions of people flittering about, going through the motions of their lives in oblivion to the beauty that's surrounding us.

"You know," I say lightly. "From up here, it's hard to believe that we have an overpopulation problem." April is wistful but silent. I ask her, "What are you thinking about?"

She looks back at me. "I just had this crazy thought."

"Which is?"

She turns her attention back to the window. "Look around you, Roman." I turn my attention to the window. April continues, "Below us lie the lives of 350 million people, spread across the Confederal Districts." I can see it. "Some of them will live forever. Some won't even live to see a day. But they're all people that touch someone's life in some way or another." She closes her eyes. "I get it: 350 million is a lot, and more than our world can sustain. But I just had this thought that maybe if we all had good intentions – if we all decided that we wanted to leave the world a little better than before – it can be our greatest strength instead of our greatest weakness."

I don't know what to tell her. With those words, she just altered my view of the world; and I don't know if there's any way that I can turn back.

April looks back at me, a smile crossing her face. "Thanks for taking me here. It was definitely worth the five-hour wait."

My insides feel like pudding. "No problem."

She turns her attention to her wrist and starts sifting through a series of prompts on her Mobiroid. "Let's take a picture."

My Mobiroid doesn't have a camera, but April's does. She attempts to take the picture from her wrist until I've deemed that her arms are too short. After struggling for another moment, she removes the device from her wrist and passes her Mobiroid to me. She gives me a brief tutorial, and I keep my finger on a digital button that she *claims* will take the picture.

"Okay," I breathe. "I'm going to count up to three. One…"

"Just take the picture already."

"Two."

She glances up at me, a grin spreading on her face.

"Three."

My thumb has barely grazed the button before I capture April's lips in mine.

CHAPTER EIGHT

# APRIL

The last two weeks have been the most surreal of my life.

Our makeup date ended well. We spent the rest of the evening watching the sun dip into the horizon until a security guard told us that it was closing time. He parked my car in my garage before he kissed me goodnight. The next day, we texted each other back and forth from the moment we woke up until we went to sleep. We talked about everything, from the monotonous details about our days (like the fact that Autumn still snores) to the big picture discussions (I asked if he finds it strange that we're not allowed to travel outside the Confederal Districts).

On Monday, it's back to reality. Roman went back to work, and I had another appointment with Dr. Gray. Dr. Gray, of course, chose this day to inquire if I had anyone "special" in my life. I tried to deny it, but the blinking red light went off. I confessed that I was indeed seeing someone (which she noted diligently).

I saw him again on Wednesday. He texted me the day before to tell me about a free concert that was happening at a community theater. We ended up spending most of the time throwing popcorn at a rowdy group of teenagers seated in front of us.

Replaying the last week is making my stomach churn. I'm starting to like Roman – really like him. He's sweet, intelligent, and considerate. He never fails to put my needs first and make me feel as though I'm the only person in the room – which is why, even though it's only been two days since I last saw him, I'm anxious to be in his arms again.

Still, I should be grateful for the time apart. Roman has been occupying most of my thoughts lately, so I haven't had the chance to focus on my schoolwork. I'm starting to fall behind. But I don't want to give him the wrong impression, which I'm not sure I have the tact to do – especially right now when he's texting me with an invitation to go out for happy hour drinks that night *('1 sterling beer!'* he tells me).

*'I can't,'* I type quickly. *'I'm not old enough to go into a bar.'*

I hit send before turning my attention back to the classroom.

I'm currently in my history class – ironically, the subject of Roman's first degree. A professor named Mr. Eastwood is presenting a timeline of the Confederal Districts' history on a projection that stretches across the front wall of the classroom.

"Can anyone tell me the name of the country that the Confederal Districts emerged from?" he asks.

Twelve hands shoot into the air. Mr. Eastwood selects a boy that's sitting in the front row.

"The United States of America," the boy answers immediately.

That's only partially correct, I think to myself. My dad once explained to me that a good portion of the United States sank underwater, thanks to rising sea levels. During the Great War of the Confederal Districts, they absorbed two other countries on the north and south respectively.

"Excellent," says Mr. Eastwood. He directs a red cursor to the front of the timeline. As he does, a photograph of a rowdy crowd burning a parchment of paper emerges. "A lot of you may know it as the United States, America, or – quite plainly, the USA. And, as a lot of you know, the Confederal Districts emerged on the day that the United States Constitution was burned. Does anyone know what lead to these events?"

I nearly volunteer to answer, but my Mobiroid vibrates before I get the chance to raise my hand. I have another text from Roman: *'I completely forgot you were only nineteen. When's your birthday? It must have recently passed.'*

"Corruption," a girl sitting in the front row answers. "The USA's government was centralized in modern-day District 1 with a few hundred representatives making all of our decisions for us. When Citizens United passed, these officials were frequently bought out by corporations – many of which didn't have the country's interests in mind. The Confederal Districts wanted to bring power back to the people."

Mr. Eastwood nods. "Very true. But what was the biggest issue that triggered all of this?"

*'What makes you think that it recently passed?'* I text Roman. My birthday is actually in a few days, but I don't want to share that information with him yet. The anniversary of my birth falls on April 30th, which is the thirty-day deadline for those elected in the first quarter. In my case, it was the anniversary of my dad's death. I doubt that I'm doing to be in a celebratory mood.

"Overpopulation," the girl answers. "This came with the invention of BIONs, which allowed people to stop their aging, eradicate disease, and become immortal."

"Good," Mr. Eastwood nods in agreement. "Now, why was overpopulation such a huge issue that it resulted in the collapse of the United States?"

Every person in the room has raised their hand, except for me. I'm still contemplating on how I'm going to tell Roman that I have no desire to celebrate the coming of my twentieth year. My Mobiroid vibrates again.

*'Well, your name is April,'* Roman had responded. *'My best guess is that you were born sometime this month.'*

"Miss McIntyre," Mr. Eastwood calls out, causing my head to shoot up in surprise. "How about if you put your Mobiroid away and tell me the side effects of overpopulation?"

I stare at the professor in contempt. I'm a bit annoyed that my conversation was cut short, but I put my Mobiroid on sleep mode anyways.

"Food shortages," I say without a second thought. "Water scarcity. Lack of housing. Global warming. Overcrowding. Conflicts. Wars between the wealthy and poor." I pause, feeling a bit dramatic. "My dad was a Member of Parliament – so none of these things are new to me."

Mr. Eastwood raises an eyebrow. "And yet, your family still opted to stop their aging."

I stand up, defiantly glaring at him. "You mean, what's left of my family?"

I wait for an answer from Mr. Eastwood, but all I hear are quiet whispers from my surrounding classmates. I cross my arms, daring him to speak further; but he refrains from commenting. Instead, he turns his attention back to the timeline. "After the burning of the constitution, can anyone tell me what happened after that?"

I turn on the audio recorder on my Mobiroid, deciding that I'll listen to a lecture at a later day. The topic of my family is still a sore subject, and I hate it when people that don't know me comment on it. I browse the internet and ignore the curious glances from my classmates. Then, when Mr. Eastwood isn't looking, I pull out my Mobiroid and text Roman to let him know that I'll be unavailable this evening.

Once the class is over, I make my way home. My commute is spent attempting to memorize vocabulary for my Biology class. We're studying the structure of BIONs, and I have my work cut out for me.

I scan through vocabulary. *Immunized ribonucleic acids, titanium ribonucleic acids.* I don't understand the difference.

As soon as my car is inside the garage, I head for the kitchen. I'm planning on microwaving a bag of popcorn, but the mechanical maid greets me. CLEO's robotic voice drones: "Good morning, Miss McIntyre. How can I be of assistance?"

I check the clock. Something is off. "It's like, four o'clock in the afternoon."

"Setting time to four o'clock in the afternoon."

"It's not *actually* four o'clock," I correct. "It's probably more like four fifteen. I don't know…"

"Setting time to four fifteen in the afternoon."

I wave a hand dismissively, giving up. With the robot frozen in place, I enjoy the freedom of cooking my popcorn without a machine following me around. I can see sunlight streaming through the kitchen window and wind that is lightly bringing the water to the shore. The nice thing about District 220 is that we're far away enough from the pollution of District 200. Sure, we wear a mask on some days, but not as often as the residents of District 200. Today is one of those days where I can enjoy the sun and the wind on my face. I don't want to waste a good day by spending it inside, so I grab my computer and move it to a table on the balcony. I'm about to turn it on when the sliding door opens.

"Mind if I join you?"

I turn my head to find my mother standing in the entryway. I want to tell her that I'd rather be alone; but before I can say another word, my mother is pulling out a chair and taking a seat next to me. She pulls out a cigarette and sets it between her lipstick-stained lips. She pats her pocket down, before realizing that she doesn't have anything to light her cigarette. "Do you have a lighter?"

I'm appalled that she even asked me that! "You do know that I quit smoking a year ago, right? Your psychoanalyst friend beat that habit out of me."

My mother eyes a pack of matches that are lying on the table. "Just checking," she says nonchalantly, as she strikes a match and lights a cigarette.

Now that my mother is immortal, she doesn't have any reason to quit smoking (other than the fact that it smells disgusting). The BIONs will just heal all the tissue damage that the tobacco causes. I, on the other hand, spend way too much time near District 200 that I'm not willing to pollute my lungs any more than I need to.

I hit a button on my hard drive. A computer screen is projected in front of me, wide enough that it takes up the entire space in front of me. I can shrink the projection if I wanted to, but I'm hoping that the screen between my mother and me will discourage any further attempts at conversation.

"So, how are your meetings with Darcy?" my mom asks, oblivious to my need for space. "She let it slip the other night that you were still seeing that Roman boy."

Just like that, the projection in front of me disappears. I can picture the therapist divulging private information to my mother, and the thought makes my fists clench. "Are you kidding me?"

"Oh, you can't blame her," my mother says, waving a hand dismissively. "She had a few drinks in her, and I did push her for answers."

"So, you two are chatting about my mental health over drinks?"

My mother takes another drag of her cigarette, confirming my suspicions. My jaw tightens in displeasure.

"That's my private business!"

"I only asked, because I'm your mother!" she counters. "I was worried about you! Speaking of which, why aren't you taking your medications? She prescribed them for a reason!"

The mention of my medication only fuels my anger. I stand up from my seat and shoot my mother a glare. "Oh really? What reason is that? A quick fix for her best friend's crazy daughter?"

"April, you have to understand that you were out of control before I sent you to her!"

"I was eighteen!" I roar. "My dad had just died! Did you ever think that maybe I was just trying to cope?"

"You're nineteen now!" my mother counters. "There's not much of a difference!"

"Of course there is!"

"How so?"

I grab my computer off the table, determined to end the conversation. "I went nine months a year without him! I'm sure I can survive the rest of my life just fine."

My mother's eyes soften. "You regret not making amends with him before he died. I can understand that." She looks away. "I'm sorry for a lot of things. Some days, I regret not following him to District 1 when he became a part of Parliament – and other days, I regret not leaving him the first time I found out that he was cheating on me."

I stop in my tracks. My mother's words find its way under my skin.

"Sometimes, it takes a lifetime to find a healthy method of coping," she continues, then she turns her attention back to me. "And I'd hardly call biting a police officer at your father's protest a healthy way of coping!"

Just like that, any sympathy I felt for her vanishes. I grab my computer and walk the opposite direction.

"Just think! You were on the news! How will that look when you're trying to find a job!"

I want to tell her that I have a job – one that isn't needed thank you very much – but I'm cut off by the sound of my Mobiroid vibrating. I glance at my wrist and read the caller ID: Roman Irvine. I hit the "Accept" button and let the call transfer to my earpiece.

"Hey, baby!" I answer, a bit too perkily. "How's it going?"

Roman's laugh fills the other end of the line. "Since when did you decide to start calling me baby?"

I shrug as I make my way back inside. I close the sliding glass door behind me. "I don't know. It feels like it fits."

"How do I fit in the same category as an infant?"

His tone is light and teasing, but I still turn red. Maybe I'll let that pet name die. "Never mind." I pause as I approach the elevator. "Give me a second. I'm about to get on the elevator. I might lose signal for a few seconds."

"Where are you?"

I press a button with an arrow pointing upwards. "Home."

"Your house has an elevator?"

"Of course. My parents are way too lazy to walk up four flights of stairs every day."

The mention of my parents brings back the sting of my earlier argument with my mother, but the elevator arrives before I can dwell on it further. "One second..."

The elevator brings me to the top floor, where my bedroom is practically beckoning to me. As soon as I close the door, I ask, "So, Mr. Irvine, what can I do for you?"

"I was wondering if you free tomorrow."

I hesitate. Tomorrow is my birthday, which means that it's also the anniversary of my dad's death. The last thing I want to is to commit myself to plans that might involve birthday cake and candles – and yet, maybe a distraction is what I need. Plus, it's not like he knows when my birthday is. I haven't told him. The chances of him knowing the significance of the day are rather minuscule.

"I'm free," I reply. "What do you have in mind?"

■■■■■■■■■■■■■■■■■■■■■■■■■■■■■■■■■■■■■■■■■■■■■■■■■■■

Roman's idea involves picking me up at noon and telling me to wear a dress. "Nothing too fancy," he emphasizes. "Think more business casual."

Business-casual is a strange term to me. They're opposites, like saying dress for the hot-cold weather. And yet, I opt to wear a black dress that I pair with heels and a leather jacket that matches my black face mask. I tip-toe out of the house in a successful attempt to avoid my mother and sister.

I'm not sure what my family wants to do. Before my dad's death, we'd celebrate my birthday by going out to dinner. Occasionally, my dad would fly in to celebrate with us. This year, the day serves as a reminder of the most trying day of our lives; and my birthday represents that. Maybe a distraction is well-needed.

Roman takes me to an Italian restaurant that's tucked away in District 230. The establishment is located in the town square of a quaint suburb, stationed near a looming clock tower and next to a movie theater. The prices aren't high, though I'm sure that Roman had to work a few extra hours of overtime to take me here. The fact that he's willing to put in extra work for me makes me feel elated and guilty at the same time.

I'm not surprised to see other patrons that are wearing black dresses and suits, but Roman is taken aback. Black clothes are everywhere we look, and Roman's red button-up shirt is beginning to stand out.

We've already ordered our food when he finally notices. He brings his voice to a whisper. "It's the bureau's deadline day."

I nod. "I know."

"Do you know anyone that was elected this quarter."

My stomach lurches. "Not this quarter."

"That's good."

I hesitate. The black suits are reminders of everything that I hoped I'd be able to avoid today. "It's the one-year anniversary of my dad's death."

Roman's face falls. "Oh."

I don't know what I expected him to say. The topic is dark, and I'm not in the mood to sadden myself when Roman had gone out of his way to take me somewhere nice. I decide that a change of topic is in order.

"The good news is, today is my birthday!" I say as enthusiastic as I can. In my ears, my voice sounds forced.

I've just revealed my biggest secret of the day. I expect Roman to look surprised. I'm sure he'll be asking me for clarification before wishing me a happy birthday and apologizing that he didn't get the chance to get me anything or take me anywhere.

Then it occurs to me that he's taking me to a restaurant that is out of his usual price range. The clothes look a bit too fancy. He's also eying me nonchalantly, un-phased by this new piece of information. The waiter is setting our food onto the table at the same moment that the pieces click into place.

"You already knew that, didn't you?" I ask, my tone more accusing than I had intended. I swallow. "How did you find out?"

Roman looks away, a guilty expression on his face. "I might have looked it up in the bureau records. I just wanted to make sure that I didn't miss it."

I stare at him.

*He.*

*Looked.*

*Up.*

*My.*

*Fucking.*

*Birthday.*

His face contours to alarm. "You're not mad at me, are you?" He looks away, thinking about it. "That probably is a little weird..."

I look down at my food. I ordered a veal cutlet. It's the first time in years that I'll be eating real meat instead of synthetic meat.

"What... what else is there about me in the bureau records?" I ask slowly, afraid of the answers.

"Nothing much," he says, avoiding my eyes. "Just – err – the usual stuff."

I raise an eyebrow. "The usual stuff?"

"You know, things like birth records and known aliases," says Roman, though he still isn't looking at me. "It's all pretty boring."

I don't know what to say, so I fill the silence my cutting my veal cutlet open. The aroma of fresh meat hits my nostrils and takes away some of the disgruntled feelings. As soon as it's in my mouth, I can feel the annoyance simmer away.

Roman, sensing my change in mood, offers me a smile. "How is it?"

The meal is the most delicious food I've ever had in my mouth, even if it is a dead animal.

"Like two decades of my life have gone by," I admit, knowing that he wasn't talking about my birthday. I take another piece. "Roman?"

He freezes up. "Yeah?"

"If you ever use your Divinity Bureau connections to look up information about me again, I'll cut your balls off," I say menacingly, holding up the knife for emphasis. I take another bite, then swallow. "Seriously. If there's something you don't know, you can always ask..."

I'm cut off by the kitchen door swinging open. A line of waiters and waitresses march out. A bald boy in the front is holding up what looks like a birthday cake. *I'm going to kill Roman.*

Roman turns red. "Please don't be mad at me."

Before I can say anything more, the wait staff has surrounded our table. The boy at the front sets the cake down in front of me. I stare at the lit candle and purple lettering – 'Happy Birthday' – unable to bring myself to look at the wait staff in the eye as they begin to sing.

"Happy birthday to you!"

I close my eyes.

"Happy birthday to you!"

Behind my closed eyelids, I can see my dad's face. Like my mother, he hadn't wanted to stop his aging, but he had different reasons. He wanted to look older, wiser, and more responsible. It was part of the image that he wanted to present to his voters.

"Happy birthday, dear April…"

"Happy birthday, April," were my father's last words to me, as he prepared to report to the bureau's headquarters. He had taken a limo because he wouldn't be a McIntyre if he didn't go down in style. He thought it would be best to go alone, so he parted ways with us from the driveway of our house. I was the only one who hadn't cried, still reeling from jail time and being cut off from my source of income. While Autumn had thrown a fit and begged him to stay, I had spent nineteen years saying goodbye to my father every time he'd leave for the capital. I wonder if my mother had taken it as a sign that I didn't care. Autumn's goodbye had consisted of a long embrace and comforting whispers that everything was going to be okay. I, on the other hand, got a pat on the back, a reminder to take care of our family, and a birthday wish.

"Happy birthday to you!"

I look up at the wait staff, who are standing too close to me. I feel like I can't breathe. Does this restaurant not understand the concept of personal space?

But they hover over me – waiting.

I blow out the candle. It barely flickers out when I excuse myself, telling Roman that I need air.

CHAPTER NINE

# ROMAN

April's threat leaves a chill up my spine: *"If you ever use your Divinity Bureau connections to look up information about me again, I'll cut your balls off."*

I realized that I had crossed the line when she hastily excused herself after blowing out the candle on her cake. I had good intentions that time. I was certain that she had told me her birthday at some point, and I was worried that I had forgotten it – so, needing a reminder, I looked it up in the database. As it turns out, she didn't tell me because it was a sore subject for her.

I spent the next several minutes lamenting over my apology. But April came back shortly afterward with a smile plastered on her face. She mentioned something about having a bathroom emergency, and we continued our night as planned.

"April," I said. "I'm sorry. I didn't know that it was a trigger for you."

She shook her head. "No, I should be the one apologizing. I know you mean well. I don't think you'd ever use your job to spy on me – and even if you did, I highly doubt you'd find anything interesting."

She laughed at this. I wanted to say, 'You have no idea, April McIntyre.'

That was ten days ago. One week ago, I deleted everything that I found on Gideon's computer. One week ago, I told myself that I would respect April's privacy and never look back.

The problem is, how do you balance someone's desire for privacy against their need for security? What if those secrets jeopardize that person's safety – or your livelihood?

So, in spite of my refusal to look through Gideon's files, I do have one source: the internet. The realization comes during my lunch hour when I realize that I hardly have any background on her family. The moment I return to my desk, I pull up an internet search engine and search for the name 'McIntyre.'

The first result is April's social media profile. I can't help the smile that comes to my face. While we haven't officially defined our relationship, April has posted several photos of us together, including the picture that we took at the top of the observation deck.

The pages after that are links to news articles. April hadn't been lying when she told me that she had come from a long line of politicians. There are a few articles about her relatives, but most are news articles were published in the following weeks following Henrik McIntyre's election. I scan the headlines:

*"Henrik McIntyre: Youngest Member of Parliament, Now Youngest Divinity Bureau Selectee."*

*"Henrik McIntyre Resigns Following Divinity Bureau Election."*

*"McIntyre Daughter Arrested at Bureau Protest."*

All of the articles are intriguing, but they're regurgitating information that I already know. I'm ready to give up on my search when a forum catches my attention. The subject reads: *'The McIntyre Curse – fact or fiction?'*

My curiosity is piqued. I click the link, but what I find is a forum for conspiracy theorists. I nearly close the browser at that. As a government employee, I can't stand conspiracy theorists. Half of what they say is simply lies, while the other half are molehills turned into mountains. I doubt that I'll be able to get any valuable information.

The post is a year old, so it doesn't take new information into consideration. But once I begin reading, I can't look away.

An anonymous user began the conversation: *"Hey – so today, District 220 MP Henrik McIntyre was elected for elimination by the Divinity Bureau. At the age of fifty, he's the youngest person in history to be elected; and the only person under the age of one hundred elected in the last fifty years. What do you guys think? Do you believe that his election was intentional? Is there such a thing as a McIntyre curse?"*

A few users chimed in.

*"The McIntyre curse was a long-held theory that used to be mentioned by the media every time tragedy hit the McIntyre family – at least until Henrik McIntyre paid off every major news publisher to keep it quiet. It just shows that even if you try to pretend that something isn't there, it still creeps up on you."*

*"Remember when Henrik McIntyre paid off a group of reality stars to run against him in the general election?"*

*"His 'over 100' rule lead to one of the greatest population spurts in history!"*

*"The McIntyre family is the greatest mob ever. Have you read their family history? If they are cursed, it's because they're despicable people."*

*"How could you say something like that? No matter what they did in the past, no one deserves the amount of tragedy that this family has been forced to endure. Henrik McIntyre has two young daughters. Do you think they deserve to lose their father at such a young age?"*

My reading is cut short by my Mobiroid vibrating. I glance at my wrist and find that I have a text message from April, who is letting me know that her mother had invited me over for dinner. I send her back a quick message: *'I thought your mom hated me?'*

I can't say for certain if Macy McIntyre truly hates me, but her feelings towards me seem to be teetering between dislike and revulsion.

April had officially introduced the two of us the day after her birthday. Macy planned a birthday dinner, and she had been adamant on meeting me. When I arrived, Macy was quick to serve me with an appetizer of shrimp with horseradish cocktail sauce. She had asked me a few questions about my work and family, but she spent most of the time chattering about a recent cocktail party that she had attended and how she was attempting to figure out if one of her neighbors was pregnant.

"She's probably pregnant," I had deduced, mainly because I was getting bored of the conversation and I wanted to change the topic.

Macy raised an eyebrow. "Oh? And what makes you say that?"

"You just stated that she was getting fat," I say, thinking that that would be the end of it. Unfortunately, that's where I made my first mistake. At 25, I learned my first rule of female code: it's never alright for a guy to use the word 'fat' to describe other women – even though it's perfectly okay for other women to use the word.

My second mistake was over dinner. Macy lit up a cigarette and blew smoke in my face. I attempted to let it go, but after the second puff, the pollutants invading my lungs were just too much to bear. I coughed and excused myself. April followed me and apologized on behalf of her mother, but I have a feeling that Macy was unaware that there was anything that needed an apology.

My third – and costliest – mistake was when I was leaving. April was walking with me to my car, which she had insisted that I park in her huge garage. Once we were away from her mother's prying eyes, I couldn't resist taking April in my arms and pressing my lips to hers. I had intended for it to be a chaste kiss until April wrapped her arms around my neck. At that moment, I could feel every bit of warmth from her body, wrapped around me like a blanket. All I wanted was to be closer. I tightened my grip around her and opened my mouth for her, ravishing her mouth. She began to pull my hair, and before I knew it, I was backing her against the wall – except it wasn't a wall. I heard a loud thud and the sound of metal hitting the floor. In our haste, we had accidentally knocked over a motorcycle – Henrik McIntyre's prized antique motorcycle – to the ground.

I feel another vibration on my wrist: *'My mom doesn't hate you.'*

"Roman!" a voice barks from behind me. I turn my chair, where I'm greeted by the sight of Finn peering at me from the opposite side of the cubicle. "Gideon wants to see you."

He leaves before I have the chance to ask why. I sit at my desk for a long while, pondering what Gideon would want with me. My first instinct is to think that Finn ratted me out.

Panic sets in. I turn back to my desk, attempting to keep myself busy – but all I can think about is what I would say and what I would omit. But I don't see any police circling the office, so I hope that I'm in the clear – hopefully.

I make my way towards the elevator and up to Gideon's floor. Gideon's door is partially open, which I take as a sign that I'm welcome to enter. But from the crack of Gideon's doorway, I can see the outline of a suit and a man that's at least a foot taller than Gideon. I decide to wait outside.

"Ten thousand names, Gideon! Ten thousand people, and you couldn't afford to put a handful of individuals on the list?"

I take a step back, wondering if I stumbled on a conversation that I'm not supposed to hear. The entire floor is technically Gideon's, so he probably doesn't think that anyone will be poking around like I am.

"I've told you multiple times: I have a protocol that I need to follow! I'm sure you remember what happened when we elected Henrik McIntyre!"

I inhale, my attention fully caught as soon as I hear the mention of April's father.

"You didn't seem to be concerned when I paid you for the job!"

"Well, you should have mentioned the fact that I'd be required to defy the bureau's standards and get approval from Nolan Fitz for every case!"

A chill runs up my spine. I remember the day when Gideon called me for the first time: *"Well, the chairman for the two hundred and twentieth district thought that it would be a fantastic idea to pay the West state a visit during election time!"* At that moment, I realize that that was a lie.

"You're the regional chairman!"

"I'm not the Minister for Population Control! Getting there requires that I have a job in two years!"

"If you finish the job, I can assure you that you will be re-elected," the man promised. "Consider it a performance bonus."

There's long pause.

"I have a lot of work that I need to do. Are we done here?"

"We're not done," the man said. "Not until the job is done."

I shouldn't be here. The last thing I want is for Gideon's frightening visitor to see me eavesdropping. I quickly go around the corner and towards the water cooler. A lump is forming in my throat.

I don't know what to do. Am I being used as an accessory to murder? Was the entire bureau being used? I wonder if similar situations arise frequently; and yet, I can't think of a reason why it wouldn't. I hover in the break room as I fill a cup with water. I can't bring myself to face Gideon just yet.

To pass the time, I think of a book I read in college – back when I was still majoring in history. I read about one religion in which God gave a man Ten Commandments to follow. These commandments include rules such as honoring one's parents and loving one's neighbor. Our class once spent an entire hour debate the clause of "Thou Shalt Not Kill." Killing would damn a person to hell for eternity. The irony was that God had killed countless people – sometimes going as far as destroying entire cities and, at one point, drowning the whole world. The debate asked one question: what gave one entity the right to decide who lived and who died?

Perhaps that's where the Divinity Bureau got its name.

I finish my cup of water and realize that I'm going to need to face Gideon eventually. Should I let him know that I overheard his conversation with the mysterious stranger? I want to demand to know who was on the list and if the man had anything to do with April's election. I could threaten to share my information with the media, the police, the Internet – anything to ensure that word got out to the public. Accepting bribes is an impeachable offense, and I'm confident that Gideon is going to want to keep his job.

But my heart sinks with the realization that it'll all be useless. The activities of the Divinity Bureau are perfectly legal, and no one will believe a lowly IT Technician over the regional chairman. I have no choice but to remain silent until I can get any further information. It'll take me some time, but I'm sure that I can save lives – including April's – if I'm successful. Until that day comes, I need to pretend that I don't know anything. That means that I need to waltz into Gideon's office with a smile on my face – which is what I do. I don't knock. Instead, I walk into the room and say, "Finn told me that you wanted to see me."

Gideon jumps. "Roman! What are you...?" He closes his eyes before he moves to close the door to his office. "I asked for you two hours ago."

"Sorry," I say. Now that I know that Gideon is in the pocket of someone, he doesn't intimidate me as much as he used to. "I was busy."

"Right," says Gideon with a nod, but he doesn't seem convinced. "Anyways, I have a special task for you. I understand that you have a background in network security?"

My heart speeds up. "Yes."

"Yes?" Gideon asks, staring at me incredulously. "Do you mind clarifying that a little more?"

"I have a degree in it," I say. That part is correct. I leave out the part that I have a degree from one of the best programming schools in the country.

"Just a degree?" he asks. "No work experience?"

I shrug. "It's a tough economy."

Gideon nods, but he hesitates on his next words. He looks as though he's having an internal war with himself. He clears his throat, and I can tell that a side has won. "Well, I suppose I can give you some experience. You see, someone hacked into our system on March 31st. I need you to figure out who that person is, and we need to have them arrested for obstruction."

I pale, knowing exactly who the hacker was. "Why is that?"

"They interfered with the election list," Gideon says darkly. "As you know, that's a crime."

I swallow, struggling to keep my composure. "How do you know that the election list was tampered with?"

"Someone that was supposed to be on the list wasn't," he says, and I feel a chill down my back. "Keep this between us. Can I count on you to get the job done?"

I swallow, attempting to remember what I promised myself I'd do. Remain silent until I can get any further information. Without anything else to say, I nod and say, "I'll take care of it."

'Sorry, April,' I think to myself. 'You might be chopping my balls off in the near-future.'

CHAPTER TEN

# APRIL

It's finals week, which means that I've spent the last two weeks
hydrated on espresso shots and energy drinks. I had requested to
take the week off work and convinced Dr. Gray to cancel our
weekly session (without a guilt trip, thankfully).

Roman came to the mansion that weekend. We had dinner with my
mom, but our time with her was cut short when she got a phone call.
We spent the rest of the time cuddled in my bedroom, watching a
movie that neither of us noticed.

After that, I spent the rest of the week focused on homework and
studying. Occasionally, I'd text Roman for help – especially with
history. But I frequently found myself texting him for help when I
didn't need it. Sometimes, I just wanted to see his name on my
Mobiroid. When I finally turned in my last exam, the first thing I did
was ask Roman what his plans were for the evening and if any of them
involve me.

That's what brings me to now: driving to his apartment at eight
o'clock in the evening. At first, he scoffed at the idea of having me
over ("There are perfectly good places downtown that we can spend
time together," he said adamantly); but he finally caved after fifteen
minutes of pleading. I couldn't understand why he was hesitant to let
me see his place. We hung out occasionally at the mansion, but we

had to worry about my mother and sister barging in. If I had an apartment (and I would – if my parents hadn't cut me off from my trust fund), I'd be inviting everyone that I know.

But the answer comes when I pass a "Chinatown" sign. The first thing that I notice are brick buildings. The buildings are twenty stories tall, but I don't miss the mismatched blocks that alter colors every few stories. Roman explained to me that the buildings used to be a lot smaller, but developers added stories over the last few decades as the housing crisis unfolded. The solution was merely a Band-Aid. Everywhere I look, I can see someone sleeping on the sidewalk or resting on a curb. I catch sight of a man urinating in the parking lot of a convenience store. These are people that had been affected by the economy, I realize. A part of me wonders if my former maid is among them. The other part doesn't want to know.

I find a parking spot on the street, where I notice a group of grungy men huddled in an alley. They eye my car conspicuously, my car standing out like fresh fruit in a compost pile. I'm surmising that a car like mine is a rare sight here. I make it a point to lock the vehicle, turn on the alarm, and ensure that my valuables are with me.

As soon as I get close to Roman's apartment, the sound of gunshots is the first thing that I hear.

*BANG! BANG! BANG!*

I jump. It would be just my luck that the one time I come to Roman's apartment would be the one time that he gets robbed. Once I catch my breath, I veer closer to the unit. I don't have anything that I can use as a weapon. I don't keep any keys on me, as both my house and car unlock whenever a sensor is within a ten-foot proximity. I'm also not carrying anything heavy that can be used as a weapon; and even if I do, I don't have enough muscle on my body to make it efficient. My only hope is that the burglar is a male and that my knee can cause him a lot of pain.

I'm less than a foot away from the door when I hear Roman's voice from inside the apartment: "Go left! Stop! Okay, now, go right! Shoot him, and that fucker can go die."

Another round of shooting follows, followed by a computer voice telling him that he has a victory. I sigh. Roman had hinted to me that he's an avid gamer, but I've never seen him in action. As soon as my heart rate slows, I knock on the door.

"I need to go," he says. "Can you finish the level on your own?"

Pause.

"I know, I know. But my girl is here."

My girl? Another pause.

"Yes, Joe, I have a girlfriend." Pause. "Well, actually, I'm not sure if she's technically my girlfriend yet, but we've been dating for about two months. She's great. Maybe I can convince her to visit home with me one of these days so you can meet her. Anyways, I've got to go!"

As soon as the words come out of his mouth, the door swings open. Roman has a VR headset covering half of his face and a remote in his right hand. I move the mouthpiece out of his way to kiss him. My lips mold into his, and he wraps an arm around my back as he pulls me closer to him. I open my mouth for him, standing in the doorway as though we're the only two people in the world.

It doesn't take long before I realize that Roman had forgotten to turn off his headset. "Gross. I can totally hear you guys!"

Roman laughs. "Bye, Joe!"

He hits a button on his headset. I follow him into the apartment. He pulls off the headset, sets it on top of a bookcase, and turns his attention back to me. A sly grin falls on his face. "Now, where were we?"

I respond by wrapping my arms around his neck and pulling him closer. I rest my head on his shoulder, relishing in the warmth of his body. He responds by running his fingers through my hair.

I peek an eye open to take in my surroundings. Roman's apartment is certainly small. The entire apartment consists of one bedroom and one full-sized room – the latter of which serves as a kitchen, living room, dining room, and bedroom. I'm not even sure if it can classify as a dining room since Roman doesn't have any tables or chairs. Instead, he has a beige futon and a coffee table cluttered with various computer cords and chips. What Roman lacks in furniture and decorations, he has plenty of electronics to compensate for that. He has a mounted projector, the screen of which takes up the entire left side of the apartment. He also has a bookshelf that has two video game consoles, a collection of games, and an internet modem. I eye it, expecting to find Roman's boasted collection of science fiction films in there, but no movies are anywhere to be seen.

I pull away from Roman. "Who was on the phone?"

"My brother, Joe," Roman says. "He lives in District 402 with my dad." He avoids eye-contact as he attempts to declutter the mess that's sitting on his coffee table. I wonder if the topic of his family is a sore subject. "I suppose I did promise you a science-fiction marathon."

I glance around the apartment. "As I recall, you told me that you owned every science fiction film produced in the last decade. If that were the case, your apartment would be overflowing with movies."

"That's because it's not in my apartment," says Roman, brushing past me to grab his computer. He points to the machine, which can fit in the palm of his hand. "It's in here."

He plops down onto the futon and motion for me to sit next to him. I oblige, resting my head on his shoulder as he presses a button and a computer screen projects onto the screen. I can't help but notice that everything looks out of date. It doesn't have touchscreen capabilities, and he can't change the size of the screen unless it's synced to a different projector.

"How come you still have an Experian?" I ask, pointing to the computer logo curiously. I would have thought that someone as interested in technology as Roman would invest in something formidable. "I figured they went out of business ten years ago."

Roman shrugs. "I don't know. This was the first computer that I ever owned. I bought it used off one of my old buddies in college. I didn't have a lot of money back then, so I couldn't afford anything better. Even now, I don't think…" He trails off, eying me nervously. I know what he was going to say: he can't afford it.

I glance at the projector. It's then that I notice that Roman's palm-sized computer has camera lenses, which is reflecting his face onto the projector. The image freezes in place. Then a computer voice says, "Welcome, Roman Irvine."

"I installed facial recognition," Roman explains. "It's pretty awesome because passwords can be intercepted. It's annoying at first, but it's perfect for keeping the hackers away. You can never be too careful."

I sneeze, prompting Roman to hand me the napkin that's sitting on the coffee table. There's a ketchup stain on it, but I'm eager to wipe the snot that's coming out of my nose.

"Anyways," Roman continues, as he opens a folder on his computer. It takes a few seconds to load Roman's impressive list of movies. "What are you in the mood to watch? I don't just have science fiction films. I also have a small collection of thriller films, some westerns, a few spy flicks…"

I sneeze again. My eyes begin to water.

Roman looks at me in alarm. "Are you okay?"

I nod. "Yeah. I just feel like I have something in my nose."

"Spring allergies?"

"No," I say, pausing as another sneeze overtakes my body. "I don't get spring allergies. I'm just allergic to…" I pause, remembering something that Roman once told me: *'I have a cat named Neville – who, by the way, is the greatest cat in the world.'* Roman has mentioned him a few times to me, but I've never seen him. Unfortunately, I don't need to. "You have a cat."

Roman's eyes widen. "Don't tell me you're allergic."

Sneeze.

"I don't think I need to," I say.

"Shit," Roman groans. He stands up from the futon. "Let me go find him. What do I need to do?"

"Medicine," I manage to gasp out. "And is there another room you could put him in?"

Roman finds the cat hiding underneath the futon and locks him in the bathroom, which makes me feel tremendously guilty. His meows echo throughout the apartment, so Roman leaves him with a bag of catnip and a few toys to keep him entertained. When he comes out of the bathroom, he has a pill jar in one hand and a glass of water in the other. I take it eagerly.

"It's what I take for my seasonal allergies," Roman explains. "It should help."

The nice thing about Roman being "normal" is that he still has medicine stockpiled in his cabinet. Once a person is injected with BIONs, things like allergies and cases of the flu disappear like magic. Unfortunately, they don't go away for the rest of us.

Roman takes his seat on the futon, working on playing with the settings on his computer screen. My vision is hazy, and my eyes are still pink from the allergen exposure, but I can't stop myself from looking at him. His lips press together, and his brows furrow in concentration. Something is appealing about a man that can get lost in the little things. I like to think that he can get lost in the big stuff – like love – as well.

He catches me staring at him. "What?"

I shrug as I take a few extra sips of water. When I finish swallowing it down, I set the glass on the coffee table and scoot a little closer towards Roman.

"When did you know that you wanted to do network security?" I ask.

Roman glances up at the projection screen to see if his movie is playing (it isn't), before turning to look at me. "I don't know. To be honest, I only went back to school for it when I realized that my

History degree wasn't getting me anywhere. But now that I think about it..." He pauses, wistful. "My parents started letting me play computer games when I was five; and every time they wanted to punish me, they would change the password. Being the bratty kid that I was, I would find ways to figure out what it was – which wasn't every hard, since they used the same five passwords for everything. I eventually figured out how to use proxy servers to..." He trails off, turning red. I have a feeling that he used it to look up things that a kid shouldn't be viewing. "Anyways, I initially majored in History; because I was curious about how the Confederal Districts came to be. There's so much that they don't teach us, particularly where North Amerigo is concerned."

"You mean America?"

He nods. "See, that's another area of debate. You see, it was named after Amerigo Vespucci..." He waves a hand. "I won't bore you with the details. Anyways, it ended up being a terrible degree choice. I was working as a clerk for a museum for minimum wage when I decided to go back to school. I thought that computer science would be a better choice. It turns out, it was only marginally better." A flash of white appears on the screen, and then the opening credits of a movie are synced to the projector. "Success!"

With that, I assume that the conversation is over.

"So, what are we watching?" I ask.

"The Avalon Predator," says Roman, setting his laptop onto the coffee table so that he has a free arm to wrap around my shoulder. "It's an epic tale of a rogue robot set on destroying humanity and a duo that consists of two people that were sent from rivaling countries to stop it. At first, they try to kill each other, but they become friends." He pauses, stopping himself from spoiling the entire movie. "I hope that's okay with you."

I nod, trying to keep myself from giggling at how adorable Roman looks whenever he gets excited over a movie. "That sounds great!"

The opening credits roll in. As it does, I can feel Roman's heart race. I wonder if it's because of the movie or my presence. The film, while tolerable, isn't quite my cup of tea. While the visual effects are impressive, the main characters have way too much testosterone for my liking. They've begun the movie with a battle scene between the two of them, both of whom prefer to fight with antique swords instead of the high-tech guns that the other characters have. It's cheesy, but Roman can't take his eyes off the screen.

Halfway through the movie, the medicine takes effect, and my allergies begin to clear. By now, the two main characters have stopped trying to kill each other and have formed a tentative alliance – and this is as much as I can figure out. They've spent a good portion of the film discussing robots and how to disable them, neither of which makes sense to me. Roman is too engrossed in the movie to notice my boredom, so I try my hand at distracting him.

I bury my nose inside the crook of his neck and plant a kiss. Roman's breath catches in his throat. "What are you doing?"

A mischievous smile crosses his lips as I continue my onslaught. "Distracting you."

"Why…" A moan escapes his lips, and his cheeks redden. He swallows. "Why would you do that?"

"It's fun," I say casually. I don't think I need a legitimate reason.

"Are you not having fun already?"

"Not as much as we could be having," I purr seductively. I don't think that Roman will take me seriously. After two months of dating, we have yet to take our relationship to the next level. I'm not sure if it's because Roman is slow at taking hints or if he isn't interested in a sexual relationship. Based on his reaction to my touch, I'm assuming it's the former.

I'm about to pull him into a kiss when he wraps an arm around my waist and turns me over so that I'm lying on the futon. I squeak, startled by the sudden movement. He hovers over me, gazing into my eyes.

"You're so beautiful," he breathes.

I respond by wrapping my hands in his hair and pull him closer to me. He buries his head in my neck, and I plant kisses on his neck, shoulder, and earlobe. As my hands find its way underneath his shirt, I find myself hoping that this is the moment that I've been waiting for. Roman is lean – skinny enough that I can feel a light trace of ribs, but meaty enough that he can hold me down if he wants to. And he's beautiful, especially as he's gazing down at me with utter adoration in his eyes.

"April," he breathes, his eyes searching mine. He touches my face, as though he's having a hard time believing that this is real. *I'm* having a hard time believing it. Never in my life have I felt so aroused, adored... and loved. Roman looks away, as he struggles to find his next words. "Listen, April. I just want you to know something. I know we don't always agree on everything, and maybe I don't always fit in your world."

*'You belong in my world,'* I want to say.

He swallows. "But I want you to know... that I..."

My heart stops in anticipation of his next words, but they don't come. He looks away from me, as though he's ashamed of himself. But I don't know why. He's beautiful, and there's not a thing in this world that can make me think otherwise.

"Hey," I murmur, cupping his face so that he'd look at me. "I know."

His eyes are soft as he gazes at me, admiring me and questioning my words, all at once. After a few moments of silence, he presses his lips to mine hungrily.

His shirt is the first thing to come off. I pry it over his head, leaving his curly hair ruffled in its wake. Once removed, he starts kissing me all over – my hair, my neck, my lips – and I can feel his hands on my body, but he hesitates like he's unsure what to do with them. It's when I feel his desire pressing against me that I pull my shirt over my head. The sight of my bare chest is the only signal he needs before his hands move down my chest and to the zipper on my pants. The rest of my clothes are soon on his living room floor, the movie forgotten.

He doesn't last long the first round. He offers an apology and tells me that it's been awhile. I kiss him and assure him that it's alright, and then he holds me close to him. We're still bare as we continue watching The Avalon Predator. Before the movie ends, Roman pulls me into another kiss; and I barely have a chance to recover from the first round before I'm underneath him again. He lasts longer the second time around, having found a steady rhythm that continues long after the credits stop rolling. I come again and again before he collapses against me.

I fall asleep quickly, my body tired from our activities and comfortable in the warmth of Roman's futon. He wraps an arm around me, and I fall into a dreamless sleep. Perhaps reality is finally better than anything that my imagination can conjure up.

In the middle of the night, I awake in Roman's arms. His nose is buried in my hair.

"I'm sorry," he whispers. "Did I wake you?"

I don't answer, nuzzling closer to him.

He lets out a content sigh. "Your hair smells amazing, by the way."

I laugh, feeling a bit self-conscious about my decision to skip a shower this morning. "Thanks."

He responds by kissing the top of my head.

"Hey, Roman?"

"Yeah?"

"I heard you say earlier that you weren't sure if I was technically your girlfriend."

Silence fills the air. I imagine Roman is turning red in embarrassment. "I guess I should have talked to you first. I just... wasn't sure what label to give this. Us."

"Well," I begin, leaning my head against his chest. "I'd like to have that talk."

He yawns. "Does it have to be right now?"

"If it counts for anything, I'd like to be your girlfriend. If that's what you want."

Roman responds by stroking my shoulder, leaving tingles on my skin. "That's what I want. I want it more than anything."

Those are the last words he says before we fall asleep. For the first time in my life, I feel complete.

CHAPTER ELEVEN

# ROMAN

I'm whistling as I walk into the bureau's headquarters. It's been two weeks since April and I spent our first night together. Since then, I'm beginning to learn her sleep patterns – or, more particularly, the fact that she hates mornings. Some days, I wake her up and make her breakfast; and other days, I forfeit my morning routine to spend the morning holding her. This morning, I chose latter. Worth it. Nothing can ruin the state of bliss I'm in.

I realize a moment later that the universe is determined to prove me wrong.

"Pardon me," a rushed voice says, followed by a small woman squeezing next to me a moment later. I brush it off as the everyday operations of the Divinity Bureau. People are always in a rush, scrambling from one appeal to the next.

But when I enter the lobby, the sight before me as anything but typical. Uniformed officers are guarding an area's roped off and crowded with a mix of people and gear. Some of them have badges that read "PRESS." Others are wearing security badges. Cameras and guns blend that I can't tell them apart.

When I approach the front desk, I'm appalled to find that no one is allowed into the office until further notice.

"What's going on?" I ask, irritated that whatever is happening will likely result in extra hours that I'll need to work.

"It's a press conference," a red-haired security guard answers. His badge reads 'Michael.' "The Minister of Population Regulation is here."

I suddenly feel underdressed. In most cases, the Minister of Population Regulation has direct authority over the Divinity Bureau. He's a member of the legislative branch, assigned by the Prime Minister to oversee the standards of population regulation. From what I remember, April's dad used to work directly with him.

I only have one question: "Why?"

Michael opens his mouth to answer, though the sound of blaring speakers cut him off.

"Ladies and gentlemen," Gideon's voice interjects over the sound system. "The Minister of Population Regulation, Nolan Fitz."

I look up in time to see the crowd burst into applause. I've never seen Nolan Fitz before, but his picture is in every corner of the Divinity Bureau. He's been the Minister of Population Regulation for as long as I've been alive. Surprisingly, he's very liberal. He's part of the Cyberocracy Party, and he is the one that pioneered using a computer to make election decisions. As a member of the national party that believes in using a computer to make decisions, he is, unsurprisingly, rarely in the public eye.

He looks a decade older than the picture that I've seen of him. He reminds me of a crossover between a snake and a lion. His hair is slicked black, stiff under the weight of all the product in it.

I soon realize that it's not his face that looks older. He was born in the same year that the Confederal Districts were erected, so he had to have stopped his aging long ago. It's his eyes – beady and black – that look older. They look resigned to a life of futility. It's a stark contrast to Gideon, who always looks like he's planning his next move.

A move to take Nolan Fitz's job, perhaps?

"Ladies and gentlemen," the man says slowly. "Thank you all for coming today."

The crowd offers a slow clap, before Fitz motions for them to sit.

"I wanted to call you here today to announce a major change in election protocol," says Fitz. "It's part of a major restructuring plan that is designed to address the country's current overpopulation problem while the bureau works out a plan for a long-term solution." He pauses, looking around the room. I swear that he's looking right at me. "As many of you know, overpopulation has been a growing concern for the last several decades, spiking rapidly upon the public release of biological technology designed to stop the aging process, known commonly as BIONs. Historically, it is what lead to the downfall of the United States of America – but we will not let it bring down the Confederal Districts."

The audience breaks into applause. I think of April's words in the observation deck: *"Below us lie the lives of 350 million people, spread across the Confederal Districts. Some of them will live forever. Some won't even live to see a day."*

"Therefore, I wanted to announce that we will be removing the barriers on the election protocol," Fitz proclaims. "This upcoming election, we will be electing five thousand candidates outside the standard restrictions. This includes anyone that has not been injected with BIONs and anyone under the age of one hundred. The change will be effective immediately and will be reflected on the next quarter's report."

My world comes to a halt.

*No.*

The audience bursts into questions.

*No.*

"Why five thousand candidates?"

*No.*

"Who will be most affected by the change?"

All I can do is stand in shock. I feel as though I'm watching myself from outside my body. A part of me is screaming at me to say something. Do something. But all I can do is look at the scene unfolding before me.

"Roman?"

Even if the Bureau announced that only one person "standard restrictions" was going to be on the list, I have a feeling that I know who it'll be. The thing is, I still haven't figured out why.

"Roman?"

April already survived the election thanks to my intervention; but given the conversation that I overheard between Gideon and the mysterious man, I know that she isn't going to be lucky the second time around. If they want her dead, she will surely be dead by the next election.

A hand is on my shoulder. "Roman? Can you hear me?"

I turn my head to see Finn standing next to me. He motions towards the elevator.

"We need to go," he says.

I can't leave. I have many questions, and I need to see the press conference to its completion, but there's nothing I can say. All I can do is nod my head and let Finn escort me past security and into the confines of the office. Some boyfriend I am, if I can't even stand up for my girlfriend.

When we're finally alone, Finn turns to face me. He says, "You're running next quarter's report."

I glance around the room, expecting for there to be a catch. "For District 200?"

"No," he says. "For the entire Midwest district."

I feel as though my knees might collapse. "What?"

"Gideon wants it in the hands of headquarters for next quarter," Finn explains. "The district chairmen will still be responsible for calculating totals and listening to appeals, but the actual report will be in your hands."

I'm still recovering from the press conference, and now this bomb is placed on me?

I shake my head. "No."

Finn's mouth hangs open. "No?"

"I can't do it!" I exclaim, throwing my hands up in exasperation. "I can't be responsible for the lives of that many people!"

"You don't have a choice."

I pace the empty office. The room, empty from the activity of the press conference, echoes back my footsteps. I don't know how many people are in the Midwest region, but I know that it's plenty. Will I be sentencing one hundred thousand people to die? A million? I think of April's name on last quarter's election report, one name out of ten thousand. A fluke, I once thought.

"Is it because of the press conference?" Finn presses. "If it is, I can assure you that the Bureau did everything they could before resorting to that."

"My girlfriend lives in the Midwest region!" I exclaim. "What if she ends up on the list?"

Finn's eyes darken. "We'll cross that bridge if it comes to it."

It's not a matter of if. It's a matter of *when*.

I clench my fists. "I overheard Gideon talking to some guy." It's a long shot, but I'm desperate. "Apparently, this guy gave Gideon a list of people – and a crap ton of money – for Gideon to elect. A lot of them are under the age of a hundred." My eyes grow wide. "I think that this whole thing about trying to fight overpopulation is a cover-up for this guy to get what he wants." It's not population control. It's murder.

"Do you have a name for this man?"

I hesitate. "No."

Finn's eyes narrow. "Roman…"

"I'm just telling you what I heard!"

Finn pauses as a realization hits him. "You said that your girlfriend lives in the Midwest region."

I hesitate, knowing where he's going with this. There's no way I can get away with hiding the truth. "Yes."

"Is it April McIntyre?"

A chill runs up my spine at the realization that Finn still remembers her name. "Yes."

Finn turns away. This time, it's his turn to pace. "Alright, Roman," he groans running a hand through his hair. "I was willing to overlook the fact that you hacked into my account and blackmailed me. I was even willing to put up with the fact that you were *extremely* condescending over it." I look away, a wave of shame going through me. "Yet *I'm* the Director of Operations – not you. And I don't even need a fancy degree in computer science!"

My stomach feels jolted by the sting of his words.

"But don't think that you're going to drag me into some crazy conspiracy against the organization that pays my bills," Finn warns darkly. "So, here's what's going to happen: instead of firing you, I'm going to insist that you walk out of this office. You're going to run that damn election report – and if I find out that you so much as corrected a typo, I will have you arrested for obstruction."

I open my mouth. "I –"

"And don't even think about running it under my name!" Finn seethes. "Or you will spend the next five years in prison."

I've never seen this side of Finn before. I wonder if it's revenge for the way I treated him when I removed April's name.

"Do you understand?" he finishes.

"Yes," I answer immediately, but I'm not quite sure if I believe the phrase that's coming out of my mouth. I think that the conversation is over, but Finn lets out a sigh.

"Listen, Roman," Finn says, his voice softening. "I know what it's like to care about someone to the point where you'd do anything for them. I have two daughters, and I know that I'd do anything to keep bad stuff from happening to them.

"But the reality is that the rest of the country depends on us. We make the tough choices between what's right and what's fair. They need us to remain unbiased, or we risk crossing the line between murder and control. Your girlfriend doesn't take priority over the future of our entire world."

I don't understand. The work that the bureau does will always be a balance of right and wrong – and lately, there's been a lot of wrongs. I'm brought back to April's words on the observation deck: *"I just had this thought that maybe if we all had good intentions – if we all decided that we wanted to leave the world a little better than before – it can be our greatest strength instead of our greatest weakness."*

"She's a priority to me," I say firmly. Then I turn to walk away.

∎∎∎∎∎∎∎∎∎∎∎∎∎∎∎∎∎∎∎∎∎∎∎∎∎∎∎∎∎∎∎∎∎∎∎∎∎∎∎∎∎∎∎∎∎∎∎∎∎∎

Over the next couple of weeks, I debate on telling April. I think that she deserves to know. If these upcoming weeks are going to be her last, she deserves to have the chance to live them to the fullest.

But I can never find the appropriate way to bring it up. If I told her that I've been digging into her family history, I risk alienating her; and I'm too selfish to do that, especially if she's on her last leg.

Maybe it's better if she doesn't know. She's been in a cheery mood lately. Occasionally, she'll gripe about things at work – but the moment that we're in each other's arms, the negative energy drifts away.

That's not the case tonight. April wanted to come over to my apartment, but I told her that I have a lot of work to do. Instead, she settled for calling me to gripe about her job.

"So, the new girl was all like, 'Don't worry, sir. I'll make sure you get extra whipped cream on your blended mocha.' I made the drink, handed it to the customer, and, of course, being the little snot that she is, she took the damn drink from my hand and insisted that I didn't have enough whipped cream on it. She pulled the lid off, added a little extra whip, and next thing I knew, it was all over her apron!"

April pauses, expecting there to be a hoot of laughter; but I spaced out halfway through the story. My mind is on coding, computer injections, and election reports.

"Roman? You there?"

I look away from my computer and attempt to bring myself back to the conversation. "Yeah, sorry. I just got distracted for a second."

"Don't tell me you're spacing out for another video," she says, disapproval in her tone. She pauses. "Speaking of which, I demand a rematch in Combat Warriors. I just looked up a whole bunch of motion combos, so I think that should level out the playing field."

I laugh, a memory coming to mind.

*"I'm so done with this game," April had said after he had defeated her in a battle for the fifth time in a row. "You win."*

*"Oh, come on. If you beat me next round, I'll take extra good care of you afterward."*

I glance around the apartment. My laptop is open, a useless algorithm on its screen. I had also searched my hard drive for the notes that I had taken in college. Currently, my old notes are projected on the screen on my wall. There's an optimistic part of me that hopes that if I make the formulas and notes bigger, I'll be able to comprehend them better.

"It's just stuff I have to do for work," I say dejectedly.

"Oh," says April. "At eleven o'clock at night?"

*"It's eleven o'clock at night!" April had exclaimed when we came home from seeing a movie. We're sitting in my car, pulling into the front of her mansion's driveway. "My mom is going to kill me."*

*"Okay," I had said. "Well, I don't want to take up any more of your time…"*

*She interrupted me by pulling me into a deep kiss. When she pulled away, she had a grin on her face. "I had a fantastic time tonight."*

I can't give up – not when there's so much at stake. I had gotten the girl, and I'm not willing to lose her.

"Yeah," I reply after a long moment of silence. "It's just this assignment." I sigh. "Listen, I should probably go. I don't have a lot of time to finish this."

"I understand," April says. "But you know, if you ever need to talk to me, I'm right here. I'd be a terrible girlfriend if you weren't comfortable enough to tell me about your day."

Girlfriend. The word brings a smile to my face. I'm still getting used to calling her that. She's likely still getting used to saying it. That fact alone nearly breaks me.

"Thanks," I say weakly. "I'll talk to you tomorrow, okay?"

She tells me that she'll call me tomorrow when she's off work. I have a feeling that my work will never end.

■■■■■■■■■■■■■■■■■■■■■■■■■■■■■■■■■■■■■■■■■■■■■■■■■■■

I get to work an hour before my shift starts, hoping to catch Gideon in a good mood. I told myself, in a burst of optimism, that I was going to come clean. I would say what I overheard, and then I'll politely request that April is removed from any list that involves the potential for election. Most likely, he's going to laugh in my face – or worse, fire me. That's okay. I'll just go to the media and expose the corruption in the Bureau. It's perfect timing, considering the reaction that I saw at the press conference. Of course, Gideon will likely laugh even harder at that – after all, I don't have any proof. But that's where he's wrong. I have the computer data saved from his personal hard drive. It's blackmail at its finest; and despite the pit that's growing at the bottom of my stomach, I remind myself that I'm doing it for April.

As soon as I clock in, my first stop is the men's bathroom. I don't need to use the toilet, but I do need time to get my thoughts in order.

I can hardly recognize the face that I see in the bathroom mirror. Who is this person that I'm becoming? Six months ago, I'd never be able to imagine myself blackmailing people into getting what I wanted, and this is going to be the second time. Had I not followed April to her workplace, would I have cared the way that I do now?

Would I have given any of the names on the list a second thought? I try to tell myself that I'm a person with principles – but when have I ever fought for anything? Have I gone my entire life standing for nothing?

But I have. I had worked forty hours a week and collected a paycheck. When that was over, I went home and played VR games. Before I met April, it was the same – day in and day out. For the first time in my life, I can change someone's life for the better.

With newfound resolve, I walk out of the bathroom and make my way towards Gideon's office. I don't bother knocking.

"Gideon, I need to talk to you."

"Yes, Morrison, I understand," says Gideon. He doesn't acknowledge my presence; and when Gideon turns his head, I can see that he's talking on his Mobiroid. "I know things didn't go according to plan, but it's done. No need to worry."

"Gideon," I say again.

"You don't need to raise your voice on me," Gideon says sharply. He waves a hand dismissively towards me, but I'm not ready to leave yet. "Yes, yes, I share your frustrations. If I had a better way to do it, I would." He turns towards me, before letting out an exasperated sigh. "Listen, I need to put you on hold for a second. The office assistant needs something from me."

"I'm not a...." I begin, but I stop myself.

Gideon presses a button on his Mobiroid to mute the person on the other line, then turns his attention back to me.

"Listen, kid. If you're here to talk about the election report..."

"I am."

"Well, you should know that Finn already ran it."

"Well, there's someone on there..." I begin, but I pause when Gideon's words register in my mind. "Wait. What?"

Gideon shrugs. "Well, Finn figured that it might get a little complicated since we'll be including people that are outside the typical boundaries. It's probably outside your realm of expertise."

I take offense to those words. "I have a Master's degree in computer science."

I knew it had little to do with my qualifications. Finn decided to take control of the situation before I could get to it. *Damn him!*

"Well, it's done," Gideon replies briskly. "It'll be released on election day. You can go back to work."

"But..."

But Gideon is back on the phone before I can utter another word out. I have no choice but to return to my desk.

I've failed. Did Gideon run the report while I was mulling over my would-be confrontation? Did my procrastination cause my girlfriend's inevitable death? Or was it done while I tried to find a way around the system?

I turn on my computer. Perhaps it's too late to see if I can find a way to have April's name removed. It'd cost me my job and put me in jail, but April will be safe. For that, it's worth it.

Finn created a new log-on for me shortly after he told me that I'd be running the report. I use it to look up the newly run election report. I do a search on the last name of McIntyre, and my heart sinks when the name generates a result.

But it's not the name that I thought it would be.

CHAPTER TWELVE

# APRIL

"Hello, you have reached the voicemail box of Roman Irvine. I can't come to the phone right now, so please leave your name, number, and message. I'll get back to you as soon as I can. Thanks."

I sigh, pacing the porch. "Hey, Roman. It's me – again. I know you're really busy right now with the election…" I wince at that word. "But I just want to hear your voice. Call me or text me when you can."

I press a button on my Mobiroid to end the call and stare out into the lake. To be fair, I've also been busy in the last few weeks. Since school is over for the summer, I've volunteered to work extra hours at the coffee shop. While the additional money isn't nearly as nice as having access to my trust fund, it's nice to have additional funds. It's also been keeping my mind off the election.

My thoughts are interjected by the sound of my stomach grumbling. Realizing that I haven't eaten all day, I make my way towards the kitchen. But just as I pass through the dining room, I notice that we have company. "Dr. Gray?"

Darcy Gray, my mother, and Autumn are sitting at the dining room table. All three of them turn their attention to me as soon as I enter the room. Autumn's eyes are red and on the brink of tears. The scene reminds me of the day my dad bailed me out of jail.

"I haven't missed a single session!" I blurt out.

All three of them frown in confusion.

I continue, "You even told me that I was doing well last week! What the hell is this about?"

Dr. Gray narrows her eyes at me. "April..."

"Do you seriously think this is all about you?" my mother interrupts, her tone rising.

"I..."

"Of course you do!" she exclaims, slamming her fist on the table. "It's always about you, isn't it?"

"Oh, I'm sorry!" I say sarcastically. "I was just having flashbacks to the last time you invited my fucking therapist over for dinner!"

"She's *my* best friend!" my mother shouts, standing up from her spot at the head of the table. "I knew her long before you were born! Who else do you think I'm going to turn to, especially if my daughters aren't going to have anyone left to take care of them! Did you even consider the possibility that Autumn might end up in a foster family?"

"A foster family?" I ask in disbelief.

"Well, I can't raise a kid if I'm six feet in the ground!"

"What the *hell* are you talking about?" I screeched, angry and confused at once. "Are you going through a midlife crisis? Is that why Autumn's crying?"

The room goes quiet. After several moments of silence, Autumn bursts into tears. My mother begins to shake. Dr. Gray clears her throat. "April, have you watched the news lately?"

I shake my head. "No." The whole room stares at me, appalled. "You know I've been busy!"

"How can you *not* know?" my mother asks in horror. "Doesn't your boyfriend work for the Divinity Bureau?"

"What does that have to do with anything?"

"You should probably watch the news," Dr. Gray murmurs. "I'm sure every station is covering it right now."

"Okay," I say, even though I'm still confused on what's going on. Without another word, I make my way into the living room and turn on the enlarged television. I feel minuscule as I watch the words appear on the screen: 'BREAKING NEWS: RALLIES HELD ACROSS THE COUNTRY AS DIVINITY BUREAU ELECTS FIVE THOUSAND UNDER MINIMUM AGE.'

Realization clicks at those words. Someone I know is going to die. A list of names scrolls at the bottom of the screen – the names of electees, sorted by the last name. I wait for my last name to appear – and it does. *Macy McIntyre.*

It all becomes clear at that moment.

■■■■■■■■■■■■■■■■■■■■■■■■■■■■■■■■■■■■■■■■■■■■■■■■■■■■■

My Mobiroid starts blowing up around five o'clock in the afternoon.

*One Missed Call.*

"Hey. Sorry, it's been a crazy day at work. I know you've probably heard what happened. Are you okay?"

*Two Missed Calls.*

"Hello? Do you want to talk about it?"

*Three Missed Calls.*

"April?"

He knew. Roman knew what was going to happen, and he didn't tell me. That's why he's been avoiding me for the last few weeks. I silence my Mobiroid and remove it from my wrist before I can receive another notification. I spend the rest of the day hiding in my bedroom, crawled into bed. My mother knocks on my door shortly after Dr. Gray leaves, but I don't respond. The chain of events leaves me feeling with an array of emotion: the shock of my mother's imminent death, fear of the future, anger over the fact that my boyfriend lied to me – and the grief that's boiling under the surface, threatening to pour out of me. She leaves me alone after that.

My family is cursed. I know my father has enemies, as he's a politician that's known to have done a few tricky things throughout the course of his career. But that's where the cycle should end. My mother is a former lawyer that gave up her career to take care of us. How far would the penance for my family's crimes stretch? How long would it be before Autumn or I end up on the election list?

My dad immediately appealed his election. From what I heard, the process is tedious. In most cases, it takes months to see a district chairman, which stretches further than the thirty-day deadline allows.

The first hearing is a request for an extension for the elected so that they aren't required to report to the bureau's headquarters by the usual thirty-day deadline. It wouldn't do any good for an appeal hearing to occur after the person is already dead. So that's where the extension comes in, but it's often denied. Still, the Bureau has a history of individuals that will appeal for the sole purpose of being granted an extension. They know that their time is running out, but they'll make it go on for as long as possible.

My dad, due to his position in Parliament, didn't need to wait for an extension. Nikolas Hemmingsworth, our district chairman, saw him within a week. My dad was also fortunate enough to be able to afford a lawyer. In this case, he chose a former colleague from his days as a private practice attorney. The two of them hired three analysts. The first that testified against the effect of overpopulation (who claimed that it was a myth). The second spoke about the long-term effects on the Divinity Bureau by electing someone – especially one with a significant role in politics – that's underage (he claimed that it would hurt the image of the bureau, thus impacting the department's influence in the long-run). The third focused on laws and tried to claim that my dad's election was illegal (as it turned out, there wasn't anything written in law that stated that the bureau could only elect those over a minimum age – but he tried to interpret a clause as such).

The final part of his appeals consisted of testimonies from his family.

*"Now, remember," Henrik had said to me. In between sessions, he had pulled me outside the courtroom to remind me that he depended on me. "The District Chairman's name is Nikolas Hemmingsworth. Don't bring up politics. Focus on portraying me as a loving and caring father. Maybe you can bring up the time we went to the Iceland's? Not a lot of people get the chance to leave the Confederal Districts. Remember that time when we got lost on the way to the ski slopes, so we stopped at a restaurant that had their own foothill? Remember how they let us borrow their gear and we got to go sledding down the mountain?"*

*"I'm not five, dad," I say, irritated that I had to spend the day in a courtroom when there was a protest happening outside the bureau's headquarters. "As I recall, we went to the Iceland's because Mom found out that you were cheating on her and wanted space."*

*My dad's eyes darkened. "Don't be difficult. Leonard says that we have a good chance of winning. Don't blow it."*

In the end, I did blow it. Both my mom and sister had testified before I did. They reminisced about the good times. It was as if my mother had forgotten that my father had ever been unfaithful to her. It was as if my sister had plenty of memories with my dad – but we both knew that he spent much of our childhoods away from home. But I wasn't angry with my father. I spent my entire life accustomed to his long absences and short temper. But I was mad at the system.

*"State your name," Leonard says as soon as I'm standing on the podium. I feel small at the moment – like the hearing room is the belly of Moby Dick, and I've been eaten alive.*

*"April Maheva McIntyre," I say, my voice shaky.*

*"How are you related to Henrik McIntyre?"*

*"He's my father."*

"Can you describe your relationship with your father in more detail?"

I pause.

"He created me, I guess," I say, my half-hearted attempt to lighten the tense atmosphere. Out of the corner of my eye, I can see my dad giving me a dark look.

"Alright," Leonard says, a smile crossing his lips. Is he amused? It seems like it. "Can you describe some of your memories with your father?"

"He took care of my family and me," I say without hesitation. "We never went hungry, and we always had a roof over our heads. Every so often, he'd take us somewhere cool – like the Iceland's. It was awesome to be able to leave the Confederal Districts for a little while..." I could never understand why we weren't allowed to leave in the first place. Don't we have an overpopulation problem?

I know that Leonard wants sensory details, but I'm not willing to share them. My memories belong to me – not a room full of strangers.

"Do you feel that your father deserves to be elected?" Leonard asks.

"No," I say without hesitation.

There's a moment of silence. Right now, I wish that I was anywhere else. I feel like a chess piece in a game where I don't know the rules. The way that everyone is staring at me – Leonard, my dad, Nikolas Hemmingsworth, Gideon Hearthstrom –

Wait, Gideon Hearthstrom?

"Well, Chairman," Leonard says, interrupting my thoughts. "I turn the floor over to –"

"My dad doesn't deserve to be elected," I say sharply. I want everyone – especially Gideon – to hear me. "You know why? It's because this whole system is fucking ridiculous! Why should one guy..." I point to Hemmingsworth. "... have any say over who lives or dies? What qualifies you to play God? The fact that you're in a fucking suit and you have a fancy title?"

*Leonard turns red. "That's enough, April!"*

*"It's not enough!" I roar. "The whole system is nothing but corrupt – and it serves no one!"*

*"That's enough," another voice interjects. I recognize it as Hemmingsworth's. "Please have Miss McIntyre removed from this hearing immediately."*

*A security officer appears at my side, tugging on my below. I pull my arm out of his grasp. I don't need to be escorted out. I'm ready to leave the room without hesitation – and it didn't escape my notice that there's a protest happening outside the bureau's headquarters. But as I'm moving, I can see Gideon Hearthstrom watching me. I'll never forget his stone-cold expression.*

My thoughts are interrupted by the sound of knocking on my door. I assume that it's my mom with another lecture. Logically, I know that my mother doesn't have a lot of time left. I shouldn't be shutting her out – and yet, what am I supposed to do? Grab tea with her and tell her what an amazing mother she is? She'd be able to see right through me.

"Go away," I spit out.

Instead, the door slowly creaks open. I expect a whiff of cigarette smoke to come in through the doorway; but instead, Autumn creeps in.

A hesitant look crosses her face. "Can I come in?"

I want to say 'no,' but Autumn is propping herself next to me on the bed before I can utter another word.

I sigh. "What do you want?"

"I don't know," Autumn admits. "I had a nightmare; but when I went past Mom's room, she was on the phone and cursing someone out."

"Probably her lawyer," I say. I have vague memories of her doing the same to Leonard last year. "She should know better than to bite the hand that's going to be saving her ass from death."

"Yeah," Autumn agrees, though her expression indicates that she's anything but agreeing with the situation. "April, do you know what happens to people when they get elected?" I raise an eyebrow. She should've learned this at least five years ago. "Like, what happens when people report to the agency? Do they line everybody up and kill them all at once?"

I cringe at the thought. "I don't know. I heard it was pretty peaceful. Someone once told me that the bureau hires chefs and lets everyone pick their last meal, but that seems a little far-fetched. I think they do it by lethal injection, though."

From what I remember, they don't report to the bureau's agency. Even at twenty stories tall, there's no way that the headquarters can house a million people. They're given some undisclosed location, and they have field agents that return the bodies afterward.

"It sound a lot like how they treat criminals that are about to executed," Autumn observes.

"It's nothing like that."

"Of course not," says Autumn, bitterness seeping into her tone. "Mom and Dad aren't criminals."

*'That's debatable,'* I want to say. My father was arrested twice. The first time was because a district chairman allegedly paid him to update the maximum age policies, and the second was for lying to Nolan Fitz when he claimed that overpopulation wasn't as big of a deal that it was (from what my mom said, he used fraudulent documents and false studies to prove his point). Fortunately, my dad was lucky enough to be acquitted both times.

"We're going to be orphans," Autumn says grimly.

"No, we're not," I say, even though it sounds hoarse in my ears. "You know that Mom is going to try and get an appeal hearing." It would buy her time, at least.

"I know – but remember how well that worked out for Dad?"

"It's two different situations."

"I'm not a kid anymore!" Autumn explains. "You don't need to tell me that everything is going to be alright when it isn't."

I feel nauseous by the implications. Once, Autumn had been a baby. My parents hired a nanny; but occasionally, I'd change her diaper and feed her a few bottles. When Autumn was a toddler, I was the only one in the household with enough energy to keep up with her. But I pulled away when Autumn grew older. Unlike me, Autumn is an introvert. While I had dreams of giving public speeches, Autumn's lifelong dream was to be a writer. When I was a kid, she was a shiny toy that I could play with. Now, she's a person with her own thoughts and emotions. We're two different people. Once, that felt like a bad thing – but seeing her now makes me think that it's wonderful. I wrap an arm around my sister, who lays her head on my shoulder.

"Remember when you were five and you were determined to break the world record for the tallest tower of toy bricks?" I ask. Autumn nods. "And remember how you spent five days building it in the backyard before it started raining and it came crashing down?"

"Yeah."

"You started crying," I reminisce. "Especially when some of the pieces ended up getting lost in the mud. Then mom came out and reassured you that it wasn't the end of the world. She said, 'When life breaks you down, you have two choices. You can either leave the pieces on the floor...'"

"'Or you can rebuild yourself so that you're stronger than before,'" Autumn finishes. "I left the pieces on the floor. There was too much mud."

I laugh. Our parents ended up buying her a new set less than a week later; but by then, Autumn had found a new hobby to keep her interest.

"We'll get through this," I promise. "If we don't, then we'll just have to find a way to rebuild ourselves."

"I don't want to live with a foster family," Autumn admits. "I heard that it's awful. I heard that drug addicts would adopt kids so that they can get money from the state to buy more drugs – or that parents will take kids and neglect them for their actual children. I'm sure there are lovely folks out there, but I don't want to take that chance."

"You won't," I reassure her.

"What if the appeal is denied?"

"You'll stay with me," I say. It takes me a second to believe the words coming out of my mouth. Can I take care of my sister? It'd be a lot of responsibility. I'd be required to attend school functions, keep an eye on her grades, and mold her into an adult.

"Will they let you?" she asks.

I think about the implications. Autumn is a smart kid, and I'd be lucky to be her guardian.

"I'm twenty years old," I say. "I'm technically an adult."

"But what about Dr. Gray? What will she say?"

"I don't care what Dr. Gray says," I say with newfound determination. My mind is made up. "I just care about keeping us together."

"So, I'll stay with you?" Autumn asks, her eyes wide and brimming with tears. "Do you promise?"

I think about the responsibilities that would come with my next words – and I don't want it any other way.

I nod. "I promise."

CHAPTER THIRTEEN

# ROMAN

"Roman!" Macy exclaims in surprise as soon as she sees me. "What are you doing here?"

I attempt to offer my best smile, but the reason for my visit is nothing to smile over. It's a Friday afternoon. I had six tickets left in my queue, but I chose to leave work early when I had gone a week without hearing from April.

"I heard what happened," I say. "I wanted to check to see how you guys were doing."

There's a chance that Macy might hate me after all this. She knows that I work for the Divinity Bureau, and she's not on favorable terms with the agency. I hope she can see past my job and recognize that I only want to offer my support.

"Oh, Roman!" she exclaims, pulling me into a hug. "You're too sweet."

Shocked by the sudden display of affection, it takes a moment before I wrap a comforting arm around Macy. When I made the decision to come to the mansion, it was to make sure that April was alright. I suddenly feel guilty for not thinking about Macy, who just found out that her life was being cut short. She didn't deserve this fate.

"Is there anything that I can do?" I ask.

"It depends on what my lawyer says."

I stop myself from saying anything more. Technically, I'm not allowed to testify at appeal hearings. According to my employment contract, it's a conflict of interest. But I'm not sure if this is the moment to bring that up.

"Listen," I say, pulling away. "I'll talk more about this later, but can you tell me where I can find April?"

Macy looks away. "She's in her room. She hasn't left since she found out…" She trails off, unable to bring herself to say the words.

"Thanks," I say making my way towards the elevator. "I just want to talk to her for a few minutes."

I take the elevator to the third floor, where April's bedroom is. There are only two rooms on that floor, and April's room is the one with a door that's been slammed shut. I give it a knock. "April?"

No answer. I try again.

"April, it's Roman."

My only response is silence.

"Listen, I know you're upset. I know you probably don't want to talk about it right now…" I pause, listening for a sound from the other side of the door. "But I was hoping that I could change your mind. Or at least get you to talk to me."

I wait for a response, but none comes.

"Could you at least open the door?"

The door doesn't bulge. I sigh and slide to the floor. I'm ready to give up when I hear a voice from the other side of the door: "Can you answer one question for me?"

I press my ears against the door, afraid that I might miss something if I stop paying attention for a split second. "Of course," I answer softly.

April's voice is so soft that it sounds like a whisper. "Why didn't you do anything to stop it?"

My mouth falls open. "What?"

"You heard me," April says, her voice growing louder with newfound determination. "Why didn't you stop my mother from being elected?"

I press my forehead against the door, wincing at her words. "April, there wasn't anything that I could do to stop it."

"You could have *tried*," she hisses.

*'She's hurting,'* I tell myself. People say awful things when they're upset. Still, my reasoning doesn't heal the sting from her words.

"Trust me," I say, pressing my brows together. "I never wanted this to happen. The last thing I ever wanted was for you – or your family – to get hurt."

"It's not just about my family."

"Then what is this about?" I ask, my voice growing desperate. "Please – tell me, what do I need to do to make this better?"

"How many people have died since you started working for the bureau?"

I'm taken aback by her question. "I…"

I don't know what to say.

Unfortunately, my silence is the only answer that April needs. "I knew it."

"Knew what?"

"You sit behind a computer all day," April says bitterly. "You see a name on your screen – not realizing that this is a person with a life, a family, hopes, and dreams. Then you destroy that life by electing them!" Her words hurt. I wish she'd open the damn door so that she could see. "I get it. There's only so much you can do. But once the day is over, you go home, collect a paycheck, and forget about it. That's what I can't seem to understand."

I slam a fist against the door. "It's not like that! Trust me, April, there is so much that you don't know – things that I want to tell you…"

I want to tell her everything: the election report, seeing her name on the list, coming to her work, the ruined hack job on her father's computer, and the research that I had done on her family. I let out a breath. "I'll tell you everything if you'll please open the door."

I press an ear against the door, not caring if I fall over. But I never do.

The last thing I hear from April is a solid, "No."

■■■■■■■■■■■■■■■■■■■■■■■■■■■■■■■■■■■■■■■■■■■■■■■■■■■■

Macy asks me if I want to join her and Autumn for dinner. A better part of me lost my appetite, but I accept in hopes that April will come downstairs to join us. Instead, her plate of food goes untouched. The sight makes me cringe.

"She's a stubborn one," says Macy, noticing the way my eyes keep drifting to April's seat at the table. "She gets it from her father." She pauses as she brings a bite to her mouth. "Do you think this chicken needs garlic? I feel like CLEO has forgotten to add the seasonings."

"It's delicious," I say, although I've barely touched my food. All I know is that its high-end synthetic chicken. "But I can look at it if you think it might need to be fixed. Just make a technical support ticket…"

As soon as I notice the look of confusion crossing Autumn and Macy's faces, I stop myself.

"Sorry," I say. "It's a habit."

Macy laughs – a sound that I never thought I'd hear when I consider the circumstances.

"How come April isn't down here?" I ask. The thought makes me angry. April knows that her mother has a limited amount of time left! Shouldn't she be capitalizing on it?

"I don't know," Macy admits in defeat. "She can be incredibly difficult to understand – at least, to me. Her therapist gets her to crack occasionally, but those times are few and far between."

"Therapist?"

"You didn't know?"

"She doesn't like Dr. Gray," Autumn interjects before I can utter another word out. "She told me."

"Why is she seeing a doctor?" I ask. Sure, April can be moody; though I thought that every twenty-year-old girl was!

"Does it need explaining?" Macy quips back. "Have you ever noticed how April goes through extreme changes in her mood? She alternates between euphoria and depression!"

I shake my head. "No, I haven't!"

She's stubborn and hot-headed, but I'd hardly blame a chemical imbalance.

"Well," Macy says, pushing her half-empty plate aside (God, there's starving children in District 560, I think with a cringe). She lights up a cigarette. "I guess you haven't been paying any attention."

"Now that I think about it," says Autumn. "I haven't seen April get depressed ever since she started dating Roman."

"That's absurd," Macy dismisses. "She has a brain chemical imbalance. That doesn't get fixed by being in a relationship." She glances at me. "It's nothing to be ashamed about. Her father also had the same problems, and he managed to lead a successful life."

The mention of April's father piques my interest. "Henrik McIntyre?"

"That would be him."

"I was reading about him," I say, though I need to censor the reason for my readings. "He – uh – came up in some news archives. It was a slow day at work, and I was browsing the internet. Anyways…" I pause. "I was doing some reading and found something called the 'McIntyre Curse.' It's ironic, considering all that's happening – don't you think?"

Macy turns white. "Autumn, can you clear the dishes?"

"I thought we had CLEO to do that!"

"CLEO is recharging. Please, Autumn?"

"But –"

"Now."

Autumn grumbles as she stands up from her seat. She grudgingly picks up my barely eaten plate – causing another cringe on my part – before making her way towards the kitchen. As soon as she disappears, Macy lowers her voice.

"I thought no one talked about the McIntyre Curse anymore," she says darkly.

The revelation is a surprise to me. "So, you're cursed? Did one of your relatives piss off a witch that did voodoo on you guys?"

"It's not a 'curse' in the traditional sense," Macy says. "It was a term that the media used to describe all of the tragedies that were happening within our family in the last few decades. There was a rumor that Henrik's great-grandfather had an affair with a witch – but we think that it's a legacy of corruption catching up with us. It's more like a conspiracy theory. Mind you; I don't know if it's true…"

"But what if it is?"

Macy glances around the house. I'm guessing she's not sure how much information she should be sharing.

"Macy," I say. "You've already been elected. I don't know what else anyone can do to you."

*'That's not true,'* I remind myself. I already saw first-hand what could happen, but it's too late to take back my words.

"They can elect April – or Autumn!" Macy says, her eyes growing wide. "Oh, God. What if I'm not enough?"

I think of April's name on the last election report. "Enough for what?"

Macy lets out a sigh, pausing as she contemplates her words. "We come from a long line of politicians. Henrik's great-grandfather made the family fortune back when he was a chairman of the Divinity Bureau. He served for some district in California – though, I'm not quite sure what it's called now. I think he was based in Los Angeles."

"The 530th district," I interject with the knowledge that I had acquired from my research about the McIntyre family. Macy glanced at me in surprise, to which I add, "Sorry – I just knew someone from that district."

Macy raises an eyebrow, though she continues, "Anyway, he made his fortune by, for all intents and purposes, selling immortality."

"That's impossible," I say immediately.

"That's what you think," Macy corrects. "He made a fortune. Upon receipt of the money, he would ensure that the person never got elected. I don't know how he did it, but I guess he just took the person's name off the list if they ever showed up on the election report."

I have an idea of how it works. I had done it not too long ago.

"Anyways, it continued for generations," Macy continues on. "It's how the family made our fortune. My husband, when he heard about what was happening, broke the chain and decided not to pursue a career in the Divinity Bureau. He opted for a career in Parliament instead, and he spent twenty years in the Committee for Population Regulation. That made it easier for him to expose the corruption happening within the bureau. Unfortunately, it caused a mass impeachment – including the impeachment of Henrik's father and grandfather."

I shake my head. "That's terrible."

"April doesn't know about it," Macy says, shaking her head. "Mind you, she can easily find out – it's all over the net – but she doesn't need to know that her legacy is built on deceit and corruption."

I think about it for a moment. "I think April knows. At least, a part of her does. She may not want to believe it, but she probably knows."

Macy closes her eyes. "I keep forgetting that she's not a child anymore. I should be proud – but instead, I'm scared."

"Why is that?"

She lights up another cigarette. I attempt to ignore the smoke invading my nostrils. "Do you know Gideon Hearthstrom?"

I let out a hollow laugh. I'm beginning to learn enough about Gideon to last me a lifetime. "Yes."

"Well, Gideon was impeached when my husband accused him of corruption."

My laughing immediately ceases. "That's unfortunate."

I know Gideon. He's terrible with computers; but he's also ruthless, determined, and ambitious – and I highly doubt that he'll stand for a lowly MP like Henrik ruining his reputation.

"Being impeached doesn't necessarily remove you from office," Macy explains. "It's just an accusation of unlawful activity. Gideon was accused of electing rivals, enemies, and people he didn't like. In the end, the charges were dismissed. There wasn't enough evidence to pursue a case against him."

"I might have a case," I say without a second thought. "I overheard something. There was a man in his office. He mentioned something about paying Gideon to ensure that a handful of people were elected. I guess you were one of them."

Macy closes her eyes, taking a drag out of her cigarette.

"We can bring it to the media," I go on, ignoring the defeat in Macy's eyes. "If you back me up, I'm sure we can make front page news!"

"Roman, be realistic."

"About what?"

Macy shakes her head. "No matter what you overheard, Gideon Hearthstrom is still Gideon Hearthstrom."

With her words, the only thing I hear is Gideon's voice: "I thought you were the office assistant." She's right. I'm merely a low-level IT Technician, and Macy's only claim to fame is the fact that she married Henrik McIntyre. We don't stand a chance.

"Anyways," Macy continues. "Gideon probably has a personal grudge against our family. That's probably going to make it hard as hell to appeal – but you better believe that I'm going to fight. The last thing I want is for Gideon's grudge to extend to my daughters."

I think about the implications. I agree that I don't want to see April or Autumn get hurt, but Macy's explanation doesn't make a lot of sense to me. Hypothetically, if I were planning a revenge plot, wouldn't I want to see that person suffer? Having that person watch their family die is the best way to make that happen – yet to do so, that person would still need to be alive. Gideon got rid of Henrik first and saved his family for last – so why would he do that if he was plotting revenge against Henrik?

I gaze at the elevator, wanting to try talking to April again. Macy takes notice and reassures me, "She'll come around."

I frown. "How do you know?"

"Because she loves you," Macy says, as though the answer is obvious. She has no idea what effect those words have on me, nearly bringing me to my knees. "And if she's smart, which I know she is, she'll see how much you love her, too."

I open my mouth to protest. I want to tell Macy that it's impossible, that it's too soon, and that there's no way April could love me if she's currently shutting me out. But she's right about one thing: I, Roman Irvine, am in love with April McIntyre. I love her, even though she's moody, spoiled, and slightly high maintenance. I love her, even though she refuses to acknowledge how kind-hearted and selfless than she is. I love her, and she's the only girl that I could ever want in my life.

I'm not about to say all this to her mother, though. I stand up in preparation to leave for the night. "Macy, I just want you to know something."

"What's that?"

"You don't need to worry about Gideon's grudge extending out to your daughters," I say, my voice low. "I'll make sure that they stay off that damn list, no matter what it takes."

Macy shakes her head. "Whatever you do, please don't do anything reckless. These are very powerful people, some of which are very dangerous." She hesitates, then continues. "This is a government agency, and you're just..." She trails off, and I have a feeling that I know what she's going to say.

"I'm just an office assistant," I mutter, repeating Gideon's words.

"No," Macy replies quickly. "I was going to say that you're too in love with my daughter to think rationally."

## CHAPTER FOURTEEN

# APRIL

The house is empty when I finally leave my room. I was hoping to waltz into the kitchen and see my mother and Autumn sitting by the nook. I was planning on grabbing breakfast – real breakfast, as opposed to the snacks that I had stockpiled in my room – and pretend that the last week never happened. But there wasn't anyone in the house.

I don't see CLEO anywhere, so I pour myself a bowl of cereal and grab an apple that's sitting in the pantry. I eat in front of the television, as my mother isn't around to scold me for bringing food into the living room. I'm relishing in the feelings of freedom when I turn on the television.

My mother's face fills the projection screen. I nearly spit my apple out.

"Mrs. McIntyre," a male journalist says, chasing down my mother as she's walking into the Divinity Bureau's headquarters. "Are you nervous about your hearing?"

I recognize the looming Divinity Bureau headquarters in the background, and that's when the pieces click into place. It's my mother's hearing – most likely, for an extension.

"No," she replies briskly, without slowing her pace. "I am confident that I, and the thousands of others who were wrongly elected, have a high chance of reversing the decision."

"What makes you say that?"

A wicked smile crosses her lips. "Because we're willing to fight."

I snort. So cliché.

"Like everyone else," she continues. "We have a right to live – and we want to ensure that the Divinity Bureau honors that right."

She doesn't say anything else. Instead, she and Autumn are ushered off-screen by a man that I vaguely recognize as Leonard. The coverage cuts back to a newsroom, where a man and woman sit around a desk that takes up the entire newsroom.

"That's Macy McIntyre," the woman says diligently. "One of the five thousand underage elects this quarter. She is the widowed wife of former District 220 MP Henrik McIntyre, who was chosen by the bureau last year at the age of fifty."

"It's such a tragedy that both husband and wife were elected fifteen months apart," the man remarks. "As a matter of fact, there are rumors that the McIntyre's are cursed."

*Cursed?*

"These rumors aren't anything new," the female reporter says. "As you may recall, the McIntyre curse has been going on for decades."

I nearly choke on my apple.

"Ah, yes, the McIntyre Curse," the male reporter says in a daze, as though an alleged curse is something to glamorize. "I see it didn't end with Henrik McIntyre. As I recall, Henrik and Macy are the only McIntyre's left."

"Not exactly," the female reporter corrects. "They have two daughters."

The world has indeed gone crazy. I've been theorizing that my family was a target for well over a year, and it resulted in my arrest, mandatory therapy, and the questioning of my sanity. But two reporters were nonchalantly chatting about some "McIntyre Curse" on live television, and no one is batting an eye!

"Well, let us hope that the McIntyre Curse ends with Macy," the male says. "Let's go back to Christian Henderson, who is reporting to us live from the Divinity Bureau's headquarters in District 1."

My Mobiroid vibrates. I jump, engrossed in the news that I had nearly forgotten about the outside world. At first, I think that it's Roman; but the name Tate Gallagher fills the screen.

I transfer the call to my earpiece. "Hello?"

Tate sounds astonished that I had picked up the phone in the first place. "Are you okay?"

"Yeah," I reply, though I feel anything except okay. "My mom is filing for an extension, which should hopefully go through. After that, we just need to keep our fingers crossed that the appeal goes through. She did look pretty darn good on the morning news, though."

There's a pause.

"Your mom was on the news?"

"Yeah. I guess the media took an interest in the fact that Henrik McIntyre's wife was elected fifteen months after him. They were talking about something called the 'McIntyre Curse.'"

"Your mom was elected!?" Tate asks in horror.

"Yeah," I say, confused on how he didn't know that. Then again, he's too self-centered to pay attention to world events. "Wait, why are you calling me?"

"Well, you haven't answered your phone in a week..."

"Don't you watch the news?"

Tate sighs. "No. I hear enough about current events from our customers. A lot of people were telling me that the bureau decided to elect two thousand people –"

"Five thousand," I correct.

"Five thousand!" Tate exclaims. "That's crazy." He clears his throat. "That's messed up, though. I'm sorry."

"It's no problem," I say through gritted teeth, knowing that it's a lie. "So, what were you calling me about?"

"Well, I didn't see you on the schedule," says Tate, and I'm suddenly reminded of the fact that I have a job that I've been neglecting for the past week. "And Josh told me that he called you."

I glance at my Mobiroid and pull up my inbox. Six unheard voicemails. I groan. "I'm so fired, aren't I?"

"After three 'no call, no shows?' I'm surprised you weren't fired after the first one."

"I was in over my head," I admit, thinking about the blur that my emotions have been in the last few days. "I'm not even that close to my mother. I don't know why her election is bothering me so much."

"I do," says Tate, his voice growing soft. "She's your mother."

I close my eyes. "I suppose you're right." I glance back at the television, where a reporter is interviewing the mother of the bureau's youngest person elected: a nine-month-old infant. The mother, a woman named Rosalie Hannigan, speaks to the reporter with a shaking voice. I feel a pang in my chest at the sight of her wet eyes and pain-stricken face. "Listen, can we talk later? I want to see how my mother's hearing is going?"

"Of course. Let me know how things go."

I promise him that I'll keep him in the loop and that we'd hang out when things calm down. As soon as I end the call, I turn my attention back to the news and keep my eyes glued to the screen for any mention of my family.

Two hours pass. I delete all six of my voicemails (two of which are from Roman, three from my former manager, and one from Tate), finish breakfast, and learn about several of the bureau's elects. Some are high-profile celebrities, including a reality show star. But I realize that most of them are people that weren't granted the opportunity to be immortal. Most were too poor to afford it. I think about the implications of this. Deciding when I'd become immortal has always been a looming shadow in my life. I can become immortal whenever I want; but for most, it took years of saving. For some, the choice doesn't even exist.

I'm just about fed up with the coverage when I hear the doorway open. I think about my stance. Should I apologize? Should I pretend that nothing has happened? Should I hug my mother? The latter seems cliché. I opt to say nothing and let me mother notice me first.

"You don't need to grab the door," Macy's voice echoes from the hallway. "I've been elected, but I'm still able to function."

A nervous laugh comes through the corridor – a male laugh, which catches me off guard.

"I just thought I'd be a gentleman," the male voice responds, and I recognize the voice as belonging to Roman. "April never complains about it."

"I'm not complaining either," Autumn chimes.

"Well, April is a lucky girl. The most honorable thing my husband has ever done for me was that he moved to District 1 for half the year."

I mute the television, positive that my ears are playing tricks on me. Two months ago, Roman was certain that my mother hated him; yet here they are, standing in my hallway and joking around like old friends. Have I missed something?

"I appreciate your presence at the extension hearing," my mother continues. "It's nice to know that someone understands how the bureau works from the inside."

"It's not a big deal, honestly," Roman says, his voice sincere. "Anyways, I didn't really come with, since I can't be seen with any of the elects."

"It's the same principle," my mother dismisses. "The fact that you're risking your job means the world to me. I'm sure it'll mean a lot to April, too."

*Is he risking his job?* His job is the reason that we're in this mess! I'll have to talk to my mom as soon as Roman leaves. In the meantime, I realize that I'm not past the resentment towards Roman for not telling me about my mother, and I'm not willing to talk it out with him yet.

I turn the television off and grab my bowl of cereal from the coffee table. As quietly as I can muster, I tip-toe away from the living room. I don't want to take the elevator, in fear that it'll make lots of noise. Instead, I walk up four flights of stairs, silently fuming. I'm only feet away from my bedroom when I hear the elevator ding.

I freeze. It's probably Autumn, I tell myself. It could also be my mother. Just as long as it isn't Roman – *please don't be Roman*. But when I glance towards the elevator, the one person that I don't want to see is staring back at me. His mouth hangs open, looking just as shocked to see me as I am to see him.

"Hi," he says breathlessly.

"Hello," I say, swallowing the lump in my throat. "What are you doing here?"

"What I wanted to do the last time I was here," Roman says, avoiding my eyes. "Are you mad at me?"

*Yes.*

"I don't know," I admit, my words betraying my mind. "On one hand, I know that what happened wasn't your fault; but I just can't get past the fact that you knew." My eyebrows furrow. I take a step closer to him and wag an accusing finger at him. "You knew! And you didn't tell me!"

Roman hangs his head down. "I'm sorry. I just… couldn't."

"Why not?"

"Because I'd lose my job," Roman says, and at that moment, it all makes sense. He avoided me because he didn't trust himself to keep his mouth shut. And for a guy that's already living paycheck to paycheck, losing his job would mean losing everything.

He sighs. "Do you hate me?"

"I don't know," I say, unable to find the words to describe my emotions. "I just… I'm having a hard time differentiating between you and them right now." By 'them,' we both know that I'm talking about the Divinity Bureau. "Logically, I know we need them. We're already in the middle of an overpopulation crisis – and I can't imagine what life would be like if we didn't have anyone around to decide who lived and who dies. I'm glad that I don't have to live through that, but it's different when it's someone that you care about. You can relate to that, right?"

"I can't," Roman says, flushing as though embarrassed by the truth. "Growing up, I wasn't a social person. We couldn't – not when there was work to be done. I'm still not, even to this day. I haven't been able to fathom the idea of loss because I didn't have anyone to lose - at least until I met you."

I offer a smile, trying to make light of such a big confession. "Well, I guess it's a good thing that you don't have to worry about losing me."

Roman hesitates on his next words. "That's where you're wrong."

"What do you mean?" I ask. The concept is silly to me. I'm young and healthy, even if I haven't been injected with BIONs yet. But something isn't right. Roman's face is scrunched together, as though he's in pain.

"Roman, is there something you're not telling me?"

It's my mother's election all over again.

"Roman!"

I can see that he's struggling to make a choice between telling me the truth and continuing to keep secrets from me.

"Is it about the bureau?" I press.

"Isn't it always about the bureau?" Roman asks sadly. "That's what it always comes down to."

"But…" I can't even think. "Why would you worry about losing me?"

"Because I already almost did."

My knees buckle at that moment. I hold my weight against the wall.

"Did you ever ask why I was in that coffee shop the day before the report was released?" Roman asks. "I work on the other side of town. It's well out of the way home for me. Why else do you think I'd be in the coffee shop on that day – one day before the election report was scheduled to be released?"

How close had I been to death without even realizing it?

"I was asked to run the election report for my boss, Finn," Roman explains. He blinks rapidly, the memories coming back to him. "The crazy thing is that I wasn't even thinking about the names on the list. Instead, I just kept thinking that this was my shot to prove that I could be more than just an IT Technician."

My name.

One out of ten thousand.

It was like finding a drop of iodine in an ocean.

"But then I stumbled on your name," Roman continues. He looks at his hands, as though they might have the answers. "Right next to it was your date of birth. I thought, 'That's weird. How does a nineteen-year-old girl end up on the election report?' I thought it was a glitch – a broken filter, perhaps. But just in case, I went to your workplace to get a gauge on who you were – and I knew the second that I saw you that you didn't deserve to be on that list, so I took your name out."

"I can't believe it," I breathe, my mind still in shock. Roman had saved my life, and all these months, I had never known.

"I don't know much," he admits. "But from what I've heard, your family messed with some very dangerous people."

I shake my head, unable and unwilling to believe that anyone in my family would do anything to put me in this situation. My relationship with my father was complicated, but he loved me. During the few times that he did visit us, he had spoiled me rotten. There's no way he'd sell me out.

My thoughts are interrupted by Roman grabbing my hands. "I know you don't believe me."

"I don't. I can't."

"It'll sink in."

"Will it?" I ask. "Even if it does, will it even matter? How long will it be before the Bureau realizes what you've done?"

"I don't know," Roman admits. "I'm doing everything I can, though." He looks away. "Some of it is outright illegal." I laugh at that. "But no matter what happens, I need you to trust me."

"I trust you."

Roman raises an eyebrow. "Do you? Because not too long ago, you were telling me that you couldn't differentiate between the Bureau and me."

I look away, realizing that he has a point. Despite my newly gained knowledge, there's still a part of me that may never trust Roman simply for his association with the Divinity Bureau. "I want to," I admit. "I just wish I could understand why you didn't tell me all of this sooner."

Roman sighs. "I know. I shouldn't have kept it from you – but our relationship was going so well that I was afraid that it'd scare you off. Saying that I broke a few laws to save your life isn't exactly an ideal first date topic."

I laugh. "That is a little scary."

"Then I would've never had the chance to kiss you," Roman says, his voice cracking. "Or hold you. Or be with you." He looks away. "The last few months have been the happiest of my life. I wouldn't do anything differently."

With those words, I've forgiven Roman. I get on my toes to kiss him gently – but, starved of my affection, he wraps his arms around me and pulls me close. At that moment, I realize that I can trust him. There's no safer place for me than right here.

He pulls away, taking a deep breath. His expression turns grim. "There's one more thing that you should know."

"What's that?"

"You once asked me if I ever counted how many people have died since I started working for the Bureau."

My breath catches in my throat. I've been so cruel to him. "Roman, I'm sorry. I shouldn't have said that."

"It's okay," he says, which makes me feel even worse. "I never counted how many people have died since I started working for the bureau. But I know how many people were on the list that I met you: ten thousand, four hundred and twenty-one."

I inhale a breath, the number incomprehensible to me.

"I managed to save one," he whispers. "I know that doesn't seem like a lot; but to me, it counts for something."

I pull him in for another kiss, light and chaste. As I pull away, I whisper, "Thank you."

CHAPTER FIFTEEN

# ROMAN

I'm greeted by a swarm of reporters as soon as I get to work that morning.

"Sir, do you work for the Divinity Bureau?"

"Do you have a comment?"

"Why do you think the bureau has decided to elect five thousand underage candidates?"

"My daughter was elected, you fucking prick!"

I keep walking. I'm not allowed to speak on behalf of the bureau, and I have no desire to. Michael, the security guard at the door, gives me a sympathetic glance. I tell myself that the chaos would die down as soon as I get inside.

"Excuse me," someone brushing past me says.

I frown. The voice belongs to a dark-haired man wearing a freshly pressed suit. I'm certain I've seen him before. But before I have the chance to dwell on it, I'm passed by another man in a suit. And another.

Something is off. As I make my way to my desk, I see a plethora of unfamiliar faces. While I don't know everyone that works in the bureau's headquarters, I know enough to realize that something is going on. My suspicions are confirmed when I walk past Finn's office and find a stern-faced man occupying the otherwise-empty side of the room.

I turn the opposite direction, thinking that I might be best finding answers in the breakroom. When I see a fresh-faced group of staffers standing near a vending machine, I decide to ask them. A low-level employee like me will never be able to get answers directly from a district chairperson, but I can still count on the old-fashioned way: gossip.

"Hey," I greet, stepping into their conversation. "Do you know what's with all the guys in suits?"

"Roman!" a girl exclaims, her eyes growing wide. I think her name is Amy? "I thought you were dead! I made you a ticket last week, but you never got back to me!'""

"Sorry," I say immediately. I've been neglecting my work in the last few weeks. "I, err, had a family emergency."

"Did someone in your family get elected?" a blonde-haired boy named David chimes.

"Something like that," I say vaguely. "Anyways, do any of you know what's going on? I think Theo Rodgers is in town. He's a district chairman that supposedly shares an office with Finn, but he's never in town unless something major is going on."

"Oh, something major is going on," says Amy. "The whole bureau is having a summit here – all five hundred and sixty districts. They flew everyone out and everything."

I stare at her in shock. "Why... why would they do that?"

The Divinity Bureau's central office is in District 1, which is where the Executive, Legislative, and Judicial Branches are. Wouldn't they fly them out there instead? I don't think the Midwest District's Headquarters can even house 560 chair people and their staffers!

"Gideon called it," says Amy. "Apparently, he did some calculations and found that our overpopulation problem is worse than they've let on. They're holding a big summit to address the issue."

164 · TESSA CLARE

"Calculations?" I ask, appalled. The man can barely use a computer!

"I heard that the Western districts are opposed to changing anything," David asserts. "Arielle was talking to one of their personal assistants. Apparently, the twelfth district's chairman –"

"Chairwoman," Amy corrects, narrowing her eyes.

"Chairwoman," David repeats, flushing. "Anyways, I heard that she's supposed to be giving a speech about how the answer isn't to elect more people – but to adapt."

That reminds me of something April once said: "I just had this thought that maybe if we all had good intentions – if we all decided that we wanted to leave the world a little better than before – it can be our greatest strength instead of our greatest weakness."

"How does she plan to do that?" Amy asks skeptically. "That doesn't sound realistic at all."

"I don't know. I just don't want to die anytime soon."

I open my mouth to add to the conversation; but I stop when I hear footsteps behind me, storming into the room like thunder. "What the hell are you guys doing?" Finn booms from behind me.

My coworkers immediately jump as soon as they hear Finn's voice.

"Do you *not* see this building swarming with district chairmen?" Finn barks. "Get back to work!"

The break room immediately empties out, but I'm standing there in stupefaction. Never, in my two years of working at the Divinity Bureau, have I seen Finn raise his voice. Even when I blackmailed him, he didn't sound as angry as he does now. "Finn…"

"Did you not hear me, Irvine?" Finn asks, his voice lowered.

"What's gotten into you?" I ask.

I regret my words as soon as I'm met with Finn's fiery glare.

"Is everything okay?" I correct, softening my tone.

Finn doesn't respond. Instead, he turns to walk away. I take that as a sign that I should do the same.

■■■■■■■■■■■■■■■■■■■■■■■■■■■■■■■■■■■■■■■■■■■■■■■■■■■■■■

By lunchtime, the swarm of reporters is joined by a throng of protesters. The building is soundproof, so I'm deaf to the commotion happening outside, but that doesn't stop me from hearing Gideon pacing across his office. As he paces, I overhear Finn telling Gideon that the crowd is getting rowdy.

"Call the police," Gideon growls.

"I already did."

"And?"

"They say that there's nothing we can do to stop the protesters from protesting, but they did offer to stand guard to make sure that no property damage or riots occur."

I was planning on grabbing lunch with April, but it sounds like I'm going to need to cancel. It's bad enough that I'm subject to harassment from the media. April, the daughter of Henrik McIntyre and his newly elected widow, would be destroyed out there. I take advantage of Finn and Gideon's distracted state to send April a quick text: *'It's a media frenzy outside the bureau right now.'*

"You have to understand, Gideon, that the agency headquarters is public property," I hear Finn say. "We can't just deny them their right of free speech."

"You call it free speech? It looks more like an angry mob to me!"

I shrink in my chair, determined to stay out of sight. As I do, my Mobiroid vibrates: *'No kidding! The freeway exit closed. Apparently, the protesters are taking up an entire block!'*

My eyes widen. A whole block? I want to move closer to a window, but I'm worried about catching the attention of Finn and Gideon.

"Well, it's the first time in seven years that every chairman is in the same place," Finn points out. "In light of the bureau's most recent decision, I don't think you can blame the public for wanting their voices heard. How would you feel if it was your kid on the election list?"

Gideon lowers his tone. "Don't mix business with your personal life."

There's a long pause. When Finn speaks, he sounds defeated: "I'm just saying."

Something is going on with Finn. Did someone close to him get elected? I debate on looking up his last name, but my Mobiroid vibrates before I get the chance: *'There's a Chinese restaurant on Lau Street. Meet me there?'*

I glance at the time: half-past one. I don't want to stand April up, but I don't think I'm going to have a choice. I think of the traffic she must have endured to get here and feel terrible, but there isn't any way that I'm going to be able to leave the building without either getting swarmed by the media or facing the wrath of my superiors.

*'April, I'm sorry – but I don't think I'm going to make it out of here,'* I write. I close my eyes as I hit the 'send' button.

In between texts, Gideon and Finn have moved their conversation elsewhere, so I walk to the closest window. I'm not the only one. Half of the office crams in front of the window, standing on their toes to get a glimpse of what's happening.

At the front of the pack are the reporters that I'd seen that morning. They're joined by a mass of people that stretches along the blocks and past my field of vision. Some have taken to standing in the parking lot of a nearby convenience store. Many are holding signs – an impressive feat, considering how hard it is to find the paper to make them. I can picture people scavenging the recycling bin for whatever material they can get their hands on, all so that their voices may be heard.

"Can you pop open a window?" a dark haired girl in the back requests. "I want to hear what they're saying."

"Probably, 'Hey, ho, the Divinity Bureau has got to go,'" I say dryly.

I get a few raised eyebrows, but David and Amy abide by the girl's request and open the window. As soon as the window pops open, the smell of polluted air comes in. I'm in the back, so it doesn't affect me – but David wheezes out a cough. The sound of coughing is quickly drowned out by the sound of a voice over a microphone.

"... will not rest when the last Divinity Bureau chairman is dethroned. We will not rest when this building, this institution, and everything it stands for is demolished. No, we will rest when the government stops killing our loved ones in the name of the economy! We will rest on the day that we can stand forward and say, 'No! I will not die for you!'"

Cheers from the crowd follow. I'm impressed by the speaker's passion, and I nearly bring my hands together for a slow clap – until I hear my coworkers snickering.

"Oh my God, that's so pathetic," the dark haired girl remarks. "When the government stops killing our loved ones?"

"No kidding. They should all just move to a freaking third world country if they have a problem with the way the government works."

I want to point out that neither of us has ever been outside of the Confederal Districts – namely because it's forbidden – but I hold my tongue.

"Yeah. I heard Russia sterilizes all their women. Is that what they'd prefer?"

"They're so stupid."

I wish that I had the strength to point out the flaws of allowing a government to decide who lives and who dies. I wish that I could tell them that the system is corrupt and that the corruption is happening right under our noses. But courage abandons me at that moment.

Instead of saying anything, I return to my desk and continue working. I begin working on the ticket that Amy sent me, resenting the fact I'm indirectly sending millions of people to their deaths.

By four o'clock, I'm surprised that I haven't heard from April. I've checked my Mobiroid several times to be sure; and each time, the lack of alerts astounds me.

She's probably mad. I can't blame her. She did drive a long way to see me; and I know I'd be unhappy if I'd been stood up. I send her a text message: *'I'm sorry! I'll make it up to you! I promise!'*

I'm about to put my Mobiroid on sleep mode when it vibrates: *'Dinner?'*

I let out a sigh of relief.

*'Of course. Should I meet you at your place?'*

If I leave now, I should be able to beat rush hour traffic. But before I have the chance to map out my route, a text comes through: *'I'm in front of the bureau.'*

What?

Why is April in front of the bureau? It's been nearly four hours since I canceled our lunch date, so she should've left a long time ago. Even if she did stay, everything within a quarter mile radius has been shut down due to the protests –

I have a momentary flashback of April holding a sign in front of the bureau all those months ago: *No Justice in the Divinity Bureau.* But surely, she wouldn't be that careless? She hadn't known that she had been on the bureau's list, but she knows now. She surely couldn't be foolish enough to bring attention to herself – especially right now, when the agency's headquarters are swarming with chairmen and women. Then again, she is April McIntyre.

I send her a text: *'I'm coming to get you.'*

I'm out of my chair before I can finish hitting "Send." Finn gives me an odd look as I pass him in the hallway. I mutter an excuse about an emergency, which I doubt Finn believes – especially since I don't even bother waiting for an elevator. I run down the stairs, and it takes every effort in my body to not trip over my own feet.

As soon as I'm past the swiveling doors, I'm greeted by the sight of a massive crowd in front of me; and for a moment, I lose my breath. No reporters are swarming around me, but the crowd of bodies hunched together is enough to overwhelm me.

It hits me that the crowd is all wearing facial masks, but I had left mine in my office. My eyes water. Pollutants infiltrate my lungs. I should run back and grab it – especially on a hot, humid day with high levels of pollution – but I need to find April first.

"Excuse me," I mutter, making my way past a few shirtless men that are holding signs that say 'I DESERVE TO LIVE.' I push my way through the crowd, nudging anyone that gets in my way and perking up whenever I catch a sight of brunette hair. But most of the time, I'm slowing down to catch my breath.

It's hopeless. I check my phone in hopes that I might have a text from April, but the lack of notifications is frightening. There are too many people, and April is probably wearing a facial mask. Even if I do manage to pull her out of the crowd, there's no guarantee that she'll heed my word. The only thing that I can do is hope that she'll listen.

I find relief when I see a clearing. My nose, my chest, and my eyes hurt; but the momentary lack of sweaty bodies around me is what I need to breathe. The clearing itself is the parking lot of a convenience store. A middle-aged employee keeps trying to shoo them out; but whenever he turns his back, several people make their way back into the parking lot.

I contemplate on going into the store to buy a face mask when I see her: she's standing on a curb with her brown hair pulled in a sideways braid. She's wearing a mask, but I recognize the sign in her hand. 'NO JUSTICE IN THE DIVINITY BUREAU,' it reads. I didn't realize that she's kept it all these months. I push my way past the crowd. As soon as I'm close enough, I grab her arm. "What are you doing?"

Reflexively, April pulls her arm away; but her expression relaxes when she sees that it's me. "What are *you* doing? I thought you were working!"

"We need to go," I insist, tugging at her arm.

April doesn't bulge. "Why?"

"Because the bureau is swarming with chairmen and women right now!" I say, exasperated that she doesn't realize the danger of what she's doing. "The last thing we need is for you to catch their attention!"

April pulls her arm out of my grasp, barely registering the fact that I said 'we.' I'd like to think that we're in this together, but April doesn't seem to notice this. "Well, maybe I want to catch their attention! If that's what it takes to make a difference, then I'll happily do it!"

"You can make a difference without drawing attention to yourself!"

"See, that's where you're wrong."

I take a step back, unable to believe her words. I'm wrong? I'm the one that's spent two years working for the Divinity Bureau! I'm the one that's spent all these months working hard to keep her under the radar so that she can stay alive!

April is stubborn, but she doesn't always listen to logic. She follows her heart, and I usually admire this about her – but right now, it's infuriating.

"I see where you're coming from," April continues, her voice softening (probably taking notice of my shocked expression). "You work in IT. You're used to fixing everything behind the scenes. The thing is, I'm not. The only thing I have is a poorly drawn sign, and I don't want to live my life on the sidelines. Especially if there's a chance that it might get cut short."

"It won't get cut short," I insist. "That's why I asked you to trust me."

April touches my face, her hands brushing against the stubble on my chin. "I do trust you, Roman. I am confident that you'll do everything you can to keep me safe. I just don't trust that it will be enough."

After months of putting in late nights and long hours – and possibly stunting my career growth – her words sting.

"The other day, you asked me to trust you," says April, her voice low. "I need you to trust me, too."

I stare back at her, unsure of what to say next. I trust her in most things. I trust her words and that she'd never lie to me. I trust that she'd never do anything to hurt me. I trust her with my heart. But April is too selfless to be trusted with her own life.

I don't answer. Instead, I move my hand to stroke April's cheek. She stares back at me with the gray eyes that I love so very much. I move the mask away from her face. Dirty air be damned, this love is the purest thing I've ever known – so I slide the mask off her face and press my lips to hers. I hope that my message comes through.

When she pulls away, a mischievous grin has crossed her face. I'm not sure if I like it.

"What?" I ask.

"I have a crazy idea. Can you hold my sign for a few minutes?"

I glance at her sign as though it's poison. "I don't think that's a good idea."

"Why not?"

"What if someone sees me?"

April rolls her eyes. "They won't. It's only for a few minutes – plus its way too crowded for anyone to see you."

The idea of spending any more time in that sweaty, dirty crowd is unappealing. My chest is still sore from my last coughing fit. But before I can utter another word, April is shoving the sign into my left arm and pulling on my right.

"Excuse me, sorry!" April says, half-politely – a bit ironic, considering she's practically shoving people out of her way. "Coming through! Excuse me…"

"Where are we going?" I ask.

"You'll see."

She appears to be pulling me towards the bureau's headquarters. As soon as I'm within the confines of the crowd, I start coughing again. The ache in my chest returns with a full vengeance.

April stops. "Why aren't you wearing a mask?"

"I... couldn't..." I attempt to speak, but my lungs are on fire.

"Here," she murmurs. She pulls off her own mask and places it on my face.

As soon as it's covering me, I gasp. "No, April! I can't..."

She tugs on my arm again before I have the chance to protest. I'm finding that it's easier for her to navigate through the crowd. April McIntyre gives off an aura of royalty, and people clear a pathway for her as soon as they see her coming. But the building comes into view, and my eyes dart through the crowd in search for a way out. The last thing I want is to associate myself with a group of protesters. But April's grip on my arm is strong.

"You know, this trust thing doesn't work if the other person is keeping secrets about what you're being dragged into," I say dryly.

She doesn't answer. Upon a closer look, I realize that she's holding her breath.

She stops in front of the staircase to the bureau's headquarters. I recall seeing the man with the microphone standing on that stairway; but it's empty right now, despite the dense crowd just a few feet away. The bureau's headquarters is less than thirty feet away.

"This is a little too close for comfort," I say, in another attempt to pull out of her grasp.

April takes a breath.

"It'll only be for a few minutes," she says, then she resumes holding her breath.

My eyes widen. "You're just going to leave me here?"

April glances at the sign and back at me. She looks as though she's contemplating on what she's about to do, but she's still not saying anything. Considering how well she's been holding her breath, she must have the lungs of a fish. After a moment of contemplation, April gives me a half-shrug and disappears into the crowd. She holds out a finger. If she could talk, I imagine she'll be reiterating that she'd only be gone for a few minutes. I want to know what her interpretation of a few minutes is.

I think about making small talk with the protesters that are standing near me. Most are conversing already. I overhear a man talking about superhero movies, and how an actor that was supposed to play the main character had been elected by the Bureau. "They're already six months into filming! What are they going to do without him?"

I turn my head to remark; but as I do, I catch a glimpse of April walking up the stairs. I let out a breath of relief as soon as I see her face, but my relief disintegrates when I see that she's walking towards the bureau's headquarters.

'What are you doing?' I mentally scream at her. Standing feet away from the Bureau's office is not the way to avoid bringing attention to oneself. As she makes her way to the top of the steps, I can see the faint outline of a wireless microphone in her hand. That is not a good sign.

I push my way through the crowd. "April! Don't!"

The protesters immediately push me back. I don't have the same power that April has.

"April!" I call out again, but she doesn't hear me.

Instead, she brings the microphone to her mouth. I try to call her name again, but I'm drowned out by the sound of her voice: *"Hello, Divinity Bureau!"*

CHAPTER SIXTEEN

# APRIL

I bring the microphone to my lips, a rush of fear and exhilaration coursing through my veins.

"Hello, Divinity Bureau!" I call out into the microphone. My voice sounds crystal clear, as though I'm merely having a conversation in a coffee shop with the crowd.

I stop when I hear my voice. My throat is dry; but considering I'm not wearing a face mask in the middle of a high-pollution and high-humidity day, that's expected. But I'm loud and incredibly nervous. It doesn't help that the crowd has immediately gone quiet. I clear my throat and try again.

"I understand that you have a few concerns about overpopulation," I say. I try to sound calm, but I've never been good at hiding my emotions. "And you think that you can have some big meeting to fix it. Well, that's fine and dandy – but we, the people, have a few things that you need to hear! So, listen up!"

I mentally rehearsed this speech while I was walking through the crowd with Roman. It sounded far differently in my head, but the crowd is erupting in applause. From the corner of my eye, I can see several people sticking their heads out of the bureau's windows in curiosity. A smile crosses my face.

"You're all probably wondering, who the hell is this brat that thinks she can stand around with a microphone and tell us what to do?" I continue. "My name is April McIntyre. I'm the daughter of Henrik McIntyre – who, one year and three months ago, you murdered."

I'm not sure how relevant my dad's name is nowadays; but apparently, it's enough to keep the crowd's attention. My eyes dart around the crowd, finding expressions of awe and curiosity. I catch a glimpse of Roman, standing in the front row with my handmade sign in his hands.

"You probably think that 'murder' is a strong word, and maybe it is. You call it an election, as though getting elected is an honor! But I've got news for you. At the end of the day, you're still taking millions of lives. Whether or not you wrap it in a fancy title doesn't change the fact that the names on your list are dying at your hands."

I hear cheers from the audience, but I'm not paying attention to them. Instead, my eyes are on the employees that are crowded in front of the windows and staring at each other in confusion.

"You think you can have some fancy summit to decide how you want to play with our lives," I continue. "You think that it's all okay, as long as you're doing it in the name of the greater good. Well, unfortunately, that's not okay with us. If you think you can use the threat of the election to intimidate us, it's not going to work." I shake my head. "No, if we make it on that list, we're not going to come quietly. We're going to fight and claw our way out! And we're going to fight until we have a say in how we live and how we die! If that doesn't scare you, then let me remind you of this: when you have nothing left, you don't have anything to lose." I pause, turning my attention back to the audience. "Thank you."

There's more that I want to say, but the rest of my words leave me. Instead, I turn off the microphone. With shaky legs, I walk down the steps. As I do, the crowd cheers, oblivious to the tingling in my fingers and toes. I feel several pats on my back.

"Amazing speech!"

"That was incredible! That'll show the Divinity Bureau who's in charge!"

"Miss McIntyre! My name is Sandra with the CBCN Morning News! Do you have a few minutes for a comment?"

I'm grinning from ear-to-ear, unable to believe that I've managed to pull this off. But I'm also a bit overwhelmed. I've been waiting for over a year to call the Divinity Bureau out without being sent to the psychiatric ward.

I find Roman and collapse into his arms. Coughs rack throughout my body, and I realize that I need a face mask. His arms wrap around me and encase me, patting me on my back as I cough out the pollutants in my lungs.

"I can't..." I begin in between coughs. "I can't believe I just did that."

"I can," Roman says sincerely.

My eyes start to water. "I guess I've always been a little crazy."

Roman shakes his head. "You just inspired hundreds of people to stand up to a major government agency. I think that makes you a leader – a fearless one."

I laugh in astonishment. I've never been described as fearless before. Usually, my parents would call me stupid when I'd do anything outside of the norm. Unfortunately, the laugh erupting through my chest brings me more pain.

"We need to get you some water," Roman mutters, placing the mask back on my face. "And we need to pick up an extra cover."

I nod, agreeing that he might be better off buying one than going back in the bureau's headquarters right now.

"I still can't believe I did that," I exclaim, my heart beating erratically. But my moment of triumph is interrupted when I think about the future repercussions of my actions. "Oh my God, my mom is going to kill me." I can already imagine my mother choking on a cigarette the moment she sees my face on the news. "Shit. Do you think this will affect her chances of getting the appeal?"

Roman falls silent. I suspect he knows the answer, and that I'm not going to like it.

"Roman…"

"Let's not worry about that," he interjects before I can worry any further. "You nailed it up there. How did you even convince them to let you up there?"

I shrug. "It's a public protest. There aren't any 'leaders,' so anyone can speak. I just found the guy that spoke last and asked if I could borrow his microphone."

"That's incredible," Roman breathes.

Silence falls between us, the repercussions of our earlier conversation still weighing on our minds – or at least, it's weighing on my mind. We need to get out of here quickly, but a larger part of me wants to clear the air first.

"Roman –"

"You're right," Roman whispers, his voice hoarse. I'm not sure if it's because of the pollution. "I shouldn't have doubted you." He looks away. "From the moment I've met you, I've tried to play the hero in your story. But the closer I get to you, the more I realize that you don't need one."

He's wrong. I do need him. But I don't need him the way one needs air to breathe. I need him the way I need a face mask: a filter to make this dirty world a little more bearable.

"You're still a hero to me," I say. I grab his arm, slick with sweat. "Let's get out of here. I'm in the mood to celebrate."

Judging by the look on Roman's face, he doesn't seem to be in the mood to disagree.

■■■■■■■■■■■■■■■■■■■■■■■■■■■■■■■■■■■■■■■■■■■■■■■■■■

Once we've fully recovered from our pollution exposure, we celebrate with a dinner at an Italian restaurant near the waterfront. Roman attempts to sneak me a glass of champagne; but we end up catching the eye of an inquisitive waitress and thus spend a significant portion of our celebration begging the manager not to kick us out. After that, I suggest to Roman that we visit my old work for coffee, which he obliges.

I'm hoping that Tate is working so that I can formally introduce him to Roman, but I also secretly hope that Tate wouldn't mind sneaking us a few drinks at no charge. I ended up covering our celebratory dinner since Roman's rent was almost due, but the lack of income was starting to hurt – and after the last few weeks, it doesn't sound like my mother has any plans of letting me access my trust fund after she's gone. Fortunately, Tate doesn't disappoint me.

"I call this the coffee rainbow," he says as he hands me and Roman two large cups that smell like a combination of peppermint and caramel. "It has every single syrup on the rack – but in varying doses. I was a little nervous about adding peppermint and raspberry, but it seems to add a crisp taste – assuming you dose it correctly."

I take a sip and determine that it is *not* dosed as well as Tate had hoped. The taste nearly makes me throw up. I glance over at Roman, who looks as though he wants to do the same.

"It's... interesting," Roman says, as politely as he can muster. "It seems to have a lot of caffeine in it."

"Triple Espresso," Tate says proudly. "This will give you a sugar high on top of a caffeine high."

I wait until Tate isn't looking to toss my drink into the trash bin. The concoction is already starting to give me a stomachache.

"So, Roman," Tate asks in between measuring a cup of coffee grounds. "I'm kind of curious to know how you got your name. Are you actually of Roman descent?"

I have a momentary flashback of asking Roman the same question the first time I met him – ironically while standing in the same location that Tate is standing in now.

Roman shrugs. "Not really. I'm one of the many Confederal District citizens that haven't been allowed to leave the country in the last two hundred years." He gives me a side glance. "Unlike April."

I shift uncomfortably. Citizens of the Confederal Districts aren't allowed to travel outside of the country, as the government claims that it's too dangerous. My dad did bring me to The Iceland's, but I was twelve years old at the time, so I hardly remember it.

"My parents couldn't agree on a name," Roman goes on, oblivious to the fact that I've spaced out in the last few minutes. "So, they had a bet on whether or not I would be a boy or a girl, and the winner would get to name me. You see, my mother's family was from the Southern continent – Mexico, it was called before the war – and she has a strong connection to her heritage. But my dad had recently uncovered some old history textbooks and was doing some reading about a guy named Julius Caesar. That's what he originally wanted to call me."

"So, I take it your mother won?" Tate asks.

Roman laughs. "No. My mother was adamant that I was going to be a girl. I would have been named Alejandra Rosa de Maria Irvine-Martinez."

"She was even going to hyphenate your last name?"

Roman shakes his head. "My surname was hyphenated for twenty-five years. But it was a pain every time I needed to sign something, so I started going by my dad's last name. My brother and I made a compromise. He'd go by my mother's last name, while I'd use my dad's."

I wonder if that is why he initially majored in history. I could easily imagine his family pouring over history textbooks after a long day of work.

As soon as Tate disappears into the back room to replenish his stock on syrup, I take Roman's hand. I bring my voice to a low whisper. "How come you don't talk about your family all that much?"

Roman looks away. "I don't know. I figured that there wasn't much to talk about." He eyes me nervously. "It's nothing like being the daughter of an infamous politician."

I snort. "It's overrated."

Roman laughs, but it's a nervous laugh. "To be honest, it wasn't the same after I went to college. We used to be close. My brother and I would go to school; then we'd spend six or seven hours in the ArgiTower. It wasn't terrible because I was usually working with Joe and my friends. We'd go home and have dinner. The adults would drink themselves under the table. As soon as we were old enough, we'd join along with them. Then we'd go to bed and repeat." He looks away. "Then one of my friends had an asthma attack while working. He would've made it, but he spent years exposed to the chemicals. So..." He trails off, not willing to talk about it any further. "To my family, that was a regular thing. But I was curious to know if there was another life out there – so, as soon as I turned eighteen, I packed my bags and went off to District 530 for college. That was almost ten years ago. We still keep in contact, but it's not the same as seeing my friends and family every day. I drifted apart from most of my friends; and occasionally, Joe will pester me about coming home."

"Do you want to go home?" I ask, suddenly curious.

Roman shrugs. "I'm not going to lie: I've thought about it a lot. I moved out to District 200 with my girlfriend from college, but we broke up shortly after I got here. After that, I was convinced that I was fooling myself and that I'd be better off in District 402. I had bills to pay, a pile of student loans, and it just didn't seem worth it to stay in District 200 when I can hardly afford to live here." He turns his attention back to me, a lopsided smile on his face. "Until I met a particular barista."

My chest flutters, but I can't resist the urge to ask, "You mean Tate?"

Roman laughs. "Obviously." He turns his attention back to him. "He seems like a great friend."

Said great friend emerges from the back room a moment later with three bottles of syrup. I watch as Tate rearranges the syrup rack to make room for the additional cylinders – destroying my alphabetical system, I think remorsefully.

"The second quarter deadline is tomorrow," Tate murmurs.

"I know," I say.

"How's your mom handling it?"

I think about it for a moment. Last week was the first time that I've spoken to my mother since I found out that she was elected, and it ended with her calling me an ungrateful brat. I can't say that I don't deserve it. But other than that skirmish, I haven't seen her do much, other than yell at Leonard and smoke two packs of cigarettes each day instead of one. "I think she's handling it pretty well. She was granted an extension, so her appeal hearing is in three weeks."

"Well, at least you've got an extra few weeks with her."

"It'll go through," I say. "That'll give me a few extra decades."

The room falls silent. Roman and Tate eye each other – something that I already decide I don't like. Roman is the one to break the silence: "What are you going to do if it doesn't?"

"It will," I say, my eyes narrowing. Didn't I already prove him wrong once today? "All we need to do is show that corruption is happening within the bureau. Then they'll have no choice but to let her go. Now that we know it's a legitimate thing, getting evidence should be easy."

Roman shakes his head. "It's not that simple."

"Why not?" I ask. "We know that it's happening. Hell, you can probably use the evidence from Gideon's computer!"

"You can't win a courtroom case by calling the judge corrupt!" Roman exclaims. "It's the same concept! And your speech probably just diminished her chances!"

I take a step back, unable to believe what I'm hearing. Just a few hours ago, Roman had told me that he was proud of me. I didn't realize how important his approval was until now when it's being retracted from me. And I'd never forgive myself if my actions sent my mother to an early grave...

"I think what you did was an amazing thing," Tate interjects. "You should be proud of yourself. But..." He pauses to glance at Roman. "I think your boyfriend's right. The timing wasn't the greatest."

I'm in disbelief that my boyfriend and best friend are practically on the same wave-length. Under normal circumstances, I'd be elated. Right now, it's causing pain in my chest.

I pull out the key sensor to my car out of my pocket. "I want to go home."

Roman is the first to protest. "April..."

I hold my hand up to keep him from speaking any further. "No, you're right. I guess I should stop being a brat and spend time with my family."

Roman smiles. "Your mother loves you. You should know that."

I shrug. I know that every parent loves their child in some way, but some have different ways of showing it than others. My mother is a blunt, chain-smoking piece of work – but I suppose she's only human. As am I.

"Will you be okay driving home?" Tate asks.

"Yeah," I answer. "Roman and I took separate cars." I had driven to the bureau's headquarters for lunch earlier that day, and neither of us was willing to leave them at their respective locations when we finally met up.

"I think I'll hang out here for a little bit," says Roman, glancing at Tate as he makes another drink.

I nod. I have a feeling that this can either bode poorly or greatly for me in the future. In spite of this, I kiss Roman goodbye and promise Tate that we'll see each other soon. As I walk away, I overhear Tate offer Roman a drink known as the "Zebra." I try to stifle a laugh as I get into my car and drive to the mansion.

Throughout the ride, I think about what I'm going to say to my mother. She already called me a selfish brat in the last conversation that I had with her (which was really me asking her if she knew where CLEO went and my mother letting her frustration with me from the last few weeks come loose). I can't just walk up to her and start talking about shopping and boys, as my mother would immediately think that I had an ulterior motive. I couldn't just launch a pity party, as neither of us would want that. The only thing I could do is the one thing that leaves me with a feeling of dread in my stomach: apologize.

I'm still dwelling on it as I pull into the driveway. I attempt to park in the garage, but my mother's car is blocking my way. It takes every ounce of my body not to be irritated by this, as I'm forced to put my car in manual mode to park in the grass.

*She doesn't have a lot of time left, she doesn't have a lot of time left...*

But when I jump out of my car, I notice something is wrong. As I walk past it, I see exposed wires throughout the car's dashboard. I squint my eyes and take several steps closer, certain that my eyes are deceiving me. The computer screen is missing from the panel. The steering wheel has been permanently mounted in front, near a pair of pedals that I've been taught to only use in case of emergency. Bags and boxes are stacked in the backseat, lining the car from floor to roof.

I dash to the mansion. I don't bother waiting for the elevator – instead, I bolt up four flights of stairs until I find myself standing in my mother's bedroom. My mom is in the middle of zipping up a suitcase when I find her.

"What are you doing?" I demand.

My mother looks like a deer caught in headlights. "What are you doing in my room? I thought I raised you better than that!"

"I came up here because I saw that the entire front dashboard of your car was ripped up!"

My mother finishes zippering up the bag. She avoids my hard gaze. "I took out the computer and GPS. It was Leonard's suggestion to make sure that they're not able to track me."

"Who's able to track you?" I ask, but a part of me already knows the answer.

My mother is silent.

I eye the bags. "Where are you going?"

"I can't tell you," my mother says, her lip quivering.

The logical part of me knows what's happening, but my heart can't seem to accept it yet. "Will I see you at the appeal hearing?"

Macy turns to face me. Her lip stops quivering, and her voice is devoid of emotion: "I'm not coming back."

With those words, my heart can't deny what my head already knew. My mother isn't intending on coming back for the hearing; and judging by the number of suitcases and empty dresser drawers, she's not planning on turning herself over to the bureau. "You're running away."

"I'm sorry, April," my mother says. She looks numb, as though she had spent all of her emotions mulling over this decision. "But I can't die. I won't."

"You won't die," I say, weakly. "You've got one of the best appeal lawyers out there! And... Roman! He knows the Divinity Bureau better than anyone. If there's one thing that I know, it's the fact that this is all a mistake!"

"It's not a mistake!" my mother shoots back. "Don't you get it? The McIntyre Curse is real! We're targets, April!"

Her words hang in the air, like the pollution in District 200.

"I don't believe it," I say breathlessly. "I said the same thing last year when Dad was elected, and you made me spend a year in therapy." I close my eyes. "Why?"

My mother glances around the room. I can't tell if she's looking for items that she's forgotten or if she's avoiding looking at me.

"I knew about the McIntyre Curse before I married your father," my mother says, her voice low. "Your grandparents and great-grandparents did some dishonest things, but your father was a good man."

I snort. I have a hard time believing that the man who practically slept with every harlot that walked through the Parliament doors was a good person.

"We didn't always get along," my mother says, noticing the disbelief on my expression. "But I have no doubt in my mind that he was innocent in all of this. It's a shame that we both had to get dragged into this as well."

"Will we still see you?" I ask, my voice helpless. I feel like a child begging my father not to go back to District 1.

My mother looks at me as though she expects me to know the answer.

"Were you even planning on saying goodbye to Autumn and me?"

"I left a note for Autumn," my mother answers. "I would've waited for you, though." My mother hesitates on her next words. "I... I know you had regrets that you never got the chance to reconcile with your father before he died. I'm sure you know as well as I do that regret is one of the most crippling emotions. So, if there's anything that you want to say to me now, please do it. I don't want you to spend your life with the regret that's haunted me ever since your father died."

"So, that's it?" I ask, unable to believe the words that are coming out of my mouth. "You're okay with Autumn having regrets, but not me?"

"She wouldn't have had them," my mother answers. "She knows I love her, and I know how much she loves me. She'll feel a lot of grief;

but grief will only destroy you temporarily, while regrets will haunt you until you die."

"I'm having a hard time believing that you're doing this out of selflessness," I say bitterly. "I can hardly hold down a minimum wage job down! I don't know how you can expect me to take care of a kid!"

"Because you love her," Macy whispers. "And she worships you." She takes her bag and makes her way towards the door. "When the police come, don't tell them that you saw me leave. As you know, harboring a fugitive of the Divinity Bureau will land you prison time. Just pretend that you know as little as possible. Maybe you can even suggest that I'm staying at our vacation home in District 180."

"I don't need to pretend."

Macy offers me a small smile. "Last chance to get your regrets out of the way. Anything you want to say? Are you going to tell me what an awful mother I am?"

I blink back tears, my head and heart fully comprehending the situation that's happening in front of me. I have only one question: "Why are you doing this?"

"Because when you have nothing left," my mother murmurs. "You don't have anything to lose."

CHAPTER SEVENTEEN

# ROMAN

I n the next few weeks, the McIntyre Family has taken over my entire life.

April has stayed busy following Macy's departure. In the weeks that followed, I expected police to be swarming at her door; but April has decided to keep her disappearance a secret from everyone except for me. Together, we worked out a cover story: Macy decided to spend some time at her family's lake house to find a sense of peace and serenity before her appeal. Little did anyone know – including Autumn and, allegedly, April – that she wasn't planning on coming back. This would give Macy time before anyone started looking for her.

When I'm not with April, I'm hearing about her on the news. Her speech in front of the bureau's headquarters has been playing on repeat wherever I go.

The first time caught me by surprise. After April had left the coffee shop, I spent some time chatting with Tate. Before I knew it, an hour passed; and I needed to head home to feed Neville. As I was walking back to my car, I noticed a projector in front of an electronics shop. More particularly, I saw April's face on the projector, standing in front of the bureau's headquarters with subtitles that read: "Whether or not you wrap it in a fancy title doesn't change the fact that the names on your list are dying at your hands." That caught me by surprise, but I brushed it off as a daily recap of the news. Pretty soon, the media would find something else to talk about.

But they didn't.

The next day, someone had figured out that the girl in front of the bureau's headquarters was Henrik McIntyre's daughter. Shortly after that, another newscaster figured out that Macy McIntyre was up for election that quarter. From there, the media dug up everything they could find about the McIntyre family, and they wasted no time in unraveling every bit of information that they could find.

There were varying opinions about April's speech.

Some were in full support ("It's refreshing," a presenter named Svana Stapleton commented enthusiastically. "The Divinity Bureau doesn't have a choice but to listen to a McIntyre."). Others were in complete disagreement ("You think that 'murder' is a strong word?" a late night talk show host had asked rhetorically. "Well, I think that crazy is a strong word, and that's what April McIntyre is!"). But most could agree that April McIntyre was unforgettable. On several occasions, I've heard the words, "I daresay she might even be following in her father's footsteps!"

The McIntyre Obsession followed me to work. Since the speech happened in front of the bureau's headquarters, everyone at the bureau couldn't stop talking about it – which brings me to now: grabbing a coffee and running into a group of coworkers huddled around a projector in the break room.

It doesn't take long for me to recognize April's speech blaring in the background. I know that April didn't write down or rehearse what she was going to say – other than the five minutes while we were making our way through the crowd – but it seems like the public remembers her speech more than she does.

"You call it an election, as though getting elected is something to be proud of," April's voice echoes. "However, I've got news for you."

"At the end of the day, you're still taking hundreds of thousands – if not millions – of lives," I repeat, not surprised that I've managed to memorize every word of April's speech. Several heads shoot sideways to glance in my direction. I recognize David and Amy.

Amy is the first to speak up. "Do you know her?"

I swallow. I don't want to deny my association with April, but I'm treading on dangerous waters. "I…"

"Of course he does!" David chimes in. "Everyone knows who April McIntyre is!"

"I knew who she was before anyone else did," Amy points out. "I voted for her father."

David rolls his eyes. "I wouldn't be proud of voting for a right-wing serial cheater that cut the bureau's budget by 25%. Remember those layoffs five years ago?"

"But think of the good he did for our social safety net!"

I want to laugh at this. Our social security went from mediocre to somewhat-functional. It was an improvement, but it hardly made a difference.

"Has Gideon said anything about it?" I interject, not in the mood to get into a political debate.

David eyes me as though I just emerged from a cave. "I take it that you haven't checked your email?"

I shake my head. "No, I haven't."

Judging by the look on David's face, I have a feeling that it isn't going to be good.

I return to my desk and turn my computer on. At the top is an email from Finn, who asks me to set up the projectors for the appeal hearings scheduled for today. I feel a twang on my chest. Four are scheduled, and one of them is for Macy. April told me that she'd show up anyway and try to have the hearing without Macy. It'd contribute to their alibi of believing her to have gone on a soul-searching mission. Unfortunately, this would be when Autumn finds out that their mother wasn't coming back.

The second email is a company-wide email sent by Gideon.

*From: Gideon Hearthstrom*
*To: All Employees of the Divinity Bureau*

*As many of you are aware, there have been several disturbances that have been occurring in front of Divinity Bureau headquarters across the country. While we are not at liberty to deny citizens the right to free speech, it is important to acknowledge that these disturbances directly affect the bureau's ability to conduct business – many of which are vital to the health of our economy, our planet, and our health.*

*This notice is to inform all employees that any participation in any protests and any association with notable leaders of the movement will lead to termination of employment. This change in policy is effective immediately. We do not believe that this change in policy will detrimentally affect anyone that is currently employed with the Divinity Bureau – however, if it does, this notice serves as a warning to choose your actions wisely.*

There has to be a mistake. I read and reread the email twice, three times, four times – all in an attempt to find a loophole to keep my job and stay with April. But it's apparent that being in a relationship with April would count as an "association with a notable leader of the movement."

"Roman, can you hear me?" Finn asks, calling my name from the opposite end of my cubicle space. It hits me that he's been calling my name for the last minute or so.

I turn my head. "Sorry. I – err – was just reading the email that Gideon sent."

As soon as the words come out of my mouth, I realize that Finn knows about my relationship with April. Karma is about to ruin my career. It wouldn't be hard to prove that we're together. There are pictures on the internet of us, both of us are in a relationship with each other, and there are plenty of witnesses that have seen us …

"Can you please start setting up the projector?" Finn asks. "We've got one person that says they'll need it."

I nod. Something about the look on Finn's face tells me that he won't turn me in.

I make my way into the hearing room. It's hidden behind a pair of plastic doors that have been stained and textured to look like wood. Once the door opens, I'm greeted by the sight of an old courtroom. Wooden benches line up neatly in the back. A small gate and divider separate the spectators from appeals. A podium sits in the middle, where the chairman sits.

I find a lift in the maintenance closet and crank it to the top so that I can reach the ceiling. I work aimlessly, struggling not to think about how I'm going to explain to April that I can't date her without getting fired. I'm still going to date her, of course. Disassociating myself from her is not an option. But I'm going to need to be discreet. That meant that I wouldn't be able to talk about her to my coworkers. I can't bring her close to the office, which means that midday lunch dates are out of the question. I also can't go anywhere in public with her, as someone would surely recognize her. That leaves only places that we could go: her house and mine. I hope that it's only temporary.

Without warning, the door is flung open and knocked against the lift. My footing shakes. I cling to whatever I can find – in this case, the projector – until my footing stabilizes. I glare at my intruder: a red-haired security officer that I know as Michael.

"Michael," I say in irritation. "I'm working here."

Michael shrugs, unfazed by the fact that he nearly knocked me to the ground. "Sorry. There's a huge crowd outside, and they're blocking the hallway. I was hoping that I'd be able to start letting people in."

I glance at the projection system. It's already synced to our main internet line, but I need to sync it to our backups. "Can you wait a few minutes? The hearings don't start for another hour."

Michael shakes his head. "April McIntyre is here, so we're going to need to get her seated pretty soon."

Those words nearly knock me over again. "What?"

"We're having her and her sister wait in the security office," Michael replies briskly. "Apparently, someone threw a shoe at her while she was coming in. We need to have someone escort her in."

My initial instinct is to demand to know who threw the shoe at her, but I hold my tongue.

"Roman," Michael says, his face turning serious. "She asked for you. Do you know her?"

I know her – every freckle, what makes her laugh, and the way her nose scrunches up when she's annoyed. The thought makes it hard to spit out the lie through my teeth: "We're acquaintances, but I don't know her. I can't."

With the projector synced to one of the bureau's five networks, I'm able to sync it to my Mobiroid for testing. I scroll through the commands on my wrist and see if it will turn on, which it does. Then I leave the courtroom as quickly as possible.

Michael wasn't lying when he said that the hallway was jammed up. It took a significant amount of effort just for me to squeeze my arm through the doorway. Once a part of me is out, people move out of the way momentarily for me to get out, but space quickly fills back up. As I squeeze past the crowd, I glance at my Mobiroid and notice that I have several texts from April.

*"Meeting with my mom's lawyer at bureau's headquarters. When's your next break? Let's grab a coffee!"*

*"I think he may have been the one that told her to run away...he's giving me shady vibes."*

*"Someone freaking threw a shoe at me! What the hell!"*

*"Dude, they're having me wait in the security office – but the security guards are talking shit about me in the next room! Apparently, I have crazy eyes?"*

*"Told the guy to keep it down, and that I couldn't hear my thoughts over the sound of his voice. That shut him up. I miss you."*

I burst out laughing at the last text. I momentarily daydream about pushing my way through the crowd and finding April in the security office and declaring my love for this woman, damn the Divinity Bureau! But I have bills to pay. And as much as I hate to admit it, I need to be here. This is the best place for me to be if I'm to keep her safe.

■■■■■■■■■■■■■■■■■■■■■■■■■■■■■■■■■■■■■■■■■■■■■■■■■■■■■■

I expect April to call me out on the fact that I've ignored her all day. It's not like me to not respond to her. Usually, it's the other way around. But once the hearing begins, my phone goes silent.

As soon as her allotted time begins, I know that I'm not going to be able to focus on work – not when I already know how the day is going to end. I search the internet for a live feed of the hearing. I find one, joining six hundred thousand people that are tuning in.

There are seven cameras in the courtroom: one point at the chairman, three at the podium, two towards the audience, and an eagle eye (the latter of which I had installed ten months ago). As an audience, we can select the which camera we want to focus on, but it defaults to whoever is speaking. I, of course, choose the one that is towards the audience, which is where April and Autumn are sitting. They sit next to a man in a gray suit, whom I'm presuming is their lawyer. Autumn is glancing around the room nervously, as though hoping that Macy was merely running late. I suddenly feel terrible for not telling her the truth.

The camera screen moves to Hemmingsworth, who is clearing his throat. "Alright. Next up, we have the Divinity Bureau versus Macy McIntyre –"

April shoots out of her seat before Hemmingsworth can finish talking.

"Counsel, will you please step up to the podium and identify yourself?"

The man walks briskly through the gate, before taking a seat in front of a table facing Hemmingsworth. He breathes into a microphone, before he states, "Leonard Kavanagh, representing Macy McIntyre."

Hemmingsworth glances at the empty seat next to Leonard. "And where exactly is Miss McIntyre?"

I hear Autumn suck in a breath. April grabs her hand.

"She is unavailable, sir. Due to the circumstances with Miss April McIntyre, she did not deem it safe to make an appearance at the bureau's headquarters," Leonard states plainly. "For that reason, I am requesting to invoke Article 23 of the Divinity Act. As you know, Article 23 states that if the elected is unable to make an appearance at the bureau's headquarters for reasons pertaining to physical danger, physical ailments –"

"I have a hard time believing that Article 23 should be invoked," Hemmingsworth says, taking note of April sitting in the audience. "April McIntyre did not have any qualms with coming here today."

"That was her choice, sir," Leonard points out. "I don't believe that my client should be held accountable for circumstances outside of her control."

"That's her daughter," Hemmingsworth remarks. "She should have been able to control that 'circumstance' from childhood." From the corner of the screen, I can see April's jaw drop. "Never mind the fact that Macy McIntyre chose not to show up at her own hearing. Tell me why I should grant her a second extension when her daughter took it upon herself to embarrass the Divinity Bureau, shake the foundation of our very existence, and, in her words, 'fight and claw her way out of election!'"

April stands up from her seat. "That's not what I said!"

She doesn't have a microphone, but her voice still carries across the room.

"And then, she adds insult to injury by making an appearance inside our very courtroom!" Hemmingsworth adds, throwing his hands up in exasperation. "Tell me, Miss McIntyre: does your mother think that she can fight and claw her way out? Or is she merely hiding?"

The views on the live stream are starting to pick up. Eight hundred and one thousand, eight hundred and two thousand…. The comments are coming in faster than I can read them:

*'Wow!'*

*'April McIntyre is a badass.'*

*'April McIntyre is a psychotic lunatic with no respect for authority.'*

Autumn tugs on April's dress to get her to sit down, but April is refusing to back down. "What does that make you?" April asks defiantly. "You're hiding behind a fancy title and a claim to have authority. How do you make decisions during these appeals? Do you have a checklist of criteria that they need to meet? Or do you just go with whatever feels good to you?"

Leonard looks as though he wants to shrink in his chair and ever be seen again.

Hemmingsworth turns away. "The request for a reschedule is denied. I want a warrant out for Macy McIntyre's arrest." He glares at April. "This hearing is adjourned."

"So, you're pulling that card then?" April presses. "You think it makes you big and powerful?"

"The hearing is adjourned," Hemmingsworth repeats icily. "Michael, please have April McIntyre escorted from the premises."

Michael is next to April in an instant. He grabs her arm, but she pulls it out of his grasp and mutters a few choice curse words. Autumn quickly trails behind her.

On the other side of the screen, I'm pressing my hand to my temple. My optimism that everything would blow over has been burst. Gideon is never going to forget this incident, and there's no doubt that he won't let anyone else forget it either.

CHAPTER EIGHTEEN

# APRIL

I don't have the closest relationship with my sister – primarily because we have an eight-year age gap between us, but also because our personalities are nearly complete opposites. I'm loud, brash, stubborn, and outgoing; while my sweet and shy sister prefers to obsess over the fantasy novels on her tablet. She dreams of being a writer. I can't even remember the last time I've read a book for pleasure. I don't understand her, but there's no way in hell that I'm letting anyone else take care of her.

"I don't need a babysitter!" Autumn whines as we ride to Roman's apartment. Once I catch a glimpse of graffiti and pop-up homeless camps, I'm attempt to keep Autumn distracted from the sights outside of her window with conversation. "I'm almost twelve years old!"

"Someone is going to have to cook for you," I say pointedly. "Plus you'll get bored spending all afternoon in that mansion by yourself."

"I will not!"

"Roman has VR games and a cat," I say. "Two things that we don't have at the mansion."

My parents were strict about letting us having any form of a gaming console, thinking that it'd prevent us from being productive. Occasionally, I'll look at Roman and believe that it was probably for the best.

"Can we please get a cat?" Autumn asks, her eyes growing wide. No doubt, she's looking to take advantage of her change in guardianship. "Mom said that she didn't have time to take care of one; but if we get one of those self-cleaning litter boxes, I think we should be okay."

"I'm allergic."

"I'll keep in my room."

I shake my head. "I don't want to suffocate every time I enter your room."

On the topic of changes in guardianship, I'm impressed with how well Autumn is handling everything. I sat her down after the hearing and told her everything: the corruption, the fact that Roman saved my life when he first met me, and the fact that our mother is on the run from the Divinity Bureau. Unlike her older and allegedly wiser sister, she didn't throw a tantrum. Instead, she asked if we could get ice cream.

"What?" I had asked, in shock that after hearing everything, that was the first thing that came to mind.

"Ice cream," Autumn repeated. "Preferably real ice cream. Monika keeps telling me about how much better 'real' ice cream is better than synthetic ice cream, but I heard it's super expensive. So, I understand…"

"Hang on," I said, confused. "Did you not hear anything I said? You know, about Mom being on the run…"

Autumn looked away. "I'm sad about it. I'll miss her a lot. But I think being on the run is better than being dead." She offered me a smile. "It's better than what I thought would happen. And you said that I get to stay with you, right?"

I nod, still in shock.

"Whenever I'm having a bad day, Mom usually takes me out for ice cream," Autumn says.

I roll my eyes. "She does not; don't forget, I grew up with you for the last twelve years. But we can get ice cream anyways."

In the last few weeks, Gideon signed off on a warrant for Macy's arrest. An old picture of her is on every news feed, along with a promise of a five thousand sterling reward for information leading to her arrest. The next thing that needs to be figured out is where my sister and I will go. While I don't need a legal guardian, I do have a meeting with Leonard today to go over the specifics in my mother's will. I'm hoping that I'll be able to regain access to my trust fund. I'm also hoping that Leonard will look past the fact that Dr. Gray is technically listed as mine and Autumn's legal guardians.

The car is parking in the lot when my Mobiroid goes off. It's a text from Roman: *'Can you circle the block for a few minutes? My neighbors are outside – and they're way too camera-happy.'*

Seriously?

Shortly after the hearing, Roman broke the news that he wasn't allowed to be seen in public with me. I can respect that. I've been in the public eye frequently lately – especially after the hearing – and it's not a secret how I feel about the bureau. But Roman's paranoia is threatening to test my patience. A week ago, we agreed to meet at the mansion for a night at home. He was an hour late, claiming to take a detour so that no one knew where he was going. A few days after that, we ordered take-out, and he refused to let me pick up the food – although the restaurant was literally on my way to his apartment.

"Where are we going?" Autumn asks as soon as she notices that we've changed course.

"We have to circle the block."

"Why?"

"Roman's neighbors," I reply, irritated. "He's worried that they'll see him with me."

"How come he doesn't want to be seen with you?"

She could have worded that a little more tactfully. The question is innocent, but it does little to help my agitated mood. "It's because Roman will lose his job if he's seen with me."

I expect Autumn to ask why Roman is willing his job over our relationship – I've been asking myself the same question over and over again – but Autumn nods in understanding. "That reminds me of this book I'm reading."

"Oh?" I ask, intrigued to know how a fictional book correlates with my life.

"Yeah. This vampire – Lukas is his name – is in love with a human girl named Marsha. He's part of this elite vampire coven, who basically rules the entire supernatural underworld of vampires, werewolves, witches, etcetera. He can also do magic. Anyways, his coven tells him that they're going to strip him of his magic and disown him if he continues to see this girl since they don't want their bloodline tainted."

The book is a bit too peculiar for my tastes, but I feign interest anyways. "So, what happens?"

Autumn shrugs nonchalantly. "His brother kills Marsha by sucking all her blood out."

I nearly choke on my own saliva. I barely have a chance to recover by the time Roman sends me a message to let me know that it's all clear. I reprogram the car to drive and park outside of Roman's apartment building.

"You don't need to walk me inside," Autumn says when she notices that I'm putting on my face mask and stepping out of the car. "It's apartment 514. I'm sure I can find it easily. It's probably on the fifth floor."

"You might want to wear a face mask," I point out. "The amount of pollution in Roman's neighborhood is ridiculous."

Autumn gives me a sideways glance, but she pulls a pink mask out of her bag and sets it on her face. In spite of the mask covering half of her face, her eyebrows are furrowed in annoyance. I can tell that she doesn't want me hovering over her. "I want to see Roman," I insist. "It's quite common for girls who have boyfriends. You would know if you've ever had one."

I also want to kick Roman in the nuts for making me drive around his crime-ridden neighborhood to avoid his neighbors seeing me. The object of my annoyance is waiting for us in the doorway of his apartment. As soon as I step into the apartment, I remove the mask – a huge mistake, as I haven't taken any allergy medications. My eyes are watering, and the cat dander feels as though it's invading my lungs. Autumn, on the other hand, is quick to find the cat lounging on Roman's futon and darts over to pet him.

With Autumn's attention captured, Roman pulls me into the kitchen area and wraps his arms around me. "I missed you."

Just like that, my irritation has vanished from my system. I close my eyes, willing myself to find the words to express my annoyance with Roman; but when I thought about it, I realized that it's not his fault. He needs his job, and he needs to take precautions. But he also cherishes me enough to keep seeing me in spite of this.

"I shouldn't be gone for too long," I say. "I promise that as soon as this meeting is over, I'll take allergy medication, and we'll spend the rest of the day together." I glance at Autumn, who has taken to stroking the cat's belly. "We'll probably have company."

"That's fine," Roman says, before planting a chaste kiss on my lips. "I suppose I'll have to get used to it being the three of us."

I shift my feet. "Yeah, I guess so."

I realize how strange the situation is. Roman and Autumn haven't spent a lot of time together, other than a few dinners at the mansion.

"Autumn is low-maintenance," I blurt out. "She'll probably play with the cat for an hour – but after that, all you need to do is throw on a movie and call it good. I'm not sure if she likes science fiction as much as you do, but she loves fantasy novels…"

Roman cuts me off by planting another kiss on my lips. "I think we'll be fine."

■■■■■■■■■■■■■■■■■■■■■■■■■■■■■■■■■■■■■■■■■■■■■■■■■

I find Leonard's office – a small office in District 209, located just a few blocks away from a run-down baseball stadium. It takes an hour and a half of traffic, but I manage to snag a parking spot just a few blocks away. His office is on the seventh floor of a modest-sized tower, noticeable only by the metal plaque with his name on it. When I push the door open, I find myself standing in a sparsely decorated waiting room. I assume he's hiding behind the door on the other side of the waiting area, so I approach it and raise my hand up to knock – until I hear voices from the other side.

"Twenty-five? Why did you make me seven years younger than I was when I stopped aging?"

"It'll last longer. The younger you are, the less likely anyone will be to ask questions."

"And I can still get to the Iceland's with this?"

"Yes. I've made sure to include a visa. Getting back into the Confederal Districts, however, will be another story."

The Iceland's.

The Iceland's is north of the Confederal Districts. My father took me there once when I was twelve years old. It was after my mother found out about one of his affairs – that time, it was remarkably scandalous since the media found out that he had allegedly paid a prostitute – and she needed space to decide if she was going to stay with him. I later learned out that the trip also doubled as a business trip. My father, Nolan Fitz, and several other high-ranking MP's were there in hopes that the Iceland's would join the Confederal Districts. From what I remember, my father had to pull strings to allow me to come with him. It's rare for anyone in the Confederal Districts have a passport, as it's reserved for high-ranking government officials and the occasional business person. It doesn't surprise me that one would need a lawyer, as Leonard is. But from what I knew about my mother's disappearance *("It was Leonard's suggestion to make sure that they're not able to track me,"* she had said), a part of me wondered if there was more to the transaction happening before me.

"Do you need anything else?" Leonard asks, his baritone voice carrying through the doorway. "I've got an appointment with a client in about five minutes."

A door opens – the one that I had entered the office from. Not wanting to be caught eavesdropping, I move to one of the waiting room chairs. My eyes dart towards the front door, where Darcy Gray is walking in. She's donned in black high heels, a pencil skirt, and a silk blazer. Glancing down at my t-shirt and nylon pants, I suddenly feel severely underdressed.

"What are you doing here?" I ask. I was under the impression that I was scheduled to have a one-on-one meeting with Leonard.

"You're challenging my rights as yours and Autumn's legal guardian," Darcy states, matter-of-fact.

"You aren't anyone's legal guardian," I spit back. "Not mine, and after today, you sure as hell won't be Autumn's!"

Darcy stares at me. I'm guessing she's thinking about all the therapy sessions that I've missed in the last few months. "I don't understand why you feel so much animosity towards me."

"You don't understand?" I hiss back. "For the last year, you made me think I was crazy! You prescribed medicine after medicine, giving me all these lectures about how we all need help, blah blah blah. But I was right the whole time!" I cross my arms pointedly. "There is no way in hell that I'm letting you put Autumn through that!"

"I never intended on making you feel that way."

"Of course not! You and my mother just wanted a quick fix instead of listening to what I had to say!"

Before Darcy could say anything more, the door to Leonard's office opens. Given everything that I know, I'm curious as to who his client is. I meet his eyes – and gasp.

"I know you!" I exclaim.

The man's eyes widen. He glances around the room in a panic, but the fear subsides when he takes another look at me. "I'm sorry, miss. But I don't recall meeting you."

"No, you probably don't," I clarify. I've never met the man either, but I've seen his face. "You were in a movie – or, rather, a series of movies. Isn't your name Neal O'Donnell?"

The room falls silent.

Neal O'Donnell had been elected a few quarters ago. I had attended a protest for his election, which was where I ran into Roman. The words of the protest ring in my ears: *"Hey, ho! The Divinity Bureau has got to go!"* At the time, I was more concerned with the message than the person whose election I was protesting for; but seeing him in front of me, it becomes apparent. His hair looks remarkably different – it's grown to his shoulders now. He also has a beard. But I've seen those eyes on too many posters not to recognize them.

"I'm sorry, miss," the man says apologetically. "But you have the wrong person."

"Yeah, April," Darcy chimes. "Neal O'Donnell is dead. Didn't you hear the bureau denied his appeal?"

But he isn't dead. He's standing right in front of me. Everything is making sense now.

My mother had used Leonard's services to get a new identity.

"Sorry, my bad," I apologize, brushing it off. "It's been a long day."

Darcy gives me a wary look as Neal O'Donnell brushes past us and exits the waiting area. As soon as he's gone, I notice Leonard let out a relieved sigh. It only lasts for a second, though, before he ushers Darcy and me into his office.

"Now…" he begins, but I quickly cut him off.

"What is she doing here?" I ask, pointing to Darcy.

"I thought we had already established this," Darcy responds in a huff.

"Miss Gray is–"

"Doctor Gray," Darcy corrects with narrow eyes.

"*Dr.* Gray is listed in your mother's will as the legal guardian of you and your sister," Leonard clarifies. "Obviously, we have a unique situation at hand. You see, we don't typically go over the details of someone's will unless they're deceased –"

'*I'd hardly call it unique,*' I think with a huff. Neal O'Donnell's image is still fresh in my mind.

"Yet given your mother's status," Leonard continues. "We deemed it necessary so that we can ensure that you and Autumn are properly taken care of."

I raise an eyebrow. "We?"

"Dr. Gray is not only named as the legal guardian, but she is also named as the benefactor of your family's fortune," Leonard explains slowly. "As your fortune is to be divided equally between you and Autumn, you will have control of your half by the end of the day today."

That is what I hoped. I've been waiting for this for almost two years. Gone are the days of stressing about finding another job. If I play my cards right, I'll never need to work again. Except – I don't like the tone that Leonard is using like he's about to tell me something that he knows I won't like.

"Autumn's half will be under the control of Dr. Gray until she turns eighteen," Leonard goes on. He stops. I know he's waiting for my reaction.

"Are you telling me…?" I begin, but I can't finish.

I can see a mixture of emotions on Dr. Gray's face. The surprise is the most dominant one, but there's no hiding the tell-tale smile of her face. Custody of Autumn will ensure that she won't need to work for a long time.

"It's your mother's wish that Darcy Gray has custody of your sister," Leonard says nervously. A layer of sweat forms on his brow.

If a reaction is what he's anticipating, I sure as hell am about to give him one.

"Are you freaking kidding me?" I exclaim, jumping out of my chair. "This woman – my family's psychiatrist?" I brush my hand through my hair. "Do you have any idea how difficult my life has been because of her?"

"April –" Leonard begins, but he's caught off by a humorless laugh from Darcy.

"I didn't make you get arrested," Darcy says, bemused. "And if going through therapy once a week is hard, then you clearly have no concept of what the real world is really like!"

I stop, rendered speechless by her words.

"Do you really think Autumn needs someone like you right now?" Darcy continues. "Someone that loses her temper just because she hears something that she doesn't like?"

I feel as though the air has been forced from my lungs. My voice is weak, barely breaking the silence: "What?"

"I understand you're upset," Darcy says, her voice sympathetic. "I lost both of my parents to the Divinity Bureau. But Autumn is hurting just as badly as you are. And I think you still have a lot of growing up to do before you can take her on full-time."

I close my eyes. "You... you don't understand. For the past few weeks, I've watched her cry herself to sleep every night..."

But did I do anything about it?

I haven't done much other than hovering in Autumn's doorway for minutes at a time. I've always figured that she'd want space – much like the way I grieve. But we're opposites. While I grieve by asking for space, Autumn probably needs someone to tell her that everything is going to be alright.

I can't breathe.

"You're twenty years old, April," Darcy says. "You're still trying to figure yourself out. How do you expect to know what an eleven-year-old girl needs?"

My chest hurts. Air enters my lungs in short puffs, but it feels like oxygen is out of my reach. I collapse to the floor. I wrap myself in a ball as I struggle to find air. Leonard and Darcy are at my side in an instant.

"Are you okay?" Leonard asks, brushing a lock of hair away from my face.

I'm not okay. My body is breaking out into a sweat. It's at this moment that I realize that the Divinity Bureau isn't the only thing dangerous to my health. If I'm to die, it could very well be at my own hands.

"She's having a panic attack!" Darcy exclaims.

"What do we do?"

"Do you have a bag?"

"A – what!?"

"A bag!" Darcy repeats, growing frustrated. She brushes a hand through my hair. "Can you find me one?"

Leonard scrambles out of the room without a second thought. I feel Darcy's hands – small with elongated fingers – on my back. She rolls me so that I'm lying on my side. I close my eyes. Under the weight of the world, I feel as though I'm being crushed to death.

CHAPTER NINETEEN

# ROMAN

"Prepare to die, little girl," I growl.

Autumn isn't about to let me get my way. She quips back, "Not a chance!"

A moment later, our match begins. Autumn starts with the first punch. I take a hit, but I find my weapon and strike her in the chest. I jump in the air and attempt another blow, but she blocks me. Then, without warning, my foot collides with the end of a table. Real pain – not the simulated pain of the VR system represented by a health bar on the corner of my vision – shoots through me. The distraction is all Autumn needs to strike a few more blows until a voice bold proclaims, "Player Two Wins!"

I pull the headset off my head so that I can nurse my throbbing foot.

We've been playing VR games all afternoon, which caused Neville to spend the last few hours hiding under the futon. At first, I suggested something that was more kid-friendly; but the only kid-friendly game I have is a digital version of chess. I beat her in three rounds with minimal effort, which caused her to whine about being bored. That's when she found my fighting game collection. I ended up moving my furniture around so that we can simulate a battle between our avatars without hurting each other. I was planning on going easy on her.

Thanks to years of playing VR games, I know almost every motion combo by heart. Autumn, on the other hand, had never owned a VR system. Still, she managed to flail her arms around and kick my ass. When I told her that swinging her arms around without a strategy was cheating, she called me a sore loser. That was when war was declared.

"Let's play again!" Autumn exclaims.

I shake my head. The problem with VR gaming is that it's exhausting. Unlike Autumn, I can only move my body around so much before I lose energy.

"Have you heard from April?" I ask. It's close to eight o'clock, so I'm worried that something is wrong.

Autumn shakes her head, but her focus is on adjusting her avatar. I can see her screen on the projector. "No."

"It's pretty late. Do you think something is wrong?"

"I don't know. Obviously, I'm not there." Her words are bitter, and I'm guessing she isn't okay with her fate lying in the hands of a bunch of grownups.

I sigh as I set the controller onto the coffee table. Coming from a family of divorced parents, I can relate to her situation. "Where do you want to live?"

Autumn shrugs. "I don't know. I love our house. I love my sister. But I feel like I'm a burden on her at times."

"That's impossible."

Autumn turns her head back in my direction, momentarily forgetting about the VR headset on her face. "Is it? I've known April my whole life."

"I've known her for long enough," I quip, but a part of me knows that it's been less than a year since I met her. Still, I refuse to believe that April doesn't love her sister with all her heart.

"One time, when I was eight, our nanny called in sick," Autumn says, and I have a feeling that I'm not going to like where this story is heading. "April had a date with this guy that went to her high school – who was a total loser, by the way," she adds hastily. I think she's only saying it to appease me. "Anyways, they were going to a movie. My dad was in town, so my parents had to go to some function. My mom and April got into this huge argument over who was going to take me – and April lost because she got stuck taking me along. So, her and her date took me to see this lame kid's movie. Ten minutes into it, they said that they were going to the bathroom and never came back. I tried calling and texting them for an hour after the movie got out. Eventually, April finally texted me back and said that she'd come and grab me. I was so scared that she left me, though."

A large part of me wants to defend April. I want to dismiss it as typical sibling antics, but I know that Joe would never intentionally leave me behind. Still, it's a younger version of her and not the one that I know; though I'm not sure if Autumn will believe me.

I pick up the VR headset from the coffee table, deciding to change the topic. "Let's see who the champion is, once and for all."

Before the fight has a chance to begin, the apartment door swings open. I jump to my feet until I realize that it's April. Tears stain her cheeks. I jump to her side, but I quickly see that she's not alone. A professionally-dressed brunette appears beside her.

"Autumn," April croaks. "I'm going to need you to go with Darcy."

Autumn jumps to her feet. "What? Why?"

"She's going to take you home," April explains slowly. "You're... you're going to be living with her for a little while."

Autumn's eyes widen in horror. "No! I don't want to go with Darcy! I want to stay in our house and go to my old school and stay with you!" Tears stream down her face. April's face crinkles in agony.

"Are you abandoning me again?" Autumn whispers.

April winces. "I'm not abandoning you."

Autumn shakes her head. "It wouldn't be the first time."

"I'm not abandoning you!" April repeats, bringing her voice to a hiss. "I'm not Mom and Dad. Mom left because she wanted to save her skin – and Dad was just, well, Dad!" Autumn's sniffles immediately cease. "I will get you back." April shoots a glare in Darcy's direction. "So, don't think for a single second that I'm giving up on you. We're all that we have left."

Autumn glances between me, April, and Darcy (the latter who looks like she wants to intervene, but is waiting until it's necessary). Autumn asks, "Do you promise that I'll get to come home?"

April gets down on one knee and wipes a stray tear from Autumn's face. "Yes. That house is way too big for one person. I'll even let you get a cat." Autumn's eyes go wide in excitement, causing April to grow nervous. "Um, as long as it stays out of my bedroom – and probably the kitchen and living room are off limits as well."

"We'll make it work," Autumn says, squeezing April's hand.

"We always do. We're McIntyre's."

"April," Darcy interjects, resulting in a fiery glare from April. "I hate to cut your moment short, but I have to work early in the morning – plus we still need to grab Autumn's things."

"Hang on," April says, before turning her attention back to Autumn. She brings her voice to a low whisper, preventing Darcy from hearing her. "Right before Mom left, she said something to me." A small smile crosses her lips. "Actually, she plagiarized my words, but she said: 'When you have nothing left, you have nothing left to lose.' I think there's a point in everyone's life where they realize that despite their best efforts, they have no choice but to surrender. That carrying on will only bring them more pain or heartache. I don't think there's any way that we can avoid these moments. But I just want you to know that I'm not quite there yet."

She glances back at me, and I realize that she's not just talking to her sister. She's talking to me as well, reassuring me that she isn't done fighting for her right to live and love. And I'm not either.

"I'll see you soon," April promises, wrapping her sister in a hug.

Autumn hesitates to leave, but she pulls away with a heavy sigh and makes her way to the doorway. Darcy puts a hand on Autumn's shoulder, before turning to April. "I wish you the best."

212 · TESSA CLARE

As soon as the door closes, April glances at me. I'm still thinking about her words to Autumn, and I wonder if she's going to say something that will resonate with me as much as it did with her. Instead, April takes five steps towards me. Then she collapses into my arms and cries.

■■■■■■■■■■■■■■■■■■■■■■■■■■■■■■■■■■■■■■■■■■■■■■■■■■■■■

As the hours' pass, April tells me everything that happened in the last several hours – Leonard's office, the conversation with Neal O'Donnell, Darcy, and, finally, her panic attack.

"I can't do this, Roman," she whispers. "Darcy's right. I'm twenty-years-old. I can't even hold a minimum wage job. Hell, I can't even go out in public!"

I stare at her, realizing her words to Autumn are a lie. There's a very real chance that she made that promise to appease her sister. After spending the last several hours with Autumn, I can't help but be upset.

"Why would you promise your sister that she'd get to come home?" I ask. In spite of the fact that I have little to do with the situation, I feel betrayed. "You know that she's going to hold you accountable to it."

April shakes her head. "Because I'm going to make it happen. It's just... going to take a bit of time."

I offer to let April stay in my apartment that night, and she willingly accepts. I imagine the last thing she wants is to go back to a mansion that's far too big for one person. I give her a dose of allergy medication, and she falls asleep in my arms.

She's still knocked out when I leave for work the next morning. I kiss her forehead and tell her to text me if she needs anything, but she never does. Instead, when I come home, I find April sprawled in front of the projector.

"You're still here?" I ask in surprise. It hits me that in the time we've been dating (almost half a year, I realize), we've never spent more than one consecutive night together – until now.

April turns red. "Sorry – I just... well, I woke up to an empty bed. I was going to get ready to leave, but I was comfortable... and next thing I know, it's five o'clock..."

I glance at my bathroom. The medicine cabinet door is wide open from April rummaging through it, probably in search of allergy medicine. I walk over to the bathroom to close it. The last thought that crosses my mind is how she's going to need to get used to not having a CLEO around – and then, I make my way on the couch next to her.

"Do you like Southwestern food?" I ask her.

"Sure, why?"

"Well, I got a text message from the restaurant down the street. The owners think that their computer got hacked. I said I'd look into it, in exchange for free food..."

We spend the next few nights alternating between tacos, burritos, and tostadas. Much like the first night, April falls asleep in my arms. By the third night, she isn't crying herself to sleep, but she does wake up a few times throughout the night. By the fifth night, I've taken to tightening my arms around her whenever I feel her move – mainly out of annoyance that April keeps waking me up, but also because I want to remind her that I'm there for her. She sleeps soundly after that.

On the sixth day, I come home with our last bag of bartered take-out. She's on a video call with Autumn, who had gone back-to-school shopping that day. Autumn would need to transfer schools, as Darcy lived in a District 230. She's nervous, as she isn't going to know anyone at her new school – but April reassures her that she'll be okay.

"Just tell everyone that you were the most popular girl at your old school," April advises.

"But I wasn't."

"Well, obviously you weren't. But your new classmates don't know that."

Weeks pass. Every morning begins with April curled up in my arms, and every night ends the same way. Once we've exhausted our free take-out food, April takes it upon herself to start cooking us dinner ("You need to eat more than boxed meals!"). I'm more than happy to oblige – but it hardly goes well.

The first time, the smoke detector goes off – resulting in my neighbors knocking on my door.

The second time, April misreads a recipe and ends up adding a little too much salt. If I didn't spend the last twenty-five years battling food scarcity, I would've thrown it out. But I suffer through it and insist when I finish that I'm helping her cook next time.

The third time, we agree to cook together. April will chop the vegetables, and I'm going to make sure that nothing gets burnt. As I watch the synthetic beef sizzle in the pan, a thought occurs to me.

"April?"

She stops what she's doing to glance over at me. "Yeah?"

"I didn't see your name on the last election report."

To be honest, that was a couple of weeks ago. Unlike the previous election, I didn't spend a month agonizing over it, as I was too distracted by work, my houseguest, and the drama with my houseguest's sister. I mulled over it for a night, but I stopped thinking about it when she didn't appear on the list the next morning. I can tell that she doesn't want to think about it, either. She shrugs and turns her attention back to chopping vegetables.

I glance around the apartment. Several of April's belongings are littered everywhere: her clothes, her computer, and even pictures of her family are stationed on one of the shelves. Another thought occurs to me.

"Are we living together?" I blurt out.

April nearly slices a finger off at that remark. "What?"

I immediately turn red. "I'm not saying you are because we've only been dating for, like, seven months? Or is it eight? I mean, I know people that move in around that time, so it's not a bad thing. I just want to make sure we're on the same page. To be honest, if we do live together, I'd rather live in your mansion than this crappy apartment –"

"Roman, breathe."

At April's instruction, I take a deep breath.

"Better?" she asks.

I nod.

"I can go home tomorrow, if that's what you want," April assures me, breaking eye contact. "I guess I've probably overstayed my welcome."

"What?" I ask, confused and not wanting her to leave anytime soon. "No, that's not what I meant –"

I'm cut off by the sound of sizzling beef and the smell of burnt food. I let out a groan of annoyance that yet another meal is burned. Still, April assures me that it's our "least crappy" meal yet. To her, that means that we're making progress.

I leave early the next morning to get an early start. I have three high-priority tickets that need to be resolved, in addition to a handful of tickets that need to be fixed before the week is over.

As I get myself situated, I realize that my desk has a lot more space than I'm accustomed to – likely because something is missing: my laptop. I check my cubicle, hoping that it might appear somewhere. But my computer is nowhere. I know that I didn't take it home. I also noticed that whoever had taken my laptop had left my file backup drive and charger. Something is wrong.

"Hey, Finn!" I call out as soon as I see my boss walking through the office. "Do you know who took my computer?"

Finn offers me a sympathetic glance. "Gideon is asking to see you."

Whatever is happening, it isn't good. I feel a pang in my stomach, as though I've been punched. I take the elevator to the top floor and make my way towards Gideon's office. As soon as I approach the door, I can see my computer lying on Gideon's desk, in the same spot where I had seen his computer all those months ago. I know what's happening before I step inside.

"Gideon," I begin, but Gideon raises a hand to stop me from saying anything further.

"Close the door."

I obey without complaint, as though the single act would make up for my disobedience in the last several months. I close the door and slink into the nearest chair. Gideon begins slowly, "I gave you an assignment a few months ago. Do you recall what it was?"

"Look into a security breach."

"Yes," Gideon acknowledges with a nod. "Do you recall what the findings were?"

I had sent him a report a week after Macy was elected. I never got a response to it, so I assumed that my answer was acceptable. "I said that there was nothing out of the ordinary, sir."

"Except that was a lie."

Humiliation overcomes me. I want nothing more than to shrink in my chair and never be seen again.

Gideon points to the computer on my desk. "We were forced to confiscate your computer after rumors emerged that you were involved in a conspiracy."

I stare at him. I have absolutely nothing to hide. If being with April and trying to keep her safe is a conspiracy, then I'll happily make my case against any judge. "What conspiracy?"

"The one to bring down the Divinity Bureau," Gideon states plainly.

Several thoughts occur in that exact moment. It's never been my intention to bring down the Divinity Bureau. All I want – and all I've ever wanted – was to protect the girl I love. Did it mean doing a few dishonest things? It did. But to me, it was a noble cause.

But if the roles reversed – if it were April that worked for the bureau instead of me – the events would have unfolded quite differently. April would have happily taken the information from

Gideon's computer to the press. She would have done everything she could to undermine the Divinity Bureau. She has every reason to hate them. But until now, I didn't.

Not until this very moment.

"We heard from a few sources that you were involved with April McIntyre," Gideon continues. "Also, your browser history indicates that you, personally, had her name removed from the first quarter election report. You were at a protest rally." He crosses his arms and glares at me. "Also, let's not disregard the fact that you managed to obtain confidential records on your computer! Did you decide to steal my files when I trusted you with my belongings?"

"I…" I begin, but I trail off. I don't know what to say.

"Interfering with the election report is a misdemeanor," Gideon continues. "But stealing confidential information, on the other hand, is guaranteed to get you a minimum of ten years. Conspiring to bring down a government agency, on the other hand, will land you there for life. A short one, I might add."

My close my eyes, knowing that the moment I've been dreading has come. *'I deserve this,'* I tell myself, crossing my arms and wishing that I could make myself disappear. Everything started with my decision to follow a girl to work.

*No,* if I'm honest with myself, it started because I'd once been desperate to prove my worth.

*But I did.* I think of the nights that I've held April in my arms. For whatever reason, this strong, magnificent woman thinks I'm her hero.

At that moment, I realize that I did prove my worth. It just wasn't to the Divinity Bureau.

I stand up from my seat. "You're the worst at revenge plotting. You know that, right?"

Gideon looks astonished by my words. His eyes quickly narrow, his voice turning to ice. "What did you say, boy?"

I take a deep breath, trying to remember what Macy had told me.

"I know what Henrik McIntyre did to you," I say, trying to sound more confident than I feel. "I have a Master's Degree in Network Security. Retracing people's steps is the first thing I do when I diagnose tech support issues. That's how I managed to figure out that April's name didn't show up on that election report by accident. But really, what else can you do to Henrik McIntyre? He's dead! Seeing his family get elected won't do anything for him now!"

Gideon lets out a hollow laugh. "Do you think this has anything to do with a twenty-year-old grudge?"

"He ruined your reputation," I say, crossing my arms. Still, Macy's explanation is making less sense by the minute, and I'm starting to lose confidence. "And he ruined your chances of taking Nolan Fitz's job."

"You don't know what you're talking about, boy!" Gideon hisses. "This is a matter of national security!"

"How?" I ask, pressing for more answers. "She's a twenty-year-old kid!" A realization hits me. "No. She's not a danger to national security. She's a risk to your political power."

His hand quickly moves a hand to his Mobiroid. "I'm calling security. As regional chairman, I am invoking Article 19. I hereby place you under arrest –"

But I'm not done talking. "I still have your computer files."

His hand freezes in mid-air.

"If you throw me in prison, all those files are going to be in the hands of April McIntyre," I say, growing more confident by the look of horror on his face. "I can tell you right now: she can't even figure out what she wants to major in, much less how to bring down a government agency. But you've brought this upon yourself. You took away her father, her mother, and – hell – even her sister. Take away the man she loves..." I hope that statement is true. "And, well, you know what they say about people that have nothing to lose. Throw me in prison, and I guarantee that there will be nothing stopping April from getting those files."

Gideon evaluates my claims for a moment. I'm mentally prepared to go to prison, but at least I'll have done everything I could.

He glowers at me. "Get out."

My eyes widen, positive that I'm hallucinating. "What?"

"You're fired," Gideon says coldly. "Get your things and get out."

I don't need to be told a third time.

## CHAPTER TWENTY

# APRIL

"Worst. Hand. Ever."

"I agree," says Tate, tossing his Mobiroid onto the plastic picnic table. "I'm folding."

Roman rolls his eyes. "Oh, come on, you two. Don't be sore losers."

In the weeks that followed Roman's unceremonious sacking, he's been learning to make the most of the situation; and that means spending his new influx of free time with me, Autumn, and Tate. Today, it's a Saturday afternoon that we decided to spend at a lakefront park. The weather report has promised us record low levels of pollution. Combined with sunny days and warm temperatures, it's the perfect day to be outside. All of us left our face masks in my car so that we could enjoy the feeling of fresh air.

I've managed to convince Darcy to let us take Autumn for a few hours; which Darcy agreed to under the condition that Autumn was home at dinner time and that I didn't corrupt my sister in those few hours. I figured that downloading Texas Hold 'Em on her Mobiroid and teaching her how to play was harmless enough.

"Forget it," I say, closing out the screen on my Mobiroid. "I've already had to lick a light post, tell a homeless woman that I loved her, and ask a bicycle cop if I could ride in the basket. I don't understand why we can't place bets with real money."

"Because you and Autumn have enough money to buy the Eastern state," Tate reminds me, as though I need reminding. "This evens out the playing field."

"Your boyfriend's unemployed," Autumn points out. "That wouldn't be fair, would it?"

Roman turns red. "Thanks for the reminder."

Thanks to my newly regained access to my trust fund, I've been able to cover Roman's rent while he looks for another job. It's the least I could do, considering he got fired because of me.

"You," I say, directing the conversation to Autumn. "You don't have access to your trust fund yet, so don't even talk. Until you turn eighteen, that's been given to Darcy."

"And I doubt Darcy would appreciate you teaching her how to gamble," Tate says dryly.

"It's better than drinking and smoking. I was doing all of that when I was Autumn's age."

"And you wonder why Darcy didn't want you taking her for a couple of hours."

"I'm not telling her to do it!" I say defensively. I turn my attention to Autumn, who's staring at her Mobiroid in concentration. The app is projecting a two-sided image: one that simulates the back of the card, and the other simulates the number and suites. "What kind of cards do you have?"

I've been giving Autumn pointers throughout the game, so I'm surprised when she turns off the screen of her Mobiroid. "None of your business!"

"Are you kidding me?"

Autumn flushes. "Sorry. I just don't want anyone to see them."

"Oh, come on! I've been helping you throughout this entire game!"

Tate gives Roman a sideways glance. "You might as well fold. Autumn's poker face is as obvious as a mime's."

"Don't listen to him," I say. "I don't want to lick another light post."

"You know, the rules of this game are unclear," Tate points out. "I get that if we all fold, we're all stuck doing the same dare. We make bets on atrocious and embarrassing tasks, and raise the stakes with tasks that are even more atrocious. But what if Roman loses? Do we all need to lick a light post?"

"It doesn't matter," says Roman. "I'm not going to lose."

"In your dreams, Irvine."

"I think you should fold," Tate suggests. "It'd be embarrassing if you lost to a twelve-year-old."

"Name your price, Miss McIntyre," Roman says, ignoring Tate and turning his attention to a smirking Autumn.

Autumn glances between Roman and me, before she decides, "You've got to kiss a stranger."

"No freaking way!" I protest. "Pick another one."

"It's okay," Roman says, winking in my direction. "I'm not going to have to kiss anyone except my beautiful girlfriend."

"You sure as hell aren't kissing anyone!"

He turns his attention back to Autumn. "And if I win?"

Autumn raises an eyebrow. "What do you want?"

"I want you to ask Danny Lundell out," Roman responds without hesitation. "By the end of next week."

I glance between the two of them. "Who's Danny Lundell?"

Autumn turns red. "No way."

"Who's Danny Lundell?" I repeat.

"He's a boy at Autumn's new school," Roman answers, grinning at the sight of Autumn's red face. "He's got golden hair, bright green eyes, and all of the girls adore him – especially Autumn."

My jaw drops. "You've got a crush?"

Autumn throws Tate's Mobiroid at Roman. "You weren't supposed to tell anyone!"

"You've got a crush? On an actual human being?"

"Hey, don't throw my Mobiroid!"

"Why did you tell Roman and not me?" I ask, offended.

"Because he's a guy!"

"I'm the better candidate!" Tate chimes agitated at being excluded from the conversation. "I'm a guy, and I'm gay!"

"Oh, please! You haven't gotten any action since Armando moved!"

Autumn looks as though she wants to crawl into a hole. "I don't want to talk about this anymore." She glances at my boyfriend. "Roman, I accept your offer."

Roman grins. "Sounds like you've got a date next week."

Autumn shakes her head. "I don't think so." She presses a button to reveal her cards. "I've got two tens. There's one on the board, thus bringing me to a three of a kind. Think you can beat that?"

"That's cute," Roman says haughtily. The virtual cards turned over. "I've got a nine and a seven. Both are clubs. There's a six, eight, and a ten on the board. I'm not sure how familiar you are with poker, but a straight flush has officially beaten you."

Tate raises a hand to give him a high-five. "Nice!"

I glance between Roman and Autumn. Roman is ready to rub his victory in her face; Autumn is beet-red and looking around for any excuse to get out of the date. But before either of them can say anything, a meek voice cuts them off: "Excuse me?"

The four of us turn our attention to the source of the sound: a skinny short-haired girl that's standing at the foot of our picnic bench. I assume that she's no older than sixteen. The girl is alternating her gaze between me and the ground.

"I'm sorry to bother you," the girl says, her voice so quiet that I have to strain to hear her. "But you look a lot like April McIntyre…"

What?

Did I hear her correctly?

"That… that would be me," I say slowly. Everyone is looking just as shocked as I am. "I'm sorry, but have we met?"

The short-haired girl's eyes widen in amazement. "So, it is you!" She turns her head and calls out, "Madeline, come over here! It's April McIntyre!"

I watch as a red-haired girl practically skips to our table in excitement.

"I saw the speech you gave in front of the bureau," the girl goes on as the red-haired girl joins the conversation. "And from that moment on, I had a whole lot of respect for your activism work."

Activism?

I've never considered myself an activist of anything. Rather, I thought I was just opinionated.

"Madeline and I are members of your discussion group," the girl continues. "Although, I guess we can't consider it a discussion group since we're all basically on the same page. I guess you can call it a fan club..."

My mouth nearly falls to the floor. "I have a fan club?"

"When will you make your next public appearance?" the girl asks, oblivious to my bafflement. "It's been a few months, right?"

"I... I don't know."

"Well, when you do make another appearance, can you let the group know?" the girl asks. "You can probably just search for your name on the net. We're on the second or third page, once you get past all the news articles. And we'd love to come out and show our support!"

The red-haired girl named Madeline presses a few buttons on her Mobiroid. "Can we take a picture with you?"

"Yeah, of course," I reply quickly, attempting to recover. "Do you two have names?"

"I'm Veronica," the short-hair girl says. She points a finger to her red-haired friend. "That's Madeline."

Madeline is scrolling through the prompts to turn her Mobiroid's camera on, shaking out of nervousness.

"Nice to meet you," I say, shooting a look of pride towards Tate and Roman. I can't wait to rub this in their faces.

"Alright, the camera is ready," says Madeline. She glances at Veronica and me. "I guess we should probably get close."

Both look like they're about to get close to a king cobra.

"I don't bite," I say jokingly, even though I'm mostly serious. A second later, I pull the girl's arms and close the distance between us. Before the camera finishes taking a photo, I decide at the last moment to plant a kiss on Veronica's cheek. I'll never forget the resulting grin.

I send them on their way with hugs and a promise to get into contact with the "fan club." By the time they leave the table, I'm smiling from ear-to-ear. Unfortunately for me, my best friend, boyfriend, and sister are sitting at the table – and they're ready to bring my ego back down to earth.

"What was that?"

"Do they not realize that they're idolizing a girl that burns everything she cooks?"

"And used to call me a 'stupid jerk face' on a regular basis!"

"Can I get your autograph and sell it on the internet?"

The last comment comes from Tate, and I can't tell if he's serious. I have a feeling that he is.

"It's probably nothing," I brush off, but my cheeks are flushed, and my heart is pounding. I have supporters. Lately, I've felt like I was in this alone *('Well,'* I think, glancing over at Roman. *'Not entirely alone.')*. Would they stand behind me if I were to be elected? Would I daresay hope that they'd help me bring down the Divinity Bureau?

"Oh no," Tate says, cutting me off from my thoughts.

"What?" I ask, confused.

"You have that look on your face," Tate observes. "The one that says you're thinking of a crazy plan."

"I am not!"

Roman is in the middle of resyncing our Mobiroid's when he turns to give me a warning look. "April, whatever you're thinking – don't

226 · TESSA CLARE

do it. I narrowly escaped prison last time. If something happens, I can't protect you."

I scoff. "I'm not thinking of anything. I was just thinking how I'm going to kick your ass next game."

Roman laughs. "Are you challenging my title as Poker Champion?"

"Oh yeah. I went easy on you last time, but I'm about to show you how it's done..."

■ ■ ■ ■ ■ ■ ■ ■ ■ ■ ■ ■ ■ ■ ■ ■ ■ ■ ■ ■ ■ ■ ■ ■ ■ ■ ■ ■ ■ ■ ■ ■ ■ ■ ■ ■ ■ ■ ■ ■ ■ ■ ■ ■ ■ ■ ■ ■ ■ ■

I wasn't lying when Tate caught me thinking of a crazy plan. Most of my stupid decisions don't involve any planning whatsoever. I go with my gut; and so far, it's been working well.

But this time, my gut is telling me to investigate. To my knowledge, I'm not anything special. Once, I had believed that I'd be able to change the world; but that dream died with my father. I'm not an elected politician. I don't know the first thing about saving the world. All I know is that I'm cursed with an overactive mind and a few strong opinions. I've been adamant about making them heard. Before my encounter with Madeline and Veronica, I'd been content with that. I could sleep well, knowing that I've done everything in my power to change the world. But I'm not sure if that's going to be the case for much longer.

"Roman," I whisper into the darkness of Roman's apartment.

It's four o'clock in the morning. We're sprawled out on Roman's futon, but I'm not sure if he's asleep. Ever since he lost his job, our schedules have become sporadic. Sometimes, we ate our breakfast in the middle of the afternoon and didn't eat dinner until the early hours of the morning. There's a chance he's awake, but I assume otherwise when I hear nothing but silence.

"Roman, I can't sleep."

Roman opens his eyes at those words. He shifts his arm around me and pulls me closer.

"I don't know what I'm going to do if I'm elected," I whisper. "I know it's coming up. I feel like I should be doing something; because right now, it just seems like all I'm doing is waiting to die."

Roman's eyes flutter, but he remains quiet.

"I want to see what this group is about," I admit. "I know you're probably going to tell me that it's egotistical. You probably think that I'm just interested in having a group of teenagers put me on a pedestal – but it's more than that. Maybe they know something. Maybe they can help me figure out why the bureau is so interested in my family and me. Hell, perhaps with their help, we can even bring down the Divinity Bureau..."

"Don't do it," a sleep voice mumbles.

I'm startled out of my thoughts. When I turn my head towards Roman, a pair of deep brown eyes are looking back at me.

I roll towards him. "I feel like I have to. That could be my one shot to leave my mark in the world." I pause, waiting to see if he has any input. When I'm met with silence, I continue, "You don't understand. I've spent my entire life thinking that there was something wrong with me. I could never understand how my family – or anyone's family, for that matter – could idly stand by as someone they cared about was sentenced to their deaths. It's not like death row, where people are sentenced to die for committing crimes. No, they're sentenced to die to make room for other people. It's sick."

"Most of those people have already lived long lives," Roman murmurs. "Your family was just the unlucky exception."

I open my mouth to protest, but Roman is quick to interrupt.

"I know it sucks," Roman says, caressing my face softly. "But I think we might be best leaving this alone for now. You weren't on the last election report. Will you be on the next one?" He bites his lip. "I don't know. But if something were to happen to you, I can't protect you. The only thing we can hope for is that this whole thing will blow over and the bureau will find other fish to fry."

"I don't care about me," April insists, her increasing volume a stark contrast to the silence around us. "But what if Autumn's next? Or you? They already know I'm with you…"

"We're at a stalemate," Roman says. "Remember, I have Gideon's files. Pissing off the bureau will only ruin that." He pauses. "Besides, maybe instead of trying to save the world, you can focus on a more manageable issue first."

"Like what?"

"Like trying to regain custody of Autumn."

My face flushes. "Oh."

"She asked me about it today," Roman says. "She wanted to know how long it would be before she could come home."

I look away, shame threatening to overtake me.

"I told you that you were still in the beginning stages," Roman continues. "I told her that you had an application to fill out. I didn't tell her that it's been sitting untouched on my hard drive for weeks."

I blink away tears. "I was starting to think that it might be better if Autumn stayed with Darcy."

"Why would you say that?"

"Look at us, Roman," I say. To me, the answer is obvious. "I'm a twenty-year-old trust fund brat on the verge of election. We're both unemployed. I don't think I'm able to raise a twelve-year-old."

"You love her," Roman says. "I think that's the most important thing. Though she won't feel loved if you break your promise to her."

My father's image comes to mind. I'm all too familiar with the betrayal of broken promises.

"Okay," I agree, hesitating but knowing that I need to try. "I'll fill out the forms. I think I should probably wait until after the election, though."

Roman kisses my forehead. "Go in the morning. Are you going to be so afraid of death that you forget to live?"

*No,* I think. I won't.

■■■■■■■■■■■■■■■■■■■■■■■■■■■■■■■■■■■■■■■■■■■■■■■■■■■■

True to my word, I use our neighbor's internet to fill out the application and submit it to the courthouse. I need to have it notarized, though. I leave in the morning to go to the courthouse. I expect it to be a seamless process – show my ID, sign a few documents, get a date in front of the judge that's hopefully sooner rather than later. It takes twice as long as I anticipated, though. I need to show my ID to two different clerks. One makes me redo the application when I accidentally sign the form with the wrong date (and I have to pay a small penalty for the waste of paper). I need to fill out paperwork to serve Darcy with a notice that I intend to obtain custody, another to certify that the information is correct, another to confirm that I don't want to lawyer... by the end of the day, I could have signed my soul to the devil, and I wouldn't have had the faintest idea.

Thanks to my early morning discussion with Roman, I'm running on little sleep. Groggily, I type in the only coffee shop I can think of into the GPS system – Dang Coffee – with the intention of paying Tate a visit. What I don't expect to see is Darcy and Autumn ordering a pair of strawberry smoothies at the same shop. Autumn recognizes me before I have the chance to notice that it's her pink jacket that's in front of me. "April!"

"What brings you out here?" Darcy asks. She has the same tone that she used during our sessions – halfway between curiosity and condescension.

I shrug. The lack of sleep is making words come out of my mouth faster than I can stop them: "Nothing much. Just filing the application to get my sister back." Autumn's face lights up. That gives me more bravery. "You should be getting a visit from the sheriff's deputy pretty soon. They've got all the details."

I don't think I've ever seen Autumn look as happy in her life. "Did you really?"

I don't answer, anticipating a response from Darcy. I expect an argument to start; but to my surprise, Darcy smiles. "I guess I'll be on the lookout for that."

I stare at her, speechless.

"The court will determine what's best for you two," Darcy replies, raising her hands up in surrender. "And that's all I want. Must I remind you that your mother was my best friend?"

I don't need the reminder, as the fact was practically beaten into my bed throughout the years. For a moment, I wonder if I'd ever feel the same way towards Tate's kids, should he end up having them.

*Speaking of Tate…*

I glance around the shop. "Have you seen a blonde haired guy around? He's about my height, talks with a lisp, and looks kind of like a frat boy?"

Darcy opens her mouth to respond, but we're interrupted by a man approaching our group. "Excuse me?"

"You can cut in front of us," I say absently. We are hovered in front of the cash register, probably interfering with any line formation.

The man waves a dismissive hand. I can't help but notice the wrinkles around his eyes. No doubt he hasn't been rendered immortal yet. "I just couldn't help but ask: are you April McIntyre?"

Twice!

I've been recognized twice in the last few days! I can't wait to tell Roman and Tate.

"I am," I reply. My chest puffs out in newfound confidence. I hold my hand out. "It's a pleasure to meet you. What's your name?"

The man's gaze hardens. "You ought to be ashamed of yourself!"

I retract my hand away quickly. "Sorry. I didn't mean to offend –"

"It's already hard enough out there!" he spits back. "The last thing we need is another BION Bot whining that they can't have live forever!"

"That's not what –"

It's no use getting him to listen. He isn't willing to hear anything that I have to say.

"You deserve what you got," he hisses. "In six weeks, we won't have to listen to your shit anymore!"

Autumn steps between the two of us. "Listen, you weathered waste of space –"

Darcy's mouth drops in horror. "Autumn!"

But I can't help but hear the last part of what he said. In six weeks?

"What are you talking about?" I ask. I take a deep breath. Roman's words from this morning race through my mind. I won't be afraid of death. I won't forget to live.

The man gives me a toothless smile. "Oh! You don't know, do you?"

"Know what?" I ask, stepping around Autumn. I've spent the last few months in paranoia that I'd be elected. He has to be messing with me. The election report isn't even due to be released yet!

"There was a leak at the bureau," the man says. I hate the look of triumph on his face. "A few names were released early."

Leak? But the bureau's system was impermeable!

Unless...

No.

It wasn't a leak. It was intentional.

"How... how do you know?" I ask.

The man glares at me coldly, before he turns to walk away. "Everyone knows."

CHAPTER TWENTY-ONE

# ROMAN

I wake up to the sound of someone knocking at my door. Maybe it's just my imagination. I roll to my side, willing the pounding in my head to go away. It knocks again. And again. I glance at my Mobiroid: 1:45 PM. I've slept in. I don't have any plans for the day, but I do have job applications to mull over. To do that, I need breakfast. Eggs and breakfast sound good, no matter what time of day it is. Hopefully, April won't mind.

*Speaking of April...*

I glance around the room. She's nowhere to be seen. Another knock comes, and I sigh. It looks like I don't have any choice but to answer it. With a yawn, I grab the closest shirt I can reach and make my way towards the door. I call out, "Who is it?"

"We're looking for April McIntyre," a male voice on the opposite side of the door answers. "Is she here?"

That's peculiar, I think. Then again, this is a girl that allegedly has a fan club.

"She's not," I reply. "I can take a message, though."

There's a pause.

"Are you her boyfriend?" the man asks.

Something clicks in my mind. Who is that man, and why did he say 'we?'

"Who are you?" I ask slowly.

"My name is Carter," he answers. "My partner and I are with High Life. We just had a few questions. Perhaps you might be able to help us out?"

*High Life.* Why does it sound familiar?

"Isn't that the celebrity gossip blog?" I ask.

"Yes, that's the one."

I sigh, breathing out a sigh of relief. "Listen, I'm not interested in a subscription. I don't follow celebrity news at all, and I know April doesn't either."

To my surprise, Carter laughs. "My dear boy. We're not here to sell you a subscription."

"Then what do you want?"

A moment of silence passes. I imagine the bemused grin on the other side of the door. Carter retorts, "Haven't you seen the news?"

■ ■ ■ ■ ■ ■ ■ ■ ■ ■ ■ ■ ■ ■ ■ ■ ■ ■ ■ ■ ■ ■ ■ ■ ■ ■ ■ ■ ■ ■ ■ ■ ■ ■ ■ ■ ■ ■ ■ ■ ■ ■ ■ ■ ■ ■ ■ ■ ■ ■ ■ ■ ■ ■

"Hey, it's April. Leave a message."

It's the third time I've heard April's voicemail greeting in the last hour. By now, I've taken to hiding in the bathroom. Neville is curled up against my feet.

"April, it's Roman," I say, growing restless. "I'm not sure if you're getting these messages – but if you are, can you please call me? I think it's urgent, but I don't know what's going on. Anyways, call me when you can."

I barely end the call when my Mobiroid vibrates. I hope that it's April returning my calls, so I transfer the call to my earpiece without a second thought. I'm disappointed when I hear Tate's voice on the other end. "Roman! Have you seen the news?"

I press a hand to my temple. "It seems like everyone's asking me that these days." I glance at the closed door and lower my voice. The last thing I need is Carter listening to my conversations. "What's going on?"

"You haven't seen it yet?"

"I don't have cable."

"It's also all over the internet."

"I don't have that, either."

I'm positive that Tate is grimacing at that statement. "How do you survive without cable and the internet?"

"I don't know," I say, growing irritated that the conversation is keeping me from knowing what's going on. "I guess it's the same way I survived being unemployed and broke."

Tate makes a noise like he wants to comment, but he holds back by the realization that we have more important things to discuss. "Okay. Well, April is on the news."

"I gathered that."

Tate lets out a sigh. "To be honest, up until April started showing up, I didn't pay a lot of attention to current events. Now, I'm glad that I do. Apparently, there was a leak at the Divinity Bureau –"

"That's impossible," I dismiss. Right after Gideon thought that they'd been hacked, he made it a point to tighten security. Several of my tickets were about tightening loopholes. At this point, the bureau's system should be impermeable.

"April's been elected."

I don't know what to think. On the one hand, I've been anticipating this moment since the moment I met April. It's haunted me – keeping me awake on some nights and giving me nightmares on others. Hearing those words makes me feel as though like I'm in one of those dreams.

"How do you know?"

Tate hesitates. Clearly, this is the last question he expected to hear. "Well, I was browsing the net –"

"No, not that," I clarify, pressing my hands to my temples. "How do they know?"

"Like I said, there was a leak…"

"Are you with her now?"

"No, I'm sitting in traffic on my way home from work. I left about an hour ago…"

She was planning on going to the courthouse, which is only a short drive away from the coffee shop. She likely would have stopped in. If she did, Tate must have missed her. I'm about to ask him to turn around and see if she's there, but my Mobiroid vibrates. I glance at my wrist: 'Incoming call: April McIntyre.'

I feel as though the air has been sucked out of my lungs.

"April is calling me," I tell him. "I'll keep you posted."

"Thanks." There's a long silence, and I think he's about to hang up – but he stops me. "Roman?"

I don't have a lot of time before April's call forwards to voicemail, but something about his tone prevents me from ending the call. "Yeah?"

He hesitates. "When you have nothing left…"

"'You have nothing left to lose,'" I say, having heard the line more times than I can count. "I know."

"I know you're scared of what she's going to do," Tate says quietly. "But she still has something to lose. She has you."

I swallow, the words lost in my throat. The truth is, I'm not scared of what she's going to do. I'm scared of what *I'm* going to do.

Fortunately, I'm spared from elaborating on my feelings when I answer the call on the other end. I let out a breath of relief. "April! I'm so glad you called…"

"This is Darcy Gray," a monotone voice on the other end interjects. "Is this April's boyfriend?"

My mouth hangs open for a moment, but I clear my throat. "Yes. Yes, it is." I glance at my Mobiroid, wondering if I've misread the caller ID. "I'm sorry, but why do you have April's Mobiroid?"

"You must not remember me," the clipped voice says. "We met when April brought me to your apartment to pick up Autumn."

"No, I remember you," I clarify. "I'll ask again: why do you have April's Mobiroid?"

There's a sigh on the other end. "She had a panic attack. She started losing her breath, and then she fainted. Her earpiece came out of her ear..."

So, she knows.

"We ran into her at the coffee shop," Darcy continues. "I'm not sure if you know..."

"She's been elected," I say hopelessly. I want to say that I was surprised, but I knew this day would come. I thought that I'd feel worse, but I don't know how long we could've gone stressing out every three months and continuing to look over our shoulders.

"There's a reason why I'm calling," says Darcy. "I was wondering if you could pick her up from my office. I brought her here, but it's getting late – and I don't think she should be alone."

I peek my head out the bathroom to see if Carter and his partner are still outside of my apartment. I don't hear anything, but I can see the shadows of their feet in the doorway. "I can't go anywhere. There's paparazzi outside my door."

"Then make them leave!"

I hesitate. "I don't think April should be here either. Not until they leave."

"How long do you think it will take?"

"I... I don't know."

I can hear a growl of frustration on the other end. "What kind of boyfriend are you?"

Not a very good one, apparently – but I don't know what else to do. I don't have gates to keep the paparazzi out. And in her current state, there isn't any way that she'll be able to talk to the press.

"Please," I beg, my voice cracking. "Bring April back to the mansion. Her house has a pretty good security system, so it should keep the paparazzi away. Tell her that I'll let her know when it's safe to come home."

That's the last thing I say before I hang up the phone and curl into a ball. The knocking on the door lines up in sync with the pounding in my head.

■■■■■■■■■■■■■■■■■■■■■■■■■■■■■■■■■■■■■■■■■■■■■■■■■■■■■■■■■

The knocking ceases by sunset. It may have stopped a few hours before that, but that's when I finally muster the bravery to stick my head out the door to make sure that Carter and his partner are gone. When I do, I send April a quick text: *'They're gone. It's safe to come home now.'*

It doesn't even hit me until that moment that home isn't just my apartment. It's ours.

I don't know what I'm going to do if the election goes through. Right now, the apartment – as small as it is – feels empty without April lounging on the futon as she paints her nails and without the smell of food burning in the kitchen. It's lonely to cook a meal for one person, and even more desolate to eat with nothing but my own company – as I'm doing now.

I send April another text message: *'I'm sorry that I wasn't able to get you today. If you saw the way the paparazzo was trying to hound me, you'd understand. I know you're going through a rough time right now; but please, let me be there for you.'*

A memory comes to mind: April kissing me in the middle of a protest and telling me that I was a hero to her. Could I still be that man for her?

An hour goes by. No response. Soon, the sun has fully set into the horizon, and it's been a few hours since I told April that she could come home. She still hasn't. I contemplate on sending her another message, but something doesn't feel right. I don't think I'll be able to get a straight answer from her over text message, so I do the only thing that does feel right: I grab my keys and drive to the mansion. No matter what I do, it doesn't feel like I can get to April quickly enough.

The traffic congestion before me is suddenly unbearable. Why can't they build better roads? I give up the façade of pretending that my car's self-driving feature is working and speed past the cars that get in my way. I'll probably have a few traffic tickets in the mail before the night is over.

It's dark when I find myself in front of the mansion. I vaguely remember the door code and let myself through the iron gates. I pull into April's driveway and park next to her car. But when I step outside of the vehicle, I stop in my tracks.

In a moment of déjà vu, the scene before me looks familiar. April's car door is swung open. Two suitcases are in the backseat. Her computer screen is completely ruined, exposed wires floating in the dashboard. It looks like someone had taken a hammer and smashed the front interior to pieces. I can't place my finger on why the scene looks familiar. Did it appear in a dream? Or did someone describe it to me once...?

Someone has. April did, shortly after her mother was elected. She must have taken inspiration from her mother.

I kick the front door down and make my way up the stairs.

"April!"

No answer.

"April!" I call out again.

So far, she's nowhere to be found; but her house will take hours for me to search in its entirety. I decide to start with the most logical place: her bedroom. The elevator is too slow for my patience, so I run up the stairs to the top floor. When I reach the top, I call her name again: "April!"

April emerges from the bedroom a few moments later, her eyes wild and her body ready to pounce on the intruder. She relaxes a second later when she realizes that it's only me, but confusion remains. "Roman? How did you get in here?"

I don't answer. Instead, I walk up to April. She's shaking. I do the only thing I can think of: wrap my arms around her. I press my lips against her temple. Everything is going to be okay. I'll do anything to prove it. I kiss her neck, her hair, her forehead – and I'm all but ready to take her in the bedroom, but she's not reciprocating my affection.

I pull away and tilt her chin so that she's looking at me. "I heard what happened."

"Everyone has," April says flatly.

"I just want you to know that it doesn't change anything," I declare earnestly. "No matter what happens. Elected or not, you're the last girl that I'll ever be in love with."

She sucks in a breath like she's been punched. It hits me at that moment that I had yet to tell her those words until now. In all fairness, I never thought that I needed to. I figured it'd show in every touch, every kiss, every stolen glance...

But April is biting her lip. Something is wrong.

"What's on your mind?" I ask, brushing a stray hair from her face.

"We need to talk," April says, not meeting my gaze. "Can we sit down somewhere?"

I shake my head. "No. Every time a conversation starts with 'we need to talk,' it usually means that something is going to end."

I've only heard it once in my life. I had hoped to never hear those words out of April's mouth.

"Roman –"

"Just tell me that this isn't going to end," I plead, grabbing her hands. They feel clammy to the touch. I told myself that I'd keep her safe. I anticipated the possibility that death would break us apart; but *never,* in a million years, did I think we'd end because of something as juvenile as a breakup. The thought makes me dizzy. "Tell me that it isn't over. And I'll sit down anywhere with you. We can talk about everything and anything; but please, tell me that it isn't over."

April looks away. "I didn't know how to tell you this. I had a letter written out that I was going to stick under your door."

"A letter?"

*No,* I think to myself. My knees grow weak at the implications. April can't have thought about breaking up with me with a fucking letter under my door!

"I'm leaving," she says quietly, averting her gaze. "I'm taking a page from the Macy McIntyre handbook and getting the hell out of here. I'm going to get a new name and a new identity. I'll be on the run, but it's better than the alternative."

I take a deep breath to calm my racing my heart. But at that moment, my mind is made up. My jaw tightens in resolution.

"I'll come with you," I say without hesitation.

April's mouth drops in shock. "You'll – what?"

"I'll come with you," I repeat slowly, taking another step towards her. To me, there's no other choice. "There's no place I'd rather be than by your side."

I wait for a response, but she doesn't give me any. She's still not looking at me.

I continue, my voice growing louder in determination, "Listen, I know it's a terrible situation. I understand what you're going through, but you can't just run away from your problems and expect them to go away. Is that what you want? Or do you want to stay and fight?" I ask this because I know April. She's a girl who stood in front of the bureau's doorsteps and boldly proclaimed that they wouldn't have her. She's a girl who once dreamt of following in her father's footsteps. "Either way, no matter what you choose, I'm going to be there with you."

I stare at our conjoined hands, willing her to never let go.

"What will I be fighting for?" she whimpers, her voice meek. Her hands are shaking. She's holding back tears. "They've already taken everything from me."

I tighten my grip on her cold hands. "You'll be fighting for your right to live!" I say in disbelief, refusing to accept that this is the end. I hope a raised voice will help her listen to reason. "You'll be fighting for your right to love! Your right to grow up, finish college, and have a normal life! Isn't that what you want?"

April is silent, but she finally looks at me. At the sight of her wet eyes, I wonder if I've gotten through to her. I must have because she'd be arguing with me if I hadn't.

I release her hands and cradle her cheeks. "April, I love you. I've always loved you. I thought I'd get plenty of chances to say it, but I'm scared that I won't. So – please – whatever you decide, let me stay with you. I don't care if it's here or in District 560. My home is wherever you are."

With that, I lean in and kiss her, feeling the tension in my muscles relieved. I've gotten through to her. She wouldn't be wrapping her arms around me if I didn't. She wouldn't be opening her mouth to me. She wouldn't be pulling me close as though I'm the missing part of her soul – and I must be because she's a part of mine. Home is wherever April McIntyre is, and I'll spend the rest of my days showing her that.

But she pulls away.

Tears are streaming down her cheeks.

"I'm sorry," April says, her voice hoarse. "But I was never cut out for a normal life. Not since I was born a McIntyre."

I inhale a breath.

*No.*

I take a step closer to her, but she steps back. Pain overtakes me, clouding every sense in my body. It's like a hundred needles have pierced my skin – and my heart.

"And I can't bring you with me," April says, wiping away the tears on her cheeks. "You'll only hold me back, and I can't risk that."

As April's eyes dry, mine start brimming with tears. "So, that's it?" My voice is hoarse. I feel pathetic, crying in front of her just minutes after telling her that I loved her for the first time. I use the sleeve my shirt to wipe my face and muffle the sobs that are threatening to overtake me. I lean on the wall for support, my knees too weak to hold my weight. "You're just going to run away and give up on us – *because I hold you back?*"

*'Please correct me,'* I silently beg. Please tell me that I misheard her. No, please tell me that today is just a horrible dream that'll be over as soon as I wake up.

But all she says is, "I'm sorry."

With those words, I'm broken.

CHAPTER TWENTY-TWO

# APRIL

The thought of being in control of a two-ton machine is terrifying. But if I can have control over a boy's heart – at least, the power to break it – then driving should be a piece of cake. I wanted more time to practice, but the desire to get away from the image of Roman's tear-stained cheeks as fast as possible is more pressing, even if it kills me.

I know the basics of driving. It's part of the relicensing process every year, as I need to know how to take control of the vehicle in the event of computer failure. But it's been awhile. It takes some time before I remember what the letters of the clutch stand for, how hard to press the accelerator and brake pedals, and how to steer. Fortunately, District 220 doesn't have the same amount of traffic as District 200. By the time I'm ten miles from home, I think I'm getting the hang of it.

I don't know where I'll be going. I think I eventually want to make my way North to head to the Iceland's, but the downside to that is that the Iceland's sterilizes citizens above a certain age and below a certain rank. It's also a developing country. I vaguely remember houses made of ice blocks, enough to make Roman's tiny apartment look like a mansion. Still, at least I won't be on the run.

There are three places that I need to visit before I can go anywhere.

The first stop is Roman's apartment. The thought makes my heart clench. I'm a monster for hurting him, and I'm even worse for thinking that I could end it with a note. But I was petrified that my resolve would break if I saw his face – and it nearly did. The light at the end of the tunnel was that I had transferred a substantial portion of my trust fund into his bank account. In the note, I explained that it'd get him through the next few years and that I hoped that he'd use some of it to spoil a girl that could give him the love he deserves.

My second stop is one that I've wanted to visit for a while, but I've never had the courage to do so – until now.

It's close to midnight when I call Leonard. He has barely answered when I tell him coolly, "I'll have a nice check waiting for you if you meet me at your office in fifteen minutes."

Leonard is pulling in front of the office in ten. It's the first time I've seen him without a suit.

"Good evening, April," Leonard greets, as though it's barely dusk and not the middle of the night. "I was going to call you in the morning. I'm a little surprised that you'd decide –"

"I need two things from you," I interrupt. If I'm to get to where I need to be by dawn, I don't have time for small talk. "The first thing is a new driver's license, birth certificate, and anything else I might need to form a new identity." I pause. "I will also need a way to get into the Iceland's."

Leonard doesn't blink. "I beg your pardon?"

"Don't play dumb," I say firmly. "I know that you help people get new identities. You helped Neal O'Donnell. Now, I need you to help me – preferably in the next hour or so, because I'm on a tight deadline."

Leonard's lips press together. His expression goes from shock to denial to annoyance to acceptance of the situation.

"Very well," he agrees. "Though typically, it takes several days for me to create new identification."

"You saw my inheritance," I point out. "I'll make it worth your while if you can make it happen."

Leonard's eyes go wide, but he quickly regains his composure. He clears his throat. "That was more than two things."

I take a step closer to Leonard to look at him square in the eye. "That's because the second thing is personal. I'm looking for someone. She's about my height, brown hair, and stopped her aging when she was in her early forties. The last name she went by was Macy McIntyre."

"You're a clever girl."

"It doesn't take a genius to figure out that she'd come here before she disappeared," I reply curtly. "You were one of her trusted friends." Leonard's mouth drops slightly, honored by the revelation. "Not that I understand why."

Leonard laughs. "You are definitely Macy's daughter."

"That's funny," I say bitterly, thinking of the press coverage that I've seen recently. "Lately, people have been saying that I'm more like my dad." I sigh. "Anyways, can we go into your office? I'm getting cold."

I follow Leonard into the office building, which looks remarkably different at night. The lobby looks like an abandoned museum – empty desk and the shell of a hallway that was once bursting with life. Leonard's office is dark; the only source of light is a small solar-powered lamp at his desk.

"Are you sure you need it today?" Leonard asks, concerned. Just in case, he clears some space on his desk. "This will take several hours. You might be waiting until morning."

"I'm sure."

Leonard stops moving to press lips together. My guess that he does it to hide his emotions. "Then you might want to go to the store and pick me up a few energy drinks. It's going to be a long night."

I pick up a case of fusion drinks from the convenience store a few blocks away. I drink one with the intention of driving away as soon as my new identification cards are ready, but Leonard reminds me that it'll be a long while. He explains that the cards contain sixty types of paper and more than thirty security features – ranging from bar codes, MICR ink, holograms, and printing techniques. The paper used wasn't readily available, so he used a substitute of his own creation. As a result, he was always careful to avoid wasting material.

"How did you get into the forgery business?" I ask. I don't want to distract him, but I can't help but be curious.

Leonard, whose eyes are focused on recreating a barcode, shrugs. "I was in college. I worked as a clerk for the state court, and I had access to just about every record available. I decided to use that info to help me pay off my student loans."

I think of Roman. "I knew someone like that; except he used it to help people. Well, he helped me, at least."

"Isn't that what I'm doing now?"

I don't answer him, knowing that I'm treading in morally ambiguous waters. When is breaking the law right, and when is it wrong? He's making money off my situation, but where would I be without his services?

Leonard explains that while he was working as a clerk, he slowly downloaded their records. He did it slowly and in small chunks, which took him years. What he does is give his clients the name and identity of someone that already exists and replaces the picture.

The thought makes me grow cold.

"But what about the person whose identity is getting stolen?" I ask. I've seen advertisements about people who have had their identities stolen, and it sometimes takes them years to get their lives back.

"I make all my clients sign a waiver that they won't partake in illegal activities and that they'll stay under the radar."

Well, I have no intention of doing that. I'm still determined to take down the bureau when I get the opportunity. I'll just have to do it from the sidelines.

"But they're already partaking in illegal activities."

Leonard sighs. "Do you want to stay alive or not?"

Leonard's database is relatively out of date, and he needs to check the election list every quarter to make sure that the person is still alive, but the good news is just about everyone on his list will never age. He can give me the identification of someone that's five hundred years old, and no one will think twice. In my case, I'll be taking the name of a woman named Elisa Meeks. She's one hundred years old, but she stopped her aging when she was young. I try to imagine the rest of my life in this woman's shoes.

It's four o'clock in the morning when I finally fall asleep while curled up in the corner of his office. When I awaken a few hours later, I have a blanket draped over my shoulders and a pillow underneath my head. Leonard is sitting in his swiveling chair behind his desk. The desk is cleared out completely, save for a large yellow envelope – one that looks as though it's been scribbled and torn a few too many times – that's laying in front of Leonard.

I stand up – *ouch*, I think I slept at the wrong angle – and make my way towards Leonard's desk. As I approach him, I can see the bags under his eyes and the way his hair is sticking up in the back. I should be thanking him for his hard work. Instead, the only thing that comes out of my mouth is, "How much do I owe you?"

"Nothing."

My mouth nearly drops in shock. "You pulled an all-nighter for me."

"You said you knew someone that used his position to help people," Leonard says. "I knew someone like that as well, and you remind me a lot of her. So, save your money. You're definitely going to need it."

I don't know what to say. "Thanks. I – uh – I have one more thing..."

"Information about your mother is in the envelope as well," Leonard continues. "She's going by the name of Miranda Tonkin. She had me list the address on her driver's license at Burnside Street, in District 205. That's all I know."

I pick up the envelope. A part of me wants to hug Leonard for all that he's done for me, but I decide that it might be weird. Instead, I say, "Thank you." He meets my eyes, so I continue, "Thank you so much. I... I'd be royally screwed if it wasn't for you."

Leonard nods, but he doesn't say anything else. I think he's in dire need of sleep. After a moment of silence, I take the envelope and walk out of the office. By now, a hint of sunlight is peeking over the horizon. That gives me just enough time for my third and final stop.

■■■■■■■■■■■■■■■■■■■■■■■■■■■■■■■■■■■■■■■■■■■■■■■■■■■■

Autumn's voice is muffled by sleepiness when she finally answers her Mobiroid. "Hello?"

I can tell that she must have reached for it and clumsily placed it around her ear. Her voice sounds far away.

"Autumn, I'm outside your house."

"What? Why?"

"Just come outside," I insist. "Hurry up! I don't have a lot of time!"

A few minutes later, Autumn emerges from the back entrance. She's still wearing her nightgown. I'm leaning against my car with my arms crossed when Autumn approaches me, still wiping the sleep from her eyes. "April? What are you doing here in the middle of the night?"

'Night' is a subjective term, I think with a glance towards the rising sun.

"It's punishment for all those times you woke me up to crawl into my bed in the middle of the night. Remember that time when you kicked me off the bed?"

Autumn crosses her arms in a huff. "I did not! You rolled off!"

"I know how I sleep. I most certainly did not roll off the bed."

"Well, when I go home, I'm going to prove to you that I definitely do not kick in my sleep. You, on the other hand..."

Home.

Right now, that place seems as far away as a foreign country. I look away, unable to bring myself to see my sister's face when I break the news to her. "Listen, Autumn... I think you're going to have to stay with Darcy."

Autumn's eyes widen. "What? Why?"

"Because as you already know, I've been elected!"

"So? You can fight it!" Autumn insists, and I realize that our optimism and determination must be hereditary. "They'd have to let you live! People know you, and you're only twenty years old! You'd have to win!"

I bite my lip. "It doesn't work that way."

"But you promised!" Autumn screeches, her nostrils flaring. She's crying now, but it's not tears of grief. They're hot tears of anger. "I knew you'd do this!"

My mouth drops. "Do what?"

"Leave!" Autumn cries, stomping her foot. "Just like you always do! Just like Mom and Dad!" She wipes an angry tear away. "I don't even know why I bothered getting my hopes up! I just thought that Mom leaving would make you a better person, but I guess —"

I clench my fists. "Don't you fucking dare compare me to Mom and Dad!"

"You promised!" Autumn screeches.

"Shh!" The last thing I need is Darcy waking up.

"You promised that you'd fight for me and that I'd get to go home!"

"It's different now, Autumn!"

"How is this any different from Mom leaving?"

I stop myself from saying anything more. I have every right to run away. My life is in danger, and I won't do Autumn any good if I'm dead. But I can easily recall the way it felt when my mother left – how abandoned I felt. But it's different this time. Now, I'm leaving Autumn on her own.

"So, you're... you're leaving then," Autumn asks, and her voice breaks. "Is... is that it? Did you come to tell me goodbye?"

To be honest, I was coming to say goodbye; but the word feels wrong to say. I take Autumn's hands and get on one knee so that we're nearly eye-level (or at least, we would be if Autumn weren't so tall).

"Listen to me," I say slowly. "Just because I'm leaving right now doesn't mean that you're not going to see me. It doesn't mean goodbye."

"What does it mean, then?"

I offer her a half smile. "It means that I'll see you later."

Autumn eyes me skeptically. She has every right to mistrust me. I've broken many promises to her, and I'd deserve it if she doesn't believe a word I say. But I'm going to keep this one, even if it kills me.

"Are you sure?" Autumn asks. Her voice quivers, betraying her emotions.

"I'm positive. As a matter of fact..." I reach into my pocket and pull out the tattered envelope that Leonard had given me. "I have something to show you."

Autumn, who has probably never seen an envelope in her life, gazes up at me questioningly. Then she opens it. The first thing she notices is a photocopy of what appears to be a driver's license.

"Paper?" Autumn asks.

"Read what's on the paper."

"It's a copy of a driver's license for someone named Miranda Tonkin."

"Look at the picture."

"I don't see the…" But Autumn gasps as soon as she recognizes the face on the picture. I grin in satisfaction. "Is that Mom?"

"It is."

"So, she's alive?"

I want to say that she is, but I have no way of confirming until I see her with my own eyes. "It looks like it. I'm going to find her, though."

"How will you do that?"

I point to the address on the license. "For one, I'm going to start there. If that doesn't work, then who knows? I'll probably just have to do it the old-fashioned way and ask around."

"That sounds complicated."

"I'll make it work."

With those words, we stand in silence as we think about the implications. I can see the sun starting to rise high on the horizon, and Darcy will be awake soon. That means that I'll need to say goodbye.

I brush away a stray tear that's fallen onto Autumn's cheek. "I'll see you again. That's a promise." Autumn tensed at those words, so I continue, "I know I've broken a lot of those. I hope you don't hate me for it."

"I could never hate you."

"I'd deserve it if you did," I admit quietly.

"Why do you think that?"

I glance at the rising sun, bringing the rest of the world hope and shrouding me in darkness at the same time. "Because I'm selfish. I'm hurting two of the most important people to me in the name of staying alive." The sun is blinding me, so I need to look away. "I used to blame Mom for abandoning us in the name of staying alive. I was so angry with her; and yet, here I am, running away. But I don't want you to think that I'm abandoning you forever."

Autumn doesn't say anything. Together, we glance towards the house. In the window, Darcy is brewing a pitcher of coffee. I think about the fact that Darcy doesn't have a CLEO to assist her with simple household tasks – not that she needs it because her house is so small. It hits me that Darcy could have easily used Autumn's trust fund money to purchase upgrades to make her life more comfortable – but she didn't.

Instead, Darcy is giving her something that I can't: a normal life.

"We should probably go," I whisper. "Darcy's going to be looking for you soon."

Autumn throws her arms around my neck. In my arms, she's a toddler again. Not too long ago, I was able to carry her with one arm. Now, she's practically a woman that's standing on her own two feet. We pull apart at the same time. As soon as Autumn turns to walk back towards the house, I climb into my car. My hand moves to plug in the address to my next destination, until I remember that I don't have a GPS console anymore – nor do I have a place to call home. For a moment, my hand hangs in the air – lingering, waiting. And then, it balls into a fist. I bring it to my face to cover the choking sobs that wrack through my body.

CHAPTER TWENTY-THREE

# ROMAN

For the first few days, my routine is consistent: sleep, eat, and wish I was asleep. Occasionally, I'll fill out a job application; but when I do, self-doubt fills me. All I can hear are April's last words to me: *'You'll only hold me back.'*

I spend those days trying to figure out what she meant. Once, being with April empowered me. It made me strive to be a better person, and the fact that I hold her back guts me. Have I been a burden to her? What could I have possibly done to make her think that?

One week after April's departure, my Mobiroid starts buzzing on a regular basis – probably my parents, though I don't have the courage to talk to them right now. I turn it off and remove it from my wrist. It finally dies after it goes two weeks without being charged.

It's two weeks after April's departure when the Divinity Bureau finally releases their election report. I do everything I can to ignore it, but I make the mistake of using the internet to fill out a job application on that day. On every site I visit, the news is determined to follow me: *"LEAK CONFIRMED: APRIL MCINTYRE HAS BEEN ELECTED BY THE DIVINITY BUREAU."* At that moment, I decide that I can be unemployed for a little longer.

A few days after that, I hear a knock on my door while I'm in the middle of cooking dinner.

"She isn't here," I groan loudly, certain that it's another round of paparazzi.

"Roman?"

I recognize the voice on the other side. Hastily, I rush to the door and pull it open. Usually, when Tate is around, April isn't too far away; so I open it in hopes that he has news on her. Unfortunately, he doesn't; but he does have a bottle of vodka in his hand. It's the next best thing.

I find out that Tate has been calling me in the last few days. He learned of April's departure over voicemail.

"She called me a few times in an hour," Tate admits. "I couldn't answer because I was at work."

In her last call, she left him a voicemail to explain the situation. She told him that she loved him, and she thanked him for being there for her. Then she spent the last sixty seconds begging him to look out for me. That only confirms my theory that I was a burden on her.

"By the time I tried to call her back, her phone was disconnected," Tate says regretfully.

When I turn my phone back on, I have three voicemails from Tate, one from my mother, and another from a phone number that I don't recognize. I give it a listen and find, to my surprise, that I have a job interview at a computer hardware store. I call them back the next morning, and I have an interview for that afternoon. By the time the day is over, I have a new job.

Tate is the only person I can think of sharing the good news with. He asks me, "Do you have to wear a uniform now?"

I think of the hideous polo shirt that they handed me at the interview. "That's the only downside. Still, it's a job!" I would be working as a computer repair technician for an electronics store. It isn't warding off hackers – though the situation with April did force me to sharpen my skills – but it'll pay the bills. "Let's head to the bar to celebrate!"

That is what we do. After spending the last several months with a twenty-year-old, it's liberating to be able to go to the bar across the street from my apartment. Tate and I drink until we can barely remember each other's names. By the time the night is over, Tate is unable to remember his address to plug into his car's computer system, so I let him sleep on the floor of my apartment. I'm forced to half-drag, half-carry him through the apartment lobby and keep him from stepping on a man that's passed out in the middle of the hallway. I sit him on the futon while I look for my stash of extra pillows and blankets. In a slurred voice, Tate points to a letter that's sitting on my coffee table. "What's that?"

I glance at the letter, debating on burning it at that moment. "It was my breakup letter."

"Do you know what it says?"

"No."

"Why not?"

I hesitate, before I admit, "Because I don't want to know." When Tate tilts his head in confusion, I continue, "She wasn't going to break up with me in person. If I hadn't come to the mansion, she would've just left."

*'You'll only hold me back.'*

"I don't know what she'd say if I hadn't been standing right in front of her. Considering how much it hurt then, the last thing I want is to make that wound any bigger."

Tate closes his eyes and falls against the futon. "There's a chance those words could also heal you."

I'm not ready to bet on those odds. Once I read that letter, I'll never read April's words or hear from her again. I'm not willing to close that door yet.

I begin my new job a few days later and quickly find myself growing accustomed to my new routine. I work longer days (twelve hour shifts), but the tradeoff is that I have more days off. Those days are typically spent grabbing drinks with Tate, hanging out in my apartment with Neville, and catching up on sleep. Occasionally, I'll eye the letter that continues to sit on my coffee table. While I'm at work, I tinker on computers while the projector blares in the background. The work is easy: fix computers and occasionally explain things to customers. As a result, I spend a lot of time staring at the projector. I absently notice the lack of media coverage on April's disappearance, though they seem very keen on covering her election.

"We're standing outside the McIntyre Mansion, where authorities believe April McIntyre is hiding following her tragic election."

I change the channel with a click.

"Mr. Fitz, you said that the removed barriers were only temporary. Why are we still electing underage citizens?"

"Well, Shelly, these are dark times. Sometimes, dark measures are needed..."

Click.

Weeks pass this way. A flipped switch here, a replaced wire there – but the job requires minimal supervision, and it keeps my mind occupied for a long while. I keep the projector off news stations and talk shows. If I hear *'The Divinity Bureau'* and *'April McIntyre'* one more time...

"Roman, a customer wants to talk to you," a customer service agent says, popping his head into the backroom.

"Who is it?"

The boy shrugs. "I don't know. He just says that he needs you to look at something."

I glance at my latest project – a palm-sized hard drive that's hardly salvageable – and decide that I can take a few minutes to talk to the customer. If a few moments is all it takes to keep whoever's computer that I worked on from coming back to me, then maybe it's worth it. I emerge from the backroom and find myself standing feet away from someone that I was hoping I'd never see again.

"Hello Roman," Finn greets cheerfully. "How do you like your new gig?"

I stop in my tracks. "Did you not hire my replacement yet?"

"Yeah, but they're not nearly as good as you."

"For twelve sterling an hour?"

"Your pay rate wasn't my decision," Finn says. "Neither was firing you." He glances around the room before lowering his voice. "Listen, is there anywhere we can go that we can talk privately?"

I shake my head. "I'm working. If you had anything that you wanted to say to me, you had two years to do it."

"I got fired," Finn blurts out.

I'd feel sorry for him, but he knew the McIntyre's were being targeted and didn't do anything about it. "Welcome to the club. Unfortunately, I'm not interested in recruiting new members."

Finn runs a hand through his hair. "Listen, Roman. They elected my daughter. My nine-month-old daughter! She hadn't even learned to walk yet!"

I remember seeing an infant on the news when the Divinity Bureau first started electing people outside of their guidelines. She was the youngest person ever elected.

His voice lowers. "I learned some things. Some of it isn't pretty. I hope I can make it up to you by telling you everything I know. A lot of it pertains to April."

My first instinct is to assume it's a trap. I can relate to Finn's emotions, and I can't imagine holding a funeral for my child, a healthy child that had to be sacrificed to make room on the planet for other people – and that's exactly why I don't trust him. Someone has to know that this is one way to lead me into a trap: catering to my emotions.

But something about Finn's face makes me trust him. I've seen that look before: I've seen it on myself.

In the end, I decide to meet with Finn when I go on my lunchbreak. I ask a sales associate to watch the service desk and text me if anything urgent comes up, but I doubt that will happen. With my bases covered, I put on my face mask and follow Finn outside the store

"So…" I begin as we walk, but I'm immediately hushed.

"Not here," Finn says gruffly, passing shoppers as though they might be poison.

I close my mouth and follow Finn. I'm not sure where he's planning on taking me, but we walk through a parking garage. He finally stops in front of a red four-seater vehicle. "Get in."

I glance at the shopping mall hesitantly. "I only have an hour-long lunch break."

"We won't be gone long."

Hesitantly, I climb into Finn's car. I notice that his self-driving car is no longer self-driving. The dashboard has been smashed in. I think of the state that I'd seen April's car in before she left.

"I feel like that's starting to become a trendy design," I say dryly, pointing to the loose wires. I'm careful not to touch them.

"Do you have your Mobiroid on you?"

I glance at my wrist. "Well, yeah. Of course, I do."

Finn lets out a groan. "We'll have to wait to talk then."

I stare at him, a chill running down by back. "Finn, please don't kidnap me. I don't have any wealthy relatives. The only ransom you'd be getting out of me is my student loan debt."

That's a bit of a white lie. I didn't miss the large deposit April had made into my bank account shortly before her departure, but I transferred it into a savings account with the determination that I'd never touch it. That money is tainted.

Finn shakes his head. "I can't risk anyone hearing us."

"Who could hear us?"

Finn doesn't answer – instead, he takes the highway and drives for a few miles until he finds an exit that's pointed to a national park. After a few minutes, we're parked outside of a forest preserve.

"Leave your Mobiroid in the car," Finn instructs as I climb out of the car.

I hesitate. "I'd rather not."

Finn rolls his eyes. "Roman, I'm not kidnapping you."

"Then why are you acting weird, bringing me to a forest preserve, and telling me to leave my phone in the car?"

"I'll explain in a second. Hurry up!"

I weigh my options. Then, after determining that Finn is smaller than me and that I can overtake him in a fight, I pull my Mobiroid off my wrist and follow him on a trail towards the forest.

"Sorry if I scared you," Finn says once the car disappears. "It's been a long few weeks."

"It's okay," I say, even though I'm not sure if it is. I think of the smashed dashboard. "What... what happened?"

"You know what happened."

"Yeah – but... how does this relate to April?"

Finn looks away. "It doesn't. Well, at least, my daughter didn't. But I was confident that I could find a loophole to keep her alive." There's a pause like he's lost in thought. "You have no idea how it felt. My daughter – my beautiful, healthy little girl – was on the verge of death, and there wasn't anything that I could do about it."

My throat goes dry. "I'm sorry."

"I found other things, though," Finn continues. "Correspondence between the Divinity Bureau and the National Security Division." I swallow. The National Security Division is another agency of the Confederal Districts. They're responsible for keeping the country safe from threats, such as terrorism. "I thought, 'well, that's odd.' What does combatting overpopulation have to do with fighting terrorism?"

"Let me guess: they're related?"

Finn shakes his head. "They're not just related. They're one and the same."

"I don't understand."

"Think about it, Roman: overpopulation wouldn't be a problem if the world were overpopulated with citizens of a particular... ah... type, I should say. If we had three hundred and fifty million saints occupying this world at one time, the world would be a far better place. The problem is that humans are selfish and destructive, which is how we ended up in a mess in the first place. Maybe we should have just started electing the raging criminals of this world before we elect innocent children."

"But that's…" I can't even find the words.

"Morally ambiguous? Subjective?" Finn finishes. "Well, yes. It is. And that's why we have the Divinity Bureau." He stares right at me. His gaze is cold. "Imagine the pollution worsened and you needed to give people ventilators to live. There's only a limited supply of ventilators, so you can't save everyone. Who would you save? The youngest? The sickest? Or would you leave it up to fate?"

"I don't know…"

"Would you save a kind-hearted doctor before you save a stone-cold criminal?"

"Maybe. I've never thought of it…"

"Or how about if you had to choose between that same doctor and your girlfriend?"

I clench my fists. "Why are you asking me this?"

"The reason why we elect District Chairmen is that they've already made that decision. And so has Gideon. You think it's random selection, but it isn't. Sure, most of it is – and they throw in a few names to ensure that the public thinks that's the case. And they hold appeals to make sure that the wrong people don't get elected. The 'over 100' rule didn't apply until Henrik McIntyre took office. He was petrified that he'd outlive his daughters, so he made sure that that didn't happen."

"But what about…" I want to ask him about his daughter, but I hold back. I'm worried that I might be bringing up a sore subject.

"Ginny?" Finn asks, his voice breaking. "Well, it turns out, Gideon was planning on giving her an appeal due to her age. She was just an accident. But as soon as I learned what was happening, I confronted him." A weak smile crosses his face, but his eyes are vacant. "We buried her next to her grandfather."

My heart breaks for him. It was hard enough losing April. I can't imagine what it'd be like to lose a child, to bury a coffin big enough to fit in your arms.

"I know April is on the run," Finn says solemnly. "Everyone at the Divinity Bureau does. And they're coming after her with a vengeance. They're worried that she might try to bring the bureau down."

I don't doubt that she will.

"They'll never find her," I say. "She's got a new name and a new identity. Her phone line is disconnected. Her GPS is out. What else can they possibly look into?"

"BIONs?"

"She hasn't been injected with any."

It never occurred to me until that moment that BIONs are a computer. Computers can be hacked...

"They know where she'll go," Finn says, looking away.

I tilt my head in confusion, unable to believe that the bureau knows where she's going to go. I don't even know, and I know her better than anybody. But if there's a place I imagine she'd go...

Oh no.

"Do they have a location on Macy McIntyre?"

Finn gives me a solemn look. "Yes."

I turn white. "I need to get back to my Mobiroid."

April is in danger. I can't even think.

"You can't call her to warn her," Finn says. "Her line is disconnected."

April is in danger.

"Do you have an address for Macy?"

"Well, yeah, I do, but – wait, where are you going?"

"I need you to drive me back to my car!"

I remember when April told me that I'd always be a hero to her. Now, it's time I do something to save the day.

## CHAPTER TWENTY-FOUR

# APRIL

The most difficult change isn't the fact that I had to leave my old life behind – and don't get me wrong, that part's hard. I can feel the absence of my loved ones like a physical ache in my body, but it was like severing an infected leg before it killed me. As I watch the outline of District 200 disappear in my rear-view mirror, I feel the loss of everything I'm leaving behind; but a part of me is excited for the opportunity to build a new life. The road trip is an adventure. I'm driving for the first time in a long while, stopping in road side diners, chatting with the wait staff, and buying an occasional souvenir. It isn't until a man walks up to me at a restaurant and asks if I'm "the girl that did that speech in front of the bureau" that I realize that I'm going to need to make another change. That brings me to the most difficult change: my hair.

I pick up a pair of scissors and a box of hair dye from the closest drunk stop, and then I book a motel room under my new name and head straight to the bathroom. As I prepare to unwrap the scissors from its wrap, I glance at the mirror.

Standing in front of the mirror is April McIntyre. April McIntyre is a brunette with wavy hair, twenty years old, an Aries, the eldest daughter in the McIntyre family, the older sister of Autumn, and the girlfriend of Roman Irvine (or, ex-girlfriend now). I have flaws: I'm moody, stubborn, impulsive, and a little arrogant. But I'm strong and fierce – even to the point that I had started a movement. Sure, it's small. It'll likely get squashed with my absence. But for the first time in my life, I've managed to inspire a group of people. I may not be perfect, but I like the person that I had been on the verge of becoming. Because of Divinity Bureau, I'm forced to give up being that person. I pace the bathroom for a few minutes. As I do, I start second-guessing my decision to throw away my Mobiroid. But I soon talk myself into doing what I need to do. When I emerge from the bathroom, I'm Elisa Meeks: 127 years-old, blonde, and a Cancer. I have no idea who I am, and I realize that losing myself hurt far more than losing the people that I love.

I spend the next few days driving to the address Leonard gave me. Traffic is stop-and-go throughout the way. When I finally make it, I find myself standing in front of a looming tower that overlooks the city. That's when fear threatens to overtake me.

I wonder what my mother's reaction will be. Surely, she'll be disappointed to know that she's the parent of a fugitive. Would she blame me? Would the disappointment be so intense that she won't want anything to do with me? I hope that won't be the case. I don't have anyone else to turn to in this new life.

I pace the halls for what turns out to be emotionally grueling fifteen minutes. I watch as people come and flitter through the halls, eying me as though I need help. By the time I garner the courage to knock on my mother's door, the door to the apartment has swung open.

I stare at the person in front of me. "I…"

A young man stares at me back in confusion. "Can I help you, miss?"

"Yeah, I'm looking for my… friend," I say slowly. "Is she here? Her name is Miranda Tonkin."

The man shakes his head. "I'm sorry, but I don't know who that person is."

I thank him for his time and walk out of the building with a heavy heart. How is this possible? I thought for certain that Leonard would know where she was! What do I do now? I'm in a different district with a name and identity that I can hardly remember. I don't have a Mobiroid anymore; and even if I did, I don't have any friends or family that I can contact. My mother is my last lifeline. I don't know the first thing about being on the run or how even to function, but my mom has managed to evade capture for months. I'm going to need her if I want to survive.

With newfound determination, I check into a motel and spend my days on the internet in search of anything that relates to my mother. I find out that the original Miranda Tonkin is a stay-at-home mother with nine children, which reminds me why we have an overpopulation problem.

Two days after I check in, I pop into the rental office of the apartment complex. I ask the administrative assistant if she's seen anyone by the name of Miranda Tonkin.

"Miranda Tonkin?" she asks, her eyes going wide. "Yeah, I recognize that name…"

Unfortunately, she's not allowed to disclose any personal information.

I try again a few days later and get a different administrative assistant, who pretends that a person named Miranda Tonkin has never lived in the building. On the third visit, the office manager threatens to call the police on me. It's around this time that the motel staff informs me that I've overstayed my welcome, explaining my room was booked by another guest. I take this as a sign that I should end my search.

I pack my bags with the intention of driving away as possible, but I don't know where to go. Do I want to live my life as a fugitive? No, not at all. And I especially don't want to live it on my own. At the last minute, while I'm passing the apartment building, I pay another visit to the rental office. I keep my fingers crossed that a different administrative assistant will be working. To my luck, a fidgeting young woman is sitting at the front desk when I walk in with a box I had taken from the dumpster and an idea.

"Excuse me," I greet politely, causing the girl to nearly jump out of her seat. "I have a package for Miranda Tonkin, but the label doesn't have an apartment number. Can you tell me where she lives?"

It's a desperate plan, and it probably won't work. I'm not even wearing a mail carrier uniform.

The girl's attention piques. "Miranda? That name sounds familiar. Give me one second..." She turns to her computer to do a search, while I do my best to resist a smile. It appears that my plan may be working after all. "Miranda Tonkin. She doesn't live here anymore. She broke her lease, so we've been having a dispute over her deposit. I guess that explains why the name sounds familiar."

"Do you have a forwarding address?" I ask. "I'd like to get this package shipped off to her."

"Oh, of course!" the girl exclaims. "Give me one second..."

■■■■■■■■■■■■■■■■■■■■■■■■■■■■■■■■■■■■■■■■■■■■■■■■■■■■■

It takes another two days of driving to reach my destination: District 190. The locals call it Fort Wayne. Having spent the last few weeks on the road, I was worried that it might be another dead end; but confidence strengthened when I was doing a routine search on the internet. I was stopped in a diner, and I found a review for a legal office in District 190. The review was written by a woman that was going through a divorce. She raved about a legal assistant that consoled her when she broke down in the middle of a meeting: "Miranda Tonkin got me a cup of coffee and let me cry on her shoulder while I babbled on about my ex-husband and his new girlfriend. It was a small gesture, but it was much appreciated!"

266 · TESSA CLARE

I thought of my parents and their turbulent marriage. Any doubts that I was on the wrong path diminished from my mind. The drive to District 190 is long and muddled with traffic – but it's not long enough. I pass the address that I was given – a blue townhouse on a busy intersection – but, wanting to avoid the disastrous scene from my first failed confrontation, I drive to the legal office where I had seen the review.

I wait in a parking garage for the day to pass. As I do, fear threatens to overtake me. I've been holding onto the hope that my mother would take me in – but what if she doesn't? We weren't close, but she was still my mother. And I don't have anyone else.

I'm holding onto these thoughts when I find myself standing in a lobby at 4:30 in the afternoon. I watch as people come and go into the office. More people leave as the day progresses. It's after an hour of waiting that a petite figure with brown hair and large grey eyes emerges from the elevator – and that's when I knew I had found her.

My mother hasn't changed much. Her hair is slightly shorter, but the biggest change is that she isn't wearing a lot of makeup. I've spent twenty years living with her, so I know how my mother looks bare-faced – but most people don't. Most people know Macy McIntyre to be polished, as one would expect the wife of a politician to be (I, of course, know differently). Here, she doesn't have that expectation to live up to. I realize that this is likely the life my mother would have lead if she hadn't met my father. Should I interfere? Would it be selfish?

*Yes.*

But I've come too far to give up now.

"Excuse me, uh, Miranda," I call out.

My mother turns her head. "Yes?"

She doesn't recognize me at first: I changed my hair and might have unwittingly changed my posture and attitude. I can no longer be April McIntyre. But she takes a few steps towards me; and as the seconds pass by, her eyes widen in realization.

We don't say anything at first. No words need to be said, as I'm sure my mother can put two and two together. We've had an emotional fallout, and the first step is acknowledging that we'll need to pick ourselves up again.

"Mom," I whimper, my voice weak. "I'm sure you know why I'm here."

I'm met with silence. She knows. How can she not? My face is plastered all over the news. I'm standing in front of her with a new hairstyle in a place far from home. But I know she never wanted this life for me. And I never wanted it for her.

"I'm sorry," I breathe, tears trailing down my face. "I know you must be so disappointed in me. I can't imagine what it's like to have a fugitive for a daughter." I bite my lip, unable to look at her in the eye. "I know you tried so hard to keep me from this life, and I just want you to know that I'm sorry. *I'm so sorry!* I should have listened to you…"

I don't get the chance to say anything further before I'm pulled into a crushing hug.

"I missed you," my mother whispers. Tears are staining my sweatshirt.

"I missed you, too," I say. I bury my face in her shirt. "I'm sorry," I say again because I'm not sure if saying it enough times will make it any better. "It's all my fault. I got us into this mess."

"You didn't," my mother whispers. "Even if you did, it doesn't matter. I'd do it all over again."

I'm brought back to my speech in front of the bureau: *'We're going to fight until we have a say in how we live and how we die!'* Despite the pain, I'm starting to think that moments like this are worth fighting for.

"You're my daughter," Macy whispers. "And I love you." I feel her grip around me tighten. "I can't believe you're here!"

I smile. "We're McIntyre's. We're willing to fight – even if it's over stuff like security deposits."

■■■■■■■■■■■■■■■■■■■■■■■■■■■■■■■■■■■■■■■■■■■■■■■■■■■■

My mother takes me back to her townhouse. She's renting a two-bedroom home, but one of the rooms has been converted into an office. She promises to turn it into a bedroom if I stay with her for a while. In the meantime, I'm stuck sleeping on the couch.

I learn about my mother's new life. She decided to move to her hometown in District 100, though she struggled to find work. Unlike me, who made a significant cash withdrawal before leaving, my mother decided to start fresh. She withdrew enough to get by for a few months, but she left the rest to Autumn and me. She didn't want anything to do with her old life, not even the money.

"I still missed you and Autumn, though," she murmurs as we eat our dinner of Chinese take-out. "I thought of you two every day."

Suddenly, my order of orange synthetic chicken feels stale in my mouth. I swallow, before I ask, "Then how come you weren't planning on saying goodbye?"

My mother looks away. "It was hard. The last thing I wanted to do was hurt you. I thought that by disappearing, I'd be saving you from the pain. I think I just made it worse, though." She pauses as she takes a bite of food from her plate. "How did you do it?"

I think about the fact that I was so close to cutting ties with a note for Roman and realize that I'm a hypocrite.

"I just told them that it was something I had to do," I admit sheepishly. "I didn't want them to think that I abandoned them."

"Did you and Autumn think I abandoned you?"

I bite my lip, realizing that there's nothing I could have said that would alleviate the feelings of abandonment. "It might've crossed our minds."

My mother stands up to clear the empty plates from the table. It's an odd sight to watch, as we're used to having a robot or maid do it for us.

"Poor Autumn," my mother says remorsefully. "I hope Darcy is taking good care of her."

"She is."

"I know what it's like to have abandonment issues," Macy continues. "It only goes away with time. I know that you probably don't fully trust me right now…" I look away, knowing that those words ring true. "But if we give it enough time, I'm sure you will. We have eternity, after all."

*Eternity.*

My mother is implying that I'll have BIONs injected in me to freeze my aging. Once that happens, I can technically live forever – especially if I play my cards right and avoid capture by the Bureau. But I'm not sure if this is the way I want to live my life.

I swallow. "It's been a long day, so I'm going to hit the sheets. Can you please leave a spare key tomorrow? I need to go shopping."

My mother smiles. "Of course."

■■■■■■■■■■■■■■■■■■■■■■■■■■■■■■■■■■■■■■■■■■■■■■■■■■■■■

When I close my eyes, I expect to fall into a dreamless slumber. The last few weeks have taken its toll on me, and I'm exhausted – emotionally and physically. But I welcome the chance to have a fresh start. Everything in my life is changing, but I hope that it will be for the better. For the first time in my life, I can live a normal life.

The dreamless slumber never comes. Instead, all I can think about is the way Roman held onto me and the pained expression on his face as I let him go.

*"I was never cut out for a normal life. Not since I was born with the McIntyre surname."*

*"So, that's it? You're just going to run away and give up on us – because I hold you back?"*

After hours of tossing and turning, I get up and grab a glass of water. I sleepily make my way into the kitchen, but I can't find a light switch. I fumble around for a few minutes, but then I give up and navigate by feeling my way around. The soft glow of the streetlights keeps me from falling on my feet. I'm successful at finding a glass in the cupboard and turning on the faucet. As I sip on a glass of water, I notice that several figures are standing outside the house.

I frown. Well, that's odd. Roman's neighborhood has had its share of late-night congregations, but I never expected it to be in my mother's sleepy district. But this group isn't like the rowdy hooligans of District 200. They're huddled in a circle, and they're whispering quietly amongst themselves. Then, abruptly, they turn around and start walking. They're stealthy. Had I not been looking right at them, I would have missed them. But then I glance down the street: police cars. The group consists of uniformed officers – and they're headed straight for the house!

I spill the glass of water onto the floor as I run towards my mother's bedroom. I shake her awake. "Mom! Wake up!"

An eye slowly opens. "It's still dark…"

"I think they found us."

"Who did?"

I open my mouth to answer, but I don't need to. My suspicions are confirmed by the incessant pounding on the front door: "Confederal District Police!"

She immediately jolts awake. "What's going on?"

"Open the door. We have a warrant for the rest of Macy and April McIntyre."

"It's the Divinity Bureau!" I exclaim, too shocked and numb to think. I don't want to die. I've barely lived! "What do we do?"

"You have ten seconds to open the door," the voice calls out. "If the door isn't open, we will be forced to kick it down."

We sit there in silence, fear crippling us from any further movement.

*10.*

*9.*

*8.*

My mother's eyes narrow. "Run."

I don't need to be told twice. By the time the door is knocked down, we are on our way towards the back door. "Put your hands in the air!" he orders, but we don't listen. We run out the door faster than we can think.

We're barefoot and unprotected from the autumn chill as we run through the garden and into the street. What will we do? Where can we run? As our legs push us forward, my mind is wondering what we'll do next. We can't stay here. But I can't start over if we have nothing more than the clothes on my back.

Still – it's better than giving my life to the Divinity Bureau.

*'If we make it on that list, we're not going to come quietly.'*

Footsteps follow closely behind me.

*'We're going to fight and claw our way out!'*

I push forward.

*'And we're going to fight until we have a say in how we live and how we die!'*

I'm getting blisters on my feet. A sharp rock punctures my foot, but I ignore the blood seeping through my wool socks and the gnawing pain in my leg. I need to get away. I need to do everything it takes to survive.

*'If that doesn't scare you, then let me remind you of this…'*

I only stop when I hear a gasp and realize that my mother is no longer behind me. When I turn my head, I see that my mother has tripped over a curb. "Mom? Are you…?"

The split second is all that's needed for the officers to reach us. At once, three of them point their guns at me.

"Put your hands in the air!"

I look around and realize that I don't have a choice. I put my hands in the hair, letting my head hang low.

"I said, put your hands in the air!"

My head shoots up, and I realize that my mother isn't complying. Instead, she stands up and glares defiantly at the officers. For the first time, I regret the words that I spoke in front of the bureau. At this moment, I'll do anything to take them back.

*'When you have nothing left, you don't have anything to lose.'*

My mother doesn't have anything to lose, except for me. I'm not religious, but I'm willing to pray to any deity that will listen that it's enough.

My mother glares defiantly at the officers. "Make me."

The response is three resounding gunshots that echo throughout the otherwise quiet neighborhood. I cringe. I don't want to watch, but a part of me needs to know if it's real. I regret it the moment the bullets pierce her body. My mother gives me one last helpless look, but by the time I look away, her eyes have glazed over. She falls to the ground a moment later.

"No!" I cry out. "No, no, no!"

I immediately move to reach out to my mother, but another gun points in my direction. "April Maheva McIntyre, you are under arrest for evading the election process, harboring a fugitive, and conspiring against a government agency. You will have your rights read to you. You have the right to remain silent…"

I can't stay silent. I will never be silent to these atrocities. I scream, agony echoing into the night.

CHAPTER TWENTY-FIVE

# ROMAN

My plan was to formulate a plan of action on the road. All I know is that I need to reach the address that Finn had given me. My first thought is that it'll be the first time I've seen April in months, after believing that I'll never see again. My second thought is chastising myself for allowing my mind to venture in that direction, not now when the situation is dire. My third thought is how I'm going to need to get them out of the house as quickly and discreetly as possible. After that –

My thoughts are interrupted by Tate using his Mobiroid to change the music. A synthesizer and auto-tuned singing replaces the sound of banjos and guitars.

"I'm vetoing this selection," says Finn.

"Why?" Tate whines. "You vetoed the last three songs I picked!"

As it turns out, my plan for peace and quiet was disrupted as soon as Tate caught the wind that April was in danger. Finn had also insisted on coming along; I'm glad he did because I wouldn't know where to go without him. Considering the circumstances, I was expecting us to talk about what we expected to do when we got there. It's practically our last stretch before we go into battle. Instead, all we've done is make awkward small talk and bicker about what songs were playing on the radio.

"This isn't music," Finn says pointedly. "This is a computer playing a bunch of loud noises."

I do my best to hold in a snicker.

I don't trust Finn completely, but I'd be stuck if it weren't for his knowledge and help. Finn had spent years working directly under Gideon, and if there's anyone who knows the Divinity Bureau inside and out, it's him. Tate, on the other hand, only seems to be there for moral support. He cares about April, but I'm not sure how that will help us get her out of danger. Still, I wasn't able to say no when Tate called out of work for the next week and hopped into Finn's car.

"How much longer do we have to go?" I ask. We've been driving for days, switching off drivers on occasion. Right now, it's my turn; and I'm growing impatient.

"Another hour," says Finn. "Macy had moved to District 205 initially, but she came here shortly afterward." He eyes me conspicuously, before asking, "Do we know what we're going to do when we get there?"

I think about my answer for a long moment before answering: "I'm going to talk to her."

Tate coughs loudly in the backseat, though it sounds suspicious.

My eyes narrow. "What?"

Tate shakes his head. "Nothing. It's just..." He trails off, much to my annoyance. I've barely slept and barely eaten in the last few days, so I don't have the patience for half-answers.

"It's just, what?"

"I don't think April will go with you unless you prove that she needs to go," Tate admits softly.

"Why not?"

In my opinion, it should be pretty obvious that we're not driving a few hundred miles for a field trip.

Tate looks away. "You know how April is. She's too headstrong to let anyone help her. Why else do you think she'd want to do this on her own?"

"She didn't have a choice!" I shoot back, frustration getting the best of me. Finn is forced to take control of the wheel momentarily to keep us from swerving off the road.

"Did she?" Tate quips back. "What did she say when you offered to come with her?"

I had spilled the details about April's departure when we were drunk one night, and I'm beginning to regret it.

*"You'll only hold me back."*

The rest of the car ride is spent in silence. Tate and Finn have given up on fighting for control of the music, leaving me alone with my thoughts.

As the miles go by and bring me closer to my destination, I wonder if Tate was right. At the moment, she'll probably think that I'm an overly attached boyfriend clinging for any chance to stay with April – and I can't deny that a part of me is. I wouldn't mind leaving my life behind for her. What do I have? A 250 square foot apartment that I can barely afford and an hourly job at an electronics store? I'd need someone to take care of Neville, but I don't have much else going for me. Maybe April has the right idea in wanting to start over.

Finn breaks the silence by reminding me that the exit is rapidly approaching. As I prepare to switch lanes, my heart races in my chest. Still, I can't afford to let my emotions get the best of me. April's safety comes first.

"We're almost there," Finn says grimly.

I nod in acknowledgment.

Finn instructs me to turn into a neighborhood, but we're stopped by a police car blocking the road. I roll the window down when an officer approaches the car.

"Take your hands off the wheel," Finn whispers.

Right, I realize. Manual driving is illegal, after all.

"My apologies," the officer says once he's within hearing distance. "But this area is blocked off."

I glance at Finn, whose eyes widen at the same that mine does.

"Can you tell me…?" I begin to ask where we can find a detour, but I'm quickly cut off.

"We're from the Divinity Bureau headquarters," Finn interjects before I can get another word in. He pulls his work identification card out of his wallet, much to my confusion. Hasn't it been deactivated by now? But I suppose the officer wouldn't know that. "We were sent here by Gideon Hearthstrom, as we heard there was an ongoing investigation. Is that here?"

The officer glances between the three of us before his eyes fall on Finn's identification card. "You guys got here pretty quickly."

Finn shrugs, as though our efficiency isn't something that should be questioned.

"Well, there was a shootout," the officer explains. "One person is dead."

I think of the implications.

We're just a few houses away from where Macy McIntyre was allegedly staying. April went to find her. Did that mean that April was dead? But that can't be…

My stomach feels as though it's been shot by an arrow.

"No! That can't be right!" I exclaim. "April…"

Finn shoots me a warning look, before resuming his conversation with the officer. "What caused the shootout?"

The officer's gaze lingers on my expression – no doubt wide in panic. "Are you guys here for the McIntyre girl?"

Finn nods. "That's correct." He shoots me another look of warning, daring me to question him. "I apologize. He's new to this. He's – uh – my intern. They both are."

Tate is suspiciously quiet, but the officer brushes it off and returns his attention to Finn. "Do you guys want to come to the station? We can give you a full report there."

"We'll more than likely stop by," says Finn. "But we'd like to investigate the scene first."

"Suit yourself," the officer says, stepping out of the way to allow the three of us to pass through. I'm still staring straight ahead, white-faced, trying not to throw up. Finn has to remind me to press the gas pedal. It doesn't cross my mind to hide the fact that we're manually driving from the officer.

Yellow tape blocks the townhouse. We park the car between two police vehicles and step into the scene. Curious neighbors surround the area, and I can hear whispered rumors over disbelief that April McIntyre had been living a mere few doors away from them. I'm unsure where to go, but Tate and I follow Finn's lead, who is pushing through the crowd and into the house. When we're alone, I turn to Finn to ask what's going on, but Finn corners me before I get the chance.

"Roman, I'm going to need you to stay calm," Finn hisses, glancing over his shoulder to make sure that no officers are near.

"Stay calm?" I gawk, forgetting to lower my voice. "I just found out that my girlfriend might be dead!"

"Shh!"

"She's not dead," Tate answers. "At least, not that we know of."

"Tate's right," Finn replies. "We don't know what happened. For all we know, it could've been a bystander."

"Or Macy," Tate chimes in quietly.

"Oh, that's just lovely!" I exclaim, letting my hands rise and fall. I'm forced to bring my volume down when I see the stern expressions on Finn and Tate's faces. "Instead of my girlfriend being dead, it's just her mother! No big deal!"

Finn places a hand on my shoulder to steady me. "Roman, you need to stay calm. If anyone finds out that you're with April, the whole thing is over."

I'm not sure if I can stay calm. The weight of the situation is threatening to overtake me and bury me alive. But I can't deny that Finn's right. I need to keep myself together if I want us to be alive by the time the week is over.

I look at Finn, taking a deep breath to calm my racing heart. "Do people run often?"

Finn closes his eyes. "Yes."

"What happens to them?"

"It's up to local law enforcement to take them into custody. Once the person is in custody, we have field agents that are responsible for transferring them to the care of the Divinity Bureau."

"What happens after that?"

Finn's gaze softens. "You know what happens."

I nod. It's a silly question to ask, but a part of me is still in denial. But one glance at the scene around me – from the police tape to the sparsely decorated townhouse to the back door that's still wide open – and I can't deny the truth any longer: April McIntyre could be dead by the time the week is over if she didn't die already.

"Let's get out of here," I say.

Tate and Finn glance around the room before they nod in agreement. Together, the three of us walk out of the house and prepare to face the uncertainty of the future.

■■■■■■■■■■■■■■■■■■■■■■■■■■■■■■■■■■■■■■■■■■■■■■■■■■■

Our plan is to pose as Divinity Bureau field agents and get the local police to release April to us. Finn has spent an hour going over the basics of what we need to know: the structure, procedures, and jargon. I'm surprised how little knew about my place of work. The most important thing that Finn tells me is that field agents usually work undercover, which is why we don't arouse any suspicion when we walk into the police in our plain clothes. Unfortunately, we're an hour too late.

"It looks like your headquarters made a mistake," a plump-faced desk sergeant explains. "Two field agents came by and took the McIntyre girl about an hour ago." My face falls immediately, which leads the woman to eye us conspicuously. "You said you're from headquarters?"

"Yes, ma'am," Finn responds immediately.

"Which McIntyre girl did they take?" I ask, doing my best to keep my desperation under control.

The desk sergeant raises an eyebrow. "The alive one, obviously. Didn't they tell you what happened?"

Finn glances back at me, and he has a glint in his eyes. I recognize that look: it's the one he makes when he has a new idea.

"We're not here for her," Finn replies curtly. "We're here to collect the body of the other one."

The idea makes me want to throw up. I don't like the idea of driving with a body in the backseat of Finn's car, much less the idea of transporting it to an undetermined location. I'm not even sure if it'll fit! Where will Tate sit? But I know what Finn is doing. If we see the body, we'll be able to narrow down who is still alive; but what will I do if it's April's body lying in the morgue?

The woman's dart between the three of us. She eyes me for a while longer, noting how I'm squirming under her scrutinizing gaze Still, she must have dismissed any suspicions, because she calls another officer over to bring us to the morgue.

"Finn," I whisper as we make our way down a narrow hallway. The closer we get, the lower the temperature drops.

Finn steps closer to me, bringing his voice down. "Yeah?"

I take a deep breath, before I admit, "I don't think we can fit a body in the car."

Finn stifles a laugh – one that's quickly stopped when we make eye contact with the uniformed officer that's leading the way. When he finally manages to contain himself, he whispers, "Don't worry. I was already planning on making up an excuse after we saw who it was." He pauses, noting my troubled expression. "What are you going to do if it's April?"

"I don't know," I admit softly. "I'll be devastated, but I'll keep it under control. I have to."

"And if it's not?"

I offer him a half-smile, but I don't feel it in the rest of my face. "Does it sound wrong if I say that I'll be relieved?"

I don't get the chance to hear Finn's answer. The officer stops in front of what appears to be our destination: the morgue. "Well, this is it."

The statement sounds simple, but it holds so much weight in my mind.

I push a swinging door open, where I find myself surrounded by gray walls, tools, books, and measuring instruments. A pungent odor fills the air. It smells like a concoction of chemicals and decay. I glance around the room, my eyes falling on a gurney that's lying in the middle of the room.

That's when I see her: Macy McIntyre, helpless and lifeless on the gurney. I've never seen her without makeup; and even if I did, I imagine she'd look nothing like this. She's paler than I've ever seen her. Her lips and eyelids are purple. Three holes puncture her chest, but I assume that the one closest to her heart is the one that killed her. Saying that she looks like a ghost would be inaccurate; though to a stranger, the image in front of me wouldn't be too far from the truth. But I knew her. She lived. She gave up everything – from a promising career to a chance at happiness with a man that would stay faithful to her – for her daughters. But the thing in front of me doesn't remind me of a ghost. It reminds me of an abandoned house: memories and hopes to lie to waste, falling apart. Brick by brick.

I told myself that I wouldn't break down, but I can feel hot tears coming. Finn quickly recognizes what's happening and asks the officer to leave the room so that we can discuss "confidential" information. As soon as the three of us are alone, I collapse and cry. Tate joins me, grasping Macy's hand – cold as ice. I feel ashamed for thinking that seeing Macy's body would be a relief. Death is never a relief when it comes too soon.

Minutes pass before I feel a hand on my shoulder. For the first time, I'm grateful for Finn's presence. I wouldn't have made it this far without him.

"Thank you," I say weakly. My throat is hoarse.

"Don't thank me yet," he replies, pulling Tate and me up. "What should we do about April?"

"We need to get her out," I say. There's no doubt in my mind that it'll be done. We just need to figure out how we're going to do that. "Finn, do you still have your work badge?"

"I do."

"Good, we're going to need it."

Tate glances between the two of us, shuffling his feet. "Guys, not to ruin your epic plan, but weren't those deactivated when you guys got fired?"

"I can reactivate your badge," I assure him. "That should be a piece of cake, and I should be able to get us into the Divinity Bureau. The office locks and unlocks using facial recognition software – which I happened to program." That meant that my face was hardcoded into the system, so it'd still let me in. I turn my attention to Finn. "It's a good thing you made me fix that stupid door, Finn. You know, the one that gave me hell for six months."

Finn laughs. "I knew you'd thank me someday. Granted, I pictured it under different circumstances." He pauses as another thought comes to him. "That only works for the office, though. The bureau keeps a holding area for runaways in the basement, and that's got a whole different system."

"Roman's got a Master's degree in network security," Tate chimes in. "If anyone can figure it out, it's him. Right, Roman?"

I'm not sure about my skills; but for April, I'm willing to try.

"As Gideon once said," I say, and I can't help the smile on my face. "I'm just an office assistant. I guess it's about time I show him what an office assistant can do."

CHAPTER TWENTY-SIX

# APRIL

I don't know how much time has passed.

All I know is that the sky is dark when I'm thrown into the backseat of a police car.

It's still dark when I'm brought to a police station and thrown into a windowless cell.

It's been a long night – physically and emotionally – and yet, every time I close my eyes, all I can see if my mother's lifeless eyes as she fell face down onto the pavement. Rather than lay my head down, I huddle into a ball and stare blankly at the walls. I don't want to think. I don't want to feel anything. All I want is to slip into nothingness. When the door to my cell opens, and two men in dark clothes explain that I'm being transferred to the custody of the Divinity Bureau, I realize that I'll be getting my wish.

Once the men finish filling out forms on their tablets – many of which require my signature, which I find ironic – I'm placed into handcuffs and escorted to the back of a black van. One of the men disappears into the front seat, while the second sits with me in the back. He attempts to make small talk with me, but all I can think about is the gun hoisted against his waist. I respond to his questions with silence until he eventually gives up.

The trip to the bureau's headquarters is expected to take a day and a half. I'm exhausted, but I want to stay awake. Soon, I'll be sleeping for eternity. I stare out the window and watch the sights pass me by - cornfields, billboards, and truck stops. Occasionally, something will pique my interest: a landmark, a unique looking shop, or a striking piece of land. During those moments, my stomach twists in pain. A few years ago, I had plenty of opportunities to do and see anything that I wanted. Instead, I wasted those opportunities on regrets and bitterness, and I'll never get them back.

As the drive goes by, I think that maybe the scenery is a metaphor for my life. I've always defined my life by major moments – the ones of life, death, happiness, and sadness. But life isn't about those moments. Most of life consists of the mundane moments in between, much like the cornfields that are passing me by.

When the skyline of District 200 comes into view, I realize that I only have a few hours left to live. For almost a year, I've skirted on the edge of death – and there it is, staring at me in the face.

The van comes to a stop.

I can't bear to look out the window because I know what I'll see. It seems like a lifetime ago that I was standing in front of the building, calling for a fight against the Bureau. The irony isn't lost on me. I had begun my fight in front of that building, and I'll be defeated in the same place. Maybe that's the reason why, the moment I step outside of the van bound in handcuffs, reporters swarm around me.

"April, do you have any last words?"

"What made you think that you'd be able to escape?"

"Do you blame yourself for what happened to your mother?"

I stop in my tracks at the last question, my knees weak. My escort glares at me in annoyance, urging me forward, but all I can think about is my mother's lifeless face. The truth is that I should blame myself. I was the one that sought her out; and if it wasn't for me, my mother could've lived a long and peaceful life. Her demise had been an unfortunate outcome of my actions.

But I've spent most of my life feeling guilty. I can't change what happened to my mother – but surely, I'll be able to change something else. If there's one opportunity that I don't want to waste...

Roman's face is the first thing that comes to mind. His words will haunt me until my last moments: *"I love you. I've always loved you. I thought I'd get plenty of chances to say it, but now I'm scared that I won't."*

I clear my throat. "Hey Roman!"

The swarm around me goes quiet. I glance around the crowd until I see a camera. I stare right at it, pretending that it's Roman instead of a bulky piece of equipment.

"Don't worry," I say firmly, even though I know that he'll worry even more. "I haven't given up the fight. If I get out of here, then I'll find you, and we'll run away together. I'm better with you than without you." I glance at my bound hands. "But in case I don't, I want you to know that I love you." I take a deep breath. "I love you." Another breath. "I'm sorry that I'm saying it on the news instead of you, but I..."

"Let's go!" my escort urges on, pulling my arm and preventing me from saying anything more. But I can't help but take pleasure in the looks of confusion that are pressed on the paparazzi's faces. When my escort brings me to a holding cell in the Divinity Bureau's basement, I don't hesitate to lay my head on the cot and fall into a dreamless sleep.

■■■■■■■■■■■■■■■■■■■■■■■■■■■■■■■■■■■■■■■■■■■■■■■■■■■■■■

I thought I'd be dead by the time the day is over, so I'm surprised when I awaken in my cell. Without exhaustion clouding my perception, I'm able to get a better picture of my surroundings: empty walls, linoleum floors, a cot – the one I was sleeping on – surrounded by sterile equipment. One of them appears to be an IV. When I glance at my arm, I realize that the IV tube is inside me.

I panic. I attempt to tear it off, but it hurts so much that I can't. Maybe I can wiggle it out, a little at a time. What is the pain in comparison to dying? But the task is harder than I can manage. Whatever they had stuck into me, it runs deep – and it's slowly killing me.

That's when I notice the label on the bag: Biological Immunization of Neutrons. BIONs. I'm confused, unable to understand why they're injecting me with the very thing that will stop my aging and make me immortal if they're trying to kill me. I ponder on it for a moment, and then I decide that I don't care anymore. I need to get out of here. I make my way to the door and find that it's being guarded by a red-haired man that I don't recognize.

"Excuse me," I whisper. I hate how desperate my voice sounds.

The guard glances in my direction, but the only response I get is a grunt. I press my hands to my temple and decide to try again.

"Look, I know you're supposed to keep me here until..." *Until I die,* I think with a grimace; but I can't bring myself to say the words. "Listen, if you get me out of here – I have money. You can have a lot of it. Hell, you can have all of it. I just don't want to die. I can't. I'm twenty years old. I'm supposed to go to college, get a job, get married, and have a healthy life..."

I push the image of Roman's tear-stricken face out of my mind.

"I don't think you'd be able to have a normal life, even if you wanted to," a smooth voice interrupts.

I cock an eyebrow to figure out where the voice had come from. It certainly didn't come from the stone-faced guard. My answer comes a moment later when Gideon Hearthstrom emerges from behind him. I back away as he glides past the guard and unlocks the holding cell. He's much shorter than I anticipated him being. In my nightmares, he's the size of the bureau's headquarters. But standing in front of me, he's only a few inches taller than me – yet every inch of him is intimidating. His eyes are dark as charcoal; and if I wasn't already dying, I'm certain I'd be dead by the way his gaze is piercing into me.

"What... what are you doing here?" I sputter out.

"I'm here to sign your paperwork, of course," Gideon says, his pleasant tone a stark contrast to the bleak ambiance. "We are a government agency, which means we need to maintain checks and balances." As if making a point, he turns to a tablet hoisted against the wall and flips through a few screens. I briefly catch a glimpse of my picture. "You'll also need to sign a few forms."

"I'm not giving you permission to kill me."

"It's not a permission slip," Gideon replies, amusement dancing in his eyes. "It's so that we can release your family for a proper burial." *I don't have any family left, because of you,'* I want to say. But I don't want to give him the satisfaction. "Though we can also donate it to science if that's what you'd prefer."

I shake my head. "No."

Gideon turns back towards me. "Suit yourself. But I must advise you; Silicon Labs is searching for acceptable candidates for their latest-"

"Why are you doing this?" I whisper. My voice quivers. I feel weak from the day's activities.

"Well, I'm sure you're aware of the side-effects of overpopulation..."

"Don't bullshit me!" I hiss. He stops what he's doing long enough to look at me. Under his scrutinizing gaze, I feel like I might turn to stone at any moment. My heart is racing as I continue, "This isn't about some utilitarian greater good. You wouldn't have gone out of your way to bring me here if it was."

Gideon chuckles. "Wouldn't it be easier to view me as some hapless villain preying on a poor innocent girl?"

"You already are a villain," I spit out. "I just want to know why."

Gideon remains silent, much to my annoyance. I clench my fist.

"Look, I'm already dying!" I press. "Why don't you just tell me the truth?"

"That's precisely what I'm worried about," Gideon replies before he walks across the room to check my IV. "Do you know what a white lie is?"

I stare at him in confusion. Does he think I'm an idiot?

"Of course I do."

"Have you ever told one before?"

I think of Autumn's tear-stricken face. "I have."

Suddenly, his hands are on my face, stroking my chin. I get a whiff of garlic on his breath, and it makes me sick.

"This is for the greater good, April McIntyre," he purrs.

*Oh no.* This doesn't look good.

Gideon laughs. "As I recall, you said that you were going to 'fight and claw your way out.' Where is your fight?"

I can feel a cold hand on my thigh. The feeling makes me want to vomit.

I do my best to kick him away, but I've hardly eaten or slept in the last few days. My thrashing hardly moves him. Gideon laughs – loud and booming that it echoes throughout the corridor.

"Come on," Gideon goads. "You said so yourself that the threat of election wasn't going to intimidate you!" I kick him again, but his hands find its way onto my buttocks. "You said that you were going to fight until you have a say in how you live and die!" He starts to tug on my pants. I squirm under his grip. "'When you have nothing left...'"

I just manage to pull an arm out of his grasp. I use the split second of freedom to punch him in the nose. The IV in my arm is jolted, causing a searing pain in my arm. I move away from him, still in shock at having nearly been violated at the hands of the Regional Chairman of the Midwest Districts.

Gideon takes a step closer to me. "You're just a little spoiled brat. A stubborn, hot-headed one. You're a fool to think that you could change the way the world works."

"So, is that it?" I ask, staring at him in disbelief. "You're trying to make an example out of me?"

"You're a liability!" Gideon accuses, taking another step towards me. "Just like your father!"

"Why?" I shout, meeting his gaze with as much ferocity as I can muster. He has me backed into a corner. "Because he damaged your reputation? Because he saw you for what you are: a corrupt fucking BION bot!"

At those words, Gideon's hands meet my throat – so hard that it feels like he's squeezing the life out of me. I gasp for air, desperate for the relief of oxygen. None comes.

"Is that what they told you?" Gideon sneers. "That *I* was corrupt?"

I ache to respond, but no words come.

"Well, let me advise you of this: your *family* has had more positions of power than any other in the history of the Confederal Districts," he hisses. "They also have the longest history of corruption. I've never broken any laws. I've never done anything outside of standard operating procedures. Your father on the other hand…."

I gasp for air.

"Well, his policies have made the election process rather difficult," he continues. "Your family sold immortality to some very dangerous people. He did everything not only to continue that tradition but also keep the people he loved off that list – and what an idiot he was! We're in the middle of an overpopulation crisis! We can't afford to let our emotions get the best of us!"

I think I might faint from the lack of air.

"You think your father was a good man," Gideon goes on. "But your father amassed a fortune selling immortality to some very dangerous people. Being in Parliament allowed him not to be restricted to a single district! He played favoritism, and it practically destroyed our world. And he accused *me* of corruption!"

When I'm positive that I'm going to pass out from asphyxiation, Gideon releases his grip on me and throws me to the ground. As I cough and struggle to recover, Gideon steps over me and glares at me. "You're a McIntyre. If it weren't for government regulations, I'd kill you right now." He glances at the IV bag. "But unfortunately, I have procedures to follow. Usually, it's a lot faster than this. All we have to do is deactivate the BIONs in one's system, and it's an instant death. However, since you didn't have any…"

Once I find breath, I let out a bitter laugh. "So, that it? That's how you say that you've never broken any laws?"

It hits me that just because someone is a law-abiding citizen doesn't mean that they're a good person.

"Government regulations," Gideon replies curtly. "It doesn't matter, though. Soon –"

He stops when a light goes out. Another goes out a split second later, and another. Within seconds, the room is pitch dark. Through the darkness, I can hear the door creaking open.

Gideon barks, "What the hell is going on?"

"It appears that there was a power outage, sir."

"Well, fix it!"

"We're working on it, sir. It should be –"

He's cut off by the sound of a crash, followed by a grunt. Another crash echoed throughout the hallway. A gunshot fires. I have a momentary flashback of my mother's face, and I cringe in the corner.

"We have intruders!" a voice yells. "Get them!"

Another shot is fired.

This is my chance to get away. I attempt to crawl towards the open doorway, but I'm held back by the needle in my arm. I cringe at the thought of what I'm about to do. I rip the needle from my arm. It's long, and it feels like I'm pulling it through the muscle. Blood spills out. It hurts so much that I want to crawl into a corner and nurse my arm, but I need to keep moving if I want to get out alive.

As I crawl towards the door, I'm stopped by a large hand pulling me back.

"Where do you think you're going?" Gideon sneers.

That's when I hear the undeniable sound of someone getting punched and the crack of a nose breaking. Gideon's hand falls away.

I'm ready to back into a corner, fearful of the intruder – until I hear an all too familiar voice: *"Get your hands off my girlfriend!"*

CHAPTER TWENTY-SEVEN

# ROMAN

As soon as April hears my voice, she bursts into tears. "Roman? Is that you?"

With Gideon rendered unconscious from the force of my punch – one that, under normal circumstances, I'd be a little proud of – I take a slow step towards her. I'm too relieved to speak.

My silence only causes her body to rack with sobs. "Oh, Roman, please tell me you're there."

It occurs me that she can't see me. I can see her, thanks to the night vision goggles I picked up on the road, but part of the plan was to shut off the power to keep the Divinity Bureau's security guards from seeing us.

I kneel to the ground and take her hands in mine. "I'm here."

I get a glimpse at her arm. Blood is gushing out, the smell of it filling the air. The smell makes me want to vomit; but instead, I tear a piece of my sleeve off and wrap it around the wound. She'll need stitches later, but that's only if we make it out alive.

"Roman!" Finn's voice barks in the earpiece connected to my Mobiroid. "Six guards are coming your way!"

I pull April to her feet. "We need to get out of here!"

I realize that I don't have an extra set of goggles. I can't expect April to run without knowing where she's going. Without a second thought, I lift her into my arms and dart out of the cell and through the hallway.

Footsteps trail behind me.

"They're trying to kill us!" Tate screeches, his voice echoing in my earpiece. "They're actually trying to kill us!"

"We are breaking into a government agency," Finn points out. "I don't think it gets more illegal than that."

Finn has tucked himself away in our old office and keeping his eye on the security cameras. When we got here, I made a few adjustments to the bureau's security systems. The first was disabling the bureau's AI security systems, which would've killed us instantly had I not known my way around thanks to my two years of employment here. The second was adjusting the security settings on the office door so that it stays locked until it scans my face.

I also let left Finn in charge of one of my projects – one that I had spent the entire car ride from District 180 programming. I created a virus to cripple the Divinity Bureau's systems. All I need to do is transmit it over a WiFi signal. Fortunately, I know the bureau's networks better than I know myself. One push of a button, and it'll all be over. Finn and I had argued whether such a method would be necessary. Finn pointed out that it was dangerous and untested. Neither of us knows what the repercussions will be. I argued that it was what needed. In the end, we compromised on the old-fashioned search and rescue tactic; and we left Finn in charge of the virus. He'd press the button if it were necessary, which we all hoped wouldn't be the case.

"Finn, which way do we go?" I press as we run through the hall.

"Keep going until you hit the stairs. It'll take you to the main floor, where – shit!"

I tense at those words. "What is it?"

"They're all moving towards the exit. They know you'll be headed that way."

"Well, is there another exit?"

"You're in the basement. The only way out is up."

I struggle to remember the layout of the Divinity Bureau, but I'm running on little food and sleep. And my arms are aching from carrying April. But I've spent two years working for the Divinity Bureau. *I must know of another way!*

A thought occurs to me. I turn on the heels of my feet and bolt in the opposite direction.

"Roman!" Tate calls out, confused by the sudden change in direction. "Where are you going?"

"Follow me!"

"There's guards chasing us from that direction!"

"Trust me on this, Tate!"

The guards shoot at us when they hear our footsteps, but they can't get a good hit without knowing where their targets are. I realize that the security force is practically helpless without their AI security system. I manage to knock one guard out by swinging a piece of equipment – it looks like a slab, but I don't know what it's used for – into his head. For every bullet that swings past us, April cringes in my chest. Her reaction is unexpected. The sound bothers me, but I don't cower in fear the way she is – and she's typically far braver than I am. Something inside her had changed since I had last seen her.

At last, I stop in front of my destination and hit a button to take us up. Tate is gasping for air by the time we've arrived, and his mouth drops when he sees why we stopped. "We're taking the elevator?"

I don't say anything. It's the only solution that I have.

"We were almost to the stairs, and you made us turn around to take the elevator?"

"The stairs are surrounded by guards," says Finn through our earpieces. "I think the elevator is a safer bet."

"We're coming to get you, Finn," I say.

"I appreciate you not forgetting about me," Finn replies lightly, as though oblivious to the tension happening a few floors below him. "Though what are you planning on doing about the exit?"

"We're not taking the exit. We're taking the elevator to the second floor and jumping out the closest window."

April and Tate's eyes widen, just as the elevator bell rings and the doors open to take us to our destination.

"No way!"

"I'm not jumping from the second floor!"

As soon as we're in the elevator, I gently set April to her feet. Blood circulation comes back into my arm, and I do my best to hold in the pain. April looks away guiltily. Once I have my thoughts in order, I explain, "Look, I know it sucks; but the way I see it, it's better to risk a few broken bones than dying. You know there's no way they're going to let us walk free."

April's mouth opens to respond, but she's cut off by the sound of the door opening. We thought we had reached the second floor; but instead, we're greeted by the sight of Gideon Hearthstrom – and the guards that surround him. Before we have the chance to register what's happening, we're forced out of the elevator and onto our knees.

"Roman," Finn's voice had lowered in my earpiece. I strain to hear him. "I think we have a problem."

"You think?"

"Guards are trying to get into the office," Finn says, his voice trembling. "They're threatening to kick the door down."

I look straight at Gideon. We're in trouble. April will die. Tate, Finn, and I will likely be imprisoned for the rest of our lives. It'll take a miracle to get us out of the situation that we're in. Fortunately, I spent the drive from District 180 to here programming one.

"Finn," I say quietly, while Gideon discusses with his guards on what they are to do with us. "You know there's a way out."

Finn sighs. "I can't. You programmed it while you were half-asleep. I'm not saying that I don't have faith in your programming capabilities – but you could've easily made a mistake! I'm not about to risk it with my life!"

I close my eyes, thinking back to the conversation that we had earlier.

■■■■■■■■■■■■■■■■■■■■■■■■■■■■■■■■■■■■■■■■■■■■■■■■■■■■■■■■■

*We got lucky coming into the bureau's headquarters. None of the guards knew that Finn and I had been fired. When Tate, Finn, and I approach their desks, Finn distracts them by asking about their children and making small talk about the latest pollution levels. After twenty minutes of chatting, I excuse myself and tell them that I need to check a router so that I can complete one of my tickets. For the first time since I was sacked, I feel like my two-year tenure at the Divinity Bureau has paid off.*

*It's after hours, which means that the call center is empty. As expected, the facial recognition software in the office door recognizes my face – thanks to a few updates that I had made several months ago – and lets us in without hesitation. Once we're alone, I unveil my plan – and the reason why I was silent throughout the drive.*

*I hold out the chip in my hand. "This is a virus – but it's a special kind of virus. It temporarily shuts down any computer when transmitted over a signal. It doesn't damage the files or anything. It just puts everything on pause." Finn and Tate glance at each other. I'm guessing they're debating on who is going to break the bad news that it likely won't help us rescue April. Fortunately, I already took that into consideration. "One more thing: it also works on BIONs."*

*I thought of my conversation with Finn when he had first found me: 'She's got a new name and a new identity. Her phone line is disconnected. Her GPS is out. What else can they possibly look into?'*

*'BIONs?'*

*The three of us stand in silence. I watch as their faces contour from shock to disbelief to confusion to awe to a reaction that I did not expect: disgust.*

*Finn is the first to speak: "That's pretty invasive, don't you think? We're talking about hacking into someone's body."*

*"And sentencing millions of people to die every quarter isn't?"*

*In my mind, it all made sense. BIONs are computers. Computers can be hacked. I have a Master's degree in this. I've spent years and money perfecting this art, and I'll finally get my chance to use those skills.*

*"You can't," Finn says flatly. "It's too dangerous. You don't know what the repercussions will be!"*

*"I know what will happen if I don't do it!"*

*"What about me?" Finn screeches, clenching his fists. "I'm immortal! If this ship breaks, I'm going down with it!"*

■■■■■■■■■■■■■■■■■■■■■■■■■■■■■■■■■■■■■■■■■■■■■■■■■■■■■■

I can hear the guards through my earpiece. The four of us are trapped. Only Finn can get us out of here. I press a hand to my earpiece and let out a breath. "Finn, I'm going to need you to trust me."

Finn lets out a bitter laugh. "Should I? Because last time I checked…"

He's cut off by a high-pitched squeal in my earpiece. I groan in pain and throw my earpiece to the ground before it can do any further damage. I glance at Tate, who has done the same. When I look up, Gideon is standing over us with a triumphant smile on his face.

"Sorry about that, gentleman," Gideon says smugly. "But we couldn't have you co-conspiring your escape." He moves to where April is hunched onto the ground and grabs her by the hair. She winces in pain as he sneers, "It seems like I can't ever be rid of you."

"Let her go!" Tate cries.

His response comes from a guard, who kicks him in the stomach. Gideon chuckles as Tate falls to the ground, clutching his stomach in pain.

Gideon then waltzes over to me, hovering over me like a looming tower. I refuse to look him in the eyes. It's bad enough that he forced me to choose between my morals and my income. It's even worst that he nearly killed the woman that I love. But the worst feeling is the realization that I'm completely helpless against him. Gideon is an elected government official with the power to determine who lives and who dies – and we can all be dead by the time the day is over.

"I expected better from you," Gideon muses. "You were brilliant, especially considering you were just an office assistant."

*'Just an office assistant,'* I think with a grimace. They were the first words I had ever heard from Gideon's mouth, and they could very well be the last.

"Who do you think you are, boy?" Gideon taunts. "This isn't a university. This is the government. We've been around far longer than you've even been alive."

I remain silent, hanging my head in shame.

"The police have been called," Gideon continues. "If it were up to me, I'd have you joining your precious girlfriend – but if I expect to have a job in two years, I'll just have to settle for having you spend a very long time behind bars. You'll be –"

"Sir!" a voice calls out.

Gideon glares at the guard who had interrupted him. "What?"

"Bobby just fainted!"

My eyes widen, daring to hope. Did Finn pull through?

Gideon rolls his eyes. "Well, get him out of here then!"

Suddenly, another guard falls to the ground – then another, and another. Gideon's expression turns from jeer to astonishment as he watches his guards go from alert to unconscious in a matter of seconds.

"What the hell is going on?" Gideon roars, turning to glare at us.

Tate and I glance at each other with knowing smiles on our faces. We know precisely what's going on. With newfound confidence, I stand up to glower at Gideon in triumph. "You asked me who I thought I was. I'm just going to remind you for the millionth time: I'm the IT guy."

Tate and April stand up as well. April glances around the room in confusion, unsure why the guards that surround us are fainting and why we don't seem to be panicking. "What's going on?"

Tate grins. "Your boyfriend is a genius."

"Hacking into computers is what I went to school for," I explain. "BIONs are computers – and they happen to be in the bloodstream of anyone that has opted to become immortal. All I had to do was take a virus and distribute it over a wireless signal – like the bureau's internet connection – and anyone with BIONs in their system takes a nap."

April stares at me in astonishment. "I can't believe it."

Gideon's face turns red. I brace myself for a harsh remark, but no words come. Instead, he crashes to the ground next to his security personnel.

"We have to get Finn," I say. "He's got BIONs in his system as well!"

"So, he finally decided to trust you," Tate says dryly.

I nod. With security disabled temporarily, April is looking at me as though she's ready to run into my arms and kiss me senseless. By the way her flushing cheeks and hitched breathing, I think she might do it. I wouldn't have minded it. After all, we're safe until the police come.

But before she can take another step, she collapses to the ground.

CHAPTER TWENTY-EIGHT

# APRIL

I can feel myself floating.

I drift in and out of consciousness, willing myself to wake up; but I can't move anything beyond my fingertips. I try to tell myself that it'll all be okay. I'm with my boyfriend and my best friend – and together, we'll be able to live long and prosperous lives. I'll get us new identities. I have enough money for us to live comfortable lives. We can live under the radar until the end of our natural lives.

"We have to get to a place with internet!"

I recognize the first voice as belonging to Roman, and I want to laugh. We barely escaped death, and the first thing he thinks about is getting to a place with internet. I wonder how we managed to survive not having it in his apartment.

Tate scoffs. "Are you kidding me? April passes out, and that's the first thing you think about?"

It's not a big deal, at least to me. It's just a sign that our lives are returning to normal.

But Roman's voice is strained. "She was injected with BIONs. We need to stabilize them."

That's when I realize he has a point: the BIONs in my system aren't programmed to give me eternal life. They're programmed to kill me.

And that's when it hits me: I'm dying. I've spent months – even years – fearing this moment; but now that it's finally here, I'm not afraid. I'd be reunited with my parents. If I become a ghost, I can even use the opportunity to pull some pranks on Autumn. I don't mind the idea of dying at all.

"Can you get Finn?" Roman asks, his voice shaking. "I'll meet you in the car."

Tate doesn't need to be told twice. I feel a rush of air as he moves past me.

Roman lifts me into his arms and carries me through the lobby of the bureau. His body is hot, like the feeling of the sun beating down on me. By the time Roman stops to unlock the car, his body is drenched in sweat. But when Roman sets me into the backseat of the car, I still feel as though the sun is beating down on me. I realize, then, that Roman isn't warm. I'm running a fever.

Tate joins us shortly after with Finn's unconscious body in tow ('Finn?' I ask myself, wondering what could have prompted Roman's former boss to rescue me). Roman gives Tate the car keys, hops into the backseat, and they drive off without another word.

"The BIONs…" Roman says with a wince. "They're releasing this chemical. I don't know what it is, but I think it's poisoning her."

I want to laugh at the irony. I've spent decades believing that BIONs are the key to immortal life; but right now, they're the key to my death.

"It's probably the Divinity Bureau's doing," says Tate. "Can you undo it?"

"I… I don't know."

I move my fingertips – then my mouth. "Roman…"

Through half-open eyelids, I can see Roman stationed in front of a laptop with his dark eyebrows furrowed in concentration. As soon as he hears my voice, however, he looks away from the screen and into my eyes. A smile spreads across his lips. "Hey, April."

I swallow. "I'm dying."

Roman shakes his head. "No! No, you're not!"

Tate stops the car in front of what appears to be a restaurant. "Can you connect to the internet here?"

Roman nods. "Yeah, there's a signal here, but…" He trails off.

"Well, hurry up and do something!"

I want to hug Tate. I didn't get the chance to say goodbye to him before I left, so perhaps this is my opportunity. "Tate…"

Tate isn't willing to hear any of it. He gives me a half-smile. "Shut up. You're only going to distract him."

A part of me wants to protest, but the rest of me is too tired to do anything but drift to sleep.

■■■■■■■■■■■■■■■■■■■■■■■■■■■■■■■■■■■■■■■■■■■■■■■■■■

When I awaken again, tears are streaming against Roman's face. I don't know how much time has passed, but his determined expression has turned to despair.

"I… I can't do it," he rasps out.

By now, Finn has already awoken. He's glancing over Roman's shoulder, staring at the screen with his lips pressed together.

"Yes, you can," Finn offers in encouragement. "If you can knock out the entire bureau in one sweep, you can save her."

I sigh. "It's okay."

They both turn their attention to me, unaware until now that I had awoken. I swallow the lump in my throat as I continue, "I'm okay with dying. I've finally accepted that it's inevitable."

Roman shakes his head. "Don't say that."

"Why not?" I ask, my voice dry and weak. "I'm… I'm so hot. And everything hurts. I just feel so weak. I think it'd be easier if I…" I trail off, unable to finish the sentence.

They both alternate their stares between me and the computer. Maybe they've finally decided to let me go – until I feel Roman's hand against mine. He places it against my chest.

"Do you feel this?"

I feel a pounding in my chest. "It's my heart."

Roman nods. "It's your heart, beating stronger and faster than ever before. Right now, your body is regenerating the lost blood cells and fixing the broken parts of you, faster than you and I can even comprehend." He swallows, willing himself to continue. "I know you're in pain. But pain makes you stronger, wiser, humbler, and kinder..." Roman's voice is hoarse. "You know this. You've been through more loss, heartbreak, and setbacks than one person should ever go through in a lifetime; and for this, you're one of the strongest people I know. So, don't think for a second that what you're feeling makes you weak. Pain is your advantage."

I watch him before my eyelids begin to flutter. I feel myself slip back to sleep. When I do, I hear Roman say, "I think I've figured something out."

∎∎∎∎∎∎∎∎∎∎∎∎∎∎∎∎∎∎∎∎∎∎∎∎∎∎∎∎∎∎∎∎∎∎∎∎∎∎∎∎∎∎∎∎∎∎∎∎∎

It's dark by the time I awaken again. When I do, the first thing I notice is that the sweat sticking to my body feels cool. I shiver when a gust of wind brushes against my skin. I also notice that the car is empty.

Feat strikes me. Have we been caught? Have they given up on me? I stand up and kick the door open. When I do, I find myself in the middle of a camping ground.

"Roman?"

No answer.

"Tate?"

Silence.

"F... Finn?" I ask, even though the name sounds foreign on my lips.

Not a soul in sight. I want to curl into a ball and let out a wail. After everything we've been through in the last few days, I just want someone to pull me into their arms and tell me that it's going to be okay. Maybe it won't be. But I don't want to be on my own.

I notice a tent perched next to the car. Exhausted and desperate for answers, I pull it open.

When I do, I see Roman, Tate, and Finn. All three of them are sleeping soundly. They're hunched together, practically spooning each other. I smile. It's been a long day for them as well, and I don't know where I'd be without them. I'll need to find a way to thank them for everything they had done for me – but until then, the only thing left to do is rest. I squeeze between Roman and Tate and close my eyes. For the first time in a long time, I drift into a peaceful slumber.

■■■■■■■■■■■■■■■■■■■■■■■■■■■■■■■■■■■■■■■■■■■■■■■■■■■■■■

I'm the first one to awaken the next morning. My stirring causes Tate to wake up. I offer him a smile – the only thing I can give him right now – and motion for us to move outside the tent, so we don't wake Finn and Roman. Once we do, I ask for him to explain everything that's happened.

"Roman and Finn spent a day trying to figure out what was going on," Tate explains as we snack on granola bars that Finn had packed in the trunk. Neither of us questions how old the bars are, as we're too hungry to care. "As soon as we were within WiFi range, Roman was able to deactivate the BIONs to keep them from doing any further damage. The thing is, there was still poison in your system that was slowly killing you. They were trying to figure out how to reverse it, but what Roman figured out was that he didn't need to program the BIONs to absorb the poison. They wouldn't, as that's not what they intended to do. What they're supposed to do is automatically detect if there's something wrong and help you. I guess he basically reset it to their factory settings – kind of like that one time when your computer broke, and we had to reset it."

I nod in understanding, but I also understand the implications of his words. "I'm immortal, Tate."

"Well, not really," he says. "You're not safe from injury – and knowing you, you'll probably get yourself into trouble."

"You know that's not what I meant."

Tate goes quiet, knowing full well the implications behind my words. I'll never age, and I'll be safe from diseases for the rest of my life. At the same time, I'll never have children, and I'll forever be twenty years young. Considering the age difference between Roman and me, the thought terrifies me.

Tate lets out a sigh. "I guess it could always be worse."

We don't get the chance to continue our conversation, as Roman and Finn emerge from the tent a moment later. Without a second thought, I run into Roman's arms and pull him into an embrace. I want to cry. I haven't felt this weak in such a long time. During my worst hour, Roman had come through and made me strong again. Twice, he had saved my life. At least this time, I can properly thank him for it.

"I love you," I whisper in his ear.

Roman responds by kissing my forehead. "I love you, too."

"I'm sorry that I said you hold me back. I was stupid and prideful."

"It's okay," Roman assures me. Something about his tone indicates that it isn't okay, and it's understandable. I hurt him. But we have an eternity to work through it.

"Not to cut this reunion short," Finn interrupts. "But we should probably try to put as much distance between the Midwest and us as possible."

I pull away from Roman to look between Finn and Tate. Tears fill my eyes, and I'm overcome with gratitude. These three have risked everything to save me. I don't know what I had done to deserve it.

"Thank you," I say, tears threatening to spill out of my eyes. After everything they had done, those two words don't seem to be enough. "You guys saved my life. I… I'd be dead if it weren't for you three."

Finn smiles. "Don't worry about it."

"Well, we probably should worry," Tate points out, shuffling his feet. "What do we do now? I'm guessing we won't be able to go back to our normal lives."

Finn shrugs. "Normal is overrated."

I glance between the three of them, an idea coming to mind. I don't think I'll be able to personally repay them for everything they had done, but I know someone that can. "I have an idea."

■■■■■■■■■■■■■■■■■■■■■■■■■■■■■■■■■■■■■■■■■■■■■■■■■■■■■■

Leonard is an early bird. The four us wait outside his office, expecting to wait for another few hours before we see him walking through the elevator doors – but it isn't even seven o'clock in the morning before he walks by, whistling. His whistles stop as soon as he makes eye-contact with me. He glances between the four of us – our bodies sweating, aching, and bleeding – before he takes another glance at me. I open my mouth to explain, but before I can utter a word, he opens the front door and gestures for us to come inside.

"I hope you plan on paying me this time around," he says with a huff as he begins his work.

■■■■■■■■■■■■■■■■■■■■■■■■■■■■■■■■■■■■■■■■■■■■■■■■■■■■■■

By the end of the day, the four of us have new identities. Leonard gives the new identification cards to me, who writes three checks. The first is to Leonard, who had canceled his appointments for the day to help my friends and me out of a bind. The second and third are placed in the envelopes that Leonard had given me. One goes to Tate, and the other goes to Finn. Both of them nearly faint when they see the amount.

"Holy shit."

"Who's Elisa Meeks? I think she forgot to add a decimal point."

I roll my eyes. "Did you think that I was going to give up my fortune when I went on the run?"

306 · TESSA CLARE

Tate shifts uncomfortably. "Well, isn't that what you're doing now?"

I think about what Gideon had told me: *"Your father amassed a fortune selling immortality to some very dangerous people."* The money is tainted. If it weren't a necessity, I'd burn it in a heartbeat.

"Consider it payment for everything you guys have done for me," I say stiffly.

I part ways with Tate first, who insists that he doesn't need to return home. He'll be able to buy everything that he needs. I pull him into a hug and thank him for being the greatest friend that I've ever known. I hope that I'll be able to see him again.

Finn is much more difficult. We've never met before him rescuing me from the bureau, but I still owe my life to him. I give him an awkward hug and tell him to take care of himself. During the car ride, Roman had filled me in on his story. I wonder if he'll be able to leave behind his wife and older child.

I tell Roman that we have two last stops before we hit the road.

The first stop is to his apartment. He stays on the lookout to make sure that law enforcement doesn't come chasing after us. I emerge from the building carrying Neville, who is squirming in my grasp and causing my entire face to turn pink. It's a miracle that I can even breathe.

It's this moment that Roman starts to cry. He's stroking Neville's fur throughout the car ride to our destination and whispers goodbye's that I'm not able to hear. He murmurs, "I got him when he was a kitten. He was my best friend for the last four years."

I look away guiltily. If I weren't allergic, I would've been more than content bringing him along. The only thing I can do is the next best thing.

Our second destination is Darcy's house.

I use a torn piece of an envelope to wrap a message in Neville's collar: *'Still not giving up on my promise.'* Once I catch a glimpse of Autumn playing in the garden, I let the cat hop out of the car. I hold

Roman's hand as we wait. It takes several minutes for Neville to realize that he's no longer in Roman's apartment. It takes even more for Autumn to take notice of the creature that's in her front yard. When she finally recognizes him, she rushes over to him. We drive away before she has the chance to see us.

Once we're on the road, I tell Roman, "You need to sleep. You've been up for a long time."

Roman stretches on the seat, not needing to be told twice. "I will."

"But before you do that, you need to tell me where to go."

"Anywhere is fine with me," he says with a content smile. He leans his chair back and prepares to fall asleep.

I sigh, wanting to tell him that his answer isn't very helpful, but if I'm near Roman, I don't mind.

"Hey, April?" Roman murmurs as he drifts to sleep.

"Yeah?"

"Remember when you said that you weren't capable of living a normal life?"

Feelings of guilt rush through me. "Look, I said I was sorry for that…"

"I know," Roman interjects before I can beat myself up for it more than I already am. "I just wanted to let you know that I hope I could prove you wrong. We can be happy. We can live a normal life, now that everything is over."

But it isn't over – not in my mind. Our destination has yet to be determined. We can go anywhere and start fresh. We can live our lives under the radar, and we can be happy, but it'll never be over. Our destination is the same place we're leaving: The Divinity Bureau. But when I come back, it'll be to bring the bureau down. That's a promise I'm making to myself.

Still, I smile to myself. We have this moment of victory, and I'm not about to ruin it. I say, "I am happy."

# ABOUT THE AUTHOR

Tessa Clare is the author of *The Divinity Bureau*.

When she's not writing, she's the Managing Director of Asset Creative House, where she's known for her enthusiastic speeches and being one of the few authors with a passion for marketing.

Throughout her early career, she was a concession stand attendant, a busgirl, a barista, a player's club representative for a casino, and an administrative assistant. She also spent years working as a manager for Vacasa, whose business model and revolutionary marketing strategies would later inspire the groundwork for Asset Creative House.

*The Divinity Bureau* is Tessa's debut novel about a forbidden love between a young activist and a government employee working for a corrupt bureau, set in a dystopian world. Originally self-published in 2016, the story was taken off the market when Tessa decided to retell it as a first person story.